Our Way Back

To my lover,
you are my happy ending.
Always come home to me.

A NOTE FROM KYLA FAYE

This book contains situations that may be uncomfortable for some, including child loss, depression, an on-page affair, strong language, detailed sex scenes, and mentions of suicide.

Please keep an open mind as you're reading and enjoy the emotional rollercoaster.

PLAYLIST

"exile" – Taylor Swift (feat. Bon Iver)
"Flames" – Mod Sun (feat. Avril Lavigne)
"Let Her Go" – Passenger
"Fallen So Young" – Declan J Donovan
"Two Ghosts" – Harry Styles
"Dumb Love" – Mimi Webb
"Out Of Love" – Alessia Cara
"Lips of an Angel" – Hinder
"Higher" – Tems
"All or Nothing" – Theory of a Deadman
"Six Feet Under" – Billie Eilish
"How to Save a Life" – The Fray
"Before It Breaks" – Brandi Carlile
"Under the Bridge" – Red Hot Chili Peppers

PROLOGUE

DRIP. Drip. Drip.

The sound of raindrops hitting metal is the only sound I can focus on. In the distance, there is a faint whining, but I can't quite make it out. It's too far away, too faint for it to hold my focus.

The only sound that I can familiarize is rain hitting metal.

Metal? *Where am I?* I don't remember anything.

Cold. I am so cold, and my fingertips are numb. My vision is blurry. I can make out the blurred yellow, red, and black view, but can't make out any shapes that could give me a clue as to where I am.

There's just darkness. Lots and lots of darkness.

I can't remember what happened; my head hurts too much to think or register what is happening. What sounds like rain hitting metal continues, but I can't decipher what it really is.

Suddenly, a faint crying sound catches my attention.

Am I crying? I don't think so.

The cries are small, too small to be of an adult. They are child-like cries. I want to get to the source of the sound, but I can't move. I can't feel my body.

An unrecognizable scream rips through me, and with all the

strength I can muster, I bring my hands to my face and rub my eyes with the heels of my palms. My head throbs, and my chest aches. *Is someone sitting on me, or is there something heavy on me?* I don't think so. But why does my chest ache? I can't get a deep breath, no matter how hard I try.

There is too much darkness around me, which isn't helping anything—especially my vision.

My hands move to my chest as I try to figure out what's restraining me, and I quickly discover it's a seatbelt. I am being held back in my seat by a seatbelt.

That means I'm in a car.

My fuzzy mind slowly works to piece the puzzle together.

My fingertips follow the seatbelt down to the buckle and push.

Nothing.

The seatbelt isn't loosening.

Stuck. I'm stuck.

I'm not sure why, but I scream.

That faint cry floats back to my ears. It's a soft cry followed by a small voice. "Mommy!" The voice is screaming now. I struggle against the seatbelt, clicking the lock repeatedly to no avail. It isn't loosening. I've never felt so trapped.

"Mommy!" The small voice sounds fearful now, screaming again, blending effortlessly with the ringing in my ears.

Where is the voice coming from? It's so close, yet so far away.

My eyelids flutter. The cries continue, the small, scared voice calling out for their mommy like a mantra.

Taking slow breaths, I close my eyes, praying I can clear my fog and confusion.

The cries continue.

"Mommy!"

Some of the haze lifts, and I realize...it's a familiar voice.

I know that voice. I've heard it every day for the past two and a half years.

Gasping, I rub my eyes harder, getting rid of my blurred vision to take in my whereabouts.

My vision comes back, but only causes me more confusion.

Why is my vision upside down?

Wait. No. My vision isn't the problem; I am the problem. I'm upside down.

Why am I upside down?

The cries that fill the air and blend in with the heavy raindrops are now my own. I begin to remember where I am and what has happened.

"Mommy!" the voice cries out louder than my screams, and my own cries instantly stop when I hear it. I realize exactly where I am and what is happening with my now clear head.

"Luca! Luca, baby. Mommy is here!" I struggle against the seatbelt; I have to get to him.

To Luca. My son.

We were in the car, driving home, when we were struck by another vehicle and flipped.

My baby is scared. I have to get to him anyhow. I scream, struggling against the seatbelt that won't budge. It's tight against my chest, locked into place, suspending me against my seat upside down.

We were in an accident. I'm still in our car, and it's still upside down.

"Luca, baby, keep talking to me. Do you have an owie?" I yell, needing to keep him calm and talking until I can get to him and fix whatever injuries he may have. The fear in his voice makes my chest ache, and I know I have to keep him calm. We both need to remain calm.

"Yes, Mommy. My tummy hurts bad! Where's Daddy?"

Daddy?

Declan. Fuck!

I remember the accident, and he was driving. Looking to the side in hopes of seeing Declan, I gasp at the sight.

The driver's seat is empty.

Where's Declan? Is he okay? I'll get our son and then I'll find my husband.

"Baby, Mommy loves you so much! I'm going to come get you!" I'm getting out of this fucking seatbelt, no matter what.

"I wuv you too, Mommy. My tummy hurts."

"It's okay, baby. Mommy will kiss your owie and make it feel better. Where are you, Luca?" I feel around the car for anything that I can use to cut myself out of the seatbelt.

"Luca! You need to talk to Mommy, okay?"

"O-o-okay, M-mommy!" His sobs are choked, causing us both pain. My fingertips brush over a shard of glass, and I want to jump in joy. Holding the shard tightly, I begin working it back and forth over the seatbelt fabric across my chest. The glass is cutting into the palm of my right hand, but I am numb to the pain. I don't even notice it until I see the blood dripping down my arm.

"We'll have ice cream for breakfast, okay, sweetie?" I hiss as the glass digs deeper into my hand. The stubborn material of the seatbelt is barely budging. I can't cut it fast enough.

And I can't keep Luca talking.

The faint cries stop.

"Luca? Baby, talk to me."

Silence.

"I said we can eat ice cream. Are you excited?" He begs to have ice cream for breakfast every morning, so why isn't he answering me? He should be excited and saying something.

Anything.

"Luca?"

Silence.

"Luca?!" I am screaming his name into the darkness.

No response.

Nothing.

Only silence.

There is too much silence.

The rain stops, just like the distant cries. "Luca!" I scream louder than I thought was humanly possible. I am likely going to rip my vocal cords, but I don't care. I have to get to my son, and he isn't responding to me. I can't hear him anymore.

In the distance, I can hear the faint whirl of sirens just as my heart drops into my stomach.

That is the last thing I hear before dizziness comes over me, and everything fades to black.

ONE
NOW

Camille

"How are you sleeping? Are the dreams still keeping you up?" Dr. Meredith Reynolds always asks meaningless questions she already knows the answers to. Yes, I still have nightmares that wake me every night. I wake up in a cold sweat, and yes, she already knows that. How does she know? Because I've told her this during every session over the last few months.

Nothing has miraculously changed since our last appointment a week ago or the several appointments before that. My nightmares haven't magically gone away in that short time.

"Of course they are. Nothing's changed," I snap at her in annoyance. I'm always so quick to snap at her even when I know she's only trying to help me, but let's face it, she's doing a terrible job at it.

I want a quick solution to my pain. All I want is the medication that suppresses my emotions and numbs my mind. To get my prescription refilled, I must endure these weekly therapy sessions. I don't want to talk, especially not today.

I've been seeing Dr. Reynolds for nearly a year now. My mother recommended that I attend therapy to discuss my trauma with someone.

After the accident, apparently, I wasn't acting according to other people's expectations after the loss I suffered. I was struggling to deal with the pain that was inside of me. There was too much going on, and I was hollow inside, so I shut everyone out, keeping my emotions to myself. Dr. Reynolds says if I don't deal with my trauma now, I'm at risk of having a mental breakdown later.

I call bullshit on that, though. It's been a year today, and so far, I'm doing fine, aside from my dreams. I should really check into her degrees and licensing.

Can you blame me for not being the same person I once was? Or not wanting to sit around and talk about my feelings every day?

Trauma can do that to you. I experienced something horrific.

Losing someone changes you. Every day I find myself fighting to remain standing on the invisible ledge. Although, I'm not going to tell her that. With my luck, she'd toss my ass into a mental hospital and put me on suicide watch.

As long as she continues prescribing the magic pills to numb my emotions, we'll be just fine.

Believe it or not, I'm thankful for Dr. Reynolds, even though I don't express my gratitude toward the woman who helps me in more ways than one. She gives me what I need to get through the day.

For a long time, my nightmares stayed away. Now, the dreams that force me to relive the worst day of my life are back. Most nights, I wake up in a panic and have to shower to clean myself from the sweat that covers my body. I have to physically wash away the horrible memory of my dreams. But lately, even that hasn't been helping me.

Every night for the last month, I've heard his voice and relived every detail of that tragic night. I become paralyzed in my sleep, forced to go through that night detail by detail until it ends. I can't wake myself up from the dreams anymore.

I'm stuck in my own personal hell, to the point where I'm afraid to go to sleep because I know what awaits me.

It's bittersweet. I want to sleep because I miss the sound of his voice, but I don't want to relive that night, or even see his face. Not in that memory.

I don't want any memories of him. I'm not strong enough to think about him, so I don't; instead, I focus every waking hour on my work.

I've been fine managing myself...until now, until today.

"Today is the one-year anniversary, and you're facing it alone. It's normal for memories to taunt you like this around the time of an anniversary," Dr. Reynolds says, making me raise my head and look at her for the first time during our session.

I'm hoping she's right. I'm fucking hoping that once I get through today, the dreams will stop. I can't take it anymore; I already blame myself more than anyone says I should.

"Talk to me, Camille. Tell me what you're thinking." Damn, this woman knows me. She always knows when I get lost inside my head.

Dr. Reynolds raises her perfectly sculpted eyebrow at me, giving me a *well, speak out loud* look. I can't help but laugh, and God bless this woman for dealing with my shit for the last year. I know I haven't been the easiest patient.

"I was thinking that you might be right. Maybe once the day is over, my dreams will stop." I tell her what she wants to hear, even though I don't believe the words coming out of my mouth. I'll tell her anything to get what I want.

"There's a support group for grieving parents at the Downtown Community Center. I know that you've turned down the idea in the past, but I think it could help you if you were to share your grief with others who would understand. Try it, just once." She leans forward and hands me the pamphlet, and I surprise us both by taking it.

"No promises, but I'll think about it. Thanks, Doc." I force a smile, and she happily changes our conversation topic.

By the end of our session, we say our goodbyes, and I leave with exactly what I came for—another refill of happy pills.

. . .

My phone rings after leaving the pharmacy directly across the street from Dr. Reynolds's office. A quick look tells me that it's my mother.

Perfect timing.

My family isn't aware that I'm still taking medication, and I don't see a reason why they'd ever need to know. They'd worry about me, and no doubt wonder if I'm truly doing as well as I claim. And honestly, I don't want their voiced concern, so I keep it private.

I climb into my car and secure my phone into the dash phone holder and answer the call via Bluetooth. "Hey, Mom, what's up?" I pull out of the pharmacy parking lot and into traffic.

"Hi, sweetie, I'm just calling to see how your session went."

"It was good, and you're right. I should do something to help myself, especially tonight." My mom has been begging me to take some action to help me through the day. She said avoiding it wasn't an option, but nothing feels right.

Why do we even celebrate the anniversary of someone's death? That seems like a fucked-up thing to do. Like, hey, congrats on being dead for one year; I hope heaven is great!

I roll my eyes and suppress a laugh.

"That's great, sweetie! What did you decide to do?"

"Dr. Reynolds suggested a support group. It's tonight at seven, so I'm going to go. Want to grab lunch now?"

"That makes me so happy. I think it'll be a great thing for you. Lunch sounds great, and I'm here at the club with your father. I'll call Spencer and we can all have lunch together."

"I'll head over there now. Love you, Mom."

"I love you too, sweetie. I'll see you soon." I press the end button on my steering wheel and lean back against my seat while driving in silence.

I've always been ridiculously close with my family. I'm incredibly close with my mom, but I've always jumped at the chance to spend time with my dad and sister, too. Ever since I moved back to Seattle last year, my mom has been my biggest ally. I can't go a day without talking to her or my older sister, Spencer.

Our family is close, and I believe that's because my mom and dad were young when they had us. Their parents weren't supportive of them having Spence and getting married, so they didn't have the best relationship. Mom and Dad both vowed to be better than their parents.

She likes to joke that the two of us are like Lorelai and Rory from *Gilmore Girls*. We're often mistaken for siblings, plus we're best friends.

I tell my family everything, well, almost everything. I'm an asshole for not telling them about the shiny bottle of pills in my purse that I can't go a day without. But we're all entitled to having a few of our own secrets.

THIRTY MINUTES LATER, I ARRIVE AT THE ELITE AND WAY TOO expensive country club that my parents are members of.

Before turning my car over to the valet, I take a quick moment to pop one of the holy grail blue pills I rely on into my mouth and wash it down with a sip of water.

As I finally walk inside the extravagant building, I send a quick text in a group chat with Mom and Spencer to tell them I've arrived.

We meet in the dining room and exchange quick hugs, getting a table for four. Mom tells me that Dad is busy somewhere socializing with a friend he ran into, so it's just us girls to start.

"So happy to see you, sweetie. I've been thinking a lot about you today," Mom says, reaching across the table to take my hand.

"How are you holding up, sis?" Spencer jumps in, taking my other hand in hers.

I force a smile, knowing they're already aware of how I'm feeling today. I don't need to tell them that today is the second worst day of my life. They already know.

Not wanting to spend any more time focusing on myself, I don't bother answering and instead change the subject. "So, how was your date last night, Spence?"

My sister rolls her eyes dramatically. "He couldn't stop speaking about himself in third person. And he stared at my tits all night." Poor girl. She has no luck when it comes to men, and knowing my sister, I'm sure she told him how terrible she thought he was.

"We were talking about our work, and he literally said, 'Martin wants a woman who stays home and keeps him fed and the house clean.' When I told him that women can be more than just homemakers, he said, 'Martin thinks you need to submit and let him teach you what to do.'" She huffs, rolling her eyes. "Who the hell talks about themselves in third person?"

A genuine laugh escapes me. "You must've done something terrible in a past life in order to have such shitty luck with dating."

Spencer narrows her eyes at me. "He was a fucking idiot."

"Language," Mom chastens, holding back her own laughter. "Perhaps you should stay off dating sites and allow me to set you up with my handsome doctor."

"Mom, for the love of God, you are not setting me up with your gynecologist." Mom and I collectively laugh at Spencer's misery.

The waiter arrives with our drinks, just as Dad finally appears. He greets me with a kiss on my head and takes the seat beside Mom.

"What's new with you, Cammy Bear?" Dad asks, using my childhood nickname that's followed me over the years. "How are you holding up?" He places his hand on top of mine across the table, giving me a reassuring squeeze.

"Well, actually, I just met with Dr. Reynolds. She suggested I attend a support group," I admit before hesitantly explaining the support group to my family. Of course, they're all thrilled and on board with the idea of me attending a support group to interact with other grieving parents.

"That's fantastic, sweetie. I hope it'll be beneficial for you," Mom says, smiling, her bright eyes full of hope.

Dad had suggested that I attend a group when I first moved back home, but at that time, I wasn't willing to consider it. Dr. Reynolds also mentioned it a few times, but I vetoed it just like Dad's idea.

I feel like I'm finally semi-ready to attend.

The rest of our lunch goes by quick, and thankfully, our conversation is light. We avoid the elephant in the room. I know it's a hard day for everyone. I'm not the only one who suffered a loss one year ago today.

My sister lost her nephew.

My parents lost their only grandchild.

And I lost my son.

After lunch, I hug my family goodbye and drive straight home to get some work done and shower. My nerves and anxiety become higher than ever. I don't like group activities or talking about myself, but I'm going to suck it up and step out of my comfort zone, even if it kills me.

And there's a good chance it might.

By seven o'clock sharp, I arrive at the community center downtown, sit in a circle, and watch as men and women fill the empty chairs around me.

"Hi, mind if I sit here?" a woman asks in a soft voice, almost a whisper. I barely spare her a glance before I nod my head, gesturing for her to sit beside me. It is the last seat available, and I must admit, I hadn't expected the meeting to be so full. I hadn't realized there were so many parents with dead kids near me.

Five minutes later, a woman with beautiful dark skin and curly hair stands from her chair and begins speaking, "All right, let's get started. I see a lot of new faces, and I'm glad you've all decided to join us today. I'm Eliza, and I put this group together three years ago after my daughter died from leukemia. This is a safe space where we can all laugh and cry together. Your pain is our pain, and we will help each other heal. Now, let us all introduce ourselves." Eliza takes her seat, nodding toward the man on her left to start us off.

I'll admit; I'm skeptical. Sharing my feelings in a room full of strangers doesn't seem appealing to me, but I'm willing to try.

With a heavy sigh, the man nods his head and waves before standing. "My name is Jerome, and six months ago, my eight-year-old son was riding his bike and was killed by a drunk driver. His death caused my wife to miscarry our daughter, and honestly, I'm struggling to take it day by day." He sniffles, wiping the tear that falls down his sad face. "I blame myself every single day. I was supposed to be watching him, but I took my eye off of him for a minute so I could go inside and get another beer." When he's done speaking, he sits back down after taking a tissue from Eliza and using it to wipe his face.

One by one, everyone in the room shares the reason they're here. Some parents lost living children; others experienced a miscarriage or stillbirth. Nonetheless, they are all parents in pain. I would know. Pain recognizes pain.

And I can feel their pain.

I shift in my chair, suddenly feeling uncomfortable. Everything about this is heartbreaking and suffocating, and I make the decision that I will not be coming back.

I hate this.

This isn't going to help me, and my little blue magic pill isn't doing anything for me right now. I need to get the fuck out of here and fast.

The woman beside me is already sobbing before it's even her turn. I hear the sniffles from her and everyone else. A quick look around the room tells me that I'm the only person with dry eyes.

The woman next to me clears her throat, and I glance over at her, taking in her whole appearance for the first time. She's beautiful, with her blonde hair cut into a short bob that brushes the tops of her shoulders, her eyes big and blue. She gives a small smile to each person before she speaks. "My name is Karina, and my baby was born sleeping at thirty-two weeks. Since then, I've had two miscarriages, and now my husband and I are struggling with getting pregnant again. We've done multiple rounds of IUI and IVF, but nothing has been successful. It's been hard. I feel like it's my fault, and month after month that I'm unable to get pregnant, I feel broken." She wipes the tears from her eyes. "I thank you all for welcoming me here tonight. I appreciate being able to share with those who understand." She speaks with an accent I hadn't noticed earlier.

Fuck. Now it's my turn.

All eyes are on me, so I slowly straighten my posture in the chair, avoiding eye contact with everyone. Most people stood when it was their turn for introductions, only three old people had remained seated. I choose to remain seated.

With a deep breath, I open my mouth to speak. "My name is Camille," I say, feeling like I'm in an AA meeting and not a grieving parents' support group, and all I want to do is laugh hysterically.

I know everyone wants me to react a certain way and share my sadness, so I give them what they want. I am a people pleaser, after all. I look down at my hands in my lap with narrow eyes and finger the hem of my shirt. "A year ago today, my four-year-old son died in a car accident." Saying those words out loud does something to me that I hadn't expected. I'm overwhelmed with emotion and my voice is clogged.

Keep it together, Camille. Don't cry. I will myself not to show my emotion, but I can already feel the unshed tears stinging my eyes. I clear my throat and stop speaking so I don't completely lose my shit in front of a room full of strangers. I didn't think bringing up Luca would affect me this much.

The blonde woman who introduced herself as Karina reaches over and takes my hand in hers, giving it a gentle squeeze. I look up to meet her sad blue eyes, then slowly pulling my hand away.

Thankfully, Eliza gets the hint that I'm not going to continue speaking and takes over.

I remain silent for the remainder of the meeting, and the second it ends, I'm the first to fold my chair and place it on the rack before hightailing it toward the door. I can't get out of here fast enough.

"Hey! Wait!" the accented voice calls behind me, but I pretend I don't hear anyone and continue walking. "Hey! Camille!" A hand on my shoulder is what finally stops me.

Fuck. So much for getting out of here quickly and unnoticed.

Doing my best to avoid snapping at the woman or showing my annoyance, I turn to face her.

Karina.

"Hi, it is Camille, right?"

"Yes. Karen, right?" Okay, that was rude. I know what her name is.

The blonde woman lets out a little laugh. "Karina. This is going to sound completely bizarre, but would you like to get a cup of coffee? I'm new here and could use a friend." Her British accent is beautifully prominent with each word. "I promise not to rape or murder you," she adds, causing my lips to curl with a genuine smile.

Hmm. She's funny.

"Or drug and kidnap me?" I add, getting an obnoxious laugh from her. Her laughter is so loud that I wonder how something so boisterous can come from her tiny figure. I realize I'm laughing too, but I'm chuckling at her ridiculous laugh, not her words.

"Yes, I promise." She raises her pinky finger to me, so I raise mine and loop it around hers.

"Okay, deal. But if I end up missing, I have people who know I was here," I warn with a grin. She grabs her stomach and leans forward, wiping away invisible tears as she lets out a full belly laugh.

Geez. It wasn't that funny. Dramatic much?

I'm unsure what compelled me to say yes, but there's something about his woman that's inviting.

"Come on, new friend, let's go." She loops her arm around mine, and we both walk across the street toward the Starbucks on the corner.

We order our drinks, then claim a quiet table in the corner.

"So, where are you from?" I ask, sipping my steaming cup of black coffee. I shouldn't drink coffee at night, but I'd rather stay awake than go to sleep in an empty bed and face my nightmares.

"I'm from London. My husband moved us here a month ago," she says with a sparkle in her sky-blue eyes.

"Well, welcome to Seattle. I'm happy to be your first friend."

"Thanks! He tried to set me up with the girls in his office, but I'm not a child who needs playdates. I can make my own friends, and he'll be thrilled to learn I did."

I can't help but laugh. Damn, this girl is forward and way too open. Must be the blonde in her.

I can relate to needing friends, though. After the accident, my friends didn't know how to speak to me anymore, and then I moved back home to Washington on a whim and deleted my personal social media accounts. I haven't talked to my so-called friends in nearly a year. All I have is my family. I guess when you think about it, I'm also alone.

Shaking my head and willing the thought away, I brush a piece of my black hair behind my ear and focus on the woman in front of me. Something tells me she enjoys talking about herself, so I ask, "So, Karina, what do you do for work?"

"I'm a housewife. My husband is an architect who travels a lot, so I book all his trips. Keeps me busy, but once we have children, they'll be my full-time job. What do you do?" she asks after her proud declaration. I watch the moment her eyes light up and her lips curl into a grin. I know what she's staring at. "What a gorgeous ring! Are you married?" She pulls my hand across the table toward her, inspecting the large diamond on my left ring finger.

Great. Here we go—one of my two least favorite topics.

17

"Uh... um... wow, look at the time." I pull my hand away, and her confused blue eyes meet mine.

Nope. No.

No fucking way am I having this conversation with a stranger.

I'm about to make up a bullshit story when my phone begins ringing.

Thank you, Jesus. Perfect fucking timing.

Picking up my phone from the table, I smile when I see Spencer's name on the screen. "Sorry, Karina, I must get going. I'm late for something. It was great to meet you." I decline the call, sending a quick text to my sister, telling her I'll call her back in a few minutes once I get to my car.

"I understand. Can I get your number? Maybe we can do lunch this week?" There's an abundant mixture of hope and loneliness in Karina's eyes. There's no reason to rain on her parade. She's clearly a bored housewife needing a friend.

"Sure, you can text me, and we can arrange something." I grab a pen from my purse and write my number down on a napkin.

Waving her goodbye, I stand and run across the street, slipping behind the wheel of my car once I reach it. Taking a deep breath, I call Spencer back.

"Come over. I'm waiting for you. I've got wine, ice cream, and I just ordered Chinese food," she says as soon as she answers the phone, not even bothering to say hello first.

For the first time all day, I'm silent, overwhelmed with the emotions that I've been holding in for far too long.

I'm not a robot, although I wish I was. I feel so much sadness and heartbreak, even when I don't want to. I've just become an expert at burying my feelings.

I was fifteen when I began pushing my feelings aside. And all the feelings I had left were buried along with my son.

"Camille, come to me. Let me take care of you," Spencer says. She knows exactly how I feel and what I need. I nod, aware she can't see me. Hanging up, I pull out of the parking lot just as the first tear rolls down my cheek.

With shaky hands and teary eyes, I drive to my sister—my lifeline.

Twenty minutes later, I pull into the driveway of Spencer's two-story townhouse and park in front of the garage. She's standing in the doorway with her arms outstretched, waiting for me.

My car is barely even in park when I jump out and run toward her on shaky legs. She pulls me in for a tight hug and lets me collapse against her and soak her gray T-shirt with my tears.

She holds me tightly against her, stroking my dark hair away from my face. "It's okay, baby sis. Cry until you can't cry anymore. I've got you." It's been so long since I've cried, and now that the flood gates are open, I can't seem to close them. It feels good to let out my pain.

I cry for myself.

I cry for my sweet baby boy, Luca.

I cry for failing to protect him.

I cry for everything that I've been through over the past year.

I cry until I can't cry anymore. And Spencer is there holding me the entire time.

My sister, my lifeline.

TWO

NOW

Camille

Me: Running a little late. I'll be there ASAP!

Karina: Okay! I just got here. I'll get us a table

KARINA TEXTED ME THE DAY AFTER WE MET AND ASKED IF I could do lunch on Wednesday. She said her husband was leaving town for an overnight work trip, and it just so happened my afternoon schedule was clear for Wednesday, so I agreed. She suggested a new seafood restaurant, and it sounded way too good to pass up. I'm usually not the type of person to engage with strangers, but something about Karina's sad blue eyes makes me want to be near her.

Ten minutes after texting her, I arrive at the restaurant we agreed on. Upon entering, it takes two seconds to scan the dining floor and find Karina. She's practically jumping out of her seat as she waves at me.

This woman is a little bizarre, but I like it. It's refreshing to have a new friend who is so open and knows nothing about me or what I've been through the past year.

All she knows about me is that I lost my son, and that's all I plan to share with her.

There's no sympathy from Karina, and I appreciate that. I'm tired of everyone acting sympathetic toward me. I'm not the fragile little bomb that everyone thinks I am.

I want to be treated normally. I *need* it. Not handled like I'm made of glass. Even my family walks on eggshells around me.

"Camille, you look beautiful!" Karina says with a bright smile, pulling me in for a hug once I'm within reach. I'd been working in my home office, so there was no need to dress up for the day. I'm wearing a powder-pink silk blouse, tight denim jeans, and red bottom heels.

It's the perfect lunch attire.

My dark hair is pulled back into a sleek ponytail, not a hair out of place, and my face contains minimal makeup. For the first time in a long time, I feel as good as I look.

Last night I didn't have any dreams, and today I feel refreshed and badass. For that, I'm thankful.

"You too, girl!" It's true; Karina's a natural beauty. Her oval-shaped face and round, doe eyes are enough to be any man's wet dream. Her husband is indeed a lucky man.

We take our seats, open our menus, and instantly, she opens her mouth and overshares. "I'm getting salmon. I read that it's good for fertility, and I should be ovulating this weekend." She grins, wiggling her brows at me from across the table.

I snort, taken aback from the sudden information I hadn't asked for. Wow, this girl is open. I'm positive her filter is practically nonexistent.

"Well, good luck to you. When does your husband return from his business trip?" I force a smile, shifting in my seat from being uncomfortable with this topic of conversation. Maybe I'm a bitch, but I'm not interested in hearing about her fertility journey with her husband.

"He'll be back on Friday. We have an event this weekend, so he'll be back in just enough time to attend. So! Do you have any tips for me about getting pregnant? Since I'm assuming you had a healthy pregnancy."

The thought of my pregnancy is painful. It was the best time of my life, but thinking about it reminds me that I'm now childless. The constant ache in my chest intensifies.

Karina must take my silence as a sign that she's overstepped because she immediately apologizes. "Oh God, I'm so sorry! I should think before I speak. I didn't mean to pour salt on the wound." She reaches across the table and grabs my hands, her blue eyes full of sorrow.

"No, no, it's fine. Yes, I did have a healthy pregnancy. But I don't have any tips for trying to conceive. When I got pregnant, I was on birth control, and it happened so fast," I explain, laughing to cover the fact I'm uncomfortable speaking to her about my past. It's not like I'm going to tell this strange woman that I had an unplanned pregnancy with a guy I barely knew. I smile to myself, remembering how Luca came to be. He was unplanned but so very loved. I pull my hand away from her grip and grab the glass of lemon water in front of me, gulping down half of it to calm my nerves.

My anxiety is high, and I'm desperate for the magic pill that I took on the way over to kick in.

"Do you and your husband plan on having more children?" She sits back in her chair, asking a personal question casually as if it's any of her business. But I answer her anyway. No fucking idea why.

"No. We had our son, and now we're done."

"Aw. Why not? Does he not want more?" God, how much more personal are we going to get? Is her next question going to be how many times a week we have sex? I wouldn't put it past her.

The more she talks, the more I'm beginning to regret my decision of agreeing to lunch.

"No, I'm the one who doesn't want more children. One was

23

enough for me. We should order." My tone is a little snippy, but I can't find it in me to care. I'm done with her questioning. You'd think I was in a fucking interrogation.

Luckily, Karina doesn't bother asking any more intrusive questions.

The remainder of our lunch is filled with light questions about my career, London, and the fun things we both like. I realize right away that we don't have a single thing in common.

We're complete opposites.

Yeah, I will not be seeing her again.

ON FRIDAY, MOM, SPENCER, AND I MEET UP AT THE SPA FOR a full body pamper treatment. Mom is dragging Spencer and me along to a charity gala that she and Dad must attend tonight, so she's bribing us with a trip to the spa. We'd always have to attend the galas that our parents' high society friends hosted when we were younger. And now, even as adults, we're still being forced to attend.

Okay, maybe not forced, but highly encouraged and expected.

I've always hated attending these types of events. It wasn't so bad as a kid because I had someone to face it with, but now, I'm going solo. Yes, I'll have Spence, but she'll be too busy on the prowl for her future husband to pay much attention to me. She won't find a man she likes, but that won't stop her from trying. Spencer is three years older than me, and I know it hurt her ego when I got married first. She'd always said she'd be married by twenty-five, but now, she's twenty-nine without a prospect in sight.

Without her holding my hand, I'll have no protection against the high society vultures tonight, and I'll be faced with a million and one questions. I've done well enough to avoid the Seattle socialites since I've been back home, but my time has run out now, and soon I'll be in a room full of them.

"Mom, I think I'm getting the flu. I might be contagious, so I think I should sit this one out." I fake a cough, looking over at her, giving her the sad puppy dog eyes I used as a child when I wanted to get my way.

"Nice try, Camille. You're going, no ifs or buts." Mom scoffs, not even bothering to look in my direction. She knows I'm being dramatic and don't want to attend.

"I'm a twenty-six-year-old woman, and you can't force me to go." I huff, my voice high-pitched and whiney. Spencer laughs stiffly from underneath her mud face mask.

"Wanna bet?" Mom raises her perfectly threaded eyebrows at me, and I surrender with a sigh. "Good. Now sit back and let Leigh finish your brows." I do as I'm told. I recline in the cosmetic chair and allow Leigh, my assigned spa specialist, to continue threading my eyebrows, shaping them into perfection.

Six hours and threaded eyebrows, a Brazilian wax, a manicure and pedicure, a hydrating facial mask, and a massage later, I feel like a brand-new woman. I'm perfectly groomed and ready for the long night ahead of faking smiles and pretending to care about people I don't even like.

Today has been a good day, but I've been unable to shake the gut feeling that something is going to happen.

The dark cloud that hangs above my head is in place, ready to rain on any chance of having a good night.

SPENCER CAME OVER TO MY CONDO TO GET READY A FEW hours ago.

Now we stand side by side in my master bathroom at the double vanity, applying makeup to our faces and sipping red wine.

She applied my eyeshadow, giving me the perfect smoky eye with winged eyeliner, and I applied my foundation and contour, painting my lips a deep shade of matte red and contouring my face to perfection. Spence even does my hair in a chignon bun with tendrils framing my face.

As children, Spence loved to dress me up and get me ready for whatever gala we'd have to attend, and that hasn't changed.

I've just finished putting the diamond earrings in my ears, courtesy of our mother, when Spencer steps behind me and wraps her arms around me from behind. We stare at our reflection in the mirror, and I see her glossy muddy green eyes staring back at me. "Spence, what's wrong?" With a frown, I turn to face my sister.

"Nothing, I'm fine. I'm just so happy that you're back home. I missed you so much." She pulls me in for a hug and squeezes me a little tighter, then steps away and fans herself with her hands, willing her tears not to fall.

When I left Seattle for school years ago, I did my best to see my family as often as I could. I even called every day, but I missed them deeply. My sister, most of all.

She's three years older, and I know that siblings often have their rough moments where they fight and argue, but that's never been the case for us. She's been my best friend and protector since the day I was born. Mom and dad told me that when they brought me home from the hospital, Spencer declared that I was her baby, and her three-year-old self would get up every night with Mom when it was time for my feedings. Where most older siblings hated having their younger siblings around, she loved when I was around. We were so inseparable that she even tried to keep me with her at school on her first day of kindergarten. I had gone with Mom to drop Spencer off, and while she was speaking with the teacher, Spencer hid me in the closet, hoping our mother wouldn't notice. Obviously, her plan was flawed, and I was discovered when I started crying because the closet was dark.

"I love you, Spence. Now, no more tears. Let's smile and see how fucked up we can get tonight." She nods, then takes her wine glass from my vanity, draining it in one gulp. She sets it down and slips into my bedroom, while I go into the closet to get dressed.

"By the way, Mom sent over our dresses. You're not going to need panties or a bra!" she calls out loud enough so I'll hear her from where I'm standing inside my walk-in closet.

I nod to myself but do what I came in here to do in the first place. Grabbing my purse from the floor, I dig inside until I find the prescription bottle that I've come to rely heavily on. Quickly opening the bottle, I take out one of the little blue pills and pop it in my mouth, shoving the bottle back into my purse. I wash the pill down with a swig of wine, praying that it kicks in soon and my nerves will subside. I just need to get through the night.

Back in my room, Spencer hands me the black dress bag that contains my dress for the gala before taking her own into the bathroom to dress. I untie my silk bathrobe and let it fall to the floor, exposing my naked body to the chilly room. Goosebumps cover my flesh once the AC kicks on. Carefully removing the dress from the bag, I unzip it and step into it just as Spencer returns to the room wearing a stunning green velvet floor-length dress.

Looking over her appearance, I whistle. "Damn, sis, I'm definitely becoming an aunt tonight," I say jokingly, watching as she spins around, modeling the dress while I clap and yell out catcalls.

"Is this dress going to get me a husband? Or are you thinking I'll just end the night knocked up?"

"Knocked up for sure. Who knows, maybe you'll end up with your own Ben Stone. A guy not very attractive but can sure make you laugh." I wiggle my eyebrows, referring to the movie *Knocked Up* that she has seen a trillion times while claiming it's not her favorite movie. Liar. I know it is.

Turning, I give her my back, and she zips up my dress, then I zip hers. While moving in sync, we step into our black, red bottom heels, then stand side by side in front of the floor-length mirror to pose for pictures. Spencer loves a good selfie. Unlike me, she's crazy for social media.

My dress is a floor-length red satin off-the-shoulder gown with a slit up the left side. The color is impeccable against my flawless, smooth olive skin. It's perfect for tonight and gives me the bit of confidence that I need to be able to face the vultures known as Seattle's finest socialites.

"Holy fuck. You look like a million bucks." Spencer snaps a

few more photos and sends them to our mom, proving we're ready and will be meeting her and Dad.

Frozen in place, I stare at our reflections in the mirror. A smile tugs at the corners of my red-painted lips. I'm not conceited by any means, but I know I'm a looker. Spencer and I have our mother's looks. We have the same heart-shaped face, long, thick luscious hair, and sharp features that have caused to turn a few heads once or twice toward us.

Spencer is taller with a slimmer figure, while I'm a few inches shorter with an hourglass figure and a peachy ass. I'm surely not missing any meals or turning down dessert. Her stomach is tight and fit, and her thighs have a gap, while my stomach is soft and squishy, and my thighs touch. From all the times I've seen her in a bikini, I know she doesn't have a single flaw to her skin, while I have cellulite and stretch marks.

Not that I'm complaining, because soft or not, I love my body.

"All right, let's go so we can get this over with," I say, giving myself a final once-over.

Arm in arm, we exit my building and climb inside the black SUV waiting for us outside. Mom always insists we use our family driver, Stefan, whenever we attend events.

With my stomach in knots, I take slow breaths, dreading the night that is to come.

EXACTLY AS I EXPECTED, SPENCER LEFT ME THE MOMENT WE stepped inside the over-the-top building that's hosting Seattle's most elite residents. Mom and Dad are busy mingling with their friends and a few of Dad's colleagues from the hospital, and I'm a standing duck that's entirely out of my comfort zone.

This is the time to mingle, but there's not one single person in this room I want to associate with. I'm alone and already thinking of ways to escape without Mom noticing, although I know there's no chance. Even though she's across the room, busy in conversation, Melanie Lambert doesn't miss a single thing. I'm positive she'd know the second I fled.

To help calm my nerves, I take a glass of champagne from the tray of a passing waiter, swallowing half of the contents in one gulp. The cold bubbly drink does nothing to settle my nerves. I'm as on edge as I've ever been.

My palms are sweaty; I'm breathing through my mouth; my skin is covered in goosebumps; and the hair on my arms is standing straight. The feeling of unease is setting in, but I can't quite tell why I'm feeling so on edge.

I'm anxious as fuck.

"Camille?" A familiar accented voice catches me off guard, causing me to put aside my escape plans. Turning toward the voice, my eyebrows hit my hairline in surprise.

What the fuck is she doing here?

"Karina? Hi, what are you doing here?" *Is she stalking me?* I wouldn't put it past her, and I'm not ruling that out yet.

She laughs her throaty laugh, pulling me in for a hug. I'm willing to bet that physical touch is her love language. "I told you I had an event to attend with my husband. This is the event." She waves her hand around with a wide smile.

"Wow, I didn't realize. So, your husband is here?"

"He is! He just got back into town this afternoon. You must meet him. I told him I've made a new friend, and he will not believe me unless you meet him." She laughs, looping her arm in mine. "Are you here with your husband as well? I'd love to meet him." *Ugh. Please, for the love of God, don't bring up my husband again.* Next time she brings him up, I might throat-punch her.

"No, actually, I'm here with my family. My parents always attend these events, and I tag along."

Karina nods. "This is my first time attending. I'm so glad I found you here. I had no idea what to do. Oh, there he is! Come, you must meet my dreamy husband." She practically drags me alongside her, leading me over to a man standing with his back toward us, speaking with two other men. "Honey." She taps the man's shoulder to gain his attention.

The moment the man turns around, my heart drops into my stomach, and the color drains from my face.

No, no, no.

Time stops, and I become frozen in place. Everything and everyone else fades into the background and becomes nonexistent.

My jaw drops right along with my heart, and my wide eyes connect with hazel eyes that I've spent countless hours staring into, countless hours remembering.

"Dean?" I audibly gulp, my voice becoming shaky and my throat as dry as the desert.

"You two know each other?" Karina asks, but I pay her no attention. My attention is solely on the tan-skinned man standing before me.

Dean stands tall, his shoulders broad, his black suit perfectly tailored to fit his muscular body. Eleven years later and he still takes my breath away.

His jaw clenches as if he's grinding his teeth together, and for a moment, I'm unsure if he remembers me or not.

Not until my name leaves his sinful lips.

"Camille." His voice is deeper, but the familiarity is still there.

My name still sounds like pure sex on his lips.

"You know each other?" Karina asks again, dropping my arm to stand beside *my* Dean.

No, not my Dean.

Her Dean.

"Yes, we do. We grew up together," Dean answers when it becomes clear I'm not going to do anything other than stand here and stare at him. With his eyes on me, I watch him press a kiss to Karina's temple, all while my body becomes heated with pure jealousy.

I have no right to be jealous.

He's married.

I'm married.

30

Yet my heart aches watching him touch her so lovingly.

It's been eleven years since he walked out of my life without ever once looking back.

"Oh, wow! What a coincidence. Camille is the friend I was telling you about, the one I met at the support group." Dean's obnoxious wife giggles, clapping her hands together. "Excuse me, the ladies' room calls." She leans up, presses a kiss to his jaw that makes me want to fight her, then walks away with the happiest smile I've ever seen.

I'll remember this moment forever. Because at this exact moment, I've never been more fucking jealous in my entire life.

Clearing my throat, I find myself uncomfortable in his presence. I realize the men he was speaking with have also left, and now it's just the two of us. "It's been a long time, Dean. I didn't know you were back in town."

His eyes watch me so intensely, goosebumps form on my skin. "Just moved back last month. I wanted to be closer to my mother."

"Oh right, of course. I'm so sorry to hear about your father, and I'm sorry I couldn't attend the funeral."

"Don't be. You had a lot going on during that time, I understand." Dean's father, Paul, passed away two weeks after Luca; the same week I was preparing to move back to Seattle. I'd been so wrapped up in my own grief that I never paid my respect to Dean's family. We grew up next door to each other, his parents were my second parents, and I didn't have the decency to call his mother, Lydia, and pay my respects.

"You're married. That's... that's... wow. How long?" I shift uncomfortably from side to side. Seeing him again after all this time is fucking with my head.

Dean doesn't say anything, instead, he stands perfectly still and calm, one hand holding a tumbler with dark liquor while the other is shoved in the pocket of his dress pants. His intense gaze never leaves me, and it's as if his stare burns me with its sheer intensity.

"We've been married for four years now." Feeling out of place,

31

I nervously twist the giant diamond ring on my finger. "Is your husband here with you?" He raises the glass to his lips and takes a swig. I shake my head just as Karina returns to his side.

"This is so great. We can all be friends now. We should double date sometime, Camille. I'd love to meet your husband, too," she says with a bright smile and way too fucking much hope.

Double date. I mentally scoff. There's only one problem with that, but I'm not going to tell her. Nor will I share the details of just how well I know Dean. Not when it's so clear that he's never even mentioned me.

I'm not sure what hurts the most. The fact he's never mentioned me, or the fact that he's looking at me like he's unhappy to see me. For years I've imagined what it would be like to see Dean again, but I never expected to receive such a cold shoulder.

"Excuse us. We should find our seats." He whisks his perfect wife away, leaving me standing there with my heart in the pit of my stomach.

JUST MY FUCKING LUCK, DEAN AND KARINA ARE SEATED AT the same table as my family. His mom is also assigned to our table, but I've yet to see her. My parents greet Karina and Dean, neither surprised to see each other. Clearly, they'd already met Karina, and they knew Dean was back in town.

So much for fucking loyalty.

No one bothered to share that major detail with me.

Mom gives me an apologetic look, while Dad talks business with Dean, and Spencer speaks to Karina, giving my hand a reassuring squeeze underneath the table from where she's sitting beside me.

"Oh my God, Camille!" Lydia, Dean's mom, screeches, smiling wide from ear to ear. She pulls me up from my chair and nearly squeezes me to death in a tight hug. "It is so good to see you again. Look at you! You're so beautiful!" She holds me at an arm's length, looking me over from head to toe. I've always loved Lydia.

Dean leaving didn't change anything between Lydia and I, and we stayed close until the day I moved away. Even then, we spoke from time to time.

She hugs me again. From the corner of my eye, I see Karina shift in her seat, and I wonder about the type of relationship she has with her mother-in-law.

Lydia is her mother-in-law.

The thought is sour and causes my face to scrunch in annoyance.

"Hi, Lydia, it's great to see you." She hugs me once more before letting me go and makes her way around the table. She greets my family while working her way around. Once she reaches Dean, she leans down to press a kiss to his cheek. "Hi son, you look so handsome." She wipes her nude lipstick off his cheek.

"Hello, Karina." Lydia takes her seat, jumping back into conversation with me. *Weird.* I guess she doesn't have much of a relationship with Karina.

"Camille, I heard you moved back. To be honest, I was a little hurt that you never stopped by to see me. I'm still next door to your parents, you know," she half-heartedly scolds me, and I instantly feel like a child. "I understand that you have a lot going on and may feel a little weird coming over. But keep in mind, it's still your home too."

Lydia always told me growing up that her house was just as much mine as it was Dean's. Even when his father was alive, he said the same thing. I told Lydia I was pregnant before I even told my own mother. I'd been too scared to tell my parents, so I'd called Lydia to tell her right after I told Spencer. She was even there holding my hand when I told my parents.

Mom and Lydia are best friends; they call themselves long-lost sisters. I know I've been horrible by not visiting Lydia, especially after Paul passed away, but that house has too many memories. It's been hard enough for me to even go to my parents' house, my childhood home.

"Lydia, I'm so sorry. Please, forgive me for being horrible." I extend my hand across the table and place it on top of hers.

She cuts the air with her free hand. "I'll forgive you if you let me take you for lunch sometime. I miss you, the daughter I never had." My heart aches. I agree to lunch and promise to respond to her calls and texts.

The entire time I speak with Lydia, I take notice of the subtle shifts in Karina's demeanor, but I refuse to speak to her.

My jealousy will not allow me to.

"I didn't realize Dean and Camille were so close," Karina says to no one in particular.

"Those two were inseparable as kids. Our parents had to turn one of our guest rooms into a room for Dean because he was over so often. Going back home next door was too much distance for these two," Spencer says with a giggle, sipping from her glass of wine. Based on her giggle, I can tell she's tipsy. *Great.* Her lips get too fucking loose when she's drunk. If I'm not careful, she'll spill all my secrets to Karina.

"These two didn't understand what *calling it a night* meant. Camille has a permanent room at my house," Lydia says happily, with a smile that brightens her eyes.

"Well, that room won't be hers for long. Eventually you'll want to turn it into a nursery for Dean and me once we have a baby," Karina says, and I nearly choke on my wine. Spencer has to pat my back while she suppresses a laugh.

Karina is Dean's wife.

Dean and Karina.

They're married.

I can't wrap my head around it even when it's being thrown in my face.

The table becomes silent, and Karina and Dean exchange a look, although the meaning isn't clear to me. She's clearly uncomfortable and maybe even a little offended. She isn't aware of the *depth* inside those years of history between us, but it's not my place to tell her.

Calling what we had a "friendship" doesn't seem like enough. We were more than friends. We were always more than friends.

"So Dean, tell us, any new projects coming up?" Dad asks in an attempt to relieve the tension at our table, and I'm grateful for his ability to read the room. Dean begins explaining how he's opened a second architecture firm in Seattle, his first being in London, and how his company, CDJ Designs, will be taking over the projects for Lawson Design Firm.

For the second time tonight, I choke on my wine from yet another bombshell being dropped on me, earning a look from everyone at the table. Taking my napkin, I dab away at the corners of my mouth to clean any lingering wine. "You're taking over Lawson Design Firm?" I ask, my brows pulling together in a scowl.

Dean nods. Judging by the smug expression on his lips, he's already aware of the point I'm getting at.

"Yes, I did take over their client list. And I do believe that you and I will be working together starting Monday."

"Dean, what are you talking about?" Lydia touches his shoulder.

"What he means is that he's my architect. I'm opening a second store here. Actually, I'm moving my headquarters here. And Dean's company is apparently designing my building now," I explain, my eyes never once leaving his. In my peripheral, I see the way Karina's eyes widen.

"Oh, that's wonderful! Dean will design you the perfect building." I can only nod, knowing Lydia is right. I trust Dean fully with my building's design. He may not be happy to see me, but I know that he'll make my plan a reality, especially since it's important to not only me, but to him as well. At least it used to be...

"CDJ Designs, that's an interesting name. How did you come up with it?" I question, shooting him daggers from across the table.

I fucking named his company. Well, we named it together. Years ago. Back when he was *my* Dean.

"Randomly." He smirks. "The idea just came to me out of nowhere."

The pain in my chest intensifies, and it's on the tip of my tongue to ask him what the letters stand for, but now isn't the appropriate time. Besides, I already know exactly what CDJ stands for.

Seeing Dean again is a massive blast from my past that I wasn't expecting. I don't know how I feel about it.

Actually, I do know how I'm feeling.

Emotionally fucked.

THREE

THEN

CAMILLE, 8 years old

"I've told you, sweetie. My friend moved in next door, and we're going to go over and say hello," Mom explains patiently, despite my growing attitude.

"But why? I don't need to meet your friend, and my cartoons are on." I pout, crossing my arms over my chest with a scowl, stomping my foot to add to my childish tantrum.

My mommy and daddy have been telling me all week that their friends will be moving next door to us. Apparently they were best friends in college, but they moved hours away from each other. They'd meet up together every year and kept in contact, and now they've moved in right next door.

"Come on, Camille. Don't be such a baby. Mom is making me go, too. They have a son my age, and maybe he's cool to play with." Spencer turns the TV off, ruining my chance to watch my Saturday cartoons on Nickelodeon. She pushes me toward the door where Mom is standing with a smile and a fresh-baked pie in her hands.

Well, it's a key lime pie, so I don't know if it's baked or not. But she made it, and it's my most favorite pie ever.

"Fine. But I'm only going for the dessert, so they better share that pie." With my hands on my small hips, I march out the front door ahead of my family, scowling the entire walk next door. My scowl is still in place even after I ring the doorbell so many times that Dad has to hold my hand to stop me.

My weekends are my me time. No school, no stupid boys who pull my pigtails, just me and my cartoons. Except for this weekend, because our new neighbors are ruining my life already.

The door opens to reveal a woman who looks Mommy's age. She has dark hair and a wide smile. Instantly my scowl is gone at the sight of her, and I return her smile. She's pretty, and her smile makes me want to smile too. "Hello! You two cuties must be Spencer and Camille. I'm Lydia." She squats down to my height, forcing Spence and me into a tight hug. She smells like warm vanilla.

She lets us go and allows us into her home while she greets my parents. Miss Lydia's house smells of fresh linen, sunshine, and cookies. I like it here, and I like Lydia now too.

I stand beside Spencer, my eyes wandering around the floor-plan that reminds me of ours.

Lydia and my parents are talking in the entryway, so I take it upon myself to venture deeper inside the large house. Spencer says I'm being nosey, but I call it being curious, and Daddy always tells me that it's good to be curious.

"Girls, can you go out back and tell my son, Dean, to come inside? We're going to eat some pie and have fresh lemonade now." Lydia has a nice smile, just like Mom. She seems friendly, and since my parents like her, I'll allow her to live next door. I sure hope this visit doesn't become a weekly thing; I'm not willing to give up my Saturday cartoons more than once.

In sync, Spencer and I nod and run toward the backyard where we find a dark-haired boy playing with his football. He's throwing it in the air and catching it.

Boys are such cootie-infested losers. I wish he were a girl instead. Perhaps Miss Lydia isn't that perfect if she has a son instead of a daughter.

"Your mom says you have to go inside right now," I say, placing my hands on my hips. "Hurry up, so we can eat pie." I then cross my arms, looking him up and down. The boy drops the football and stands before me, mimicking my stance. He's taller than me, so he has to look down to talk to me.

"Who the hell are you, and what are you doing in my house?" I'm temporarily taken aback by the mouth on this boy. I wonder if Miss Lydia knows that he curses.

"You're my new neighbor; your mom let me in, and she says it's time to go inside."

"You're bossy, and I don't have to listen to you."

"Yes, you do, because your mom told me to tell you to come inside so we can eat some pie."

"You don't look like you need any pie," the loser boy says, poking my chubby cheek. Mom says I have baby weight, and that I'll grow out of it when I'm older and taller. I'm eight, so I don't think it's baby weight because I'm not a baby. But I love myself just the way I am, round cheeks and all. Mom says it's vital to have self-confidence, and I sure do.

"Camille, Mom said you have to be nice!" Spencer says, running over to the swing set, not even caring that I'm trying like heck to get this loser boy inside so we can have dessert. We haven't even had lunch yet, so I hope Mom doesn't remember that. She never lets us eat sweets first.

"Your name is Camille?"

"Yeah, and your name is Dean. Come inside, cootie boy, I want pie."

He laughs in my face, and my scowl returns. I like his laugh. He makes me want to laugh, but I don't because I'm really getting pissed off. I should be home watching my shows instead of practically being bullied here.

For a moment, the thought crosses my mind to ask him if he'd like to watch TV with me, but I veto that idea as soon as he does what he does next.

Loser boy pulls on one of my pigtails, yanking my head to the side. "Let's go, Cam. Don't want to miss out on the pie." He runs inside the house, turning his head over his shoulder to stick his tongue out at me.

I rub my head with a frown. I'm tender-headed, and that hurt. Mom says it's never okay to be violent, but Dad says it's okay to hit if it's self-defense and as long as I'm not the one that strikes first.

The loser boy better watch the heck out because he's going to get a knuckle sandwich when he least expects it.

I decide I will never, ever be friends with Dean because he's a big meanie. With my small hands balled in fists at my sides, I decide to run inside and tell on him.

Stupid Dean.

He doesn't deserve any of my mom's delicious key lime pie.

I plan not to tell on him, at least not until I get to eat some pie first. With my luck, Mom might make us go home, and we don't have pie at home.

AFTER EATING A SLICE OF THE KEY LIME PIE, THE ADULTS GO into the living room for a glass of wine and to catch up. Spencer ran back outside to play on the swing set and jungle gym while I took it upon myself to explore the house and find Dean.

Dean isn't hard to find. He's in his room, where he ran off to right after we finished our pie. He's sitting at his desk writing on a piece of paper, and silently, I tiptoe over to him and punch him right in the arm, just like my cousin, Roger, taught me.

Dean removes his headphones and spins in his chair to look at me with a scowl. "Ow! That hurt!" He rubs his arm. "What was that for?"

"That's what you get for pulling my hair." I cross my arms, scowling back at him. The little punk pulls on my pigtail again, and I gasp. "Do it again, and I'll knock you into next week!"

"You punched me, so now we're even." I slug him in the arm again.

He doesn't understand what even means. "No, now we're

even. And we're not going to be friends because you're mean," I say matter-of-fact, earning a laugh from him.

"We're going to be friends, Cam. We're going to be best friends, you'll see. How old are you, anyway?"

"No! We'll never be friends. I don't want a bully as my friend. And I'm eight. How old are you, meanie?"

"I'm eleven. You're such a baby. Isn't it past your bedtime?" h mocks me. Ugh. He's making me so angry! How can he say we'll be friends when he won't stop teasing me? Raising my right hand, I flip him the bird and stick my tongue out, just like Roger taught me to do to bullies at school.

"I'm going to tell your parents. You're in my room, in my house, being mean." He stands, and I sit down in the chair at the desk that he was sitting in. I shove my hands in the pockets of my overalls and swing my legs.

"You started it. I'll tell *your* parents," I counter with a nonchalant shrug, trying not to let him see how afraid that makes me. I don't want him to tell my parents I punched him.

"No! You started it. You were bossing me around."

With a sigh, I say, "I'm sorry I was mean. I wanted to watch my cartoons today, and instead, my parents made me come over here. Don't tell on me, please. You said we'll be friends, and friends don't tell on friends."

Dean walks over to his bed with a smile and sits on top of it. "Okay, fine. I won't tell, but you better keep your hands to yourself. Where did you learn to punch and flip people off?"

"My cousin, Roger. He's fifteen. He says I can only do it to bullies, and you were being a bully." I shrug my shoulders, turning to face his desk and snoop around, finding the paper he was drawing on.

"Hey! You can't go through my stuff." He runs over, taking the paper from my hands.

"What are you drawing? I like drawing too."

"Oh, yeah? Well, I don't care."

"Listen, butthead! We're friends now. You have to be nice, and friends share stuff like this. Now, what are you drawing?" He sighs, giving in and returning the paper to my hands.

"It's an office building. One day, I'm going to build it and have it as my office."

"That's cool. You can see my drawings sometime too. I have a pool; you can come and swim, and we can share our drawings."

"I love swimming. Maybe my mom will let me come over tomorrow."

"Yes, but you have to keep your hands to yourself. Or else I'll punch you again."

A gasp comes from the doorway, causing us to turn our heads toward the sound. "Camille! What do you mean again?!" my mom shrieks and apologizes to a laughing Lydia for my behavior.

"Oh, Mel, kids will be kids. I'm sure Dean's smart mouth provoked a punch," Lydia says, giving me a wink.

"Oh, it sure did," I say smugly, standing from the chair and walking over to my mom. "Dean and I are friends now. He's going to come swimming tomorrow if that's okay with you, Miss Lydia." Mom joins in on her laughter, shaking her head.

"That's fine, sweetie. I'm glad Dean has made a friend already."

"Well, we're still in the trial period, so we'll see how it goes if he can behave." Mom's face turns red with embarrassment.

"Let's go, sweetie. You can play some more tomorrow."

"Thank you for having us over, Miss Lydia. It was nice to meet you." I hug her, looking at Dean once more before following Mom down the stairs.

If he doesn't pull my hair again, I foresee Dean becoming my best friend forever.

FOUR

NOW

DEAN

My mind has been a fucked-up mess since I saw Camille again this past weekend. It's been eleven years since I looked into her captivating emerald eyes, yet it feels as if no time has passed at all.

I knew sooner or later I'd see her again, but I was hoping for the latter. I hadn't prepared myself to see her Friday night. And I sure as fuck didn't expect her and Karina to be friends.

What the fuck is that about?

My wife is friends with the first woman I ever loved.

I'm a bastard for lying to Karina. She had asked me on the ride home if there was more to the "childhood friends" story. I lied to her face and painfully told her that Camille was just the girl next door and never meant anything to me. The truth is, she is so much more than just the girl next door. But Karina can never know. She's already insecure and jealous enough, and I can't push her further. I know her insecurity is my fault. If I were a better husband, she'd have no need to feel insecure about anything. But I'm not a good husband. And I've been exceedingly awful this weekend after seeing Camille.

Karina tried to have sex as soon as we got home that night. She

47

said she was ovulating, and it was necessary, but I couldn't bring myself to fuck my wife while I had another woman on my mind.

Not when all I could think about was how that red satin dress clung to every curve of Camille's luscious body. Not when I could still remember what it felt like to run my tongue across every single inch of her sun-kissed silky skin. The memory of Camille, my sweet Camille, writhing beneath me, has my fucking traitorous cock hard.

Beside me in bed, Karina thinks my hard cock is for her. I'm not going to tell her otherwise, nor will I do anything about it.

It wouldn't be right to give her something not meant for her.

It's not right that I'm thinking of another woman while my wife is innocently lying beside me.

"Mmm. Someone is in the mood this morning." Karina wiggles her ass against my cock while in the spooning position we're in. Before I can respond, she pushes me onto my back and climbs on top of me, straddling me and kissing my neck in the delicious way she always does. "Let's brush our teeth and continue this." She climbs off me, leaving me with a raging boner like I'm a fucking teenager again.

Throwing the covers off myself, I sigh, looking at the tent in my boxers.

Fuck. I'm painfully hard.

Like the good husband I wish I could be, I follow Karina into the bathroom and stand beside her at the sink while we brush our teeth together. The second she spits out the toothpaste, I'm on her like a starved man.

Like a bad husband, I fuck my wife from behind against the bathroom counter with thoughts of another woman playing in my head. I have to close my eyes while I'm inside her so that I don't see my reflection in the mirror. I feel bad enough as it is.

Camille has fucked with my head, and I wish I'd never have to see her again.

That's the first lie I tell myself.

"You really gave me your all. Thanks, honey. I feel confident that we made a baby," Karina singsongs. She's so hopeful. She is always so damn hopeful.

I'm beginning to wonder if sex is even for her enjoyment anymore. Does she want me like she used to, or does she only want me for the purpose of making a baby? I know she *wants* a baby, and I want her to be happy, but a baby isn't the answer to fixing a marriage that has been broken for years. We're not happy; we've grown apart and fallen out of love, but we're too afraid to admit it to each other.

"I'm ovulating, so we'll need to do it again tonight and tomorrow to be sure we catch the egg." Karina steps out of the bathroom, holding the digital ovulation test in her hand. "If it doesn't work this cycle, I want to try IVF again."

"Karina, I think we should take a break from trying. No more tracking your cycle, no more tests, no more procedures." The words are out of my mouth before I can control myself or think about what I'm saying.

Gasping, she shakes her head, looking at me like I've gone crazy and grew three heads. "No, Dean. I don't want to stop. I know we'll eventually be successful and have a healthy baby that I can carry full term. I'm not done trying."

I'm the one that opened the door for this inevitable conversation, and now I can't close it. The discussion about her obsession with trying to conceive is long overdue and has been weighing heavily on me for a while. It's time to be honest and speak my truth. "I'm done trying, Karina." I close the distance between us, taking her small hands in mine. "We both need to step back and take a break. A lot is going on right now, and for the time being, we need to stop." It isn't a complete lie. I'm stressed from our move and with establishing my company here in Seattle. I'm jumping into two new projects today and taking over a current project that has already begun.

There's a lot on my plate right now, things she'd never understand.

"Why are you saying these things? You want a baby just as

much as I do." That's not entirely true, nor is it false. When Karina got pregnant the first time, our marriage had hit a rough patch, and during one drunken night in an attempt to rekindle our romance, we ended up creating a baby. A baby girl that never got the chance to take her first breath. Our beautiful angel was born sleeping, and Karina has been obsessed with trying to conceive ever since.

I worry about her; I do. That's why we need to take a break from trying before it drives us further apart.

"You're just saying this because you're stressed with work and the move. I knew we should've stayed in London." She pulls her hands away from mine with a sigh.

"Don't ever say that. You know my mom needs me, needs *us*. And yes, I am stressed with work. I can't stress about work and then come home and stress about getting you pregnant." I'm not looking for an argument, but I should've known this sensitive topic would lead to one. It always does.

"Your mom is fine, Dean! It's been a year since your father died. If anything, she needed you then. Not a year later. Besides, she has her *precious* Camille." I don't miss the disdain in her voice when she mentions Camille, but I choose to ignore it.

My mom and Karina have never been close. Mom did not agree with me marrying her. She never felt we were right for each other, but she respects my decision and has always been respectful toward my wife. I wish Karina would be better toward my mother, who is my number one. I'm not a mama's boy, but I'd take a bullet for my mother any day. I'd protect her with my dying breath. Karina has never understood our relationship, which caused a strain on our marriage in the beginning. She doesn't understand how much family matters to me.

Even as important as family is, I'm surprised by the fact I don't want to have a child. Not now, at least.

"I'm her son, and she needs me. We'll finish this conversation later; I need to get to work." With a sigh and shake of my head, I walk toward the chair in the corner of our bedroom and pick up the freshly pressed suit Karina laid out for me last night. Picking up the clothes, I dress myself quickly, watching as she crosses the room and slips inside the closet, returning with my jacket seconds later. She helps me into my navy suit jacket and adjusts my tie.

"Fine. We'll talk later, but keep in mind that I'm not done trying. One more round of IVF, Dean. If it doesn't work, we'll look into surrogacy." She kisses my cheek and walks off toward the bathroom as if she hadn't just dropped a huge fucking bombshell.

Hell to the mother fucking no. Surrogacy is not an option.

Forty minutes later, I arrive at the construction site that will soon become the headquarters for Sinful Pleasures, Camille's clothing line. We agreed to meet here with the head of construction to discuss bringing Camille's dream to life.

I park my blacked-out Lamborghini Urus behind her Range Rover and watch her from the window like a creep.

She's standing next to Garrett, the construction crew manager I hired. They're both laughing, and something resembling jealousy takes over me. My hands ball into fists in my lap, and I grind my teeth, hating that he's getting to hear her laugh. I don't need to be beside her to remember what her laugh sounds like. I've never forgotten the sound, and if I'm being honest, it's a sound that I fucking miss. She hadn't laughed on Friday. She barely even spoke or looked in my direction. I would know; I couldn't keep my goddamn eyes off her.

I'm a bad husband.

Instead of continuing to watch her like a weirdo, I shut off my car and join them. She's wearing a form-fitting emerald dress that matches her eyes and clings to her body like a second skin. A pair of black heels wrap around her ankles. Even after eleven years, she's still able to take my breath away with one smile. She's older now; her body more mature and even more beautiful than I remember.

Her crimson lipstick has me thinking dirty thoughts. Thoughts I have no fucking business thinking.

I clear my throat and shake my head, needing to snap out of it. I need to get myself out from under the spell she's so effortlessly cast on me. "Good morning. I hope you have an idea of what you want for your building." I interrupt their conversation, jumping right to the point. For my sake, I can't make small talk with her. It's too dangerous.

"Yes, I do. I have a few rough drawings, but I trust that you can work with them." The way her plump lips curl up at the corners has my cock twitching.

Beside her, Garrett starts talking, but I'm too focused on her red lips and sinful body to pay attention to anything that's being said.

Fuck. This is going to be the longest project of my life. I'm half-tempted to tell her that I can't work with her and will set her up with someone else.

Being around her is dangerous.

While I'm willing my cock to stay down, Garrett begins sharing a few updates about his construction crew with both of us. The only thing I manage to catch is that they're to start tearing down the current building today and get the space cleaned up.

When Camille purchased this location, there was already a building here—which was once a mechanic shop—but it's been vacant, and the lot has been for sale for years.

It really is the perfect location for her headquarters. And as I look around, a strange feeling of familiarity comes over me.

I can't quite place it, but I know that I'm missing something.

We spend twenty minutes discussing the plans to tear down the current building and clean up the lot. Afterward, we say our goodbyes to Garrett, then Camille and I agree to go back to her office to discuss the design plan further.

NOT LONG AFTER, WE ARRIVE AT A LARGE OFFICE PLAZA downtown. I follow Camille into the parking lot and ride the elevator with her silently up to the twentieth floor, where her temporary office is located. The woman at the front desk buzzes us in and offers a friendly wave that Camille returns.

"A few of my staff members from New York followed me here. I'll need to hire some more, but I want to get construction started first," she explains while leading me down a hallway. Her makeshift location is not what I was expecting. I hadn't realized she was already beginning to move operations here and had staff. As we pass by the different offices, she explains what each one is for.

The first office we come across is for legal, the second for printing, the third for marketing, the fourth for design, and finally, we reach the fifth door at the very end of the hall, secluded away from the other offices. The fifth is her office, and once we're inside, I see that it fits her perfectly.

A white sectional couch is against a white wall, and above it hangs a large gold and black painting, across the room is her cherry oak desk, and near the sofa is a minibar cart. The wall directly ahead is a floor-to-ceiling window that displays the Seattle skyline. It's a beautiful view and exactly what I'd expect from Camille.

She gestures for me to take a seat in front of her desk. Unbuttoning my jacket, I take a seat, my eyes carefully watching her movements. She sits in the chair behind the desk, and frozen, I watch her pull a folded piece of paper from one of her drawers.

With a smug grin on her plump red lips, she slides the crumpled paper across to me. "This is what I want. As I said, it's a rough sketch, but I know you can bring the vision to life."

I lean forward, take the piece of paper, and I'm instantly taken back many years as I see the semi-faded ink and a very rough sketch. "You kept this?" I'm shocked, to say the least.

It's my design. A design I made for her when we were younger. Even as children, Camille talked about one day owning her own clothing company, and my plan was to design her dream building.

"Of course I did. I am a little surprised you didn't remember the location."

"What?" I ask, just as the realization hits me, causing me to laugh suddenly.

How did I not realize it sooner?

She's bringing my plans for her to life—the location we chose together and the design I made for her years ago. I'm surprised she even remembers after all these years, and I'm even more shocked that she still wants the same design.

"Okay, then let's get started. I know exactly what to create for you." Her eyes meet mine, and I know I'm not the only one feeling the sizzling electricity between us.

Camille has come into my life unexpectedly after eleven years, and I know that life as I know it will never be the same again.

FIVE

THEN

DEAN, *12 years old*

"Where are we at?" Camille pushes down the kickstand on her bike and walks toward the gate of the vacant building that I brought her to. She turned nine today, and right after we had cake and ice cream at her house, I told her I wanted to show her something, so we jumped on our bikes, and I led her straight here.

This is my birthday present to her.

"We are at the location of your future clothing company," I explain with a wide smile. For a year now, Camille has been talking about one day becoming a fashion designer and being famous. She's been talking about wanting to find the best office space in the entire city. When I was riding my bike one day, I found this place and knew that it was perfect for her. It sits on a hill and overlooks Seattle beautifully. It was once a mechanic shop that went out of business a few months ago, and since then, it's been gated up. I've never seen anyone around here.

"Dean! Are you serious?" She jumps up and down excitedly, clapping her hands.

"Look"—I pull a piece of paper out of my jacket and unfold it carefully—"this is exactly how I will design it. I'm going to build it just for you." I stand beside her, holding my hand out to offer my sketch to her.

"You drew this for me? Why?"

"I'd do anything for you, Cam. You're my best friend." She surprises me by throwing herself at me and hugging me tightly while she squeals joyously. I relish in the feeling of holding her against me, my nose buried in her silky black hair. She always smells like vanilla and coconut, and it's become my favorite scent. "I want to help you achieve your dream of having the best building for your fashion stuff."

She pulls away from me, her fingertips tracing over the lines of the blueprint on the paper I gave her. "I will, thanks to you! This will be my number one location. I'll work here and live with you, and together, we can create more so I can open several stores worldwide." Camille has always been a big dreamer. While most kids her age are talking about becoming a princess, an astronaut, a doctor in space, or any other crazy career choices us children come up with, she knows exactly what she wants. Her mind has never changed. She has her entire future planned.

We have our future planned. I'll become an architect, and she'll be a fashion designer.

"I know you will, Cam. You're going to be the best." We've known each other for a year now, and she is my best friend. We've been inseparable ever since we met. I'd shown her my drawings, and she decided that she liked them and announced to our family that we'd become best friends officially.

"I'll have my brand, and you'll have yours. I'll design clothes, and you'll design houses and all types of buildings." Her smile is contagious. Camille loves talking about the future. And even though she's three years younger than me, she knows exactly what she wants. I only hope I'll be lucky enough to be with her through every milestone of her dream to witness the greatness she'll one day achieve.

"That's the plan. We'll be power best friends."

She scrunches her nose. "You mean like a power couple?"

I shrug my shoulders with my hands in my pockets, look down at the gravel and kick a few rocks. "Yeah, like a power couple."

"CDJ Designs. That's what you should name your company." I look up at her sudden announcement, watching as she carefully folds the piece of paper and shoves it in the pocket of her pink overalls. I don't think I've ever seen her wear anything other than overalls—okay, that's a bit dramatic, but overalls are her favorite.

"CDJ Designs? What does that stand for?" I ask, my eyebrows pulling together in a frown.

With an eye roll, she pops her hip and places her hand on it. "Camille and Dean Jameson. You know, once we get married, I'll have your last name." She runs up to the gate and begins climbing up, leaving me standing in my tracks wholly bewildered. I'd never thought about it before now, but I think she's right.

One day I will marry my best friend. I've always thought marriage was gross and had once announced to my parents that I would never get married. But watching Camille climb the fence with a carefree smile on her pink lips, I decide right then and there that marriage is for me after all, but only if I'm marrying her. If marriage is what it takes to see her smile every day, then so be it.

When we grow up, she'll be mine forever.

I don't want to spend one day away from my best friend.

"Come on, slowpoke!" she yells from the other side of the fence. With a smile, I run after her and climb up the fence carefully, following her across the vacant lot of the once mechanic shop. She walks in front of me, goes right up to the door, and lets herself inside.

Scoffing, I say, "Stupid people. Someone should keep this place locked."

"If it were locked, we wouldn't be able to get in here," she deadpans, giving me her signature look with her hands on her hips. She throws her head back, rolls her eyes, then carefully tiptoes inside the building, opening a second door that leads to what looks like the former owner's office.

"My office is going to be twenty times this size." She sits on the

59

dusty, squeaky chair behind the desk, pulls her legs to her chest, and spins herself around while the chair groans and squeaks. "I need to look at your drawing again. I want to know all about your plan." She stops spinning, pulls a granola bar out of her pocket, and munches on it while pulling the drawing from her other pocket.

I swear this girl can't go anywhere without snacks in her pockets.

Taking the paper from her, I sit on top of the desk and unfold the blueprint, pointing to each drawing. "We'll remove this building and build a brand new one. It'll be huge! You'll have a perfect view of Seattle; you'll have an office on the top floor with a floor-to-ceiling window to see the city. And there will be so much room for all of your designs and everyone who will work for you." I want to be an architect just like my dad when I grow up. I want to create beautiful buildings and houses for people that will make them smile, just like she's smiling now.

From my peripheral, I see her staring at me. I like the way she looks at me. And I like that she always includes me in the plans for her future. When my parents moved us to Seattle, I had to leave all my friends behind. And being the new kid in school didn't exactly make me popular. I can count on one hand the friends that I have.

Camille.

Spencer.

Dallas.

Nathan.

That's it. See, one hand.

"Happy birthday, Cam. This is for you."

"Thank you. But I want one more thing." She sets the wrapper from her granola bar on the desk and uses the back of her hand to wipe her mouth. I wonder what other snacks I'd find if I were to reach inside her pocket. It's not like she's starving. It's a strange quirk.

"Anything for the birthday girl. What else?" She stands up from the chair, closes her eyes, and puckers her lips.

Woah. Wait. What?

I'm caught off guard. I hop off the desk and stand in front of her, wiping my sweaty palms on my faded blue jeans.

Does she really want me to kiss her? I've never kissed anyone. I thought about kissing her before, but she's too young, and I don't think she knows what she's doing, not that I do either, but I've seen it in movies. I'm almost a teenager, and according to Dad, my first kiss should be happening soon. He said he had his first kiss when he was my age. That girl was Mom.

Maybe if I kiss Camille at this age, she'll be my wife for sure. Just like my parents. Their love story is my favorite story ever told.

I pucker my lips and lean down to Camille's small figure and press my lips to hers.

Instantly, we both pull back, open our eyes, and burst into a fit of laughter.

My cheeks turn red. "Does this mean you're my girlfriend now?"

"No! I can't be your girlfriend! Mom says I can't date until I'm sixteen," she states as if I should've known. With her tiny hands, she twirls her dark pigtails.

"Okay, so we'll wait until you're sixteen and then you'll be my girlfriend."

"But you'll be nineteen. What if you get another girlfriend?" The corners of her pink lips curl down in a frown.

I take her small hand in mine. "I won't. Promise." I hold up my pinky with my free hand, and she loops hers around mine.

"Good. Because we're getting married one day, and I'll punch your girlfriend if you get one."

"Okay, calm down, Ali." I laugh at her hysterics.

"Who's Ali?" Her eyebrows pull together in confusion.

"Never mind. Come on, let's go back home."

Hand in hand, we run out of the building and race toward the fence.

That was the first day I realized just how much I cared for my best friend and couldn't imagine a future without her in it.

SIX

NOW

Camille

"Are you going to the support group again tonight?" Mom asks me from across the dinner table.

"No, not tonight. I need to catch up on some work, and a bubble bath is calling my name," I answer before shoving a forkful of lasagna into my mouth.

"She's just trying to avoid Karina, Dean's wife, who she met in the group," Spencer says with a smug smirk, knowing damn good and well that is precisely why I want to avoid the support group tonight. The night of the gala, right after I discovered that my new friend is the wife of my first love, I called Spencer and told her all about it.

Mom shakes her head, exchanging a look with Spence. "Oh, Jesus. You spent the day with him too, didn't you?"

"No, only a few hours. He's the architect who's designing my building, so of course, I'll see him. We had a meeting this morning and went over some ideas. Doesn't matter. I have an appointment with Dr. Reynolds tomorrow, so that's good enough." I wipe my mouth with my napkin. "By the way, thanks for the heads-up about Dean being back in town." I roll my eyes. "Whatever, doesn't matter anyway. Mom, this is amazing. Thanks for dinner."

I change the subject before they can continue about the support group or Dean.

It's just us girls for dinner tonight. Dad had an emergency surgery at the hospital, so it's girls' night. Mom said she was making lasagna, and I'd never miss the opportunity for a home-cooked meal. Lately I've been living on protein bars, takeout, and wine. Not exactly a healthy lifestyle, but I haven't had the time to cook.

Luckily, mom catches on to my need to change the subject, but unfortunately, she brings up another topic I don't want to discuss. "How's Declan? Have you spoken to him recently?" she asks cautiously, causing me to roll my eyes again. She's determined to go from one triggering topic to the next. If she's bringing up Declan, I know there must be a good reason. She knows things with him are off the table for discussion.

My silence is the only answer she needs to continue. "Well, he called me today. He wants to hear from you. He's getting out in two weeks, you know." Dropping my fork and letting it clank against my plate, I toss my napkin on my plate and stand up from the table with a huff.

"Yeah, I know when he gets released." I exit the dining room without looking back, and go to the living room, where I slip my shoes on and grab my purse from the hall closet.

"Come on, Camille. Don't get upset. You know Mom is only trying to help," Spencer says, following me into the living room with Mom hot on her heels.

"Please, sweetie, stay. You don't need to leave. I won't bring him up again."

"No, it's fine. I need to finish working anyway." I hug and kiss them both goodbye and leave just as quickly as I arrived.

I'm annoyed that my mother has been speaking with Declan. And I'm annoyed that my husband had to call her to tattle because I've been ignoring his calls. I don't want to see him. I don't want to speak to him.

Not yet anyway.

Fuck!

What the fuck is he doing calling my mother? Yes, I've been purposely ignoring his calls. But I have enough on my plate to deal with now, I don't need to add worrying about my husband who needs a good fucking punch to the damn face.

Fuck him!

I know my mom is only trying to help. According to my dad, my mom accepts every call and visits him as often as she can, even taking him baked goods and little gifts. She fucking spoils him and is making me look bad. I'm the one that's supposed to be visiting him. Yet I haven't seen him once in nearly three months.

My mom and I agree on most things, but when it comes to my husband and my lack of communication with him, she doesn't agree with my tough love approach, and I don't blame her. A wife should be there for her husband during the bad times and good.

Unfortunately, I can't be what he needs right now.

"How was the group? Did you actually attend?" Dr. Reynolds asks the first question to start our session.

"Yes, I went last Monday, and it was nice."

"Why didn't you attend yesterday?"

"I met a woman in the group. Not just any woman. She's the wife of someone I used to know," I explain, causing her to raise a curious eyebrow. I watch silently as she flips to a new page in her notebook to write something down. "And this woman is why you didn't go yesterday?"

I roll my lips between my teeth, thinking of what to say next. I may sound childish for missing the group just because of Karina, but knowing who she is now, I know we will not be able to continue a friendship. There's no way.

I choose to answer the question honestly. "Yes. I didn't want to see her again. Not so soon, at least." Dr. Reynolds urges me to continue, so I do. I tell her all about my history with Dean, how his wife is part of the group, and how I saw him again over the weekend for the first time in eleven years, and now he's designing my building. A building that he drew up the initial designs for when we were younger, and it's even at the exact location he chose for me on my ninth birthday. I tell her everything about Dean... well, almost everything.

When I finish speaking, for the first time since I've known her, she's speechless. She writes several things in her notebook, and I watch her brown eyes twinkle. A faint smile curls on my lips at the fact that I opened up to her.

"How did you feel when you saw Dean again after all this time?" she finally asks after several silent minutes.

"I felt like nothing had changed. It felt like he was still my Dean, and we were kids discussing our future together."

She nods, her curls bouncing from the movement. "But he's not your Dean anymore. He has a wife and a future with his wife. And you have a husband. Speaking of which, are you still ignoring his calls?"

Fuck. I don't need the reminder that I have a husband.

"I know... but it feels like he'll always be my Dean. I gave my soul to him at a very young age." I look down at my hands in my lap, twiddling my thumbs together. I don't bother responding to her question about Declan.

"Perhaps your feelings for him were reignited because you're lonely. Declan has been away for a while now and seeing a man you used to love made your subconscious realize that you're feeling lonely and confusing those feelings." Fuck. Why does that make so much sense?

Maybe she's right. But that can't be true, can it?

Actually, yes, it can. She's right. She's a hundred percent right. I'm lonely, and seeing Dean and Karina together reminded me of how lonely I actually am. I miss romantic dates and intimate moments. They seem to have a happy and healthy marriage, and perhaps it's made me a little envious. I smile brightly, choosing to believe what she's saying but knowing deep down that it's the furthest thing from the truth.

"Declan will be home in two weeks. I think he's what I'm missing." My first lie of the day. I don't miss him. I don't miss those moments with him. Not anymore. There was a point in time when I was happy and loved being married. I loved my husband and my life, but that piece of me died a year ago.

The day I buried my baby boy was when I stopped loving my life.

"I think so too. Have you spoken to him? Do you plan to work on your marriage once he returns home?" she presses. I shrug my shoulders.

"We haven't spoken in nearly three months. He's called, but I've ignored every call. I'm not ready to speak to him."

"Do you think your marriage is redeemable?"

"I don't know. We need to discuss and figure out a lot when he does get home."

"Perhaps you'll rethink attending couples therapy. It can truly help you two." I nod, no longer wanting to continue with her chosen topic.

I hate talking about Declan. I hate talking about my marriage. I hate talking about most things about my life. I prefer to keep myself busy with work because I hate dealing with or thinking about anything else. If I allow myself to stop thinking about work, then I begin to think about the hole in my heart—the emptiness.

The truth is, I don't know who I am anymore. I was once a good wife, a good mother, and a great person who loved life and living.

Now, I'm nothing.

I'm not living; I'm merely existing.

SINCE LAST NIGHT AT DINNER WITH MOM AND SPENCER, MY head's been in a funk. I had hoped today's therapy session would help me, but it only left me further confused with my feelings.

Stepping off the elevator, I greet Emily, my receptionist, and walk down the long hallway toward my office.

I've just entered and sat down at my desk when my intercom beeps. "Yes?" I answer with a sigh, not in the mood to deal with anyone. I should've spent the day working from home.

"Camille, there's a Karina Jameson here to see you."

I sigh. Elbows on my desk, I lean forward and rub my temples to soothe my throbbing headache.

"Thanks, Emily, you can send her back."

A minute later, there's a knock on my door. Rolling my green eyes, I stand and walk across my office and open the door to reveal the last person I want to see.

Karina has come to visit. Great. How fucking lucky am I?

"Hi Karina, what can I do for you?"

"Hello, Camille. You weren't in group last night, and you didn't answer my calls or texts, so here I am. I just wanted to make sure you were all right." I step aside and allow her to enter my office, closing the door behind her.

"Sorry, my phone died, and I've been too busy to charge it." I grab my phone and spare charger from my purse and plug it into the outlet beside my desk. The red battery appears on the screen showing how dead my phone is. "I had a lot of work to catch up on, so I stayed in last night to work."

"Yeah, I figured you were busy with the new building. Dean is pretty busy himself." Karina sits in front of my desk, and I reclaim my chair behind it. "How did your meeting with him go yesterday? Were you able to come up with a few ideas?"

Why is she asking about this? She's the last person I ever want to discuss him with.

Being the friendly person I am, I answer with a smile. "Yeah, we have a pretty solid plan. He's drawing up the ideas and will show me later." I pick up the sketchbook from my desk and close it, cleaning up some of the papers scattered across the top.

"Good, I'm glad to hear it. It seems you're his only client at the moment. The rest of his design team is handling his client list. He cleared everything to work with you himself. You, his old friend." There's malice in her tone. Does she not believe Dean and I about being old friends? In a way, it's true. We were only friends. We never dated, and she married him. I got the boy he once was, and she got the man he grew up to be.

I may have his past and all his firsts, but she has his future and will have all his lasts.

"That's very kind of him. I'm sorry, Karina, but I'm swamped. Is there anything I can help you with?"

She watches my movements closely for a long minute with a blank stare. Blinking, she smiles and stands up. "No, as I said, I just wanted to check on you. Perhaps we can grab lunch when your schedule clears up?"

"I'm not sure when that'll be. It's a little crazy around here, as you can tell. But I'll try. I will text you." I stand, following her toward the door. I have no intentions of contacting her to plan anything.

"Great. We do need to plan a night out for a double date. I'm anxiously waiting to meet your husband." With a smile and wave, Karina departs, and a sigh of relief washes over me.

Fuck me. I can't be friends with this woman. Not when I share such a deep history with her husband.

A history she knows nothing about, and I hope he never tells her. It's our past, our story, and it doesn't need to be retold, no matter how beautiful it was.

SEVEN

THEN

CAMILLE, *12 years old*

"Hi, sweetie. Dean is upstairs. You can go on up." Lydia greets me with a tight hug. I thank her for letting me come over, then take off running up the stairs, yelling Dean's name until I reach his bedroom. Without bothering to knock, I open his door and skip over to his bed, where he lies in the middle on his back, sound asleep. Slipping my flip flops off, I climb onto the cloud-like mattress and begin jumping up and down.

"Dean! Wake up! Dean!" I yell, giggling while I jump on his bed, causing his sleeping body to jump and shake.

"Knock it off, Cam! I'm sleeping!" he groans out, his voice raspy.

"Get your lazy butt up! It's summer, and you're sleeping. What's wrong with you?" I roll my eyes, somehow managing to jump so high I nearly touch the ceiling.

"Exactly." He pulls the blanket over his head, curling into the fetal position. "It's the first day of summer vacation, which means we should both sleep in."

"It's noon! You've slept enough. Now, get up. We're going to the lake today." I reach down, grip the blanket, and force it down from his face. His arm reaches out, and he grabs my ankle, pulling me down onto the bed on my back. Laughter flows freely from my open mouth.

Dean's hands grip my waist as he pulls me closer to him, raises the blanket, and covers us both.

"Stop, we're not sleeping. Come on, get up!" His only response is a groan. "Fine. Your choice." I reach across to his nightstand, take the half-empty water bottle, unscrew the lid, and pour it over his head. If he's going to waste his day sleeping, that's what he gets.

"Camille!" he yells, jumping out of bed, shaking his wet head of hair at me. Droplets of water land on my cheeks, causing me to laugh even harder.

"Oh good, you're up. Get ready. We're leaving in five minutes." I lie back on the bed, put my hands behind my head, and cross my legs. His furious hazel eyes look me over, but he eventually disappears into the bathroom.

While Dean is getting ready, I run downstairs searching for Lydia, finding her in the kitchen as always.

"What are you two doing today?" she asks once she spots me. She's leaning over in front of the oven, removing a tray of delicious-smelling cookies. My mouth waters from the sweet aroma. She's so like my mom, always having freshly baked goodies around.

"We're going to the lake with Spencer and Dallas. My parents are at the country club today," I explain, earning a sweet smile from Dean's mom, who has become my second mother in the few years I've known them.

"I'm meeting your parents there later when Paul gets home. I'll be sure to tell them you said hi." She reaches toward me and rubs a thumb across my cheek. "Come on, let's make some lunch for you four then." She disappears into the pantry, returning with a large picnic basket seconds later. She sets it on the marble island, then walks around to the fridge and takes out all the ingredients for sandwiches.

Side by side, we make sandwiches and pack veggies, cookies, and water.

Lydia's loading all our food into the picnic basket just as Dean comes into the kitchen dressed in black swim shorts and a white T-shirt. He takes a warm cookie from the baking sheet and hugs his mother goodbye.

"Bye, Mom."

"Bye, Lydia. We'll be home around dinner time."

"Okay, kids. Be safe and have fun. Call if you need anything." Dean and I nod in sync, and he carries the picnic basket next door to my house.

"There you are. Let's go!" Spencer yells from where she's standing and waiting with her boyfriend, Dallas, in our driveway. She's not sixteen yet, but our parents like Dallas, so they agreed to them dating because she will be sixteen in a few weeks. I asked Mom if I could date Dean since they like him, but they both said no.

It's totally unfair. I can't date, but Spencer can. I wonder if they'd change their mind if they knew that Dean and I kissed. I make a mental note to ask my sister for her advice later.

She's the best big sister. She always gives great advice, and I know she'll steer me in the right direction.

Dallas is sixteen and has his license. His parents bought him a car, so he came over today to drive us to the lake. He takes the picnic basket from Dean and places it in the trunk next to the cooler of drinks he brought. Once all four of us are buckled, we set off for the lake.

LUCKILY FOR US, THERE AREN'T MANY PEOPLE AT THE LAKE. Since today is the first day of summer break, I thought there would be a lot of other kids from school here, but there's no one. It's great because I'm not too fond of crowds.

There are only a few other people here that I can see, but

they're not in our area. Dallas opens the trunk of his car to allow us access to the swimming supplies, food, and drinks. He and Spence grab a few pool noodles and run off together.

Dean and I opt for the inflatable floats, but blowing them up takes forever because Dallas forgot the air pump.

Such a dumbass.

I give up about halfway through blowing mine up, but lucky for me, Dean takes over and finishes it. Once they're both fully inflated, we're ready to roll.

Dean holds both of our floats, one under each arm, and walks toward the water. I'm ready to follow him when I remember something and pause. "Wait, we need sunscreen first." I remove my tank top and shorts, revealing the hot pink bikini that Spencer let me borrow. It's a little big in the chest, and we had to tie it a few times to fit me since I don't have boobs yet like she does.

Once, I overheard Dallas say on the phone that he likes her boobs. Thankfully she didn't know I was listening in on her conversation. In my defense, I had picked up the landline to call Dean, unaware that she and Dallas were on it doing something called phone sex. I hung up after Dallas's boobs comment.

But now I wonder when I'll get boobs, and when I do, will Dean like them?

Shaking the thought away, I grab the bottle of sunscreen from the car. Last summer, I got a horrible sunburn, so I'm not taking any chances this time. Waving the white sunscreen bottle in the air, I yell out to Dean, "Can you lotion up my back, please?"

He sets our floats down near the water and jogs toward me. He has already taken off his T-shirt, gracing me with a view of his muscular, tan body.

Once in front of me, he takes the bottle from my hand and squirts some of the white lotion onto his hands. I pull my hair into a bun and give him my back. He warms the sunscreen by rubbing it between his hands so it's not cold when his fingers touch me. I relax against his long fingers, allowing him to rub the lotion into my back and massage it thoroughly.

Dean surprises me by rubbing down my entire body. I had only expected my back, but I'm not arguing. The feel of his strong hands is nice on my body. He makes me feel warm under his touch.

Once he's finished with me, I rub him down in exchange, my hands lingering a little too long on the washboard abs he's been forming over the last few months. He has a nice body. He works out and plays sports. He's nice to look at, but I'll never tell him that. He's my best friend, and I worry I might scare him away if he knows how much I like how he looks. So, for now, it's my secret. Spencer told me it's best to keep my feelings for Dean to myself for now, so I do. No matter how badly I want to tell him.

The last time we kissed or talked about marriage was three years ago when I was nine and he was twelve. We're much more grown now and haven't had any further kisses. Much to my dismay.

Once we're both lotioned up, we remain silent as we race toward the water. I pick up the hot pink raft that matches my swimsuit and carry it into the water, waiting until the water reaches my knees before I climb on.

Pulling my sunglasses over my eyes, I adjust myself on my back, place my hands behind my head, and allow the water to float me away.

Inhaling the warm summer air, I smile and say, "Ahh, this is the life."

"It sure is." Dean splashes around beside me, then gets on his raft.

We remain in the water for hours, taking turns splashing each other. Several times Dean even flips my float over, causing me to crash into the water.

When we finally return to shore, there is no sign of Spencer or Dallas anywhere. I'm sure they're off somewhere making out, but that doesn't bother me because I'm having so much fun with Dean.

We sit side by side on a towel in the sand, eat our sandwiches, and gulp down two bottles of water each.

"So, Dean... can I ask you something?" I ask nervously, munching on a cookie after I finish my sandwich.

"You know you can ask me anything." I can see him looking at me from my peripheral, but I'm too afraid to look at him, so I keep my focus on the cookie in my hands. "Why are you acting shy?" He nudges me in the shoulder playfully.

I shrug my shoulders, picking the cookie apart into small pieces. "I heard that Sadie asked you out," I blurt, holding my breath while I await his answer.

Dean is fifteen now, and he's the hottest boy in school. He's popular, and all the girls want to go out with him. I know this because Spencer told me. He and Spencer go to high school together, while I'm left behind in middle school because I'm only twelve.

Spencer has told me a lot about Sadie, and she doesn't like her either. I've only met her once or twice when I've been at Spence's cheer practice. They're on the cheer team together. I know just enough about her to say that I hate her. I hate her even more because she's set her sights on what's mine.

Dean is mine, and stupid Sadie needs to keep her stupid cheerleader paws off him.

"How did you... Spencer told you?" He does not deny it, which means it's true. My hands ball into fists, crumbling the cookie even further. The chocolate melts in my palms.

"So, it's true? You're going out with Sadie?"

"Well, she asked me on a date. She wants to go to the pizzeria." I'm getting angrier the more he speaks. Props to her for taking charge and asking him out. Usually it's the guy asking the girl. But girls are just as capable. Girl power and all that. But Sadie doesn't seem like the type to go to the pizzeria for bowling and pizza. She's too prissy to eat that delicious cheesy, doughy goodness.

Do you know who isn't too good to eat pizza and go bowling? The real type of woman that Dean should go on a date with? *Me.*

He's my best friend and has been since I was eight years old, but now I'm developing feelings for him. I want more than friendship.

"Well, are you going to go?" I should shut up, but I can't stop. I want to know. I want him to tell me he's not going, and I want him to finally ask me to be his girlfriend. Even though my parents say I can't date yet. I'm willing to keep it a secret for now. Parents don't need to know everything. They can't control my life. I'm my own person.

"Why are you asking? Are you jealous?" He turns to face me. I look up at him and shake my head.

Busted.

He knows me too well and will see right through me.

Scoffing, I shrug my shoulders, acting like I'm unbothered. "What? No! You can date whoever you want." He laughs. This punk is laughing at me! I shove him in the shoulder, crossing my arms over my chest, my eyebrows pulling together in a scowl.

"You're cute when you're jealous," he says, laughing his deep laugh that's been my favorite sound since I was only eight years old.

"I'm not jealous. You can date stupid Sadie if you want to."

"Yeah, sure. You're lying." He lies down on his back with his head on my lap and looks up at me with a smug grin that I want to wipe off his perfect face. "I told you, Cam, it's you and me."

"Yeah, but until then, you could want to date someone."

"Why would I want to date someone who isn't you?" My scowl is wiped away, and a smile threatens to form on my lips. My heart beats rapidly in my chest, and I can practically feel the butterflies fluttering in my stomach whenever I'm near him.

Dean reaches up and brushes the loose strands of hair out of my face, his thumb gently brushing over my bottom lip. My lips part, and a gasp escapes from his touch, and suddenly I want him to kiss me again. The longer he looks at me with hooded eyes the way he is, the more I hope we'll share another kiss.

And soon.

"Come on, let's get back in the water." He jumps up, running toward the water, leaving me on shore, panting from his touch.

Holy cow.

I really do have deep feelings for my best friend.

EIGHT

NOW

Camille

"Thanks for bringing the designs over. I'm excited to see them." I rub my hands together eagerly.

It's Thursday, and I haven't seen Dean since Monday.

Actually, I've been avoiding him since Monday. Seeing him again has been too much, and after seeing Karina on Tuesday, I haven't been able to bring myself to face either of them. It's hard enough to see him; I don't need to see his wife and be reminded that he married her.

He *chose* her.

What a childish way of thinking. It's not like we're in a competition. But if we were, she won. She won the man I love.

No, the man I *loved*.

I have a husband now, and we're not the same people we were all those years ago. We were young, foolish children who hadn't experienced life. Now we're grown adults, and both know how ugly and unfair life can be.

It would be wise for me to remember that, though it's hard.

It's hard to see Dean because he makes me feel the same way he did when we were kids falling in love. All it takes is one look at him for the color to come back into my life, and that's wrong. He shouldn't have any effect on me whatsoever.

He's not mine anymore.

Clearing my throat, my eyes connect with his captivating hazel eyes. Eyes that I stared into each time he'd thrust into me or taste me with that warm velvet tongue. The memory of him hovering above me comes back to me like a slap in the face. I press my thighs together as warmth floods my core.

No. Stop, Camille. You can't think those things.

"Are you okay?" The sound of Dean's husky voice breaks me from my stroll down the memory lane. I smile and nod, because that's all I can do.

"Yes, of course, I'm fine. Please have a seat, and you can show me the designs." We sit side by side on the couch, and I watch him unroll his design plans and lay them out on the coffee table in front of us. The blueprint design is everything I could ever want.

The amount of detail is extraordinary.

Looking it over, I find myself speechless. He remembers all the things I had told him when we were young that I one day wanted.

He remembers everything.

Everything.

My heart swells.

Dean points to different areas on the blueprint and explains every detail to me. The top floor will be my office. City view, floor-to-ceiling windows, and the space is large enough for me to have a boardroom in my office for meetings, separated by a sliding glass door. He exceeded my expectations, as I knew he would. I have complete faith in him. I trust him entirely with something so personal to me, knowing he is the perfect person to bring my vision—our vision—to life.

Maybe it's fate that brought us back together.

"I'm thinking that I should take your silence as a good thing," he says, leaning back against the plush white sofa, his fingertips brushing my shoulder innocently when he raises his arm to rest on the back of the couch. The simple touch sends electric shocks through me.

Fuck. If he can ignite my body with a simple touch or look, I already know this will be difficult.

He's awakening a part of my body that's been dead for so long.

Clearing my throat, I roll my lips between my teeth, then gather enough courage to look at him. "Yes, very good. Holy fuck, Dean. This is amazing." I can't downplay my excitement.

"I can always change whatever you want or add anything else you want. I used my old designs and memory as reference." He chuckles; the deep sound enough to turn my insides to liquid.

"No. No, it's perfect. There's nothing that needs to be changed. This is exactly what I want."

He nods, giving me one of his dazzling, toe-curling smiles. "Here is a list of interior designers in Seattle that I'd recommend if you haven't already hired someone." He leans forward, opens his folder, and hands me the list of information for interior designers. "Most have a long waitlist, so it would be smart to find someone soon."

With a nod, I take the list from him and look it over. One name feels like a slap to me across the face. "Sadie Marshall? As in, Sadie Marshall from high school?" I scoff, looking up at him with my eyebrows pulled together in a scowl.

He gives me an apologetic look. "She's rated as one of the top interior designers in Seattle and has a very elite client list and exceptional recommendations. Hate to say it, but she's the best at what she does."

Great, how lucky am I? The Sadie fucking Marshall.

As in the stupid Sadie Marshall from high school who made my freshman year a living hell by embarrassing me every single chance she got because she wanted Dean to herself, and I was his younger best friend who stood in the way. Sadie was a fucking she-devil.

Good God. I cannot work with her.

"I must've done something horrible in another life if my path is crossing with Sadie's again," I say sarcastically with a long dramatic eye roll.

He laughs at my misery, not bothering to hide it. "Keep rolling your eyes, and they'll get stuck in the back of your head."

God, I can even feel his deep laugh all the way to my toes. I clench my thighs together and lean against the soft back of the couch, covering my face with my hands. "Do not laugh at me. I'm serious. This is painful."

"Then hire someone else. I just wanted to make sure you had all the options of those who are the best."

"I sense a *but* coming." I peek at him through my fingers, still covering my face.

He grins, shifting toward me. He wraps his long fingers around my wrists and pulls my hands away from my face. "But would you really not hire someone who is clearly the best just because of a high school beef from years ago?"

"Dean! She made my life hell, and you know this. And stop laughing at me." I'm being dramatic. We both know I am. It's so easy with Dean. Everything is so fucking easy when I'm around him. It's as if no time has passed, and we're able to slip right back to the people we used to be. How we used to be with each other.

"She did it because she was jealous. And how well did that turn out for her? Sadie and I didn't end up together, did we?"

I huff out a breath of air. I've always hated when he spoke logic to me. I allow myself to look at him, really look at him. My eyes scan over his handsome face, taking in his sharp features. His oval-shaped face, thick black hair that's cut into a comb-over, longer on the top and faded on the sides, trimmed beard, and stunning hazel eyes with bright specks of gold. Everything about Dean Jameson is attractive. He's pure sex on legs.

Inhaling deeply, I pry my eyes away from him before he's able to cast me under his spell any further. "Neither of us did. Guess we both lost," I mumble under my breath, unable to stop myself, hoping he doesn't hear, but knowing that's not the case.

Dean never misses a single fucking thing.

His eyes connect with mine, his thick yet trimmed eyebrows pulling together in a deep V, his plump lips thinning. He grabs hold of my wrist, and his thumb traces invisible shapes on my skin. I'm not sure he even realizes he's doing it, but his warm lingering touch makes time freeze.

Time fucking freezes.

I know we both feel the spark. It's always been there between us.

I used to think there were invisible strings between us pulling us together, but I realize how crazy that sounds. I've always hated that mushy, romantic shit, but when it comes to Dean, I feel like a mushy hopeless romantic.

He pulls away from me quickly, dropping my wrist as if I burned him. Clearing his throat, he begins gathering the papers on the table. "If you don't want to make any changes, then construction can go ahead and get started. My guys should be ready to start with the foundation on Monday. They've got the old building torn down, and the place is nearly cleaned up," he explains.

"That's great. I'm looking forward to seeing it once they get started."

"I'll call you on Monday, and you can come and check it out if you'd like."

"Yeah, that sounds great." He has everything packed up; now, the only thing left for him to do is go. I don't want him to leave. I want to stay in his presence for as long as possible. But I know it's not wise for him to stay. There's no reason for it.

By the way he's lingering, I don't think he wants to leave either. There are so many things left unsaid between us. So many questions that I need answers to.

I open my mouth to speak, but he beats me to it. "Can I ask you something?" he asks with a sigh but doesn't wait for me to respond before he begins speaking. "You and Karina... you two are friends? Why?"

I sit up straight and put a cushion of space between us, turning slightly to face him. He mirrors me, both of us facing each other. "We met at a support group for grieving parents. My therapist recommended it. I didn't know who she was when I met her, and she just clung to me. We started to become friends before I knew she was your wife."

"And now? Are you two still friends?"

"Honestly, Dean, it's a little weird."

"Weird, how?"

"Well, she's your wife. You. Yours." I point at him to punctuate my point. He leans forward and places his elbows on his knees, letting his head fall into his hands.

"Yeah, I get your point. I wouldn't want to be friends with your *husband* either," he spits, pure venom in his tone at the mention of my husband.

"Why didn't you come back for me?" I whisper the question that has been lingering in my mind for eleven years. I regret asking as soon as the words leave my mouth, but I need to know. I need closure.

Dean drops his arms and raises his head to pin me in place with just one look. I can see the sorrow in his eyes for a split second before it becomes a look I don't recognize.

"I did." His eyes shrink into an aggressive glare.

Damn! If looks could kill.

Like the confident brat I'm feeling, I hold up my left hand and look down at my wedding ring. "No, Dean. You didn't." I wave it in his face and point toward his own silver wedding band.

"Yes, Camille, I did. I tracked you all the way to New York, and I even saw you once. You were wearing a pink sundress and had a baby in your arms and a ring on your finger. I was too late for you."

My heart drops, and my breathing stops. He came back for me... but it was too late. I had Luca and was married, which means he came back six years after he left.

Six years too late.

I'm not sure how long we sit in silence staring at each other, but I'm the one that finally breaks our silence and staring contest.

"Six years. You came back six years later? After radio silence all that time?" I stand, balling my hands in fists at my sides.

He narrows his eyes at me. "That was our deal. I told you when you graduated from school that I'd come for you because that gave me time to start a design firm and start preparing for our life together. And that's exactly what I did. I'd already met Karina, but I wanted you," he states sternly, standing to his feet.

He's acting so casual about his revelation while I'm struggling to breathe and process this new information.

Dean came back for me. He followed our plan.

"What did you do after you saw me?"

"It doesn't matter what I did. You had moved on, so I left."

"Dean, what did you do?"

"I went back to London to be with Karina!" It would've hurt less if he'd slapped me in the face. "I waited for you! I followed our plan!" My lips turn down in a frown.

"I got pregnant, Dean. It was unplanned and unexpected. But how the fuck was I supposed to know that you were across the fucking world waiting for me?" I yell, placing my hands on my hips. I'm so angry that I'm sure there will be steam coming out of my ears soon.

"We had a plan, Cam. I waited for you because we made a fucking plan."

"Yeah, a plan when I was fucking fifteen and love-drunk on you! Do you not understand that life happens and things can change? Life doesn't go according to a plan you make when you're fifteen!"

"You married someone else! You had a baby with someone else! Don't twist this around and blame me. I meant it when I said that I only wanted you. That there would never be anyone else."

Fuck. I ruined our plan, but I don't regret meeting Declan even for a second because if I hadn't, then I never would've had Luca.

My stubbornness wants to challenge him and see how far I can push him.

If we're fighting, does it mean he still cares?

At that time, we hadn't spoken in six years, not since he left me when he went away to college. How was I supposed to know that one day he would come for me out of the blue?

We were foolish kids when we planned out our life. And sometimes, things don't always go according to plan.

"You were the one that wanted me to have a typical school experience and not sit around waiting for you. So, I did, but I got pregnant." I brush my hair out of my face with a defeated sigh. "None of this matters now. We're both married to other people, and we can't change the past, and I would never want to even if I could." My hands grip my hips. "I waited for you. I had hoped that one day you'd come back for me. I dreamed about it for so long. I dreamed about touching you, kissing you, making love to you in our special place until the sun came up. I wanted to spend forever with you." I stand and take a confident step toward him, placing my hands on his chest. "I waited and wanted you for so long, Dean. Then one day, I realized that you were right when you said not to wait and to continue living. There was a chance that you would've never come for me, and so many times, I wondered if you'd forgotten me, so I allowed myself to have fun and truly live for once without thinking of you. The next thing I knew, I was married and had Luca." I give him a sad smile. "I've loved you since I was eight years old, and I'd been waiting since then for our chance to be together, but it never came. We were silly kids, Dean. Time has never been on our side, and we never were meant to be. I'm not sorry that I didn't continue to wait for you because I had Luca, and I will never ever regret the decisions I made that led me to creating him." I pour my heart out to him, letting him see me wear my heart on my sleeve. It's time I close the door on my past for good and separate myself from him. It'll be hard considering we're working together.

As I speak, I see the realization that flashes over him, causing his hazel eyes to soften. "Of course, you shouldn't regret anything. I guess you're right. We had a stupid childhood crush and fooled ourselves by thinking we were made for each other." His eyebrows pull together, and I watch his jaw clench as if it pains him to get the words out.

We both know he's lying.

"Why did you marry Karina? Are you even in love with her?" I ask the lingering question.

"I married her because I love her. Do I love her the way I love you? Fuck no. Will I ever love anyone the way I love you? Fuck no." He hangs his head. "For a while, Karina and I were good together. You moved on and got married, so I did too."

Stepping away from him, I say, "Things between us now are strictly professional." We're both liars.

"Karina doesn't know anything about our past. I want to be the one to tell her before she finds out from someone else." I can only nod. He steps further away from me, grabs his blueprints folder, and walks toward the door.

He pauses with his hand on the doorknob, and I stare at his back, his shoulders tensing up.

"I never stopped thinking about you and our time together. I still remember every single minute that we've spent together, and I'm sorry things couldn't be different." Dean opens the door and walks through it without a second glance at me.

Once again, he leaves me staring at his back.

He leaves me behind, taking another piece of my heart with him, just like he did eleven years ago.

NINE

THEN

CAMILLE, *13 years old*

"Wow! Your parents bought you a car?" Dean's parents purchased him a 2008 Mercedes G-Class for his birthday. The car came out earlier in the year, and Dean has been gushing over it ever since. His parents had previously told him there was no way they would buy him a car for his birthday, but surprise. The proof is in his driveway with a big red bow on the hood.

"They sure did! They gave it to me this morning." He smiles ear to ear, and I know mine mirrors his. I'm just as excited as he is. Dean finally has a car of his own, and not just any car. A brand-new car he's been wanting for months.

"Well, congrats, you deserve it. I'm happy for you!"

"Thanks, now get in." I don't need to be told twice. I race to the passenger side and climb in, watching through the window as Dean removes the bow and then joins me inside the car. He inserts the key into the ignition and brings the car to life, whistling at the engine's sound. He shifts the car into reverse, and then we're pulling out of his driveway, all the while beaming at each other.

Dean drives us to an ice cream shop, where we order a banana split with two spoons to share. We sit on the outside patio shoving ice cream in our faces.

"I still can't get over the fact your parents bought you a car and are letting you throw a party tonight." His parents agreed to let him throw a party with friends from school to celebrate his sixteenth birthday.

According to Spencer, half of their high school is coming, and apparently, it will be wild. I doubt it will be wild, though, because Dean doesn't like parties. He has always been invited to them, but like me, he thinks they are stupid.

"Yup! And I hope you didn't change your mind about coming. You know that it'll only be worth it if you're there with me."

The unfamiliar ache in my chest returns every time he says something sweet. "Duh, why wouldn't I come? It's my best friend's birthday. Plus, I have to make sure you don't get drunk and end up kissing some girl from your class." He laughs, but I'm serious. Dean is mine, and I won't allow anyone else to have him. I've always had feelings for him. I've been in love with him since I was eight, and lately, my feelings have been getting harder to hide. I want to believe we'll end up together like we sometimes talk about, but I worry that may not happen. Dean has so many girls after him, girls who are his age and better suited.

I'm thirteen, and I'm just a child compared to the girls that Dean goes to school with. I'm not even in high school yet. I'm just Spencer's younger sister and Dean's neighbor. No one knows that we're best friends or that I'm secretly in love with him.

No one knows but me... well, and Spence.

Sooner or later, he will want to go on dates, kiss someone, and even have sex. And I'll just be the girl who's too young for any of that.

Spencer told me all about sex last year. I forced her to after I found a package of condoms in her room, so I now know everything, and I understand that it's not something I want to do any time soon.

With a sigh, I dig my spoon into our banana split and take a massive bite. Every year for each of our birthdays, we visit this same ice cream shop and share a banana split, minus the bananas because they're mushy and gross. So, basically, it's just a split or a very large ice cream sundae. Whatever you want to call it.

"Will you wear that purple dress I like? It's my birthday, so you have to do whatever I ask you to do," Dean says around a mouthful of ice cream.

I giggle at his full mouth. "Okay, fine. So, birthday boy, what are we doing next?" I let him have the last bite of ice cream. It is his birthday, after all. He eats it without argument.

After we clean up our trash and begin walking down the sidewalk, slowly, Dean takes my hand in his, intertwines our fingers, and leads me back toward his new car.

"Let's just drive around and listen to some music?" he suggests.

"Okay!" I break free of his grip and clap my hands together. His touch is nice, but sometimes I get too nervous and unsure what to do when he touches me. I see him giving me a questioning look, so to avoid making things awkward, I stick my tongue out at him and run toward the car, knowing he'll be racing right alongside me.

I don't know how to act around him lately. Sometimes he looks at me a little too long, making me nervous. I don't want to do or say anything stupid, but I also don't want him to get the wrong idea. I've matured physically since last summer. I have boobs now, and my figure is beginning to shape nicely.

Thanks to health class and an older sister, I'm aware of all the changes that my body is going through—and Dean's body, too. But I'm not ready to do any of the teenage things that Spencer does with Dallas.

Dean unlocks the door once we reach the car, and I reclaim my rightful seat as passenger. "I'm going to call my mom and let her know we'll be out for a while," he explains, and I nod.

He starts the car, and I watch as he pulls out his phone and dials his mom to tell her that we'll be out for a while, driving his new car around. Instead of waiting for him, I climb out of the car and run across to the corner store to get us snacks for our drive. I don't know how far we are going or how long we'll be gone, but that doesn't matter. We both like having snacks around for any reason and any length of time.

After paying for our snacks with the cash my parents have given me, I race back to Dean and take my place in the passenger seat.

Minutes later, we're off on the open road.

Dean takes the backroads, and I'm pretty sure we'll end up getting lost, but I don't care. I'll go anywhere and get lost with Dean as long as we are together. It doesn't matter. We can end up breaking down on a backroad, and the only thing that'll matter is that we're together.

My heart thumps in my chest at the thought.

"What's on your mind? You're silent over there." Dean breaks our silent streak. I look over at him, a grin spreading across my face.

"Nothing, just thinking that we need some music." I lean forward and turn the radio on, flipping through the stations until I find a song I recognize. "What You Got" by Colby O'Donis blasts through the speakers while I sit back in my seat, put my feet on the dash, and sing my heart out through mouthfuls of candy.

This is freedom. This is living the good life and living freely with the person who makes your young heart beat. I'll always remember today as being one of the best days of my life.

We don't speak much during our drive, but Dean and I don't always need to be talking. We're both comfortable enough with each other to simply enjoy the silence.

He reaches over and slowly takes my hand in his, lacing our fingers together and squeezing gently. His thumb traces circles on the back of my hand while he drives. His eyes remain on the road while my eyes are on him.

This is twice today that he's held my hand and touched me as more than just a friend. I like it.

Quickly, I use my free hand to take out my pink Razr cell phone and capture a quick picture of him, setting it as my home screen. He looks over at me briefly, the shutter of my camera giving me away. Luckily for me, he doesn't mind. Good thing, because he looks so cute with one hand on the wheel, eyes on the road, and a carefree smile on his face. I couldn't resist taking the photo, especially with his hand being in mine. I want to lock this moment in time forever.

At this moment, I've never been happier than I am right now with my best friend.

We drive around for what feels like hours. When we finally return home, I wave him goodbye and run home to shower and get ready for his birthday party tonight. My parents are helping Dean's parents set up for the party next door, so Spencer is the only one home.

Knowing she's home and hoping she'll help me, I rush to her door and burst into her lavender-painted bedroom.

"Knock next time!" she yells, jumping away from Dallas with a guilty expression, her lips red and swollen from kissing. I roll my eyes and cross my arms over my chest.

"You're lucky I'm not mom or dad. You know the rules, no boys in the room with the door closed." She climbs off the bed and mirrors how I'm standing.

"What do you want?"

"I need your help getting ready for Dean's party. He wants me to wear my purple dress, and I was hoping you could do my hair and makeup." I've never worn makeup before, but Spencer just started wearing it, and all her girlfriends wear it, and she says that Dallas and other boys at school like it.

She's my big sister, so she'd know what guys like.

"Baby sis, you don't need makeup." Her scowl softens as she wraps an arm around my shoulders.

"Stupid Sadie will be there tonight, and you know that she's going after Dean. I want to look hot." I plead my case, getting a roar of laughter from Dallas. My eyebrows pull together, and I look behind Spencer to where her boyfriend lies on her bed. I shoot him a scowl, which shuts him up quick.

"Okay, fine. I'll help you. Dallas, I'll be back."

"It's cool. I'll go next door and see Dean." He climbs off the bed, his brown eyes full of humor as he walks toward us. I look away while he and Spencer kiss. Dallas and Dean had become good friends a few years ago. He's friends with Spencer too, so naturally, they formed a close bond. I'd be lying if I said that sometimes, I feel left out.

Spencer leads me to my bedroom and takes it upon herself to step into my closet, searching for my purple dress. Seconds later, she returns with my dress in one hand and shoes in the other.

"Here." She sets the items on my bed. "Go shower and then I'll do your hair. You're wearing a dress, so you'll need to shave." I nod, then skip off toward my bathroom. I strip, then step inside my shower.

I'm nervous. So nervous I end up cutting my knee while shaving because I wasn't paying enough attention. I've never been to a high school party before. I'll have Dean and Spencer, but it will be different. I'll be the youngest person there and will hardly know anyone. If I didn't care for Dean so much, I wouldn't even go.

I keep reminding myself that I'm doing this for him.

I wash my hair with my vanilla coconut shampoo that Dean likes so much. When I finish, I step out of the glass shower and towel myself off, spreading vanilla-scented lotion all over myself. It's a lotion that he gave me for my last birthday.

I'm beginning to realize that I like doing things that he likes. I'd do anything for him.

I'm standing in front of my vanity mirror, wrapped in my fluffy pink bathrobe, while Spencer is working on my hair behind me. She blow-dries my long hair, then begins straightening it, getting the flat iron too close to my scalp occasionally, causing me to flinch.

"I'm not going to put a lot of makeup on you or Mom will kill us both. Besides, you're too young and already pretty, you don't need it."

"You're young too, but you still wear makeup."

"I'm sixteen. Therefore, I'm allowed to wear makeup. Plus, I have a boyfriend, so I can do things you can't do." I roll my eyes at her.

The only makeup she agrees to put on me is a little bit of eyeshadow that's barely noticeable, some mascara, and clear lip gloss. It's strawberry flavored, and I secretly hope Dean will get to taste it tonight.

Spencer zips me into my purple spaghetti strap dress that lands above my knees, and I put on the black ballet flats she picked to go with.

Just like that, I'm ready to go to the party.

My first ever high school party and I'm not even in high school yet. Maybe by the time I get to high school, everyone will think I'm cool, and I'll have a lot of friends since I'm partying with the cool kids already.

Spencer says it's better to show up to a party late. I don't know why; the party starts at eight, and we're not going until nine. It seems ridiculous to show up late, but even Dallas, who comes back over, says that's what the cool kids do. I wonder if he knows he doesn't sound very cool calling himself a cool kid. I have even texted Dean to see if he wants me to come over early, but my texts go unanswered.

Guess he's having too much fun with his high school friends.

At nine o'clock, the three of us walk across the street to Dean's house. We let ourselves in, and I'm instantly left alone just as soon as we enter. Dallas drags Spence off somewhere to either make out or find their other friends.

I stand alone in the foyer like a loser, not recognizing a single person in the crowd.

The music is loud, and the further into the living room I get, the more I recognize the song. "Whatever You Like" by T.I. is playing. I finally see Dean sitting on the couch in the living room surrounded by a bunch of his friends, and there on his lap is Sadie freaking Marshall. I hate her even more now.

Spencer has told me many times about how Sadie is going after Dean and how he has always ignored her, but he isn't doing anything this time.

The stupid blonde sits on his lap like she belongs while he's smiling at her. He is freaking smiling at her! What the heck?! He either needs to push her off, or I'm going to really be angry.

Screw it, I'm angry at him for allowing her to sit there in the first place.

"Yeah, birthday boy, you can have *whatever you like*," Sadie yells over the music with a giggle, leaning into the side of his face. She must be whispering something in his ear because his smile grows, and his hand touches her knee.

One of the guys sitting beside him passes something I recognize as a joint to him, and I wait for him to pass it, only he doesn't.

I stand invisible in the crowd of people watching as my best friend smokes a joint and touches Sadie, who is still sitting on his lap. Is there not anywhere else she can sit?

Maybe on the floor after I punch her.

Balling my hands into fists at my side, I inhale deeply and push my way through the crowd toward Dean. His bloodshot eyes meet mine, and a stupid grin forms on his lips.

"Hey, Cam." *Hey, Cam? Really?* That's all he has to say to me?

Sadie's eyes snap to mine, and she glares at me. "Hey, Cambria." She smirks a nasty smirk.

"It's Camille, not Cambria." She waves her hand as if to say she doesn't care.

"That's a stupid name," she says to a girl sitting on the arm of the couch with a giggle. The brat isn't even trying to be quiet.

"You want to talk about stupid names, Mercedes? At least my

parents didn't name me after a car." She gasps, crossing her arms over her chest.

Yeah, that's right, I went there.

Not many people know that Sadie is short for Mercedes. But thanks to my internet skills, I found her parents online and learned her full name. I also learned that she hates her name because she was teased in elementary school about being named after a car, so she's been going by Sadie ever since.

"What are you even doing here, little girl? It's past your bedtime." I mimic her stance, crossing my arms over my chest and glaring at her.

"I'm here for Dean's birthday. But you can feel free to leave, and don't let the door hit you on the way out."

She looks at Dean and wiggles on his lap. "Are you going to let this child talk to me like that?" He doesn't respond; he's too busy laughing, as are his friends.

"What? Are you so afraid of this child that you need someone to protect you?" I challenge, standing my ground. I'm not about to be intimated by the blonde-haired, big-boobed she-devil. If she wants to go at it, I'm ready.

"You're just a stupid little girl who follows Dean around like a lost puppy. You can't take the hint that he doesn't like you. He's even told me himself. You're only embarrassing yourself, and you look ridiculous being here in that dress that's clearly too small for you and wearing makeup that makes you look like a clown. Just go home, little girl, and leave Dean the hell alone!" she yells loud enough for everyone to hear. She stands, so I have to tilt my head back slightly to look at her since she's several inches taller than me in the ungodly high heels she's wearing. At some point, the music paused, and everyone in the room has stopped what they were doing and circled around us, giving us their complete attention.

All eyes are on Sadie and me.

My cheeks heat with embarrassment, but I refuse to let her see how much she's affecting me, so I fight back. "The only one here who's embarrassing themselves is you. Dean doesn't want you, yet here you are, sitting your boney ass on his lap, trying to make him pay attention to you. You're pathetic," I hiss. My parents didn't raise me to take shit from anyone.

Out of nowhere, Sadie raises her hand and strikes me across the face. My head snaps to the side toward Dean, who I see is now standing, his fists balled at his sides and his face fuming with anger. Judging by the way he's looking at me, I'm unsure if he's angry at Sadie, or me, for potentially ruining his party.

I've never been slapped before, and holy crap, it hurts! Refusing to give stupid Sadie the satisfaction of seeing how much she hurt me, I blink rapidly, praying that the tears stinging my eyes don't fall. If I cry in front of this room filled of high schoolers, I'll never live it down.

Instead of showing pain, I smile, ball my hand into a fist, cock it back, and punch Sadie right in her stupid little face. The crowd roars with laughter. I'm positive that my hand is broken, so I use my unbroken hand to flip the bird to Dean before I turn and run out of his stupid party.

I was right all along.

Parties do suck.

High schoolers suck.

And stupid Sadie can go straight to hell along with Dean who did nothing to stand up for me.

TEN

NOW

Dean

For the second time, I fucked my wife while I had another woman on my mind.

I'm a piece of shit. A real fucking piece of shit.

And if that isn't bad enough, I don't even finish.

I faked it because I didn't want to cum inside my wife. She couldn't tell and didn't even notice that I was still painfully hard. The moment I slipped out of her drying pussy, she raised her legs in the air, hoping to help my sperm reach her eggs.

I say nothing while she lays there hoping to get pregnant.

I go into the bathroom—unnoticed—and stay in there long enough until I'm positive Karina is asleep, then I slip into bed silently and hope she won't wake up, because I don't want to talk to her. I don't want to hear about how we might get lucky and get pregnant even though she knows where she's at in her cycle, and I didn't finish inside her.

Even when she's not ovulating, she still can't refrain from talking about getting pregnant. For once, just fucking once, I'd like to fuck my wife without the next words out of her mouth being, "I feel like this time was it."

Don't get me wrong, I'd like for Karina to have a baby. I'd love

105

nothing more than to see her smile and for her to be happy. I'm willing to give her almost anything she wants, but a baby is the one thing I don't think I can give her. Which doesn't make any sense. I want her to be happy and become a mother, but I don't want to be the one she has the baby with.

As stated, I'm a piece of shit.

I know losing our daughter damn near killed Karina, and I can't pretend to imagine her pain because I wasn't the one that carried a life inside of me. My wife is a fucking superhero. *Women are fucking superheroes.*

I'm just tired.

So tired of disappointing her month after month and seeing the devastated look in her blue eyes when her monthly pregnancy test is negative. She thinks I don't notice her crying in the bathroom every time she starts bleeding, but I do.

In the beginning, she let me hold her when she cried. Now, she hides it from me, and I don't know why.

Karina and I had never discussed having children. Her first pregnancy was a surprise.

Again, not once did we discuss it. She never asked how I felt about it, and I never told her, because I could see how much enjoyment it brought her, knowing that we'd have a family one day. I don't believe you need children to be a family, but she thinks otherwise.

We've both been through every possible exam out there to test for infertility, and not a damn thing is wrong with either of us. I have a great sperm count and outstanding motility, and she has a great egg count and quality. There's no reason for our lack of success with getting pregnant. I had hoped that moving to Seattle would change things and Karina would relax, but she's still as obsessed as she was in London.

Day by day, I feel further and further away from her. I love my wife, but the spark we once had is long gone, and it has been for a while now.

With Camille, our spark was explosive. It *is* explosive.

With her, it's always been a massive fucking bomb of fireworks every time I'm near her. The times we shared have been fucking phenomenal.

Eleven years later, and with one look at Camille, it feels as if no time has passed. I remember exactly how I felt with her, and I still feel exactly as I once did when I look at her.

With Karina, in the beginning of our relationship, our spark was like sparklers. You know, the sparklers that you light on the Fourth of July. Nothing spectacular, but at least it's something that'll bring a smile to your face.

Our connection has always been sparklers, while my connection with Camille has always been the whole damn fucking firework show. The show you wait all night to see.

The fact I'm even comparing the two makes me an even bigger asshole. But am I more of an asshole for thinking of another woman or for staying married to a woman who I'm only content with? Who I've always only been just content with?

By staying with Karina, I'm preventing her from meeting her perfect soulmate and having the family she dreams of one day. We have been drifting apart for years, and instead of ending things like we need to, Karina continues to believe a child will repair our relationship.

It won't, and I know that, but she desperately wants to be a mother. She'd make a great one, so I've participated in her fantasy, all while being unhappy and hoping that her monthly pregnancy test will be negative. Hoping I can stop being a coward and ask for a divorce.

I'm not a religious man, but I like to think that we've been unsuccessful with having a baby because God knows we're not meant to be parents and is waiting for Karina to meet her person.

A person who I know isn't me.

The logical thing to do would be to ask for a divorce, but I'm a selfish bastard.

These thoughts stay on my mind throughout the night and into the following morning.

The sun is beginning to rise. I love mornings. I love the warmth of the sun on my skin and the color it paints a room as it rises.

Closing my eyes for the first time all night, I roll over onto my side and wrap my arms around my wife's sleeping body. She stirs slightly before turning on her back and exhaling deeply, signifying that she's awake.

My eyes open and land on her blue eyes staring back at me.

So often, I wonder what she sees when she looks at me.

Does she see a man who loves her but isn't *in* love with her?

Does she see a man who's been dreaming about someone else?

Or does she see a man in love with another woman, who has always been in love with another woman?

Wondering what goes through Karina's mind is honestly reminiscent of one of the world's greatest mysteries.

"Good morning, honey." Her silky voice brings me away from the many things I wonder when I look into her big blue eyes. She seals her mouth against mine, for once not caring that we've yet to brush our teeth.

Since I'm an asshole, I take the kiss and her parted lips as an opportunity to slip my tongue inside of her mouth. My dick stirs in my boxers, needing attention, still painfully hard from last night. My fingers tangle in the strands of her short blonde hair. Suddenly, Karina turns her head to the side, breaking our kiss.

"Come on, let's get ready for the day." I roll onto my back with a groan and watch her walk away from me.

No surprise there. She's good at walking away when I want her. We can only ever fuck on her terms.

I'd like to kiss my wife just once without her worrying about morning breath and her morning appearance. But that's not possible for Karina. She must be fully presentable before we can properly function.

At this point, I'm surprised we don't sleep in separate beds.

Karina doesn't like to cuddle. She likes to read and have a cup of tea in bed at night, then she faces her back to me and complains about being too hot when I try to touch her. I can't remember a time when Karina let me feel her at night or a time when she was spontaneous.

In the beginning, Karina's obsessive need to plan everything out attracted me to her. I, too, like to have certain things planned out. It's how I keep control of my day, but now I wish she could fucking be spontaneous.

Even our sex is fucking planned for the most part. She tells me when we'll have it and what position we'll do. And we only do it after we both shower, then she wears her sexy little silk nightgown, and we fuck without the pure, heated passion we once had. I've tried to fix our marriage, even brought up therapy several times. She refuses, claiming there's nothing wrong with us, and that all we need to do is spend more time together.

More time together isn't the solution. I can't force her into couples counseling, but I have tried to repair our relationship.

Minus the time we fucked against the bathroom counter, that was a fluke. I had hoped for a second round but was rejected.

No surprise, but we don't do oral because she doesn't think it's appropriate for her to suck my cock. I've tried to eat her pussy before, and she was disgusted that I'd be willing to stick my tongue in such a place.

What's a man got to do to get some pussy on his tongue? I know women who must beg for their man to eat them. Yet here I am, wishing my wife liked it.

Camille liked it.

I miss having a woman's tight little hole squeeze my tongue as I tongue fuck her pussy and coax orgasm after orgasm from her body.

I miss shoving my meaty cock down a throat, having lips wrap around it, sucking it like a fucking lollipop.

I remember the first time Camille came on my tongue. When she came, it was like a delicious waterfall. She was so embarrassed when she saw my face coated in her juices, but I fucking loved it. She tasted like heaven.

Needless to say, to this day, that's still my favorite fucking flavor.

I wonder what Karina would taste like. Probably nothing. She showers so many damn times a day that her pussy never has a chance to become seasoned. I'd like to taste her after she finishes a HIIT workout at the gym. When she's sweaty and thinks she's disgusting, that's when I'd like to lick her from asshole to clit and taste her.

I feel like a horny teenager. I'm ready to cut off my own arm for a chance to have someone sit on my face and swallow my cock.

Licking my lips, I climb out of bed, walk into the bathroom, and wrap my arms around Karina from behind, kissing her bare shoulder while she stands in front of the sink, flossing. "Come with me this weekend to California," I say, thrusting my hips against her so my hard dick can slip between her ass crack. I wouldn't mind bending her over and watching my cock disappear into her tight, puckered asshole, but I know that'll never happen. A man sure can dream.

She laughs, staring at me through the mirror. "Honey, you're going for work. You can't bring your wife along."

"My meetings are during the day. You can explore and go shopping, and when my meetings end, it'll be just you and me."

"No, don't be ridiculous. You have to work, and I have housework to catch up on." Housework? What housework? Our ridiculous, way too large, in-your-face home is so spotless you can lick the floors. Our housekeepers do a great job.

"Come with me, please." She shakes her head, wiggling free from my embrace. "Do something unplanned and out of character just once. Just fucking once, Karina," I grunt, inhaling deeply through my nose to keep myself calm. I try time and time again to rekindle our romance and remind myself why the fuck I married her, and time and time again, she lets me down. Just for once, I'd like to do something with my wife that isn't penciled in her fucking ridiculous planner. For a woman who doesn't work, she sure as fuck is busy and keeps a close eye on her schedule.

"Dean, don't you dare act like that. What's wrong with you? You've never asked me to go with you on a business trip before." She rinses her mouth, then turns to face me.

"I'm asking you now. I want my wife with me because I miss you, and you know what? I'm tired of fucking on a damn schedule." She gasps, her hand rising to her chest.

"Don't be vulgar. We make love! And why are you complaining about these things now?"

"Never mind. I don't know what's wrong with me. I need to pack." I scrub my face with my hands, leaving the bathroom and stalking across our oversized bedroom toward our closet. Yet again, my attempt to ignite a flame between us has failed. I don't know how many more attempts I have left in me.

"Brush your teeth and wash your face!" she calls out after me.

Right. How on earth can I forget that. Heaven fucking forbid I don't brush my teeth the moment my feet hit the fucking floor.

I don't know why I even bothered asking her to go with me anyway. I knew her answer would be no before I even asked. Karina never wants to do anything on a whim. Everything must be planned.

At this point, I wouldn't be surprised if she plans her shits, too.

Come to think of it, I've never seen her shit before. She probably doesn't. Karina is much too proper to sit on the porcelain throne and take a shit.

Laughing to myself, I take my duffel bag from the closet and throw it on the bed, going back into the closet to gather the clothes I'll need for my business trip.

Karina walks into the room, sets my bag on the ottoman at the foot of the bed, and begins making the bed as she always does. She's placing the final decorative pillow on top when I return with some socks and boxers in my hands.

"I have an appointment with the top fertility specialist here in Washington on Wednesday," she says casually, like this is normal everyday conversation. Well, for us, I guess it is. It's rare to have a conversation anymore that isn't about trying to conceive.

"Why would you do that? I told you that we need to take a break."

"And I told you I don't want to. We're not getting any younger, and it's a miracle to get an appointment this quick. She usually has a very long waiting list. Honey, this could be a sign."

Everything is a goddamn sign to her. "This isn't a fucking sign, Karina! I told you that I don't want to keep this shit up!" I yell, throwing my handful of clothes on the bed.

She jumps back, startled by my outburst, but composes herself. She sits on the edge of the bed with a sigh, her bright blue eyes finally meeting mine.

"You're just under so much stress, and I understand. But we need to do this, and we have to keep trying, Dean."

"No, we don't! You can cancel the appointment." I pace the room, raking my hands through my hair. "I'm not trying anymore. I'm done with it, Karina. I don't need a break; I want to be done. For good."

"You promised you'd give me anything I want! You promised to make me happy!" She jumps up, throwing her hands in the air. Now it's my turn to be surprised by her outburst.

"A baby is not the fucking answer! A baby will not magically fix us and make us happy together! A baby isn't a solution for a broken marriage!" I roar, regretting the harsh words the moment they leave my mouth. They're true, but I didn't mean to be that harsh toward her.

Karina flinches as if I'd slapped her, her blue eyes becoming glossy with unshed tears. She wraps one hand around her waist, and places the other against her chest. "You think our marriage is broken?"

"Karina, I'm sorry. That's not what I meant." She holds up a hand to silence me.

"You never say things you don't mean. You meant it, or else you wouldn't have said it." We stare at each other in silence. She's right. It's not common for me to say things I don't mean.

My words linger between us. I know they hurt Karina, but she doesn't cry or give in to whatever emotions she's feeling. No, she stands straight and smiles at me.

"Go shower and get ready for the day. I'll finish your packing." She disappears into the closet without another word, and I go into the bathroom to shower.

Here we go again.

Back to acting as if we're perfect, ignoring every single flaw in our marriage, along with the massive elephant in the room.

ELEVEN

THEN

Dean, *16 years old*

Camille has ignored my texts since my birthday party on Friday night. It's Sunday, and I'm no longer letting her ignore me. I gave her the space I knew she needed to cool down. I'm aware I messed up on Friday, and now I'm prepared to make it up to her.

The way I acted on Friday wasn't me; I should've never allowed her to be treated the way Sadie treated her, and I failed her. When Mario passed the joint to me, I'd never smoked weed before, but being surrounded by my friends and their influence, I wanted to try it. Camille is a goody-two-shoes; she never does anything stupid. Even at thirteen, she knows the difference between good and bad and never allows herself to be influenced by those around her. That's one of the many things I adore about her. I don't know why I even did it. I guess, for once, I wanted to do what those around me were doing, so I didn't turn Mario down.

Even though I knew better and wasn't even a fan of weed in the first place, I still did it. Sure, I sometimes drink on the rare occasion I'm with my friends at a party, but never had I tried weed or ever been interested in it before. When my parents got home, they weren't pleased either.

When Sadie came over and sat on my lap, the guys around me

praised me for having the hottest girl in school on my lap. Sadie Marshall is the head cheerleader, has nice tits that developed earlier than most girls, and apparently, she even has the best blowjob skills. Every guy in school drools over her, and though she's sucked a dick or five, she's never chased after a guy or wanted to date anyone until me.

And Sadie wants me, which according to the guys, is a tremendous honor. But I'm not interested in Sadie. I have never been. The only girl I've ever liked or wanted to date is Camille. But I fucked up. I should've pushed Sadie away and stood up for Cam.

I fucked up and spent all weekend thinking about how much I fucked up.

It's my affection for my best friend that has me standing at her front door right now.

"Hi, Dean. Camille is up in her room. You can go on up." Cam's mother, Melanie, smiles at me, stepping aside so I can enter their house. I thank her and run up the stairs two at a time until I reach Camille's door. We never bother knocking on each other's door, so I don't. I just open it, grinning when she jumps, startled by my sudden intrusion.

"Put your shoes on, I'm taking you somewhere." Camille is lying on her bed, resting on her stomach, propped up by her elbows with her sketchpad in front of her. She's always buried in her sketch pad or a book.

"No, I think I'd like to be angry at you for a little longer." Her bright emerald eyes look up at me, her eyebrows pulling together and her eyes squinting into a glare.

"You've been angry at me long enough, and now it's time to go. Put your shoes on." Camille climbs off her neatly made bed with a very dramatic sigh and shoves her feet into the white converse at the end of her bed.

As usual, she is wearing overall shorts with a pink T-shirt underneath. I cross my arms over my chest, leaning against the doorframe as she pulls her dark hair into a ponytail.

The movement of her hair allows me to smell her vanilla coconut shampoo. The heavenly scent is my favorite.

Camille shoves my shoulder with another glare as she walks past me, leading me outside to the driveway toward my awaiting car.

THE CAR RIDE IS SILENT, BUT THAT'S FINE. AT LEAST SHE came with me even if she does want to continue being angry with me. She got in the car, and that's all that matters. That means she still wants to be around me even if she is mad.

After taking a right, we drive for another few minutes until we reach a gravel road. The rocks crunch underneath my tires, and soon I come to a stop in front of a large blue lighthouse. We are miles away from the city, and there are no houses in sight. We're secluded in the middle of nowhere.

The lighthouse is a few feet in front of us, looking out toward the lake.

"A lighthouse?" I look over at Camille, hiding my grin by rolling my lips inward. She may be upset, but her curiosity is getting the best of her.

"It's actually a house designed as a lighthouse. It's abandoned and has been for years. The man who created it was an architect," I explain, climbing out of the car, Camille following behind me.

I take her hand in mine, lace our fingers together, and begin leading her up the gravel walkway toward the front door. I'd be lying if I said I wasn't enjoying the physical contact. It makes my skin warm up instantly on contact. Her skin is always so soft.

Once we reach the entrance, I let go of her hand long enough to kneel and reach for the key hidden inside a plastic-shaped rock and turn it over. Opening the little flap, I remove a key and stand up. Unlocking the door, I lead Camille inside, shutting us inside the naturally lit lighthouse.

The sunlight illuminates the inside of the modern style light-house-shaped house, showcasing the walls that are covered in blueprints. Walking further into the place, we find a circular table in the center, books and more blueprints splayed out. I can't keep the smile off my face as I watch Camille enter my private space and look around at all the blueprints I've been creating over the last six months, when I first discovered this place.

"Are these yours?" she asks, picking up the papers from the table and examining them closely. The lighthouse doesn't have electricity since it's an abandoned house, but I managed to get battery-powered lamps to use whenever I'm here after dark.

I nod. "Welcome to my secret hideout." I wave my arms around with a smile.

"How did you find this place?"

"By accident. I stumbled upon it one day with my dad, and then I came back on my own to explore it even further. It's sitting here, untouched, unclaimed, so I claimed it as my own." She nods, exploring the house.

The inside isn't very big, but it is perfect for me, and I can imagine it was perfect for whoever lived here. Whenever I want to get away when I'm not with Camille, this is where I come.

A few times, I've even slept here.

Camille walks up the staircase to the second level, and I follow behind her. The upstairs is an open floor space. There's another desk, a box spring, and a mattress that I brought here and covered with new bedding so I can have a place to sleep.

"Where did you get a bed, and how did you get it up here?"

"It's my old mattress. After I got my new bed, my parents were throwing it out, so I said I'd take it to the dump but brought it here instead. Dallas helped me get it inside and up the stairs." She nods again, looking at me from over her shoulder.

By the way she's looking at me, I can tell she has something to say, and is nervous by the way she's biting on her bottom lip, rocking on her heels. I know she's still angry with me, so I don't push her to speak, instead, I wait for her to get the courage to speak on her own terms.

"I hated seeing Sadie on your lap." Okay, so we are diving straight into this conversation. *Great.*

My shoulders slump, and I exhale a breath I wasn't aware I was holding. Standing in front of Camille, I lift her chin gently until her beautiful green eyes look right at me.

"I'm so sorry, Cam. I know she was terrible to you, and you didn't deserve that. I should've never gotten high or let her sit on my lap. You know that I don't like her like that."

"That slap actually really hurt."

"But you played it off well. And that was a nice right hook." She giggles. Clear as day, I can see the anger leave her petite body. We laugh together, then something changes. Our smiles fade, and we stand staring at each other, our hands holding onto each other, our fingers intertwined.

We're locked together in an intense gaze, and I never want to blink or look away from her. I want to spend the rest of my days staring into Camille's beautiful green eyes and being with her every second. She is my happiness.

Even at sixteen, I know that I want Camille to be my today, tomorrow, and always.

Camille leans up on her tiptoes, and without hesitation, our lips collide into a sloppy kiss. Neither of us know much about kissing since this is only our second kiss, but I want to practice with her to become better only for her. Her arms wrap around my neck, my hands holding her hips, our heads tilted to opposite sides, and our lips fighting against each other. It isn't the type of kiss I've seen in movies or in those late-night Showtime soft porn movies, but with Camille, it is perfect.

Everything is perfect.

We spend about two hours at the lighthouse, both lying side by side on the bed, kissing. It's sloppy. Our teeth clink together, and each time one of us pulls away for air, there's a string of saliva, and our lips are already red and bruised. We both fight for dominance, and neither of us want to give it up. But Camille being Camille, she takes control. She pushes me back, climbs on top of me, pins my hands down by my sides, and kisses me with her tongue.

I like the new position of her being on top of me and kissing, at least until the friction between us causes my dick to get hard and tent my jeans.

"Cam, stop. We should probably get home before our parents worry." Thankfully, she doesn't notice my hard dick. She climbs off me, takes my hand, and we leave our new special spot.

THE DRIVE HOME IS SILENT, BUT IT'S A COMFORTABLE silence. We hold hands the entire way, and the only time she lets go is so we can get out of the car, but once we're out, we're right back to holding hands.

All the way up to my bedroom.

My house is dark, and my parents already asleep. Thankfully, they never hover when I am with Camille, and neither do her parents. All they expect from us are calls or texts to confirm we are safe, and as long as we are home by our weekend curfews, our parents don't mind where we go. They trust us.

They trust us so much that each of our parents set up a bedroom for us at each other's house. Camille sleeps over often, and tonight was no different.

Well, except she'll be sleeping in my bed instead of hers for the first time.

While Camille is getting ready for bed in my bathroom, I lock my door and undress down to my boxers. I step into a pair of pajama pants, and moments later, she walks out of the bathroom wearing a tank top and sleeping shorts that my mom had bought her for when she sleeps over. Silently, we climb into my bed, wrap our arms around each other, and kiss until we fall asleep.

Best. Night. Ever.

TWELVE

NOW

Camille

"Karina, what a surprise. What can I do for you?" I switch my phone to speaker and set it down on my desk while organizing the pile of papers that have taken over the space. I've been avoiding her, either ignoring her texts or replying with lame excuses. It felt too weird to befriend the woman who's married to my first love. It doesn't feel right, especially considering she doesn't know the truth about Dean and me and how close we really were growing up. He said he wants to tell her, and I know that she'll stop trying to contact me and pursue a friendship once he does. And honestly, like the coward I am, I'm counting on that.

"Hey, I haven't heard from you in a while. Dean is away on business until Sunday. He left this morning. So, I'm hoping we can go out for dinner and drinks tonight." All she wants is a friend, and I'm being terrible. But I can't get close to this woman. I just can't.

"I'm sorry, Karina. I'm—" she cuts me off before I can finish my excuse.

"I'm not taking no for an answer. There's a bar that I found that I want to check out. I'll text you the details, but please, don't

123

say no. Please, you're my only friend." The desperation is evident in her voice. I sigh, my shoulders slumping as I relent.

"Okay. Fine. Sounds great. Just text me the details. I got to go. Talk later."

"Fantastic! I'm looking forward to this." I end the call with a final goodbye just as my phone rings again. This time, Spencer's name appears on the screen.

The moment I click the green accept icon, I say, "Oh my fucking hell, guess who I just got off the phone with?"

"Tell me over lunch. I'm starving, and I'm downstairs." She ends the call. I grab my phone and purse and exit my office with a laugh.

Moments later, I'm downstairs, greeting my sister with a hug. We walk across the street toward a local café that we often enjoy for lunch.

We sit, and she gestures for me to speak. "Who called you?"

"Karina! She wants to go out tonight for dinner and drinks at a bar." She looks at me wide-eyed over the edge of her menu.

"Karina, Dean's wife? Is that a good idea? I thought you were going to let her down easy?"

"I was, but she needs a friend. I talked to Dean yesterday too, and he says that he will tell her about our history together, so that means I won't have to worry about her much longer."

"She might try to kill you." I laugh, knowing damn good and well it's likely.

"Probably. She might be angry at us both for not telling her sooner that Dean and I were once..." I trail off, unsure how to describe what Dean and I were.

"Best friends who were in love with each other but never got the chance to officially date? That you were each other's first kiss, and he was the one that popped your cherry?" Spencer says casually, shrugging her shoulders while sipping her glass of lemon water.

She pretty much summed it up. "Exactly. It's complicated, but it's in the past. Now we're just working together."

"Yeah, working together to design the building he planned for you years ago, and at the exact location he chose. Camille, do you still have feelings for Dean?"

I sigh, setting my menu on the table and placing my elbows on top of it. My head falls into my hands, and I close my eyes, shaking my head. "Fuck, Spencer. This situation is fucked up."

"What happened yesterday?" I tell her about the entire conversation between Dean and me in my office. "You're married, and he's married. What do you think can happen between you two?"

"Nothing. Nothing will happen. It's just a childhood crush that was reignited because I saw him again, eleven years later, and now he's happily married, and I'm not." I wonder how many times I'll have to convince myself that I no longer have feelings for Dean. "I haven't seen him since the day he left for college. When he left, we were in love and preparing for our future. Now, I don't know what I feel. You know what I went through after he left." I sigh, unwilling to think about what happened to me and what I went through after Dean left for college. The memory is too painful, and I've buried it so far down and haven't told a single soul since. Spencer is the only one who knows my secret. "It's hard to see him after all that happened."

"I know, little sis. You were such a wreck, so I can only imagine what you're feeling now that he's back in your life."

"I'm trying not to think about it. It's in the past, and we're different people now. It'll be fine. Nothing will happen between us. We'll finish working together, and then we'll return to being strangers."

"Your building will probably take a year, maybe even longer. That's a long time to spend working with the love of your life."

Fuck. I hate when Spencer is right.

What am I getting myself info?

The rest of our lunch is spent with light and easy conversation, completely avoiding anything involving Dean and Karina. I pay the bill, then hug my sister goodbye after she walks me back to my office so I can return to work.

The rest of the day, my head is in a foggy haze. I can't focus, still replaying my conversation with Dean yesterday and Spencer at lunch today.

I'm now mindlessly working on the designs for my fall collection when my phone pings with a new text.

Karina: Bar Maroon tonight at 8 p.m. Meet you there.

I send her a thumbs-up emoji, then turn my phone off and return to work.

AT 5:30, I PULL INTO THE PARKING GARAGE AND RIDE THE elevator up to my condo. I let myself inside, kick off my heels and undress while I walk down the hallway toward my bedroom. I fill the bathtub, tie my hair in a bun, and climb into the clawfoot tub, submerging my tense body into the hot water.

I remain in the bathtub until the water goes cold, and my body turns into a prune, and still I'm not relaxed. There's no way I'll be able to until after my dinner with Karina.

As time gets closer, so does my worry.

Instantly, I begin to question if Dean has told her about our history yet. If he has, then why does she want to go out tonight? To confront me? To warn me to stay away from her husband? Oh God, I'm making myself paranoid with what-ifs. The only way to find out for sure is to go. But I need to know before that.

Stupidly, I grab my phone and send a quick text to Dean while I dry myself off.

Me: Sorry to bother you, I know you're busy. But I'm wondering if you told Karina about our history yet?

HIS REPLY COMES SECONDS LATER.

Dean: No. I haven't had the chance to tell her yet. Why?

Me: I'm getting ready to go to dinner with her tonight. Wanted to know what I was walking into.

Dean: Why are you going to dinner? We had a fight this morning, so she probably just wants a girlfriend to talk to. Isn't that what girls do? Bitch about their husbands?

Me: Why'd you fight?

Me: Sorry, that's none of my business. Don't answer that.

Dean: We don't always see eye to eye. Enjoy dinner. I'll tell her soon.

Me: Thanks, Dean. Goodnight.

Dean: Goodnight, Cam.

A simple text. A simple nickname, and I already have a stomach full of butterflies. I love it when he calls me Cam. He is the only one that ever has. Having him say it does weird things to me. Fuck. I need to get my mind out of the damn gutter. It isn't right to think of him that way anymore.

At eight, I walk into Bar Maroon, an upscale bar located in downtown Seattle. The place is packed but that's not surprising considering it's a Friday night. It takes me a while, but eventually I find Karina sitting at a high-top table in the back, so I join her, taking the seat across her. She smiles happily, sliding a menu over to me and holding up a glass of wine.

"This is glass number three. I'm already feeling tipsy," she says with a giggle the second I sit down.

"Easy girl, don't pass out or throw up on me."

She laughs, shaking her head. "Don't worry. I just really need a drink." She flags a server down, and we both order our meals, and I, too, order a glass of red wine.

Karina takes a large swig from her glass and sets it down with a heavy sigh.

I wasn't planning on inquiring about her fight with Dean, but by the way she's drinking and sighing so often, I can't help but ask the loaded question. "Are you okay?"

She looks up at me, her light-colored eyebrows pulling together for a moment as if she's in thought before finally shaking her head. "Dean and I fought this morning. I've been replaying it in my head ever since."

Fuck. I don't want to hear about it, but I want to try and help her feel better. "Okay, lay it on me. What happened?"

"He doesn't want to keep trying for a baby. I told him about my appointment with a fertility specialist, and he got mad. He said he's done trying."

Fuck. I wasn't prepared for this type of conversation. "Why? I thought you both wanted to have a baby." Over text, Dean said they didn't see eye to eye. Is this what he meant? She wants a baby, and he doesn't? But why? He loves children.

"He's been telling me for a few weeks that he wants to take a break from trying, but I guess I just haven't been listening. He's not interested in other options; he won't even listen to me. He's really done."

"Well, why don't you both just take a break? Take a step back, focus on each other, and just let it happen." Good God. Am I really sitting here giving her advice about having a baby? Perhaps subconsciously, I want her to quit trying. I don't want her to have Dean's baby.

Fuck, I really am a horrible person.

I make a mental note to book my first-class ticket straight to hell when I get home.

"That's what he says too. He says I'm obsessing too much and putting myself under too much stress. I know he's right, but dammit, I'm not getting any younger. I want a baby."

"Take a break. Even if it's short, just take one."

"For how long?"

"Start with one cycle. For one month, don't track your cycle. No tests, no obsessing, no discussing it. Just stop everything, and after one month, see where you're both at." Her eyes light up, and she looks at me with a smile so bright that you'd think I'd hung the moon. I wrap my hand around the stem of my wine glass and bring it to my mouth, taking a heavy sip.

On the way over, I'd taken a magic pill, and shouldn't drink, but oh well. I'm going to enjoy alcohol while I can.

"You're right! You are absolutely right! Okay, one month. This is good, and this can work." She giggles, swallowing down the contents of her glass in one gulp.

"See? It's not that hard. Just take it slow. One month at a time."

"I can do that. I think I've been going a little crazy anyway. I can't blame him for needing a break."

Luckily, the server brings over our dinner just in time, so I don't have to say anything else. A mango chicken salad for me, and a salmon salad for her. I stuck with something light since Karina clearly planned on drinking more than just one glass of wine. If I'm going to allow myself to get fucked up, I didn't want to eat anything heavy.

"Excuse me really quick, I need to run to the ladies' room," Karina says, climbing down from the high-top chair. I nod, waving her away just as my phone pings. I pick it up, and an instant smile comes to my lips when I see the name of the sender.

Dean: How's dinner?

Me: Good. Don't be mad because I didn't mean to interfere, but Karina told me about your fight. And she agrees.

Dean: Agrees to what?

Me: To take a break from TTC.

Dean: TTC?

Me: Trying to conceive.

Dean: Are you serious?

Me: Yup. But let her tell you. Obviously.
Me: Just being nosey, but why don't you want to keep trying? You've always wanted your own family.

Dean: That's none of your business.

Ouch.

Me: Sorry, not trying to overstep.

Three text bubbles appear and then disappear just as quickly. Karina reclaims her seat, and I sit staring at my phone for too long until she brings my attention back to her. I hadn't intended to upset Dean. I was only trying to understand. I knew he wanted a family because he's told me. Whenever we talked about our future and our plans to get married, he always said he wanted children.

Two. A boy and a girl.

Knowing he's not going to respond, I lock my screen and set my phone on the table face down.

The rest of dinner is spent listening to Karina share stories from her and Dean's days in college. She asks me questions about

Declan, and as usual, I avoid those questions. She is too drunk to even notice my sudden subject change whenever she mentions my husband.

Luckily, I'm able to sober up by the time our night ends. She is plastered, so I put her in an Uber and send her home. I didn't drink much—much less than what I had anticipated—but getting drunk with Karina because she was upset about a fight with her husband hadn't felt right.

After she leaves in her Uber, I drive myself home.

LATER THAT NIGHT, I'M LYING IN BED, AIMLESSLY SCROLLING social media on my phone. I've never been a fan of social media, but occasionally, I like to check notifications and see what is going on. I log into my business account, which my social media manager runs. I never use my personal accounts anymore. I had to download the app first, but I do it because I'm curious.

Lie.

Actually, I do it because I want to view Karina's page. And that's exactly how I end up where I'm at now.

With a glass of wine in hand, I scroll through picture after picture of Karina and some of Dean on her Instagram. Seems that she can't go a day without posting a selfie or two. There are a handful of photos of her and Dean together, but mainly just her.

What hurt the most is seeing their wedding photos and the photos of her being pregnant.

It isn't surprising that their wedding was fucking massive and completely ridiculous. The pictures make me laugh because I know it was all her doing. Dean would've never wanted such a large, pretentious wedding.

I'm just closing Instagram when my phone chimes with a new text.

Dean: Don't assume you know what I want just because we had conversations over eleven years ago. Those conversations were

between us. They were plans made between us. Things I wanted
with you.
Dean: Goodnight.

My heart stops. Is he saying what I think he's saying?

Is he saying that he doesn't want a baby with Karina, his wife, because of plans we made years ago? Is he really saying that he only wanted a family with me? Fuck. I need to know.

I'm tipsy and reading way too much into his text. Surely that's not what he's saying at all... right?

Me: She's your wife.

Dean: Yet you're the only one I ever wanted a family with. Don't act
surprised.

My heart stops. My heart fucking stops. I check my pulse to make sure I'm still alive.

Me: You can't say that. She's your wife.

Dean: We want different things. I'll never be able to give her the
family she wants.

My heart aches for him. For the boy he once was, who wanted to be a father so badly.

Me: Why not? You can have the family that you want with her.

Dean: That's not what I want.

Fuck. Fuck. Fuck.
I don't text back, I can't.
We are both stepping into dangerous territory right now.

THIRTEEN

THEN

CAMILLE, *13 years old*

It's been one month since the night Dean took me to his secret place—the lighthouse. And for an entire month, we've been more inseparable than ever before. We're on summer vacation now, and we spend every waking moment with each other. He drives us to the lighthouse, and we spend hours there.

We'll read, talk about anything and everything, or he'll work on his blueprints, and I'll work on my sketches... or we'll kiss.

Lots and lots of kissing. We've been doing that a lot lately.

We have the perfect routine, and this is already by far the best summer ever.

I love spending time with Dean.

I love kissing him.

And I love our lighthouse.

Since that night a month ago when we kissed for the second time, he's been kissing me every day. We kiss all the time now. And I freakin' love it! His lips are soft, and our lips move in perfect sync now. At first, we had no idea what we were doing, and our kissing was sloppy, but now it's magical.

My stomach fills with butterflies every time he kisses me.

I asked my parents yet again if I was able to date Dean, but they still said no, even though they know that we're best friends and always together. Mom says I must wait until I turn sixteen to have him as my boyfriend officially. She says it's okay for us to be friends, but I'm not old enough yet to date.

Little does she know that we're kissing. With tongue.

Our families think I have a crush on Dean, but they don't understand that it's not one-sided and that we'll be married one day.

Despite what anyone believes, I will marry Dean Jameson if it's the last thing I do.

Today is no different than any other day. Dean and I are hanging out together at the lighthouse as usual. Our parents have gone to the country club today.

Our dads play golf while our moms visit the spa, and Spencer is too busy spending all her time with Dallas.

We're upstairs in the lighthouse; I'm on the bed, lying on my stomach, working on some sketches on my sketchpad, and Dean is sitting at his desk across the room, working on some blueprints. His phone keeps beeping, and occasionally, he'll look at the screen and then steal a glance back at me. His smile doesn't meet his eyes, and instantly I know there's something wrong. I know him well enough to know all his expressions. Whenever he's guilty of hiding something, I know how he looks. And right now, he looks guilty.

"Dean," I call out his name in frustration. "What's going on?"

"N-nothing." His focus remains on the papers in front of him, not bothering to look at me, but I notice his pencil isn't moving. I climb off the bed with an angered huff and march over to him.

I'm beside him just as his phone beeps with another text. His hand shoots out toward the phone to flip it over, but he's not quick enough, so I see the sender's name.

Sadie freaking Marshall.

What the hell is she doing texting Dean? *My* Dean.

"I didn't know that Sadie had your number." I cross my arms

over my chest, looking right at him, but he doesn't look up at me. He keeps his eyes shifted down on his paper.

Like a jealous girlfriend, who's not even his girlfriend, I snatch his phone off the desk and run across the room. He rushes after me, but I give him my back and fight him off with one hand while I unlock the screen and click the icon for messages.

Dread fills my stomach the moment I click her name.

I regret it.

"Cam, give it back!" There, on the screen, is a topless photo of Sadie. She's standing in front of a mirror wearing shorts and no shirt. Her perfectly round C cups are out on display, and I want to smack the ugly smile from her face.

Dean grabs the phone from my shaky hands, shoves it into his pocket, and takes my hands in his.

Pulling away from him, I narrow my eyes and speak through gritted teeth. "Take me home right now. I hate you." A painful look washes over his face, and a frown curls his perfect plump lips that I love kissing.

My mind is racing. I'm struggling to comprehend the fact Sadie sent Dean a nude photo, and now I'm wondering if her stupid-ass self has ever gotten the chance to kiss his perfect lips.

"You don't mean that. Let me explain." On instinct, I ball my right hand in a fist and slug him in the arm, hoping he feels a fraction of the pain that I feel.

"Ow!" He rubs his arm, his jaw clenching as he glares at me. I pace around the room, too angry to look at him and too stubborn to leave on my own. He's my ride, and the walk home would be so long, and there's a good chance I'd either get lost or kidnapped.

I'm not ready to be kidnapped, so I stay my ass put.

"It's not what you think! I didn't ask for it, she just sent it. She keeps sending pictures like that, and I tell her to stop. I'm not interested in Sadie, and you know this."

"She must think you like it if she keeps doing it. Wait, there's more?!"

"Y-yes." He hangs his head shamefully. "After the first one, I

137

told her she needs to stop. I don't even know how she got my number. It must've been from one of our friends. But please, Cam, don't leave. She's nothing to me."

I finally look at him, pausing to take in the apologetic look on his face.

"Did you like the pictures? You could've blocked her, but you didn't for a reason. So, tell me, Dean, do you like how she looks?" I'm genuinely curious about what he thinks of her.

"No! Of course not. I don't like Sadie, especially like that."

"Especially like what?"

"Sexually." My lip snarls in disgust at the thought of her.

Suddenly feeling confident, and without taking my eyes off him, I slowly remove my T-shirt and then my white bra, letting the items fall to the floor with a silent thud. "Is this what you want?" My boobs are small, not nearly as nice and large as Sadie's, but they're bigger than every other girl in my grade. Mom says she developed earlier than others too, and so did Spencer.

Dean gulps, his Adam's apple visibly moving in his throat, his hazel eyes fixated on my smooth flesh. Goosebumps rise on my skin from his heated gaze.

"Is this what I need to do to make you interested in me? Is sex what you need?"

As if he's snapping out of his trance, Dean rushes forward, picks up my clothing from the floor, and shoves it in my hands, urging me to cover myself. "Shit, Cam, no. I don't need to have sex or to see you naked, not right now."

A frown forms on my lips. Does he not like me? Am I not attractive to him? I may be an inexperienced virgin, but I know enough about sex.

Spencer lost her virginity last year, and she told me everything I needed to know about sex. Plus, I've Googled it.

According to her, it's perfectly normal and the ultimate form of intimacy with someone you love. Spencer says giving your body to someone you love is a gift, and I should only give it to someone who will cherish me for the rest of my life. I had asked if Dallas would cherish her for the rest of his life, and she smiled and said yes.

"Would you ever want to do sexual things with me?" I ask, snapping my bra back on and pulling my T-shirt over my head.

"Jesus, Cam. I don't think we should have his conversation right now. You should wait until you're married to have sex."

"When *we're* married, right?"

With a sigh, he nods. "Yes, when we're married, I'll make love to you every day."

"Okay," I whisper, feeling embarrassed by the fact I showed myself to him. "Take me home, now, please." He looks defeated, but he doesn't argue.

He cleans up our stuff, then five minutes later, we leave.

Later that night, after I'm freshly showered and tucked into bed, I replay the day in my head and realize that he never answered me when I asked if he was interested in me or if he'd ever want to have sex with me.

I dissect our conversation into tiny pieces until I've convinced myself that he doesn't like me that way, and I'm embarrassed all over again.

With teary eyes, I reach across to my nightstand and grab my sketchbook that I'd placed there after I got home.

I open it to the page that I had saved with my pencil. A wide smile spreads across my face when I see the orange Post-it note that's stuck to my paper. I instantly recognize the handwriting.

You're beautiful, no matter what, and I'll only have eyes for you always.

Tears streak down my face, but this time, they're happy tears.

FOURTEEN

NOW

Camille

Walking into my office on Monday morning, I get a surprise I am unprepared for. Dean is waiting outside of my office door with two coffees in hand, and a bag of what I hope are donuts. I haven't spoken to him since his last text on Friday night, and honestly, seeing him right now doesn't make me the happiest.

He left me with too many thoughts and feelings that I had no business having about another woman's husband. But at this moment, seeing him standing in front of my door with coffee and snacks and a boyish grin on his lips, I'm taken back to eleven years ago and reminded of the boy he once was.

When he was mine, and we were too busy falling in love.

He's the boy who left me behind.

I relent and allow him into my office. He closes the door, sets the coffee and bag on my desk, and takes a seat in the chair directly in front of my desk. I sit in my chair, then reach inside the brown bag, instantly delighted to find my favorite.

A Boston cream donut.

"I'm sorry about Friday night. I never meant to—" I begin, but he raises his hand to silence me.

"Let's forget about it. I think we both let things get a little too—"

It's my turn to cut him off now. "Out of hand?" I offer with a shrug. He flashes his bright white smile, his eyes dropping from mine to the cup of coffee in his hands.

"It's hard, you know. Seeing you again after all these years. I remember when once we thought we were end game and would be together forever. We had a plan that we thought was foolproof." I understand what he means. Once, we thought that we were invincible, and nothing could ever stop us from being together.

Now I realize just how ridiculous our plan was. We were too young and naive.

"We were kids back then. Neither of us was prepared for the real world and how life can disrupt your plans." I sigh, saying the words more for myself than for him. No matter how often you fantasize about your future or how many times you plan, life always has its own plans for you, and things don't always turn out as expected.

"I know. I just can't help thinking about what could've been." In silence, we sip our coffee and eat our donuts, not saying another word until they're finished and I'm licking the chocolate from my fingers.

To ease the tension and make things less awkward after being silent for so long, I speak up. "Oh, so, guess what? You'll be proud to know that I called Sadie last week, and she'll take the job." His eyes go wide, his lips twitching with a grin threatening to peak through.

"You did? You actually called her? I'm so surprised." That makes two of us.

I laugh while nodding. "I did. She was also surprised that I'd called her, but she took the job. I'll have to meet with her on Thursday to discuss things."

"You can have her meet you at the construction site. That way you can both see it. If you let me know the time, I'll meet you there too, and we can discuss the plans." I nod, tossing the empty coffee cup into the trashcan underneath my desk.

"Dean... did you mean what you said Friday night?" I am hesitant to ask, but I have to know the answer. I must know if I'm why he isn't willing to have children.

Ever since he told me he went to New York looking for me six years ago, something inside me has shifted, and now I can't explain how I feel. His confession on Friday only added to my confusion.

"I had no right to say that to you. You're married, and I respect that." An uncontrollable laugh erupts through me. Yeah, he's right. I'm technically married. But where's my husband? I don't feel married, and I haven't in a long time. Although he doesn't know anything about Declan or my marriage that has been treading on thin ice for years, since the day we said I do.

Words we only said because I was pregnant.

But to regret Declan means to regret Luca, and Luca is someone I will never regret.

Do I have other regrets from my younger years? Yes, many.

Do I regret getting married? Somedays.

The only thing I don't regret is having my son. My baby boy was the center of my universe, and he was the reason I did everything. And wanting to give him a family was why Declan and I got married, although neither of us will admit it aloud.

"You're married too, Dean," I remind him, tangling my hands in my hair and pulling at the roots. Fuck. The whole situation is a fucked-up mess.

Why couldn't he just stay in London, and out of my life?

He feels the same as I, battling the same inner turmoil. I knew it from the moment our eyes connected at the gala.

"Don't remind me," he mumbles, setting his coffee on my desk and leaning back in his seat.

"Why not? It's the truth. You're married, and you have a great wife at home who only wants to please you."

"Don't do that. Don't act like you know a damn thing about my marriage. And what about you? Where's your husband? I haven't seen or heard about him once. Aren't you supposed to be madly in love with the man you had a baby with?"

"Aren't you? Last I heard, you had a baby too! You've had three pregnancies with her." He stands, his eyes glaring at me, knowing I'd hit a nerve. I stand too, refusing to let the fucker look down on me. Even though he still is because of our height difference.

"Don't go there. You already know that the pregnancies weren't planned." He grinds his teeth, his jaw tightening. "My daughter was stillborn, and the two other pregnancies ended in miscarriage."

"Stop acting as if I betrayed you by having a baby! I'm not sorry for that, and I never will be! But having a baby with someone doesn't mean you belong with that person or that you're happy. Sometimes you just want to do the right thing for your child, even if you're not the happiest version of yourself."

"Do you love him? Your husband. Are you in love with him? You haven't mentioned him once, and according to Karina, you change the subject every time he comes up."

There's a difference between loving someone and being in love with someone.

I love Declan.

I love my husband because of the life we created.

We created Luca, and I will always love Declan for giving me the greatest gift I could've ever asked for. I had four perfect years with my baby boy, and I will forever cherish those memories.

Not loving Declan isn't even an option, but am I *in* love with him? Was I ever?

The question hits hard, and I can't respond. I can't respond to a question that I've been asking myself for far too long. Deep down, I know the answer, but I can't bring myself to admit it.

We stand in a silent stare-off.

You can cut the fucking tension in the room with a knife.

"Go home, Dean. Go home to your wife."

"Call your husband, Cam. Tell him you love him."

"Fuck you," I spit, my blood boiling with anger. No one has

ever been able to work me up as much as Dean. All these years later, and he still is the only person who can spark such a reaction from me.

"Oh baby, I wish. I'd bend you over and fuck you so hard against your desk that you'd see stars, you'd be screaming my name for this entire building to hear. Then, I'd fuck you in front of that window and hope people watch what I'm doing to your body." My jaw drops at his words, warmth flooding my body, and I have to clamp my thighs together to prevent myself from dripping all over the floor.

Holy fuck. That was unexpected.

Wrong. So wrong.

Dean turns, his back facing me as he walks toward the door. "Things should've been different for us. They were supposed to be different." He may believe that, but I don't think I do. Things happened exactly how they were supposed to. If they were different, I never would've had Luca, and that's not a situation I ever want to think about.

Suddenly finding my voice, I clear my throat, hoping to shield the fact that he deeply affected me with his words. "Leave the past in the past. Now leave, Dean. As I've already said before, we'll be professional from here on out." He opens the door, walks out, and slams it so hard I'm surprised it doesn't fall off the hinges.

My hands shake, my heart aches, and my eyes sting with unshed tears.

I miss the way we were.

But most of all, I miss my best friend.

"How are you doing, Camille? Have you attended another group session?" Dr. Reynolds asks from her usual gray chair. I'm in her office for my weekly Tuesday morning meeting.

"Honestly, I've been better. I'm sleeping, but I'm restless. My mind doesn't shut off when I sleep, and I don't feel rested enough. Plus, I stopped attending those meetings."

"Let's revisit the meetings in a second. I want to talk about why you're not sleeping. Are you having the dreams again?"

I shake my head. "No, I haven't had any dreams. I've been thinking about Luca and Declan a lot and just can't sleep very well."

"Perhaps the fact that Declan will be returning home soon is why you're all worked up at night. Things will change when he gets home. You two haven't talked in a while, and now he's ready to return home. How do you feel about that?"

Honestly, I've tried not to think about it. I've been trying so hard not to think about him but always fail.

Soon, he'll be home, and we'll be under the same roof again.

"I don't know. I guess I'm nervous. It's been three months since we've been under the same roof, and I don't know how things will be." Declan has been someone who's been out of sight, out of mind. How will my life change once he's back in it?

"Do you worry that he'll do drugs again once he's back home?" That thought hadn't crossed my mind until recently, and now it's one of the many things I've been thinking about.

"Honestly, I don't know," I admit with a sigh, hoping for my own sanity that things will be better once Declan is released.

THOUGHTS OF DECLAN AND THE PAST ARE STILL ON MY MIND as I sit parked in front of the lighthouse later that night. The last time I was here was nine years ago. I was seventeen and getting ready to go off to college.

When Dean first left, I'd come here often to feel close to him, but eventually, I had to put it behind me and move on. I came here before moving to New York for a final goodbye.

This was once a place so special to me, a place where Dean and I would stay for hours and tell secrets and make promises in the dark. We promised each other forever without even understanding what that meant.

Honestly, I'm surprised this place is still standing and vacant nine years later. When I pulled up, there had been a gate in the driveway and a sign that read, No Trespassing, so I assumed someone must've bought it. But the gate wasn't locked, so I took it upon myself to open it and let my car through.

And now, here I sit in front of it. Too frozen to turn off my car and go inside.

Come on, Camille. Stop being a bitch, just get out and go inside.

With an eye roll to my inner voice, I do just that. I turn my car off and walk to the door, finding the key in the exact same spot it was years ago. Hidden inside of a fake plastic rock. Even the lock is the same.

The door is hard to open; I have to push my weight against the door to get it to budge, likely because it's an old building, and the door hasn't been opened in what I assume is nine years.

It opens with an audible creak, and right away I'm encased with memories and the feeling of nostalgia. Grabbing my iPhone from my pocket, I turn the flashlight on.

Holy shit, I walked into a fucking time capsule full of memories. Everything is the same. Dusty, but the same.

The walls are still lined with Dean's blueprints and my rough clothing sketches. The ink has faded, and they are a bit unreadable.

My fingertips trace over the lines and swirls of designs, a smile curling at the corner of my lips. Once, this place meant everything to me. I never thought I'd be back.

Coming here was a sudden decision. I felt compelled to come to the place where Dean and I shared so many memories. Now that I'm here, I realize it wasn't the best idea. My eyes sting with unshed tears, my throat is clogged with emotion, and my heart is aching.

Years of memories play through my head, and all I want to do is go back in time and press pause. Soak up the feeling of being young and carefree for a little bit longer.

Am I pathetic for being so attached to someone I loved so

many years ago? They say you never forget your first love, and I know that's true because I never have. But are you always supposed to be in love with that person? People fall in and out of love every day. How can that be? I have never loved anyone the way I loved Dean.

The way I *still* love him. The way I always will, no matter what.

I don't believe there's a single thing in the world that can ever make me stop loving him. There's nothing he can ever do or say that can change my feelings for him. No matter how many years pass or the fact we married other people, the fact will always be true that I love Dean.

I'm in love with him, all these years later.

I'm aware of how pathetic that makes me.

In college, I had flings, but I never allowed myself to let my guard down and get too close or be with them for more than a short period of time. I compared every man I met to Dean and never wanted to commit myself to anyone.

That changed when I met Declan.

He swept me off my feet from the first day, and our whirlwind entanglement began. I now question if it was him or the adrenaline that I fell in love with.

I don't realize I'm crying until I taste the saltiness on my lips. My anxiety is so high that my hands are shaking, and I realize that I haven't taken a magic pill in a few days. Not since my dinner with Karina.

I'm a horrible person. I should be preparing for my husband to come home and to see him for the first time in three months. Instead, I'm chasing ghosts from my past and torturing myself by reminding myself what it was like to be with Dean and love him.

I'm torturing myself by waving the forbidden fruit in front of my face.

I want it but can never have it.

Soulmates do exist, and mine is across the town with his wife.

I'll allow myself this one time to cry. I'll cry and get it all out and then move on. I'll mourn the loss of Dean and what could've been, and then I'll carry on with my life. I'll accept the fact that fate doesn't exist, and we don't always end up with our soulmates.

One night of crying will be the closure I need, and I can put him in my past and keep him there.

"It hasn't changed a bit." I feel his warm breath on the back of my neck, goosebumps raising on my skin. He didn't startle me; I could feel his presence long before he spoke. I wipe the tears from my face, giving him a silent nod. His long fingers wrap around my arms, and he turns me to face him. His touch sends a thousand lightning bolts through my body, and I feel it down to my toes. His hazel eyes are captivating, and instantly, I lose myself in them. Just like I have so many times before.

To make sure he's real and not a figment of my imagination, I reach out and press a hand against his chest.

Without breaking eye contact, Dean cups my face gently and wipes my tears away with his thumbs.

"I'm sorry about earlier." His voice is soft, barely above a whisper.

"Me too. I don't want to fight with you." He brushes a loose strand of my hair from my face.

"You are so beautiful." His whispered words deliver butterflies to my stomach. We're standing on an invisible but dangerous line that neither of us can cross but desperately want to.

His eyes close, and he leans in toward me. I see the pained look on his face. I know him too well and know he's fighting with himself internally. Dean is too good of a man to allow things to escalate further between us, while I, on the other hand, am not. I'm a horrible person that's currently craving his lips on mine, but I'd never push him.

If I do, he will regret it, and I never want to be someone he regrets.

"I'm so sorry, Cam. I'm so fucking sorry," he rasps, his warm spearmint scented breath fanning across my lips.

I close my eyes, and when I open them again, he's gone.

FIFTEEN

THEN

DEAN, *16 years old*

"Sadie, you need to leave."

"Why? Your mom let me in on her way out, and I wanted to see you."

"Because I'm not in the mood for company." This girl is relentless.

She hasn't taken any of the hints I've given her, trying to let her down easy, and now it's clear I'm going to have to be a dick and let her down the hard way.

Sadie Marshall is like a disease that you can't get rid of. She keeps coming back.

Stronger each time.

"You never replied to the pictures I sent." The smirk on her thin lips makes my stomach churn. She doesn't have nice lips like Camille. Hers are thin, and her top lip disappears when she smiles.

They're like thin little paper cuts, whereas Camille's lips are thick, plump, and soft to kiss.

"I'm not interested, Sadie. Get that through your head, and please leave," I say with a sigh, shoving aside my notebook and pencil.

"Why?! Is it because you like that stupid girl next door? Dean, she's a child. That's actually pretty sick." She places her hands on her hips and pops her bubblegum. I tried to be nice, but this bitch isn't accepting it.

"Get the fuck out, and I won't say it again." One more year. Just one more year of dealing with Sadie, and then I'm off to college and will be far away from her.

I'd hoped that the summer would distract her from me and allow her to find someone else to prey on, but nope. I'm not that fucking lucky.

She must have a hearing problem because she's showing no signs of removing herself from my bedroom. Instead, she lays down on my bed, her hands behind her big head while she continues chewing and popping her pink bubblegum. The piece is too big for her mouth, and each time she chews it, it sounds like she's choking.

It's disgusting, but it wouldn't be such a bad thing if she were to choke.

"Calm down, Dean. I only want to hang out for a little bit."

"I don't care. Find someone else. I already have plans." She sighs, her blue eyes snapping over to meet mine.

"Right, probably plans with your child girlfriend. Fine, I'll go. Help me up?" She holds up her arms. I don't want to touch her, but if it means her leaving, then fine.

I stand from my desk in the corner of my bedroom and walk over to her, grabbing both of her hands, and begin pulling her up.

Sadie hooks her right leg behind the back of my left leg and pulls me down on top of her, her legs moving to wrap securely around my waist, her arms around my neck, and her thin lips on mine in a matter of seconds.

"Oh, Dean, you know that you want me. Stop pretending that you don't. I see the way you look at me."

This bitch is fucking delusional.

"Sadie, stop." I grab hold of her wrists and remove them from around my neck. Sitting up on my knees, I grip onto her ankles just as a gasp sounds from behind me. I don't even need to turn around to know who is behind me.

Camille.

Shit. Shit. Shit.

The door slams shut, and Sadie unwraps herself from me with a giggle.

"Stay the fuck away from me, Sadie. I won't ask you again. Next time I have to repeat myself, you'll be sorry." I grab my phone from the nightstand and waste no time running after Camille, my heart beating in my chest with every single step.

I know what it looked like, and I know what she's thinking, and holy shit, this is bad.

"Camille, wait!" I yell, but I'm too late. I catch her just in time to see her as she climbs into the passenger seat of Spencer's car, and they drive off down the street.

I unlock my phone and select her contact, the line only ringing twice before going to voicemail.

Fuck.

I call again, each call going straight to voicemail.

I'm fucked. I'm so fucked!

This may have been the final nail in the coffin. Cam hates Sadie, and after finding the unsolicited nude photos on my phone, she was already iffy about trusting me. This will be the straw that broke the camel's back, all thanks to Sadie fucking Marshall.

IT'S BEEN A WEEK SINCE CAMILLE CAUGHT SADIE AND ME together. It was completely innocent, but that's not how it looked. I wasn't doing anything with Sadie, despite what she has been telling everyone. I blocked her number from my phone, which I should've done in the first place. Dallas told me that Sadie's been telling all her girlfriends that we hooked up, and her girlfriends told their boyfriends, and now I'm sure everyone from school knows.

According to him, Spencer told Camille, so now Camille believes that I hooked up with Sadie too, which is a damn lie.

I've never done anything sexual with Sadie, nor have I wanted to, and the only person I've ever kissed is my best friend. My best friend that isn't speaking to me, and I can't blame her. If the roles were reversed, I'd be pissed too.

I'd told Dallas that it wasn't true, and he agreed to talk to Spencer and Camille. I've tried to tell Spencer, but she won't speak to me, which I figured. She's taking Camille's side, and I can't blame her. How can Camille not believe it when she saw me on top of Sadie with her body around me? It looked pretty damning.

I've been calling and texting Cam for hours every day, but after the third day, she blocked my number.

She won't even open her bedroom door for me, and that's only when I've been allowed inside her house.

Their parents work during the day, leaving Cam and Spencer home alone. Spencer won't let me in, but once, I was able to catch their mom, who let me inside before she left for work.

Cam didn't answer, but I knew she was inside because once I knocked and asked to talk, she turned the music up.

She's being fucking stubborn and refusing to allow me the chance to explain my side. She heard a rumor and believed it.

She should know me better than that.

A week without her feels like a lifetime.

Months ago, our parents planned a summer vacation together, and we're supposed to leave in nine days. Camille has been so excited about the trip and has been helping our parents plan the itinerary. I was looking forward to it, and now I'm dreading it. I'm excited to see her again, but it won't be enjoyable if she won't even talk to me. She can't even open the door long enough to speak to me, so I know she won't speak to me during our trip.

We're going to be in the same house together for two whole

weeks. Our parents rented an ocean-front house in Cancun together. This was supposed to be a summer to remember.

The best summer ever to celebrate Camille's upcoming first year of high school, and my upcoming senior year.

Thanks to Sadie, it will be a summer to remember, but not in a good way.

SIXTEEN

NOW

Camille

"You need to pencil me in for lunch once a week," Karina says before shoving another forkful of lettuce into her mouth. She had hassled me all week until I agreed to go to lunch on Thursday.

We've barely spoken since the night at the bar. I've been trying to keep her at an arm's length, but I couldn't avoid her any longer, so I agreed to lunch since today is the only day that I have a mostly clear schedule. I have a meeting with Sadie later to discuss contracts since she'll be my interior designer, but that's two hours away.

"It's just so hard to make time these days. I've been so busy moving my operations from New York to here."

"I understand. Dean has been busy with the construction crew too. You're both working so much."

I shrug and take another bite of my club sandwich.

It's hard to try and distance myself from Karina when she so often blows up my phone like a virus. I could try harder or even tell her that I'm not interested in a friendship, but I think, in a way, I like torturing myself with the fact she's Dean's wife.

Her Dean. Not my Dean.

Not anymore.

"How have you been?" I interrupt whatever she's saying. Her lips were moving, but I wasn't paying any attention to the words coming out.

"I've been terrific since taking your advice and deciding to take a month off trying to conceive. Dean and I are doing a lot better, and now we're closer than ever. We've been out on a few lunch dates this week," she says with so much happiness in her big blue eyes, and I resent her. I hate myself for resenting her. She's innocent, just a woman in love.

I think my resentment toward her is toward myself. You know what they say, misery loves company.

I'm unhappy and apparently want everyone around me to be just as unhappy as I am.

"That's great. I'm happy for you." I lie. I'm positive that it's strictly against girl code to be in love with another woman's husband. It's against my vows, too. I'm married, a fact I seem to forget damn near daily. Guess that's what happens when your husband is nowhere to be seen.

Out of sight, out of mind.

"Camille, what do you think?"

What? Is she still talking? Damn, I missed everything she said. I'm too fucking lost inside my head. "About what?" I clear my throat, giving her my attention this time.

Karina smiles, stabbing into her salad. "I said we need to plan a double date. Now that Dean is getting more free time on the weekends, we need to go out. Me and Dean, you and your husband. I'm ready to meet your mystery husband." *Fuck.* Can we ever have a conversation where Declan isn't brought up? "I'm not taking no for an answer this time." She's only going to continue asking, and I don't think I can put it off any longer. Declan gets home on Monday, and sooner or later, I'll have to bring him around Karina so she'll shut up about him. I'm running out of excuses.

With a heavy sigh and a shrug of the shoulders, I give in.

"Okay, fine. Next Friday night? Dinner at Mio's?" She claps her hands excitedly.

"Yes, girl! Finally! Oh goodness, I'm so excited. I'll need to call Dean once I'm home and tell him the exciting news. We've both been dying to meet your husband. A husband you never talk about, what's up with that?" She winks. "Trying to keep him so private that you have him all to yourself?"

"Declan and I just aren't like that. We don't talk about each other twenty-four-seven." I shrug, not completely lying.

"Ahh, he has a name. Declan Lambert?" she asks.

Here we fucking go.

I shake my head with a wince. "No, Lambert is my maiden name. I use it for work. Valentine is my married name." I can practically see the wheels turning in her head with this new information.

"Wait... Valentine? Declan Valentine is your husband?" She drops her fork, the metal clanking against her plate. Her jaw drops, and I nod.

"As in, *the* Declan Valentine from Riot?" I nod again.

Yes, Declan Valentine, lead singer of the famous rock band Riot, is my husband.

"Yup, the one and only, that's my husband." I grab my phone from the table, unlock it, go straight to my photo gallery, and select a picture from my favorite's album. Holding the phone out toward her, I show her a selfie that Declan and I had taken a few years ago when we were happy.

Karina giggles and claps like a child who just discovered they are going to Disneyland.

"I can't believe it! I had no idea! I knew he was married, but there's not much about his family on social media." After we had Luca and got married, Declan's publicist worked overtime to keep our family out of the media. We didn't want our son to grow up in the spotlight, so neither of us posted photos of him on social media. We kept our family very private, which is why none of his fans know about our son or the fact we are married. There are no photos of the two of us together online, and when it comes to my own brand, I use my maiden name. There's been tons of speculation over the years, but nothing has ever been made public, thanks to both of our publicists.

"We both keep our personal life off social media. His Instagram is dedicated to the band, not his personal life." She nods in understanding.

"Okay, now I must know how you two met." The memory of meeting Declan brings a genuine smile to my lips.

It's a happy memory, so I don't mind sharing. "I was twenty-one and just graduated. A few friends and I had been obsessing over Riot for months, and they played a show in New York on the night of our graduation. So, we went and somehow got backstage passes. I met Declan and became a groupie." I laugh at the happy memory. "Nine months later, we were married with a baby."

"Oh, my goodness, I love that! I'm a little jealous. I've been a Riot fan for years but never got lucky enough to meet anyone from the band. And look at you, you're married to the one and only Declan Valentine."

Emotion clogs my throat, and I don't want to risk crying by strolling down memory lane and sharing stories from the simple days when I was young, carefree, and so in love with my baby boy and my husband.

"The band has been silent on social media for a while. What are they up to? Where is Declan?" Nice try, but I'm not going to share that detail. His whereabouts over the last three months is confidential. Only close family and those involved with his band know. We can't risk it leaking to the media and ruining his image. We've worked too hard to keep a clean image of him online when time and time again, he's liked to fuck it up.

"He's away, behind the scenes doing band stuff." I lie easily. "I've got to go now, but next Friday, it's a date." I set three twenties down on the table, grab my bag, and wave to Karina while rushing out before she could say anything more.

· · ·

I'd just stepped out of the elevator when I see Dean sitting in the waiting area, busy scrolling through his phone. I haven't seen or heard from him since the moment we shared at the lighthouse on Monday. I don't say anything; instead, I stand staring at him.

He must feel my presence because he looks up at me with that boyish grin of his. "Are you gawking at me?"

Busted. I nod. "I'm enjoying the view." He laughs and stands, his body standing to his full height of six-foot-five, an entire foot taller than me. I'm grateful for my heels that allow me to be four inches taller than usual. "What are you doing here?"

"I thought we could drive together to the construction site to meet Sadie. Shall we?" He gestures toward the elevator, and I nod, falling into step beside him.

The elevator ride is silent.

The walk to his car in the parking garage is silent.

The drive to the construction site is silent.

"Well, well, well... Look who it is! Dean and little Camille." Sadie greets us the moment we step out of Dean's car. She smirks, giving him a tight hug that lingers too long. Her hug to me is one armed and quick, and I'm glad.

I don't miss the way her eyes look over our left hands that both contain wedding rings, a small laugh leaving her pink painted lips. "I always knew you two would end up married."

"We're married, but not to each other," Dean speaks for the first time since we left my office. Briefly, I cringe at his snappy tone.

"Wow, I'm actually surprised. Everyone in high school expected you two to end up together." *Yeah, Sadie, me too.* "I always wondered what became of you, Dean. I never heard anything more about you after you went away to university. Anyway, let's get started, shall we? We can catch up later." She looks exactly as she did all those years ago, only now she's older and more mature looking.

Now that I don't hate her as much as I once did, I can see what all the guys in school were crazy about.

Sadie fucking Marshall is beautiful. Big blue doe eyes, long blonde hair, a figure that any girl would kill for, and boobs that I'm willing to bet money are fake. Unlike me, she knows what a gym is and doesn't have the curves and big ass like I do.

I have my mom to thank for my curvy hourglass figure, and round, delicious peachy ass.

We spend the next hour with Sadie at the construction site, signing contracts and discussing my vision for the interior. Dean didn't have to be here, but he wanted to. He chose to be here, which means more to me than he could ever know. He wanted to stay and be part of bringing my vision, years into the making, to life. I'm glad that he's here with me.

After our meeting, we say our goodbyes to Sadie, go back to his car, and he starts driving in the direction of my office.

"So, Karina said that you two had lunch together today. How was that?" This is the first time he has spoken directly to me since picking me up.

I nod. "Yeah, we did. It was good."

"But?" He knows me too well to know there's something else on my mind.

"Well, I don't know if she's told you yet, so when she does, act surprised. But she's been trying to get a double date organized."

"And you agreed?"

"I agreed. Next Friday night, we're going out. On a double date. Us, and our spouses." I hate the double date idea, but Karina proved she wasn't going to let up anytime soon, so I gave in.

One night couldn't hurt, right?

SEVENTEEN

THEN

CAMILLE, *13 years old*

It's been two weeks since finding out Dean had sex with Sadie in his room that day, and a complete silence on my end. I must've walked in at the end, considering they were fully dressed.

Either that or after he chased me, he went back to her, and then they had sex.

No, it had to be before.

Dean wouldn't go and have sex with her after I caught them.

Would he? I don't know anymore. I didn't think Dean would even have sex with anyone but me on our wedding night, but clearly, I was wrong. I gave him too much credit, and now I know that he's just like all the other horny guys at school that Spencer always tells me about.

My heart broke when I saw him and Sadie together, and it continued to break when I had to ignore him.

Every call, text, and knock on my door. I ignored it all. His apology texts were too much, so I blocked him. I cried when I blocked his number and erased him from my phone like a baby. I was impulsive and deleted all our texts and pictures together.

Spencer had helped me back up my phone a few days before, so the pictures aren't gone forever, but they're off my phone, and that's all that matters. I don't care that the photos are saved on my computer. I can delete those later, too.

I'm sitting at the airport waiting for my parents to return with my hot chocolate and snack. Spencer is away somewhere talking to Dallas on the phone again for the fifth time since this morning, and stupid Dean is sitting right across from me. His traitorous parents went to the coffee shop with my parents and left us behind.

We're going to Cancun for two weeks to celebrate the end of summer and going back to school. When we return from vacation, I'll start ninth grade, and Spence and Dean will begin their senior year. Our parents wanted to do something special to celebrate, so they've been planning this trip for months. I had been so excited and did as much research as I could on Cancun and the things the three of us could do.

Now I only need activities for two.

Spencer is upset that Dallas's parents wouldn't let him come with us, and our parents wouldn't let her stay home, so I promised her that she could hang out with Dean and me and she wouldn't even be the third wheel.

Everything was planned, but stupid Dean had to ruin the would-be fun trip. He had to go and have sex with Sadie and ruin everything, our friendship included because he is no longer my best friend.

I should make it official and tell him that, but I can't bring myself to even speak to him.

He broke my heart.

Just do it. Make him feel as bad as you. He deserves it.

After giving myself an inner pep talk, I unfold myself from the chair and walk over to where he sits directly across from me.

Standing in front of him, I cross my arms over my chest and look down at him with a scowl when his hazel eyes look up, more brown than usual.

"Camille, can we please talk?"

"Shut up. I'm doing the talking. I just want you to know that I officially hate you and that you're not my best friend anymore. And we're not going to get married. Oh, and I hope Sadie gives you an STD that you'll never get rid of, and your penis falls off." I flip him off, then turn and walk away from him before he has a chance to respond to my outburst.

My eyes sting with unshed tears, but I refuse to let my guard down in front of him and let him see my cry. The moment I run away, my tears spill over.

Breathing heavily, I run away from him and right in Lydia's arms, who is walking toward me. She wipes my tears away, holding me lovingly in her arms.

"What's wrong, sweetie?"

"Where's my mom?" I hiccup, unwilling to tell her why I'm crying. I haven't told our parents anything that's been going on, but I know they suspect something because Mom keeps asking me why she hasn't seen Dean around lately.

"She's still in line at the I with your dad. What's wrong?" I shake my head and wrap my arms around her, hugging her tightly.

Not wanting to walk into the cafe while crying, I decide to spill the beans and tell Lydia what's wrong. "Dean and I are no longer friends."

"Sweetie, what is going on between you two? You always work things out. This is the longest time you two have been apart." From behind her body, I spot Dean walking toward us, but Lydia's back is to him, so she can't see him. With a venomous snarl, I pull back, look him right in the eyes, and tell Lydia exactly what happened, all the while keeping eye contact with Dean.

"We're not friends anymore because he had sex with Sadie. In his bedroom, and I caught them," I say as she gasps. "She gave him an STD, and she might be pregnant, but that's not yet confirmed." I lie about the last part but fuck him.

"That's not true! Camille, what the hell? You know that's not true!" Dean exclaims, throwing his hands in the air. Poor Lydia goes as white as a ghost. I run off toward the cafe to find my parents, not caring if Dean gets in trouble with his mother.

167

I hope he does, but knowing Lydia, whatever happens to him wouldn't be harsh enough.

FORTY-FIVE MINUTES LATER, WE'RE BOARDING OUR PLANE.

Our parents have concluded that Dean and Sadie having sex is in fact just a rumor and that we shouldn't ruin our friendship over a rumor.

Since we're going to be under the same roof for the next two weeks, they tell us that we better change our behavior and apologize, so they make Spencer switch seats, which she does happily, and unfortunately for me, Dean is the one filling her seat.

My parents aren't too happy about me lying and saying that Sadie was pregnant and gave Dean an STD, but it is too late to cancel our trip, so even though I don't want to go anymore, they are forcing me to, which is against my rights.

Luckily, I got the window seat.

I'm sitting beside the window, staring out at the tarmac, while Dean is sitting beside me silently, but I feel his eyes on me.

"Our moms say that we have to make up so we're not miserable the entire trip." He breaks the silence. I remain mute. "Come on, Cam. Talk to me, please. You didn't even let me explain my side. Nothing happened between us." He is pissing me off now. Why can't he ever take a hint? I don't want anything to do with him ever again, and he's too stupid to understand.

Well, actually, Dean isn't stupid, but he is being a little bitch right now.

Finally, I look over at him with a scowl.

I wish looks could kill.

"I saw you two with my own eyes."

"You saw Sadie pull me on top of her and kiss me. I didn't kiss her back, and I was already pulling away when you came in the room."

"I don't believe you."

"You know what, that's your problem. You believe only what

you want to believe and are so quick to get angry with me and believe the rumors," he snaps. "Have I ever lied to you, Cam? Ever?" My scowl fades into a frown.

He's right. He's never lied to me ever. Even when the truth hurts, he's always been completely honest with me. "Answer me. Have I ever lied to you?" he demands an answer, so I shake my head.

"Exactly. I always tell you the truth, and I'm telling you the truth now. I never had sex with Sadie, and I'd never do that to you. I'm serious when I tell you that when the time comes, I only want you." Stupid Dean and his stupid way of smooth-talking me into forgiveness.

But what if he is telling the truth? If Sadie is lying about sleeping with him—and maybe she is—that means I wasted two weeks ignoring and hating him for no reason. Dean is right. He doesn't lie to me. So why would he start now?

Stupid freaking Sadie.

I'm still angry, but until we return home, and I can investigate further, I'll forgive him to please our parents and enjoy our trip. "Okay, I forgive you."

"There's nothing to forgive me for. I didn't do anything wrong." He sighs. "Next time, don't be so quick to believe rumors. You're going to high school now, where you'll hear rumors every day. If you hear something that upsets you, then talk to me. Don't run away from me." I nod as he reaches over to take my hand in his. "Jealousy and insecurity isn't a good look for you."

He intertwines our fingers together. "My little spitfire, always pissing me off," he mumbles under his breath, but not low enough that I'm unable to hear him.

"I promise I'll talk to you first and not assume the worst." I should've known better. I know I'm quick to rush to judgment. I've been told that plenty of times before.

But it's my insecurities that are getting the best of me. We only have a year left together. After the school year ends, Dean will be going away to college, and I worry about what'll happen while he's away. He'll see college girls and will want them instead of a child who's just barely starting high school.

With a sigh, I sit back against my seat and close my eyes.

Life as I know it is about to change. I've been comfortable with things with Dean for too long, and soon, our entire lives will change.

One year, and then he'll be gone.

In one year, I'll lose the person that I've spent nearly every day with since I was eight years old.

"Look at me and smile." He cups my face and pulls me in close. I look at him, and instantly, a smile curls on my lips.

"I love you, Camille. I promise I'd never do anything to hurt you or betray your trust." He seals his promise with a kiss.

My heart stops.

That's the first time Dean has ever said those words to me.

For just a little bit longer, I'll lie and tell myself everything will work out.

EIGHTEEN

NOW

Camille

I didn't think I'd be as nervous as I am right now, standing outside Harbor Point Rehab Center waiting for Declan to be released.

After ninety days, I'm going to see my husband again.

Ninety-three days ago, I found Declan passed out in our condo with a needle still stuck in his arm, surrounded by empty liquor bottles. It wasn't the first time I saw him like that, and every time I found him, he promised it would be the last. I gave him an ultimatum.

Either divorce or rehab, because I couldn't take it anymore. I couldn't sit back and watch him slowly kill himself and blame his addiction on the loss of our son.

When I confronted him, he said dealing with Luca's death sober was too hard, and he couldn't take it, and that's when I freaked out on him and gave him the ultimatum.

The truth is, Declan struggled with addiction long before our son died. Hell, he struggled with addiction before we even got married. But I looked past it all and told myself he was okay.

Yes, it got worse after Luca, but he's always had issues.

I dealt with our son's death alone because my husband was too high or drunk to function. I didn't get to numb or distract myself as he did. He took the easy way out.

Then he started blaming the doctors, claiming they started his addiction. After the accident, he was given painkillers, and it's been downhill since then.

Even though the painkillers didn't start his addiction, he lied to himself and chose to believe he didn't previously have issues.

Declan was born with addiction issues. His birth mother was an avid drug user, and he was born with drugs in his system. His first drink was at thirteen, and his first hit of weed soon after.

Declan always partied on the wild side, but nothing as crazy as heroin. That began over a year ago.

I didn't realize how deeply addicted he was until recently.

He hid it well.

The needles. The heroine. The cocaine. The alcohol. He hid it all so well.

Until a few months in, when I caught him, and he promised to stop using, and for a while, I thought he did.

Drugs, at least. He still drank himself stupid.

Then ninety-three days ago, I learned that he wasn't sober and never had been. He went to rehab a couple of days later.

And for the past ninety days, he's been here at Harbor Point Rehab Center getting the help he desperately needed.

I couldn't bring myself to go inside, so instead, I stand outside, waiting for the doors to open and for him to appear.

At first, I don't recognize him. He's gained back all the weight he lost, even gaining muscle. His skin is lively again instead of sick and pale, and his chocolate eyes are vibrant instead of hidden beneath deep bags. He looks good. He looks like the man I married and not the addict I grew to resent.

Declan's arms open for me, and I run into them on instinct, finding comfort in the familiar touch. My legs wrap around his waist, and his strong arms hold me against his warm body.

He buries his face in the crook of my neck, inhaling my scent. "You smell so fucking good," he mumbles against the skin of my neck. I pull back, take his face in my hands, and press my lips against his. They are plump and soft... and all wrong.

They're familiar, but they're not the lips I want.

The realization that I am comparing Declan, my husband, to Dean hits me like a slap in the face. It makes me sick to my stomach at the thought.

"Come on, let's go home." I remove myself from him, but he keeps hold of my hand. I lead us to my car and drive us home.

AN HOUR LATER, WE ARRIVE AT OUR COMPLEX AND RIDE the elevator up to the floor of our condo. Declan had talked the whole way home, telling me about rehab and everything he learned and the people he met. I was too lost in my head to pay attention to him. I felt horrible for not giving him proper attention, but I didn't feel bad enough because I still ignored him.

"Are you hungry? I can make us some lunch," I ask once we step inside our condo, eyeing him cautiously as he enters our home for the first time in three months.

"No thanks, babe. I'm going to take a shower and then have a nap." I nod. We are standing several feet apart, staring at each other like strangers. It's like we don't know how to act around each other anymore. "Join me for a shower?"

"No, you go ahead. I'm going to order some groceries for delivery so I can cook tonight. Is there anything specific you'd like?"

"Steak sounds good." He kisses my cheek, and I nod. He winks at me, taking his duffle bag into our bedroom.

My phone pings in my purse, and I dig it out just in time to see a new text.

Dean: Let's grab lunch? I'm in the area.
Me: Can't. Busy.

The three text bubbles appear and disappear seconds later. I sigh, turning my phone on do not disturb.

Warmth floods between my legs, and I can't tell if it is because of Declan or Dean.

Fuck it.

I walk into my bedroom, strip naked, and join Declan inside the large walk-in shower, my arms wrapping around his waist from behind.

"There's my girl." He adjusts the temperature. "Changed your mind?" He turns to face me, a smirk spreading on his lips.

I look up at him, really look at him. My heart beats in my chest, my core flutters, and I know it's Declan that I want. I want his body, his touch, only him.

At this moment, at least.

Our lips crash together, and moments later, he's filling my heated pussy with his hard cock that I'm all too familiar with. Declan and I may have our many issues, but one thing we never had a problem with is our sex life.

There's always been pure heated passion between us. Communication may not be our strong suit, but fucking sure as hell is.

Our bodies move in perfect sync, and in no time, I'm reaching my orgasm, biting down on my hand to muffle a scream.

I barely have time to come down from my state of bliss when Declan carries me into our bedroom and spreads me out on our plush king-size bed. With my legs on his shoulders, he stands on his knees, grips my hips, and impales me back onto his cock, knocking the air from my lungs.

After two orgasms and a promise for a third, I wrap myself in my bathrobe and order our grocery delivery while Declan returns to the bathroom to shave the beard he grew while in rehab.

"Groceries will be here in about an hour. I ordered a few things that I know you like." He walks into the bedroom, still in his naked glory. Gently he takes my hands and pulls me up to him, his arms wrapping around my waist.

"I'm so sorry for everything, baby girl. I'm better, and I'm home now. I'm going to be the husband you deserve." He rests his forehead against mine, his eyes staring into mine. I wrap my arms around his neck, offering him the best smile I can muster, wishing I could believe him.

The truth is, I was unhappy long before Luca died. I couldn't pinpoint the exact moment I became sad and fell out of love, I just knew it happened. I don't love him the way I should.

Not anymore, and I haven't for a long time.

I wasn't always unhappy.

At one point, I believe I was in love with him, but that hasn't been for a while. For years, I've been living solely for our son. He's the reason I stayed. And now... now I realize how unhappy I truly am. I don't want to continue living the way we were.

Not living, but merely existing under the same roof.

"Are you okay?"

I nod. "Yes. Of course I am." *Lie.* I'm not okay, but he doesn't question me any further; he never does.

"Good, I'm home now, and we can get back to us." He kisses my lips, and once again, it feels all wrong.

Later that night, we sit on the floor in the living room eating dinner on the coffee table. I engage in conversation with him, and I'm present during said conversation. He speaks more about rehab, and I tell him all about work and how the build of my new location is coming along. I even tell him about Dean. Well, I tell him that he is an old friend who just so happens to be an architect and is the one who is doing my build. He doesn't ask further questions about Dean; I knew he wouldn't. Declan isn't like that. He's always trusted me—I've never given him a reason not to, until now.

"Well, I'd love to meet him sometime. Meet the one who's bringing my wife's dream to life."

"I'm glad you say that because he and his wife want to go out on a double date this weekend."

"Sounds good. Count me in." He wipes his mouth with his

napkin. "Now, if you're finished eating, I don't plan on sleeping anytime soon." He pins me with a hungry look, slowly making his way toward me as if I were his prey.

That night, Declan fulfills his promise for that third orgasm.

And a fourth.

And a fifth.

The entire time, only one man is on my mind.

Dean.

NINETEEN

THEN

***Camille,** 14 years old*

Today is my first day of ninth grade.

I officially start high school today, and I'm nervous as hell.

Spencer, Dallas, and Dean start their senior year, and I know I'll rarely see them.

Our schedules are opposite, so my chance of getting to hang around them is a bust.

Spencer says I need to make more friends because I won't have anyone to hang out with once she goes away to college. I have two friends, but they're more strictly school friends. Obviously, she's right, so my goal for the year is to make new friends.

Starting right now, I will work on becoming more social.

I grab my phone from my bed and send a quick group text to Bex and Fallon, my only friends.

Me: Let's meet outside the school and walk in together!

Fallon: Okay! I'm so nervous!!

Bex: Me too, and my sister won't let me walk in with her.

Me: Spencer said all the seniors have to get there earlier because of some first-day stuff.

Fallon: I'm leaving now. Meet you guys out front!

Of the two, Fallon is the one I'm closest to. We've known each other since kindergarten, and we've hung out a few times during the summer, but it's been a while. She knows about my crush on Dean, too. I've told her, letting her know that I already have dibs, so she can't have him.

Luckily for me, she's more interested in girls than boys.

An hour later, my mom drops me off at the front of Cyprus High School, where I immediately spot Bex waiting outside. She waves her arms in the air the moment she sees me. I hug my mom goodbye with a smile and climb out of the car, rushing toward Bex just as Fallon's mom drops her off. After a group hug between the three of us, we walk inside of our new school arm in arm.

Luckily, my classes are easy to find. I know where most of the classrooms are because I've already been to the school several times before. I came with my parents anytime Spencer had a school function, and she would often bring me along to Dallas's basketball games, so I've already gotten a glimpse of the school.

Most of my classes are with Fallon, and a few with both her and Bex.

By lunch, I am ready for the first day to end. It seems to drag on, and all I want to do is to get home so I can tell Dean all about my first day of high school. I haven't seen him yet, at least not until I enter the lunchroom.

It isn't until I sit down with Fallon and Bex at an empty table with my lunch tray that I spot Dean across the cafeteria.

I knew it was possible I'd see him at lunch initially for the first few days since first-year students and seniors have the same lunch period in the beginning. The principal thought it would be helpful for the seniors to be around to welcome the freshman and answer questions we might have.

Afterward, the seniors would leave us and have a later lunch period.

It is the first day, and I have already heard whispers in the hallway about Dean and how hot he is. I can't disagree, but I am not too fond of hearing other girls talk about him.

I'm aware Dean has a reputation; I've heard about it plenty over the years, but that doesn't mean I am ready or prepared to hear about it.

From across the cafeteria, I sit at my table, watching him sit at a lunch table crowded with people. Spence and Dallas sit with him, which makes sense, considering they are in the popular group.

This year, Spencer is the captain of the cheerleading team, having taken the position from Sadie and bumping her down to co-captain, and Dallas is the basketball team's star player.

They are a perfect match. No doubt they'll end up married with five kids. They're perfect together, and everyone swears they'll be together forever. There's no doubt about it, especially when Spence looks at him with hearts in her eyes and like he's the reason for the stars in the sky.

My sister is madly in love.

Dean plays football. Well, played. This year he isn't playing because he wants to focus on researching colleges and spend as much at home as he can since this is his final year before going away to college. I'll miss going to his games, but selfishly I'm glad he's not playing. It'll allow us more time together.

"Why don't you walk over to him instead of sitting here and staring?" Fallon snaps me out of my thoughts, stealing some fries from my plate.

"Who? Who are we watching?" Bex asks, as oblivious as ever.

"Dean Jameson." Fallon points, and I reach out and pull her hand down.

"Don't point. You'll make it obvious. I'm just curious about what Dean's like at school. I haven't seen him at all today." They both giggle.

"We're at school, duh. He's probably busy with first-day stuff. You can't expect to see him every day, all day. Things will be different than they are during summer." I roll my eyes at Fallon.

"Yeah, yeah, yeah, I know this. I guess I just hoped he'd have more time for me."

"You're acting like a possessive girlfriend." Fallon rolls her eyes. "You're a freshman, and he's a senior. He probably won't pay any attention to you during school." She steals another fry from my plate. "We're at school, so stop being ridiculous. He can't focus on you."

"Ugh, you're right! You're totally right." I shove some fries into my mouth. After our trip over the summer to Cancun and kissing Dean every day and slipping into his bed to sleep at night, I've gotten comfortable with our routine, and I love it. And I love him.

I'm in love with Dean.

Since we've been back home, we haven't spent a night apart. I've gotten great at sneaking out, and he's gotten great at sneaking me in. I sleep in his bed and sneak out before the sun comes up and our parents wake up.

"I'll just go say hi, then come back and let it go." They both give me a reluctant nod, and like a girl obsessed, I walk across the lunchroom toward Dean and his group of friends.

We haven't put a label on whatever we are. We sleep together, make out, and say we love each other, and to me, that sounds like a relationship.

Are we in a relationship? I believe we are, even if my parents don't want me dating until I'm sixteen.

I'm halfway toward Dean's table when I suddenly feel like I'm walking into the lion's den. I've never been nervous about approaching him before, but now I am. I think about turning around and going back to my table, but Spencer spots me before I can.

"Hey, sis." She smiles, biting into an apple. I make a face at her tray of food—an apple, water, and a salad. She eats insanely healthy, always keeping in shape and rarely eating junk. Whereas

I never turn down a pizza and hate exercise, she loves it and prefers salad over pizza.

I wave at Spence and Dallas just as Dean's head turns toward me, and a smile spreads across his lips, lighting up his handsome face.

"Hey, Cam." He shifts, facing me. "How's your first day going?"

Stupid Sadie opens her stupid paper-cut mouth before I can respond. "Who let the child near our table?"

"Last I checked, it's a free lunchroom. I can go anywhere I like." I cross my arms over my chest. I don't need this crap from Sadie on the first day of school.

"Yeah, and I can sit anywhere I like, too." She slips down from the table and sits on Dean's lap, looking me right in the eye with a smirk. "Isn't that right, Dean?"

"Fuck off, Sadie." He stands, letting her boney ass fall straight to the ground. Instant laughter rumbles from those who witness her fall.

"You weren't saying that over the summer when I was sucking your dick!" she yells. The laughter stops, and the entire cafeteria falls silent.

With an annoyed laugh, Dean looks at her. "We both know that's not true. Don't flatter yourself." She stands and brushes herself off, flipping her stupid blonde hair over her shoulder. She's red with embarrassment, clearly not expecting Dean to out her lie to the entire school.

"Fuck you, Dean. Go run off with your stupid child slut!"

Spencer jumps to her feet in two seconds and is in Sadie's face.

"Talk about my sister like that again, and I'll kick your ass myself. And you can stop lying now. We all know that Dean never fucked you." Before I have a chance to hear her comeback, Dean takes my hand and pulls me out of the lunchroom.

We walk down the empty hall toward the janitor's closet, and the second we step inside, he pushes me up against the wall, and his lips find mine in the darkness.

"Let's go to the lighthouse tonight," he whispers against my lips. With my hands on his hips, I nod, laughing when I realize that he can't even see me.

"Okay," I mumble, connecting my lips with his again. His kiss is different from usual; it's aggressive and hungry.

With a groan, Dean pulls away, leaving my lips raw and swollen.

THE REMAINDER OF THE DAY GOES BY IN A BLUR.

Spencer has cheer practice after, and Dean had to stay after school, so Mom picks me up and brings me home. Since it was the first day, there is no homework, which is great considering I can't wait to get home and prepare to see Dean later at the lighthouse.

Holy crap. I really am overly obsessed with him.

Is this what all girls experience when they have their first boyfriend? Well, I don't have my first boyfriend since we aren't dating, not yet at least. And the more I think about it, that won't happen for a very long time.

I'm allowed to date when I'm sixteen, but Dean will already be away at college by then. I won't have my first boyfriend for God knows how long.

Ugh. I'm such a loser.

With that realization, I flop onto my bed and bury my face into my pillow, groaning when a knock sounds at my door.

"Go away!" I grumble, muffled by my pillow. Hearing a knock again, I remove the pillow from my face. "I said go away." I turn over, lying on my back.

The door creaks open. "Dean's downstairs with Dad. He said he's picking you up," my mom says, and I groan.

"What's wrong? Did something happen at school?"

"No, I just realized that I'll never have a boyfriend."

She laughs. "Don't be so dramatic, Camille. When you're older, you will have a boyfriend. For now, focus on school and getting good grades." I sit up with a sigh and roll my green eyes.

"Mom, I always get good grades. Dean graduates this year, so I don't understand why you can't make a special exception and let us be together. Spencer gets to date! She was dating before she was sixteen."

Mom enters my room and sits beside me on my bed. "Sweetie, Dean is too old for you. Your father and I don't mind you two being friends and hanging out, but you're too young for a relationship."

"If you think he's too old for me, why do you let us hang out? He's downstairs to pick me up right now!"

"We trust him and always know where you two are. He told me that you had a bad day at school, so he's taking you for ice cream, and you'll be home by curfew. Sweetheart, Dean thinks of you as a little sister and watches out for you, just like Spencer." She pats my head.

My cheeks are heated, and I hope she can't see the guilt on my face. Dean isn't taking me for ice cream, and if she only knew what goes on between us, she'd forbid us from seeing each other.

"You're right, and I'm just being dramatic. Thanks, Mom, love you." I jump up from my bed and rush out of my room, not bothering to wait for her response. I need to get away from her before the truth about Dean and me is revealed.

Downstairs, I find him and my dad in the living room yelling at the TV over some game. I don't pay attention to the sport, because once Dean catches sight of me, he says a goodbye to my father.

I hug my dad and tell him I'll be home by curfew. Then with matching smiles, Dean drives us to the lighthouse.

Since the day Dean showed me the lighthouse, it has become our special place, and we spend every moment we can here. This is the one place we can be completely uncensored.

No hiding our feelings for each other, no hiding our kissing or hand holding, no hiding our dreams and aspirations.

We can just be... us.

We get to be unapologetically us, and I love and cherish every second of our time spent in the lighthouse.

I'm the first to unlock the door and run inside, but Dean is hot on my heels. The moment the front door closes, he lifts me in his arms. I wrap my legs around his waist and arms around his neck, and in the next second, his soft lips are on mine, breathing life back into me.

His kiss is heaven and hell wrapped into one. It's both magic and sin.

It ignites a spark within me that I've never felt before. I can feel his kiss all the way from my lips down to my toes... and everywhere in between.

Especially my core.

The feeling is new to me. The need I feel for him between my thighs grows with each kiss. I can feel the heat, and I wonder if he can too.

Dean's intensity began a few months ago. He kissed me with more tongue than usual, and it turned into heavy petting over our clothes. Now, our making out usually results in heavy petting and getting close to the line we know we can't cross, but that doesn't stop us from getting awfully close.

Dean carries me upstairs to the bedroom and sits down on the bed with me on top of him so I'm straddling him. My fingers tangle in his hair while I kiss him, hoping he can feel my love for him.

I'm so worked up that I don't notice myself grinding on him at first. Not until I feel the pleasure between us. With a low moan against his lips, I continue moving my hips against his. The friction against my jeans feels so good on my sensitive clit. The more we've been petting, the more online research I've been doing about sex, and the more porn I've been watching in preparation for the day I give my virginity to Dean. I want to be completely prepared and know what to do.

At this point, it's likely we won't make it to our wedding night, but I don't care. He makes me feel too good to wait, and how can something that feels so good be wrong?

His hands are on my hips, and he's rocking me against the hard erection that's tented his pants while our lips fuse together, moving in perfect sync.

He's so hard beneath me, and I wonder if it hurts to be as hard as he is. This is usually when Dean stop us, but tonight I hope he doesn't.

I let my curious hand slip underneath his T-shirt. His skin is warm, and I trace the lines and grooves over his washboard abs.

As my hand lowers, I feel his breathing quicken. Confidently and curiously, I palm his crotch, and my mind slips to places it shouldn't.

I wonder what his dick would look like and if it would be as big as of the guys I've seen in porn videos.

I'm curious, and part of me wants to say screw it and cross the line that we're already dancing on.

Dean groans against my lips, and it's the most incredible sound. I made him do that. I want to hear what other sounds I can milk from him. He tangles his hands in my hair and pulls at the root, and now it's his turn to elicit a delicate moan from me.

"We need to stop right now before we do something you're not ready for," he rasps, his voice husky and deeper than usual.

Something I'm not ready for? Does that mean he's ready?

Is Dean ready for sex?

I'm almost embarrassed to ask, but I have to know. "A-are you ready for that?"

"I'm ready for you whenever you're ready for me. I will never pressure you, so please don't feel that way. We do this on your time." I gulp and pull back from him with a nod. My lips sting from his kiss, and I already know they'll be swollen and bruised.

"Not tonight. But soon." I promise with a kiss.

Holy crap.

Am I really promising to have sex soon?

Dean and I said we'd have sex on our wedding night, but when will that be? There's no telling when that would be, and now we are both painfully aware that our time together is coming closer to an end every day.

Every day we get closer and closer to the end of us.

He'll be off to college, and everything will change. I won't see him every day, and who knows when we'd get married. I have faith and love him enough to know that it will happen, but it's the not knowing *when* that I can't stand.

So yes, I am promising Dean we will have sex soon.

One of these days, before Dean goes to college, we will have sex. I'll give him my special gift that I'd planned to save until marriage.

But it's okay that we're not waiting until we're married. Because I know that Dean will be my first and my last.

He will be my first and last everything.

TWENTY

NOW

Camille

All week long, Dean has been texting me, and all week I have read his messages and deleted them without replying. As much as it pains me to ignore him, I can't bring myself to respond. Not when my head is in such a fucked-up place right now.

On Tuesday, I had taken Declan to my office to show him around, and Emily, my receptionist, told me that I'd just missed a visit from Dean and that he had left a message for me to call him.

He texted me twice after that, but it wasn't about the build, so I didn't reply.

He says he wants to talk.

It's as if he's trying to restart our friendship, which isn't possible. It can't be. Not when there are still lingering feelings between us.

We never got closure. *I* never got closure.

Our relationship was put on pause eleven years ago, and we both moved on without ever getting closure. I know that's what I need now; Dr. Reynolds even agrees.

Perhaps that's why I'm wound up so tight and stuck inside my head. I need closure to finally be set free and move on from Dean after eleven years.

They say time will heal you and that you can get over someone with time. But I don't believe that. Time isn't closure; it's just time. Just another passing day.

Since Declan came home, I've been distant, and I know he's starting to notice that I'm not as okay as I pretend to be. I've missed my recent appointment with Dr. Reynolds, and I've been working from home in a desperate attempt to avoid Dean. I don't want to risk running into him at my office if he decides to drop by again.

So, since showing my office to Declan on Tuesday, I've been home.

Home, avoiding Dean, and babysitting Declan because I don't trust him to be alone.

"Earth to Camille, baby girl, what's up?" I snap my head to the side to face Declan, the man I should be thinking about and focusing on. He wraps his arms around my waist, but the feeling isn't as comforting as it once was.

It's Friday, the night I've been dreading.

We're going to dinner with Dean and Karina.

With a sigh, I lean against Declan's chest and inhale the scent of his cologne that surrounds me. "Nothing, just can't decide what to wear." Pulling away from his embrace, I hang the dress in my hands back on the rack and grab the red dress with thick straps from the black velvet hanger.

With gentle fingers, he brushes my hair over my shoulder and presses a kiss to my bare skin.

"We have an hour before we need to leave. That's enough time for some fun." His hands push up the bottom of my towel until my bottom half is exposed; his thumb and middle finger spread my lips apart while his index finger flicks over my clit.

Declan trails his lips to my neck, and I sigh, giving in to his touch. "I need to finish getting ready," I protest weakly, making no attempt to leave. His other arm wraps around my waist, holding me back against his chest.

"Give me five minutes. We both need this," he breathes

against my neck, his lips trailing over every bare part of skin he can reach from our position. Without warning, Declan slams two fingers inside me and pumps his hand, his thumb strumming my sensitive clit.

Thankfully, I'm already wet, making it easier for him to strum my clit and glide between my legs.

We've been fucking like jackrabbits ever since he came home. Five minutes into a conversation, we end up naked and going at it like a couple of horny teenagers.

We fuck because we have nothing to say to each other. We don't do much talking; we fuck. I know it's unhealthy, and using each other for pleasure will not solve any issues, but it's all we've got right now.

Declan pulls his hand away, sucks his fingers into his mouth, bends me over the stool in the closet, and stretches my pussy with his glorious cock when he enters me in one rough thrust.

"Fuck, baby girl. I have missed your tight pussy so much," he grunts, reaching an arm around to play with my clit.

After an orgasm that leaves me sated and limp, Declan dresses and then leaves without a word. He's never had the best aftercare, but I don't mind. I prefer not to do much speaking anyway.

Luckily, his great cock makes up for the fact I have to take care of myself. At least I'm able to orgasm. Most guys don't even care if women get off. They only care about themselves. Declan isn't like that; he always makes sure I orgasm before he reaches his own. But after that, he pulls out and doesn't care about me. Like I'm a stranger that gave him a quick fuck rather than his wife.

I use a T-shirt to clean between my legs and toss it into the hamper before sliding on my panties and dressing, opting for the red dress.

I stand in the bathroom finishing my makeup when my phone beeps with a new text.

Dean: We can cancel dinner if you're not up for it anymore.
Dean: Call Karina and cancel dinner.

Dean: I can't do it.

Dean: I'm serious, Camille.

Dean: Cancel dinner.

Dean: Now.

Dean: Fucking cancel it.

Dean: Please.

With a sigh, I delete the thread of messages and send a text to Karina.

Me: We're on our way. See you soon.

Karina: Yay! I'm so excited!

Thirty minutes later, we arrive at Mio's, a popular new Italian restaurant. Declan is wearing sunglasses and keeps his head down, even though it's seven o'clock at night, and the sun is long gone.

He must always take precautions wherever he goes, or else someone may recognize him and draw attention.

Luckily for us, no one recognizes him, at least not until we walk into the restaurant and are seated.

He removes his sunglasses just as the waitress comes over to us to get our drink order. Her young face instantly lights up with recognition. Thank fuck she's professional and doesn't say a word.

Declan gives her a knowing wink.

We order our drinks, water for me and coke for him. I want to get alcohol, I need something to take the edge off, but I can't with Dec around. Unfortunately, I'm out of my magic pills, so I can't even rely on those to make me feel better.

Minutes later, Dean and Karina walk in side by side, hand in hand.

We exchange quick greetings, and then they take their place across the table from us.

After a brief exchange, Dean avoids eye contact with me and barely makes conversation, but with the way Karina takes control of the conversation, there isn't much room for anyone else to speak.

Declan and Karina fall into an instant, easy conversation, babbling on about music, London, and his touring days.

By the way they speak, you'd think that they were old friends and didn't just meet a few minutes ago.

"Camille was such a groupie," he says with a laugh, retelling the story of how we met. "She was twenty-one, hot-headed as fuck, and scared off the women hanging around backstage hoping to get to see me. I think it only took two minutes for me to realize that I had to have her. The next morning, she left on tour with me, wearing only the clothes on her back." He looks over at me with a smile, pressing a kiss to my temple.

Mindlessly I hear him and Karina speaking but don't pay enough attention to be able to add to the conversation. At least not until he squeezes my hand to bring me back to reality, and then I realize that he's still sharing our story.

Day by day, our story is reaching its final chapter.

"I've loved her every minute since that day." His smile is sad and doesn't reach his eyes. Right then, I know that he's aware of the constant battle in my head.

Declan, too, knows that our story is coming to an end, and it won't end with an epilogue and a happy ever after. We share a sad smile between the two of us.

He brings my hand up to his mouth and kisses my knuckles one by one. With our eyes locked on each other, I truly feel seen for the first time in a long time and feel like I'm looking at someone I used to know. His eyes are clear instead of foggy like they always were before he went to rehab. He's changed. I see that clear as day.

We've both changed; we're not who we used to be.

We've both known for a while now that we're doomed and heading for divorce. It's no surprise, and since he's been home, we're right back to being who we were before he went to rehab. There's too much distance between us.

"That's such a crazy story. Nine months later, you've got a baby and a wife." Karina swoons, ruining our moment. For a second, I had forgotten all about her.

Clearing my throat, I tear my eyes away from my husband and look at the blonde sitting across from me. She brings her wine glass to her lips and takes a long noisy gulp, her hot pink lipstick leaving residue on the glass when she sets it down.

Declan's eyes follow the movement of the glass, his Adam's apple bobbing in his throat. He's thirsty for a taste. I know he is—his hand trembles against mine with the desire to reach across the table and take the glass of wine for himself.

I tighten my grip on his hand and intertwine our fingers, hoping like hell I can keep him calm and take his mind off his urge for a drink.

Clearing his throat, he says, "Enough about us. How did you two meet?" He reaches over for my glass of water and downs most of it in one drink.

Dean opens his mouth to speak, but Karina cuts him off and answers. No surprise there. "We went to university together, but Dean never gave me the time of day. After graduation, the company he was working for was hired to design a building for my father, and Dean and I reconnected. We started dating, then two years later we were married." She giggles. "I wish I could say it was love at first sight, but it took some convincing for him to give me a chance. He was secretly still hung up on an ex-girlfriend." My mouth goes dry at her words.

Karina looks across at me with pure malice, and I know right in that moment that she knows about Dean and me.

My eyes shoot to Dean just in time to see him give me a subtle shake of the head.

Fuck.

Is Karina beginning to put two and two together and realize that there is more to Dean and me? Or did someone tell her about us? I'd like to think that he wouldn't tell her about our history without warning me first.

Thankfully, Declan saves me before things can take a turn. "So, Dean, Camille tells me that you two are childhood friends?" Declan sits back, his hand holding mine tightly under the table.

"Yup. We were young when my family moved in next door. Our mothers are friends from college."

Karina sits back unimpressed, gulping down the remainder of her wine. And right on cue, the waitress returns to refill our waters and her wine.

"Did you two ever date?" Declan asks bluntly.

Dean looks at me, and my heart stops. He opens his mouth to speak, but I quickly cut him off. "God, no. We were only friends. I was younger than him, so even saying friends is too much. We were nothing really. He was mostly friends with Spence and her boyfriend at the time," I lie smoothly, my heart aching as the words leave my mouth. It's physically painful to lie and say that Dean was nothing to me when that is so far from the truth. He was once everything to me.

Always has been, always will be.

And I can never admit it.

But I will get over it; I will. I'll get closure and move on from Dean, and I'll learn to be happy.

I *can* do this. I *need* to do this.

Karina mumbles something under her breath, gulping down her freshly filled glass of wine. "Karina, I think you've had enough to drink," Dean whispers not so silently. She waves him off, chugging the remainder of her fourth glass of red wine. We haven't even ordered yet, and she's nearly drunk.

"Where has Camille been hiding you? I've been trying to get her to bring you out for weeks now." Fuck. Great, just the question that I was hoping to avoid.

Karina is drinking too much, and I see how Declan's eyes follow her lips each time she takes a drink. I'm worried that seeing her drinking so much will trigger him, and the last thing I want to go through is Declan falling back into old habits. If he falls off the wagon after spending three months in rehab, I don't know what will happen.

"We should order now," I cut in before he has the chance to try and explain his absence. Knowing Declan, he'd be honest, and I can't have that.

Our waitress returns to our table just in time, so we order our meals, along with another glass of wine for Karina.

We engage in subtle but forced conversation while we wait for our food to arrive.

You can cut the tension in the air with a knife.

I know we all feel it. Even laid-back Declan seems to be on edge.

I say a silent prayer that our food will come soon, even though we just ordered so we can leave. The uncomfortable situation, mixed with Karina's endless drinks may push Declan over the edge when he's already so fragile.

We need to get the fuck out of here, and soon.

Karina's been silent for a while, leaving the three of us to carry on a meaningless conversation. It's light and fucking awkward.

Declan asks Dean about the build, I add a word in here and there, but otherwise, it's awkward.

"So, Declan, how do you feel about not having more children? I'd think that you'd want more, you know, considering the first one was short-lived."

"Karina!" Dean snaps, his booming voice earning us a couple of glances.

Declan's face pales, his hands shaking while my hands ball into fists. He has to adjust his grip to keep his hand around mine, because I'm ready to jump across the table and strangle the life out of her.

This rude fucking bitch.

I've tried to be nice, but this is it. Her comment about my son is the final straw.

Fuck Karina.

"What the fuck is wrong with you?!" I hiss. Declan's grip on my hand tightens, and his jaw clenches.

"Oh shit, I'm so sorry. I didn't mean for it to come out that way," she says with a smirk.

"That's exactly how you meant it." It's too late for a fucking apology. Fuck the bitch.

"It's fine." Declan sighs, letting go of my hand. "But yes, eventually, I do want more children."

"How will that happen since Camille doesn't want more?"

"You are overstepping, Karina. That's enough," Dean interrupts.

She ignores her husband and continues, "I'm like you, Declan. I want a baby, too. But I'm married to someone who doesn't want to give that to me."

"This is not the time nor the place to have this discussion." Dean grabs her glass of wine from her hand and sits it down on the table with force. "You've had enough to drink."

"What's it like to want something so badly but not be able to get because of the person you're married to?" Karina's glaring eyes look from me to Declan. "Let me tell you a secret, Declan. Your wife is fucking my husband."

"Karina!" Dean practically yells.

"What the fuck?" Declan shakes his head, looking between Karina and me.

"You're batshit crazy," I practically yell. Yes, I've thought about him. But I haven't been touched sexually by Dean in eleven years. This woman is fucking crazy. And she has the nerve to sit there laughing.

"I'm just joking. But you should see your faces." She giggles.

I scoot my chair back and stand with an angered huff, throwing my napkin onto the table.

"You know what, you can go fuck yourself, Karina. You would make a terrible fucking mother," I hiss, hoping my words hurt her as badly as she hurt me.

"Yeah, well, at least I would be able to keep my child alive," she snarls.

I see red.

It happens in an instant. I don't know who lunged first or exactly what happened, but one second there is a table between us, and the next second, the table is flipped over, and I'm throwing myself at her like I'm Mike fucking Tyson.

Screams erupt from those around us, but I pay no attention to the other guests in the restaurant.

I barely even register what's happening until a pair of strong arms wrap around my waist and pull me away from Karina, who is now on the floor crying, curled into the fetal position.

I'm not positive if I slapped or punched her, but I know there was definitely a physical altercation.

"Get off me! Get the fuck off me! Say something else about my son, and you will regret it!" I yell like a maniac, my body shaking with the rage coursing through my veins.

"Camille! Calm the fuck down!" Declan yells, setting me on my feet just long enough for him to switch positions and haul me over his shoulder like I'm a sack of potatoes.

I look up just in time to see Dean pick Karina up from the floor and wipe her bloody nose before he turns to speak with someone who appears to be the restaurant manager.

I'm fuming.

Never have I been so fucking angry before.

Karina's words cut me deeper than she'll ever know. Deeper than anyone will ever know. She triggered something inside me that I thought was buried.

Guilt.

Her hurtful words make me realize that my son is in fact gone, and it's all my fault.

I knew Declan wasn't acting like himself that night, and I still let him drive. His eyes were red, and his words were slurred, but I still allowed him to get behind the wheel.

Instead of making him give me the keys, I turned a blind eye to his disheveled appearance and was too distracted by our arguing.

I was so distracted that I didn't double-check Luca's car seat to ensure he was properly buckled in, and I turned a blind eye to Declan's addiction. He got behind the wheel, and our son paid the price.

Because of the decisions we made that night, our son is gone.

On the drive home, I don't say a single word. Even once we step inside our condo and Declan undresses me, I remain silent.

We sit in the kitchen, me on the island and him between my legs. He's icing my right hand—the hand that I apparently punched Karina with. "I'm sorry about what she said to you," he says with a sigh.

I roll my eyes, his words angering me enough to cause me to speak. "Don't apologize for that dumb bitch." He mumbles something under his breath, inhaling deeply.

One heartbeat.

Two heartbeats.

Three heartbeats.

Four heartbeats later, Declan asks the loaded question.

"Camille, is there something going on between you and Dean?"

TWENTY-ONE

THEN

DEAN, *18 years old*

Camille and I have been getting closer than ever before... intimately, for the last three months. She doesn't shy away when my hand goes between her legs and I rub her through her jeans, or when I hold her hips and slide her against the growing bulge in my pants, or even when I suck on her round tits and leave my mark on her.

I want nothing more than to leave my mark on her neck for everyone to see, but that's impossible, considering she's not even allowed to date yet.

When I sucked on her neck for the first time, she moaned so sweetly, and I loved it so much that I wanted to hear those sounds fall from her plump lips repeatedly. She was the one who took her shirt off but kept her bra on. Her tits are perky and round and fit perfectly in my hands, and I couldn't help but suck the skin that was exposed. She wouldn't let me take her bra off so I could suck on her bare nipples, and I know that is because she'd be too turned on and wouldn't want to stop. I have already seen how difficult it is for her to stop each time we go too far.

She is left with wet panties, and I am left with blue balls.

Every fucking time.

My right hand has never been used more than it is now.

It's winter break, so I'll be getting to see Cam for a hell of a lot longer than an hour or two after school.

My time with her is coming to an end, and it's a reality neither of us want to face... until now.

Mom and Dad are ready for me to start sending off college applications, and the number one school I want to attend isn't close by. It's the best architecture school, and I've had my eye on it for years. Camille knows about the school, but she doesn't know attending school in England is my firm plan. Tonight is the night I'll tell her. I haven't even applied or been accepted, so I may be jumping the gun by telling her, but I have a good feeling about it, and I'd rather her be prepared for the possibility of me moving a lot farther away than she originally thought.

I think Camille's been so open to letting things between us get closer to the line we can't cross yet because she knows I'll be gone soon.

But tonight, before I tell her my college plans, I'm taking her on an official date.

Last night, I told her to be ready by 10 a.m., so I'm not surprised when I pull into her driveway and see her waiting.

Like a true gentleman, I even get out of the car to open the passenger door for her. She's wearing jeans that hug her like a second skin, a sweater underneath her jacket, and flat knee-high boots. Her long, silky midnight black hair hangs freely down her back, and a gray beanie is on her head, pulled down to her ears.

Fuck. The sight of her makes my cock twitch in my pants. She looks so fucking beautiful no matter what she wears.

The girl who once wore pigtails and overalls every single day is long gone, and in her place is a young woman who makes my dick painfully hard.

"Where are we going?" she asks from the passenger seat with a bright smile.

"It's a surprise." I lean over, cup her face, and press my lips against hers, stealing the air from her lungs.

"Hurry up before someone sees us kissing." I laugh, kissing her again. I turn my attention to the road and carefully back out of the driveway with a grin.

As usual, Cam leans forward to take control over the radio and sings along to every song that plays. She's not going to audition for American Idol anytime soon, but the girl can at least carry a tune.

I love seeing her when she's in my car.

She's so beautiful, so young, so free.

Camille Avery Lambert is the definition of perfection.

And I was a goner when it came to her. I am so fucking in love with this girl that I will never recover. She has me under her spell, and she doesn't even know it. She does it effortlessly, and I don't know how I'll survive being away from her. But that's not something I want to think about right now.

We'll have that conversation before the day is done, but I want to focus on the beautiful girl beside me for now.

Twenty minutes later, we've parked, I've paid for our skates, and now I'm kneeling and helping her into them. For years, Camille has been telling me she wanted to go ice skating, and I don't know why we never got around to it until now. But today is all about her, and I want to make all her wishes come true before I break her heart.

Hand in hand, we walk toward the large ice rink. The moment we step onto the ice, she begins to wobble, so I reach out to steady her. She's not at all graceful, and even though she looks like a baby giraffe trying to walk, she's still perfect and completely carefree.

Hand in hand, we skate around the rink; slow at first, taking our time until she gets the hang of it and finds her balance. I expected her to fall once or twice, but as with everything else she does, she surprises me and stays on her feet the entire time.

We skate around for over an hour until her nose is red and her teeth are chattering.

Silently, we return our skates and climb back into my car.

Inside my car, with the heater on full blast and hot chocolate in our hands, I shift in my seat to look at her.

She giggles. "That was so much fun!" She removes the cups from our hands to place them in the cupholder, then throws her arms around my neck and presses her cold lips to mine. My hands find her small waist, bringing her body as close to mine as I can despite our position. With my eyes closed, I return every delicious kiss, devouring her mouth, willing myself to commit her lips and touch to memory.

I pull back and carefully brush the hair away from her face. "I'm glad you had fun. Are you hungry?" She nods. Of course, she is. The girl can out eat me any day. I love that about her. She never tries to be someone she's not and never tries to fit into the smallest size like all the other girls at school.

"Let's get some lunch, and then we're going to the lighthouse." Since the snow began last week, it's been too cold to go to the lighthouse, so we've stayed at either her house or mine. Yesterday, I was able to get a couple of heaters so that we'd be able to spend time there without freezing ourselves to death.

Cam pecks my cheek before settling back into her seat and buckling her seatbelt across her chest. "Let's go. I'm starving." I follow suit by putting on my own seatbelt and driving us toward our favorite diner, which is nearby.

AFTER SCARFING DOWN BURGERS, FRIES, AND MILKSHAKES, we're now en route to the lighthouse. I've never seen Cam eat so quick before, but she is dead set on getting to the lighthouse soon so we can make out for a while before we have to leave to get back home. With the snow only getting worse, it likely won't be long before our parents call and want us to return home.

Once we finally make it to the lighthouse, I'm quick to unlock the door and rush inside to turn on the heaters that I'd brought over earlier. Between both heaters and our bodies, I know we'll be able to keep each other plenty warm.

"It's freezing!" Camille says through chattering teeth. I watch her sit down, remove her gloves, and wave her hands in front of the heater. I sit down behind her, pull her between my legs, and bring her back against my chest, wrapping my arms around her. She fits perfectly between my legs, and she's exactly where she needs to be. I kiss the sensitive spot beneath her left ear that I learned was a huge turn-on for her.

Instantly I wonder if I slip my hand into her pants, will I find her wet? I've never touched her bare pussy before, but I've felt her over her cotton panties and know how wet she can get. Obviously, by now, I know what makes her wet and what fucking soaks her.

"Talk to me, Dean. You've had something on your mind all day." She tilts her head back to look at me, and I press a kiss on her forehead with a sigh. She's always been able to read me better than anyone.

"I'm sending in college applications soon," I admit; the only response I get from her is a nod. "I'm applying to the University of Cambridge." Camille goes still. Her breathing slows, and for a moment, I'm pretty sure she stops breathing altogether.

She's silent for an extended period before a very long and very dramatic sigh escapes her parted pink lips. "I knew this was coming, but that doesn't mean this doesn't suck any less. I hope you get in. I really do." I've told her about the University of Cambridge in the past. She knows it's my dream school for architecture. And Camille being Camille would only ever want the best for me.

Her body shifts in my lap until she's facing me, and her arms are wrapped around my neck. "You want to marry me, right? So, what'll happen when you go to college?"

I think for a long silent moment, wrapping my arms around her waist to bring her closer to me.

What will happen?

I will be thousands of miles away and will be gone for four

years. A lot can happen in four years. By the time I graduate college, she'll just be really getting the swing of things at her own college. I'll be twenty-two, and she'll be nineteen.

We haven't been apart from each other much. We've been practically glued to the hip since we were eight and eleven years old.

I don't want to make her wait for me. That's selfish and unrealistic, but dammit, I sure as fuck don't want anyone else trying to slip their way in to take my place.

"Let's make a promise to each other right now." I sigh. "By the time I finish my degree, you'll just be completing your first year of college, and I want you to have the whole high school and college experience. So, we'll go to school, and when you graduate, I'll find you, and we'll start our life together."

"What the fuck kind of idea is that?!" she snaps, her green eyes practically shooting daggers at me from the glare she's giving me. I hide my laugh. It's not often I hear her curse, but it humors me greatly when I do.

"Seven years. You'll have your degree by then, and I'll be able to start my design firm."

"Are you high? I'm pretty sure you've been smoking crack."

I frown. Seven years is a long fucking time. I'd never be able to even make it seven days. But I'm doing this for her. I can't hold her back from anything. She's fifteen. She's so fucking young and has the rest of her high school and college years ahead of her. I don't want her sitting around waiting for me, not experiencing life because of me. I want her to take life by the fucking balls and make it her bitch.

"Cam, you're too young to sit around waiting for me. Go to parties, get drunk, do things you might regret, and make new friends. Be young and have fun. I will not allow you to spend any time sitting at home counting down the days until I return." I press my forehead against hers. "I love you so fucking much, and it's because I love you that I'm letting you go. I want you to live."

"No, nope, no way!" She pulls back, jumps to her feet, and paces around the room. "What are we supposed to do for the next seven years? Write to each other? Call when you have time? Do I forget about you until hopefully one day you come back to me?!" she yells, furiously shaking her head, and I can see the unshed tears that are glistening in her bright green eyes. "You're an even bigger idiot than I thought if you think I'm going to follow your dumb-ass plan."

"What's your plan, then? Huh? I have four years of college ahead of me, and you're about to be sophomore in high school." I can't blame her for being angry. I'm springing this absurd idea on her at the spur of the moment. She hasn't had time to process like I have. I've been thinking about this for weeks. I've prepared myself and thought about every single possible option. I stand, extending my arms out toward her, hoping to try and calm my little spitfire.

"You're a coward. You want to date other girls. *You* are the one who wants to experience college life and parties and fuck random bitches. This isn't about me. This is about you!" she yells, stabbing my chest with her index finger with each word.

I scoff. "It's about both of us. This will be good for us both!" I sigh, taking a deep breath to calm myself. The last thing I need to do is yell at her when she's upset. The truth is, I want to experience youth and college life just as much as I know she does. We're so consumed by each other, and it's not fair to either one of us to sit around.

Anything can happen.

What if one of us gets sick and dies or gets hit by a car and dies? I wouldn't want either of us to die without ever experiencing life. My parents told me how important it is to experience things while you're young, and I want the same college experience they had.

They were high school sweethearts and broke up for two years after graduation to have freedom and the college experience because they were so young. After two years, Dad transferred to

Mom's college, and they got back together and have been together ever since.

"I must mean nothing to you if you can leave me so easily."

"It's not going to be easy, baby. But it's necessary. I'm letting you go so we can each have school experiences while we're young. That way when we're older, we won't have any regrets and wonder what if."

"You don't even know if you're going to get accepted." She crosses her arms over her chest.

"Even if I don't go to England, I'm still leaving the state."

"If you stay, it's easier for us to call and text."

"No, Cam, baby, come on." I reach for her, but her stubborn ass takes a step away from my reach.

"Go fuck yourself, Dean. You're breaking up with me because you want someone else, but you want your conscience to be clear by saying this is for the best." The first tear rolls down her rosy cheeks.

I cross the room toward her and take her body into my arms just in time for her to fall apart, violent sobs shaking her body.

"That's too long to be apart, Dean. I can't do it. Please don't make me do it." She looks up at me through her wet lashes.

"I love you, and I'll only ever want you. I promise I will come back to you. Live your life without me. Don't just count down the days waiting for me. Wherever you are, I'll find you," I promise. Honestly, I don't know if my plan will even work. It's a long time, and who knows if she'll find someone else and fall in love during that time. There's no telling what can happen between now and then.

Regardless of whatever happens, I will come back for her. I will find her wherever she goes, even if she's moved on. She's my best friend, and that'll never change.

If one day I come back to find she's moved on and is truly happy, I'll respect that and let her be. As painful as it would be to see her happy with someone else, I'd never want to take that away from her. I've always only wanted to see Camille happy.

"You'll fall in love with someone else. You'll move on and forget all about me."

"It's not possible for me to love anyone the way I love you. I will be back for you."

"Promise?" She holds up her pinky, and I hook mine around hers.

"Promise." We seal the promise with a kiss.

It's a promise I plan to keep.

TWENTY-TWO

NOW

DEAN

The moment we returned home from dinner last night, it was a complete shit show. Karina went straight into our bedroom, slammed the door, and stayed inside all night. I didn't pressure her to let me in or even try to talk to her. I was too fucking pissed about her outburst; I didn't want to risk talking to her and saying something I didn't mean. Or worse, something I *did* mean but needed to wait to say until the right time.

While she was locked in the bedroom, I dealt with the aftermath of what happened at the restaurant. It took a pretty penny, but thank fuck, the manager agreed not to call the police. The four of us were also banned from ever returning. If the police would've come, Camille likely would've been arrested for assault.

I tried sleeping on the couch that night, but the look on Camille's face when Karina brought up her son kept flashing through my mind, haunting me every time I closed my eyes.

Everything is so fucked up right now, and Karina and I are balancing on a fucking ledge that I'm ready to jump over.

Day by day, I'm feeling further and further away from her—and from myself. We're overdue for a conversation about our future, a conversation that we started three years ago but didn't get to finish because we found out she was pregnant.

Funny how that worked out.

One day you're resenting your wife and dreading the thought of coming home, ready to ask for a divorce, and the next day you find out she's pregnant and resent her even more. You resent her but love her because she's carrying your child and all you want to do is be the best father you can possibly be.

I'm a terrible husband and a complete fucking joke of a man.

How can I resent the woman I married simply because she's not *her*? I chose Karina. I'm the one that asked her to marry me and stood in front of all our friends and family and made a vow until death do us part. And many times, I've come close to breaking that vow.

We both need to be set free, but I've never been brave enough to do it. At least not until now.

Our ending has been a long time coming, and I'm ready for it. For years, I've fallen asleep with only one face in my mind. I've never cheated on Karina physically, but I've been cheating on her emotionally for years. I can't lie and say I never loved her, because I did, and I do. I love her enough to know that we're not right for each other, and it's time I set her free and let her move on to find the one she does belong with.

Her soulmate.

I've already met mine, and it's not Karina.

IT'S NOW SATURDAY MORNING, AND I'VE BEEN AWAKE ALL night tossing and turning, thinking about the conversation we need to have, but haven't been able to come up with the right words to say.

I'm lying on the couch staring at the ceiling when I hear Karina walk into the kitchen and begin preparing the coffee pot.

From where I'm positioned, I have a perfect view of her from our open-floor plan.

As usual, she's completely dressed for the day, and there's no sign of a hangover. If she is hungover, she doesn't look it. But that's Karina. She never lets her emotions be seen. Not even by me... the one person who *should* see them.

I watch her, part of me waiting to see if she'll break and show any hint of what she feels on the inside. And the other part of me is being a coward and putting off the long overdue conversation.

With a sigh, I sit up, grow a pair of balls, and walk into the kitchen toward my wife.

"Good morning, honey." She smiles, grabs a mug from the cabinet, and fills it with coffee before handing it to me.

"Morning," I mumble, taking the mug and blowing into the steaming darkness of black coffee. It's as black as my soul feels now. "We need to talk about last night."

She holds up her hand and waves it. "I already plan to call Camille later and apologize. I won't press charges against her either."

I scoff. "Really, Karina? What the fuck is wrong with you?" I snap, setting my cup on the countertop with so much force the black liquid sloshes over the sides and drips on the white marble.

White. Everything in this house is white and fucking sterile looking. I hate it. It doesn't even feel like a home.

"I don't know what came over me. I got my period a couple of days ago, and I've just been in a rut ever since." She sighs, smoothing her hair even though there isn't a single strand out of place. There never is.

"Getting your period is no excuse to bring up her dead son. That was a low fucking blow. It was disgusting and cruel."

"Are you going to ask if I'm okay? She hit me!"

"Violence is never the answer, but what did you expect? You poured salt on an open wound."

"Are you fucking her?" she asks, her face stoic.

I laugh. I laugh right in her fucking face. "Are you serious?"

"I saw how you two looked at each other the night of the gala —and last night. There's more to you two than just childhood friends." *Fuck.* "Have you slept with her since we moved here?"

"Jesus, fuck, Karina. Are you serious? You sound ridiculous." She nods, crossing her arms over her chest. "No! I have never once had sex with anyone else since we've been together. I've never cheated on you." Not physically, but we've already established that.

"Tell me the truth about you two. There's history between you, and I need to know it." I sit on the barstool and drop my head into my hands. She deserves the truth, but I'm not prepared to tell her everything.

"We grew up together. I don't know what else to say, Karina. We were friends. We lived next door, and I went to school with her sister, Spencer, and Spence's boyfriend was one of my best friends."

She sits beside me and inhales deeply. "You make it seem like you barely knew each other."

"Goddamn, it's the past. You're digging for something that isn't there. Our family is close. Our parents have been friends since college." I look up at her, meeting her eyes as I prepare to lie. "Camille is nothing to me. She was Spencer's little tag along sister." The words make me feel sick.

She eyes me suspiciously, not wholly ready to believe my lies. "When we were dating, you went to New York, and when you came back, you said you wanted to spend your life with me." I watch her face closely as she does calculations in her head. "Camille was living in New York at that time." She stands up abruptly, knocking the stool over. "Did you go to New York to see her? It matches up perfectly!" she yells, a piece of her blonde hair falls out of her perfect bun, but she doesn't bother fixing it. This is the most out of sorts I've seen her in a long time.

"Is she the reason you don't want to have a baby anymore?"

"What? No!" I stand, choosing not to answer her question

about seeing Camille in New York. "Karina, I've been telling you since before we moved here that I was done trying." It's my fault for giving her mixed signals. I told her I wanted to stop trying for a baby, yet I fucked her when she asked me to while she was ovulating, and I waited in the room while she took countless ovulation and pregnancy tests.

"Prove to me she's not the reason! Let's look into other options. Let's make a baby!"

"No, Karina, you're not listening to me. I'm done! I don't want a baby, and you need to understand that." A lone tear rolls down her cheek, and I stand, reaching out to brush it away, but she slaps my hand away. "We need a break. I can't do this anymore." I sigh, sitting back down on the stool.

She stares at me blankly. "Are you serious, Dean? No, of course you're not. Don't be silly. You're just stressed. We'll take a break from trying; I'll give you that."

She isn't understanding, and I'm apparently not making myself clear. "I'm going to stay at a hotel for a few days. We both need to take some time to cool down." Without another word, I turn and walk toward our bedroom to pack a bag.

I need space to clear my head and figure out my shit, and I can't do that while around Karina.

This is necessary before taking any other actions.

ON MONDAY MORNING, I WALK INTO CAMILLE'S OFFICE with two coffees in hand and an apology on the tip of my tongue. I've spent the weekend at a hotel drinking my sorrows away, and today I feel like a brand-new man.

Karina hasn't tried to contact me, and for that, I'm grateful. Hopefully she's beginning to process and understand my words and the fact that we desperately need a separation.

I ride the elevator to Camille's office, and the receptionist allows me back right away. The door opens before I can even knock, and her emerald eyes find mine and speak to my soul.

My dick twitches in my pants at the sight of her.

"Hi," she mumbles. She's wearing a knee-length beige wraparound dress that's doing nothing to calm my aching cock. Especially those red bottom heels she's wearing. All I can think about is pushing her dress up and sinking my cock so deep inside her warm pussy that she'll feel me there every time she walks, all while those heels dig into my ass while I thrust inside her.

Seeing Camille is like a breath of fresh fucking air, and I desperately need to breathe.

She's my oxygen, and I've been deprived long enough.

Her long hair is tied back into a ponytail. A ponytail that I want to wrap around my fist while I bend her over her desk and fuck the life out of her.

Fuck. I'm like a horny teenage boy. Every time I see her, I think of several ways I could fuck her.

I clear my throat and shake my head as if that will remove the thoughts. "That for me?" She points at the coffee cup in my hand, and I nod, handing her the black coffee that I'd got from Starbucks on my way to her office. "Thanks." She takes it with a shy smile and allows me to enter her space.

With a heavy sigh, she sits on the couch, kicks off her shoes, pulls her legs underneath her body, and sips her coffee. "I wanted to apologize for Karina's behavior on Friday night. It was unacceptable, and there's no excuse." She doesn't look at me; her eyes are focused on the cup of coffee like it is the most exciting thing in the room.

"Yeah, she texted me Saturday."

"Fuck, I told her not to. You didn't deserve any of that shit. It's completely inexcusable." I shake my head, walking toward her, needing to be close to her. I sit on the coffee table in front of her and set my coffee cup to the side of me. "She was out of line, and it was so fucked up."

"You're right. It was fucked up." She takes a sip from her cup and then sets it beside mine, her elbows resting on her knees as she buries her face into her hands.

"Talk to me. What's wrong?" I reach forward and grip her wrists, pulling her hands away from her face so she'll look at me.

"Nothing, I'm fine," she lies. She isn't, and we both know that. The tired look on her face tells me she's anything but okay.

"Talk to me, Cam." Clear as day, I see the sadness and confusion swimming in her intoxicating green eyes.

"Honestly, Dean? I'm so fucking confused. Since seeing you again, my head has been in a fog. I feel more disconnected than usual, and I don't know anything anymore." I didn't expect that much honesty, but I'm glad for it because I've been feeling the same. My life was fine until I saw her again. Since then, it feels like I'm on the outside of my life looking in.

"What are you confused about?"

"You. Declan. My life. Everything." She sighs, turning her head back to bury it in her hands.

"Let's talk it out. What's confusing about it?" The second I finish my sentence, she jumps up from the couch and flings her arms around like a crazy person.

"Everything! You ruined everything!" *Huh?* Now I'm confused, but I let her finish speaking. "You should've never come back! You shouldn't be designing my building, and you shouldn't be here right now."

"Why? I promised you that one day I'd design your building, and I'm keeping that promise. Besides, you want me here. I know you do."

"Fuck the promises, Dean! They don't mean a damn thing anymore. Those were broken a long time ago." She paces around the room with her hands on her hips. "I'm tired. I feel trapped and lost and like I'm losing my mind." She inhales, her eyes finding mine from across the room.

With such sadness in her bright green eyes, she turns away from me to keep me from seeing the tears I know are now falling. I can hear the sadness in her voice.

Camille stands in front of the floor-to-ceiling window, one hand on the glass and the other on her stomach. "I'm tired of loving you. I'm so fucking sick of it. I don't want to love you anymore, and I don't know how to stop. How fucked up is it that when Declan touches me, I picture you? For years, I've pictured you every single time I've closed my eyes. He's my husband, and I wish that it was your mouth on my body and your dick inside me instead of his." She chokes on a sob. "It's been eleven years since I've seen you, and after all that's happened, I'm still hopelessly in love with you. I've never stopped loving you, even after you left me. I went back to the lighthouse so many times hoping that I'd find you there." She sighs, now placing both hands on the window. "I'm so tired of worrying about Declan. Every single time he gets out of bed or stirs in the middle of the night, I worry about what he's doing. When I'm here, I feel guilty for not being home with him because I need to watch him and make sure he's not overdosing. Every time I go home, I worry that I'll find him on the floor with a needle in his arm." She sniffles. "Most of all, I'm tired of being treated like I'm a fragile bomb. My family walks on eggshells around me, careful not to upset me because they fear I'll explode." The irony is, she *is* exploding. She's having a breakdown, and all I can do is shut the fuck up and let her say everything she needs to.

Camille has built up emotions that she's been bottling up for so long, and now she's letting her feelings detonate.

"Sometimes, I look out this window and wonder what it would be like to jump out. I bet it would be so freeing to just fall. I picture it often; will it be like going to sleep and never waking up? Or will I regret it halfway down?" Before I can even blink, I cross the room and wrap her in my arms. "I'm falling, Dean, and no one can save me," she whispers, and I hug her body tighter.

The woman in my arms is not the carefree, happy girl I left behind eleven years ago. I don't know what she's been through, but it's clear that life hasn't been on her side, and she's experienced things I can't even fathom. I have a gut feeling that there's more damage that's been done to Camille aside from losing a child.

"You are not going anywhere, Camille. I've got you. I'm here now, and I have you. I see you. I'm here." I turn her to face me, her tears now dry and her face void of emotion. "You jump, I jump. We're in this together." I press my forehead against hers.

"I never stopped loving you, Camille. Every second of every day, you've been on my mind. It doesn't matter how many years have passed between us. It's you. It always has been and always will be." Every word I say is the truth. She's been my heartbeat since the first day I laid eyes on her... eighteen years ago.

"Get me out of here, please. I can't be here right now." She inhales deeply through her nose, then exhales slowly through her mouth.

"Let's go, Cam." I take her hand and lead her over to her desk. I find her purse and carry it, leading her out of the office after she puts her shoes back on.

Within minutes, we're outside in the parking garage, and I'm putting her into the passenger seat of my car.

She needs me now more than ever, and I'm never letting her go again.

Within twenty minutes, we're at my hotel, and I turn my car over to the valet. She hasn't said a word the entire drive, but neither have I.

Camille doesn't like to be vulnerable; she never has. In the twenty minutes we've been in the car, I can already see her slipping her mask gently back into place.

I lead Camille to my hotel room, and once we're inside, I secure the locks, then lead her into the living room of my suite.

"Take a bath or a shower, and I'll order us some lunch. Try and relax, then we'll talk some more," I instruct, helping her out of her dress. She nods like a robot, entirely on auto pilot.

I pick up the room phone to order room service as I watch her movements. She picks up her purse and reaches inside to retrieve a pill bottle, then I watch her disappear into the bathroom.

Camille steps out of the bathroom several minutes later,

wearing the white guest bathrobe, her damp hair flowing down her back.

She looks at me shyly, her fingers nervously playing with each other. I wave her over to me, and she comes to me without hesitation. "I wasn't sure what you wanted, so I pretty much ordered one of everything." I gesture to both carts of food from room service. She reaches for the wine bottle and pours herself a glass, then takes a strawberry.

Camille sits on the coffee table in front of me, and I sit on the couch as her eyes lock on mine. She looks so much better than she did there in her office. Her color has returned, and the haunted look is gone from her eyes.

"I'm sorry about earlier. I just get sad and overwhelmed sometimes."

"How often do you think about hurting yourself?" The question makes her cringe, but I need to know.

"Not often," she whispers, looking down at her wine glass. "Sometimes, I just want to feel something. I worry if I don't feel something soon, then I'll forever be emotionless, yet at the same time, I'm scared to feel." She closes her eyes. "I don't ever want to feel like I did today."

"What pills did you take?" I ask, referring to the bottle she pulled from her purse before she entered the bathroom. She looks away from me and shrugs a shoulder.

"My therapist gave them to me after I moved back here. They're the only thing that helps me through the day. I don't have to feel when I take them." Her voice is so soft and sad, breaking me apart.

What happened to the girl who was once so happy and full of life? Where did she go?

"They'll kick in soon, and then I'll feel better. I won't feel so sad." She looks at me with hopeful eyes. "My family doesn't know, so please don't mention it."

"Why haven't you told them? Cam, baby, if you're feeling sad or depressed, you need to talk to your family, too." I reach forward, taking her hands in mine.

She shakes her head. "No, I can't. They'll think I'm crazy, and I don't want them to think I'm weak."

"You're not weak for needing help." She chews her bottom lip, avoiding eye contact.

"I have bipolar depression, Dean, and they don't know. They can't know. I went off my meds for a couple of days, and my emotions got fucked up, but I'm okay now. Today is the first day back on my meds, and I'll be fine."

I don't believe her, but the vacant look in her eyes tells me that I can't push her any further, or I'll risk losing her completely. "I'm here, Cam. I'm going to take care of you. You have me and can always tell me anything," I promise, knowing damn good and well I will do whatever I can to breathe life back into her.

She doesn't respond, only nods and takes a sip from her glass of wine.

After several silent minutes, she opens her mouth and speaks. "I married Declan because I didn't want my son to have a broken home and have parents that weren't together. I wanted him to be raised with both parents present. And that's exactly what he had, and he was the happiest little boy," she says, looking into my eyes, tears streaming down her perfect heart-shaped face. "I love him, but not like that. He's my best friend, but the adrenaline and excitement always kept us together. It wasn't love, not until Luca. And then it became all about our son. We both know our marriage is in trouble, but I can't leave him. I'm scared of what'll happen if I do." I'm shocked by her sudden honesty. She's being vulnerable and opening herself up to me. I know this is a rare moment.

"Why are you scared, baby? What will he do if you leave him? Has he ever hit you?" I clench my fists, ready to kill the fucker if she says yes.

"No," she answers quickly. "Declan is only dangerous to himself." She sighs. "Dec just got out of rehab."

Rehab? What the fuck. "What the fuck was he in rehab for?"

"Addiction. Drugs. Alcohol. It got bad after our son died. He started chasing a higher high when pills weren't enough anymore. He started using heroin a year ago, and I couldn't take it anymore. So, he's been in rehab for the last three months." Fuck. This poor woman. Not only was she dealing with the death of her son, but she was also dealing with a drug-addicted husband.

My mom had told me about the accident when it happened. She was distraught when she called me and told me that Camille had been in a car accident. I felt physically ill because I thought she was going to tell me that she had died, but she told me it was her son.

Camille's four-year-old son, Luca, died on the scene. He'd been thrown from the car, hit his head, and had been bleeding out and was bleeding internally. The poor boy died before the ambulance could get to them. Camille was the only one who walked away unharmed.

I'd called Melanie, Camille's mom, to check on them, and she said that she had cuts and bruises, but she'd be fine. Declan spent a week in a coma for head trauma. I couldn't imagine what that week must've been like for her. Her son had just died, and she spent a week not knowing if her husband would wake up or die.

"You are such a strong woman, Cam. I truly mean that." I lean forward and take her free hand in mine, selfishly needing to feel her warmth and be close to her.

I *want* to feel her again. I *need* to feel her again.

"I've missed you so much." Her smile is sad.

No matter what happens, I'll never stop believing that she's my destiny. That she and I share the same soul and are meant to be.

Our timing is off, and it seems that it always has been, but I know where her heart is.

Camille belongs with me, and one day, she will be all mine, and nothing can stop that fate.

She and I—we're inevitable.

"I love you, Cam. You know I always have, and I know we'll

find our way back to each other. I promise you that." She sets her wine glass down, leans forward, rests her forehead against mine.

"Find a way back to yourself, and then find your way back to me," I whisper. Cupping her face in my hands, I lean in and press my lips against hers.

And suddenly, I am home.

TWENTY-THREE

THEN

CAMILLE, *15 years old*

Dean found out a few months ago that he'd been accepted to the University of Cambridge, as we all knew he would be. It wasn't a surprise, and don't get me wrong, I'm incredibly proud and so happy for him. But I'm sad for us. I'm sad that we're ending before we even had the chance to begin officially.

Dean's parents want him to go to England a month before school starts, to get familiar with his new scenery, so we're not even getting to spend the entire summer together.

He graduated as valedictorian of his class with a perfect GPA. Not only am I losing Dean, but I'm also losing Spencer. She was accepted to the University of Southern California and will be leaving in two weeks before school starts. We're driving to California as a family to drop her off, and then our parents and I will fly back. We're driving down so she'll be able to have a car with her while she's at school.

Dallas is going to school in Florida, so he and Spencer had a mutual breakup, and she's been crying ever since. They wanted to break up before they left so that they wouldn't make things more complicated by spending the summer together and then breaking up at the last minute.

Dean and I were able to come up with a plan, so I was surprised that she and Dallas couldn't. Their breakup doesn't make sense, not when I know they belong together and are crazy in love.

I'd pressed Spencer for more details, but she kept shushing me, telling me they both agreed to end things.

This is already the most depressing summer ever.

Dean is leaving in two days, and then Spencer will leave after. And I'll be alone. Both of my best friends will be gone. It freakin' sucks.

However, on the bright side, I don't have to deal with stupid Sadie at school any longer.

"Are you sure you want to sleep over? You can always call me, and I'll pick you up," my mom says from where she stands at my doorframe. I lied and told her that I'm sleeping over at Fallon's house. There's a party tonight, for which Spencer and Dean have already left. But Dean will leave the party and meet me at the lighthouse, where we plan to spend the entire night together.

"Yes, I'm sure, Mom. Fallon's mom already said it was okay and bought a bunch of snacks. We're going to have a horror movie marathon." I hate lying to my mom, but I can never tell her that I plan to spend the night with Dean, and I plan to give my V-card to him tonight. She'd obviously stop me. Mom is great and loves Dean, but she'd never be okay with her fifteen-year-old daughter having sex. That's why I came up with this plan, and Fallon agreed.

"Okay, sweetie. I'll be downstairs when you're ready for me to drop you off." I nod and finish packing my overnight backpack.

The plan is that I'll be dropped off at Fallon's house, then her sister will take me to the lighthouse before she goes to the party tonight. Their mom works nights, and Fallon is going on a date with Bex, so our plan works perfectly. To make it convincing, Dean even went to the party a couple of hours ago, and his parents removed his curfew since he's now eighteen and has graduated. I'm excited to spend the night with him away from our homes. But

I'm also extremely nervous. I'm going to give him a piece of myself I'll never be able to get back.

An hour later, I was dropped off at Fallon's house, and her sister Carla took me to the lighthouse. She even gave me a condom and told me to be safe before she left, laughing uncontrollably.

Now, I'm at the lighthouse staring at the condom in my hand. I know exactly where I want the night to lead. I plan to have Dean inside of me for the first time. He's leaving in two days, and I want him to be my first. We haven't discussed this, so he's unaware of my plan of seduction, so I can only hope that he's thinking the same thing as I am.

It's not like I'm attached to my virginity or anything, but it wouldn't be special with anyone else as my first. It must be him. I don't care when I lose it, as long as it is with someone I love. But staring at the condom reminds me just how unprepared I am. I've been on birth control since I was thirteen. Mom put me on it two years ago to help with my periods. I've watched so much porn to prepare myself for tonight, and I shaved every part of my body. My legs are silky, and it's bare between my legs. I wanted to be perfect for Dean.

It would be a lie if I said I wasn't nervous. I've talked to Spencer and Carla previously about their first time, so I think I know what to expect. Dean and I have fooled around enough, which never made me feel uncomfortable. In fact, I've always wanted more with him. But now we'll touch each other while naked, and I'll do something I can never take back.

With a deep sigh, I put the condom in my backpack and grab my phone, sending a quick text to Dean.

Me: I'm here. Waiting for you.

His reply comes back instantly.

Dean: Be there soon.

True to his word, Dean arrived shortly after his text. He must've been speeding because he came quick. I greet him with a hug as soon as he walks through the door.

"How was the party and seeing your friends for the last time?" He shrugs his shoulders, wrapping his arms around my waist.

"Everyone was pretty drunk, so I don't think anyone will remember my goodbyes. I'm happier here with you." He always knows the right things to say to make me smile. I wrap my arms around his neck, stand on my tiptoes, and press my lips to his. His kiss sends electric shocks through my body and makes me swoon.

"Do you want to go upstairs?" I nod just as he takes my hand and leads me upstairs. I wonder if both of us have the same thing on our minds.

Does he plan on having sex too? Better yet, is he even a virgin? I've heard so many stories at school, and after the Sadie rumor, I never asked him again if he has slept with anyone else or not. He never brought it up, and neither did I. Now I was too shy to even ask. What if he said no? I wouldn't like that answer. And if he said yes, how would I feel? I'd like to be his first, but what if he doesn't know what to do either? Or worse, what if he's been with other girls and I'm not as good as them?

Oh God, I can't do this.

"What's on your mind?" he whispers against my neck as he trails light kisses over my flesh.

"N-nothing." I sigh.

"You've got something on your mind. You're tense and worried about something." He pulls away from my neck and brushes the hair out of my face. "We don't have to do anything tonight that you're not ready for. Don't feel pressured into anything, baby."

He's never pressured me into doing anything I didn't want to do. I trust him fully. "I want to do this with you. I want you to be my first. I'm just nervous." He nods in understanding, his lips finding mine again. Gently, he leads me toward the bed, and I lay down, his body climbing beside mine.

He's on his side, and I'm on my back. His hand pushes my shirt up to rest on my bare stomach.

"Tell me to stop if you feel uncomfortable and don't want to do something." My breathing stills, but his lips crash back to mine and breathe life into me.

His tongue dives into my mouth, and the hand on my stomach is now fumbling with the button on my shorts. I feel everything so deeply. Every sensation from his touch radiates through my body and starts a fire within me. Pleasure courses through my body from his tongue fucking my mouth. His kiss is more heated than ever.

Dean moves so quickly that I don't notice when he removes my shorts and panties. His index finger strokes over my wet folds, and I gasp when his warm fingers find my clit. The sensation is new to me. Sure, I've pleasured myself many times before, but having his hands on me while bare feels completely different. It feels better.

"Do you want me to stop?" He pulls away from my kiss, his hand slowing his strokes. My hips raise on their own to meet his fingers. He chuckles, his lips finding mine again. I can smell my sweet arousal in the air and know that he can too.

One finger slips inside me while his thumb rubs circles over my clit. Unable to control myself from the exciting new sensation, I moan into his mouth.

He swallows every moan that leaves my lips, our kissing becoming even more frenzied and heated while I moan uncontrollably, his hand playing me like a fiddle. His touch is pure magic and sin. My mind is foggy, and before I know it, I'm shaking and temporarily go blind, seeing nothing but stars.

"Fuck, you're so tight," he rasps. Removing his finger from my cunt, he shoves it into his mouth, sucking it clean from my orgasm. It's the hottest thing I've ever seen.

Way better than porn.

In a flash, he removes the remainder of my clothes, and I

remove his, leaving him in only a pair of boxer briefs tented by his obvious boner.

With his muscular body hovering over mine, all I can think about is how it will feel to have him finally enter me for the first time. My head is floating, my body on fire. His touch is what I'm trying to focus on. I want him so badly—all of him. I want to feel every single inch that he has to offer.

Painfully slow, Dean kisses down my body, his velvet tongue flicking my pebbled nipples, his wet tongue trailing the length of my body until he settles himself between my legs. Throwing my legs over his shoulders, he licks up my slit. My hands tangle in his hair and my back arches off the bed. Uncontrollable moans leave my lips as he sucks and laps at my pussy.

He eats me like a starved man at a buffet, and before long, I'm seeing stars for the second time, screaming my release.

"God, Cam, you taste so fucking good." He licks me again, his warm tongue circling my clit before sucking it into his mouth. I'm overly sensitive. My body jerks at the sensation. Removing my legs from his shoulders, I pull him up, licking over his lips and chin that glisten with my juices.

"Mmm, you're right. I do taste good." He crushes his lips to mine with a devilish smirk, moving his body to hover over me.

"You're on the pill, right?" he asks against my lips. All I can do is nod. "Good. We'll do it again with a condom, but for the first time, I need to feel you raw." I should object. I know I should, but I want to feel him.

All of him.

Skin on skin.

Leaning forward, I push down his boxers, gasping when his hard cock springs free, standing proudly between his legs and pointing right at me. It looks swollen and angry, and the tip glistens with a bead of pre-cum. My mouth goes dry at the sight.

How the fuck is that going to fit inside of me?

With a smug smirk, Dean moves me until I'm flat on my back.

His hips thrust against mine, coating his intimidating length in my arousal.

"Are you sure about this, baby?" he grunts, the head of his cock pressing against the entrance of my virgin pussy.

"Yes, I want you, Dean." I kiss him because it's all I can do in this moment. I spread my legs wider, holding on tightly to his shoulders, goosebumps coating my skin, a light sweat already breaking out on my forehead.

Dean applies a little more pressure, working his hips side to side as his cock slowly begins to push inside me, breaking the seal of my virginity.

The air leaves my lungs, my body is on fire, and my core is burning. I can feel the burning deep inside my stomach. I feel like he's ripping me in half. He's large, and it hurts. But I do my best to keep my face stoic, so he can't see the pain he's causing. My eyes sting with unshed tears.

The intimacy is becoming too much for me, and I fail at keeping my emotions to myself. I turn my head away from him just as the first tear falls. I don't want him to get the wrong idea and think I'm crying because of the pain, but I can't bring myself to look at him. I'll likely fall apart even further, and I don't want that.

He kisses my face gently, kissing the tears away. "Are you okay? Do you want me to stop?" I shake my head and grip his forearms to stop him from moving.

"Please, don't. Keep going." Moving my hands around to his back, I dig my nails into his skin for encouragement.

Dean pulls out, places his thumb on my clit, and rubs it slowly as his length fills me again. The burn is gone, replaced by pleasure and the feeling of being so incredibly full.

Full of Dean.

"Why are you crying? Am I hurting you?" he asks. I look up at him and see pleasure all over his face.

"You're not hurting me." I force a smile. "I love you so much. I'm crying because this is the moment I've waited for." This is goodbye and I love you all wrapped into one. Dean is leaving, and then I'll likely never see him again. I'm emotional because I don't want to say goodbye. We kiss as he settles himself deep inside me, filling me to the hilt.

My body is tight; the foreign feel of him uncomfortable and burning. I feel like I'm being split in two, and I eagerly wait for the pain to go away.

I can feel every vein and pulse of his cock, and it's odd. I've used a tampon before and that was extremely uncomfortable. This is much worse than that.

"Fuck, baby, you're so tight," Dean grits out through clenched teeth while I struggle to breath. I hope he's enjoying it because I'm not.

I've read that the first time is always the worst, but after a few more times, I'll adjust, and it'll start to feel good. I hope I'm one of the lucky girls that adjusts quickly and feels pleasure sooner rather than later.

The air in the room is becoming moist and heavy, and our bodies are hot and sticky against each other.

Sweat beads linger above Dean's fluffy eyebrows, and a layer of sweat covers us.

"Slower," I cry out.

"Do you want me to stop?" he asks, his voice soft and full of worry.

I shake my head and wrap my arms around his waist. "No, but please, move slowly."

Dean nods, and carefully pulls back until only his tip remains inside me, then he pushes back in, inch by painful inch. "Is this okay?" he asks, his face buried in the crook of my neck and his left hand tracing my pebbled nipples.

After a few minutes and a few slow thrusts, I feel myself loosen around him. The feeling is still uncomfortable, but it's not agonizing anymore. His hands move to my waist, and he grips it so tightly that I know I'll have bruises on my hips from him, but I welcome it. I want any mark of him anywhere on my body. If I have bruises from him, I'll have a visual reminder that this happened, and this is real and not just in my head. It's too good to be true, and I need proof that it's real.

He must feel me loosening around him because he begins to push into me faster, pulling my hips up to meet him thrust for thrust. It doesn't hurt, but it doesn't feel amazing yet. At least not until he places a thumb on my clit and begins rubbing. That one simple touch is enough to make my body relax and melt into the mattress. "Ahhh! Holy fuck, I'm going to cum," he groans out the words before yelling a string of curses into the barely lit room as he quickens his strokes of his thumb on my clit.

Soft moans leave my lips because I'm feeling good now, but I know I won't reach an orgasm, no matter how great it feels having him rub me.

"Oh fuck," he groans, his body stilling as his warm seed fills my pussy, the heated sensation causing another moan to spill from my lips. With his cock still inside me, he returns to kissing my lips, flipping us over so that I'm now straddling him. I keep my eyes on him, not wanting to look down because then I'd see the evidence of my lost virginity on the sheets.

He must've read my mind and knows exactly what I am thinking. "Don't worry, baby. I'll change the sheets and clean you up. It won't hurt as much next time, and maybe you'll get to come too." *Next time.* My skin grows goosebumps at the mention of doing it again.

With him still inside of me, I lie down on his chest, memorizing the feel of him inside of me when he's hard, and how he feels when he begins to soften.

After a while of lying in the dimly lit room in silence, Dean gets hard again and asks if I'm ready to try again.

Wanting to be close to him and wanting to feel pleasure, I agree.

Lucky for me, Dean is right, and the second time is better. I still don't come on his cock, but he makes up for it by playing with my clit after he finishes.

. . .

"I LOVE YOU, CAM. I PROMISE THAT WE'LL GET TO BE together one day, and it'll be forever." He kisses the top of my head, tightening his grip around my naked body.

We spent most of the night exploring each other's bodies after he used a washcloth to wipe between my legs. He even sucked my pussy again. I'm completely convinced that he's trying to suck my soul out of my body, but whatever his magic mouth was doing last night worked because I was screaming, writhing on the bed, and fully sated in no time.

"I love you, Dean." I kiss his lips, tasting the salt from my tears that I didn't know were there.

His parents are gone when we return home, so we make love again in his bed, then shower together.

It's the most amazing experience of my life.

THE DAY I'VE BEEN DREADING IS HERE. DEAN IS LEAVING.

My parents let me sleep over last night. They thought I'd sleep in the guest room that Lydia turned into my bedroom, but during the night, I snuck into Dean's room to fall asleep in his arms and wake up next to him one last time.

It's 6 a.m., and Dean and I lie silently in his room. He finished packing last night, and his dad loaded up the car in the garage while I helped Lydia cook dinner, but now it's time to leave. His flight is in a couple of hours, and my heart is breaking. I can literally feel it breaking inside my chest.

Silently, we both climb out of bed and get dressed. We don't look at each other, and I know he's feeling everything that I'm feeling. With his back to me, I slip out of his bedroom and walk silently down the hallway toward my guest bedroom to brush my teeth and wash my face.

By the time it's seven, I've given in. I can't hide anymore. I'd already heard his parents wake up a little bit ago, and soon they'd have to leave.

Walking on tiptoes to keep quiet, I exit my bedroom and pad down the stairs. Dean is in the living room, zipping his suitcase. When he spots me, he rushes toward me and wraps his arms around me, hugging me tightly against his chest.

That's when the first tear falls. I'd been trying so hard to stay strong and not give in to my emotions. I don't want to cry, but I'm fucking failing because now I'm crying against his chest, wishing that I didn't have to let him go.

I don't know how we end up outside. He must've carried me because I don't remember moving. I'm clinging on to him for dear life, unwilling to let go of my best friend and the love of my life.

"Camille," he whispers, and I step away, tilting my head to look at him. I sniffle, wiping my snotty nose with the back of my hand. His brown eyes are full of sorrow, mirroring the heartbreak anyone can see in mine. He's crying; I've never seen him cry before. "I love you, baby. So much. Please, don't stay in your room crying over me, please, Cam." He chokes on a sob. "I need you to take life by the fucking balls and make the rest of high school your bitch. Have fun, and when you go to college, I want you to have the time of your life." His lips crash against mine, his kiss tasting of spearmint and salt from our tears. I should be worried about kissing him in front of our parents', but right now I don't care.

It's our final kiss, the final action that causes my heart to shatter completely. He's my soulmate, and I'm so deeply, madly, crazy in love with him. He's leaving and taking my heart with him, and I'll be stuck here waiting for the day he returns with my heart in his hands.

My parents and Spencer are outside with us, hugging Dean and his parents goodbye. While they say their goodbyes, I stand there, unable to move.

This is worse than death. At least with death, it's final, and yes, I'd miss him, but I wouldn't spend the next however many years thinking about him and wondering what he's doing and who he's doing it with.

His parents hug me goodbye, but I'm too frozen in place and numb that I can't recall if I say anything or even wave.

Dean hugs Spence, then returns to me, taking my face into his hands. "I've always loved you, Cam, and I always will. I promise I will come back to you, and our hearts will be one again. It's always been you, and it always will be," he whispers against my lips, kissing me once more before pulling away. I'm aware he's kissing me in front of our parents, but I can't bring myself to care.

"You better come back to me, dammit." I hiccup. Spencer comes to my side for moral support.

"I will. You can count on that. There's no way you can ever get rid of me this easily."

What a bittersweet feeling to fall in love so young.

"I love you so much, Dean. You'll have my heart forever."

"Close your eyes, baby. Picture us in the lighthouse, happy and laughing. Don't cry, because in our memories we're together, laughing and having the time of our life in the lighthouse. That's how I want you to remember me." I sniffle, closing my eyes, relishing in the feel of his lips all over my face.

He kisses my lips, my forehead, my eyelids, my cheeks, and nose.

When I open my eyes again, he's gone, and my vision becomes blurred by tears.

I think I scream. I'm not sure. I'm breaking down. That much I know for sure. I don't even remember Spencer leaving, but when I look up, I see my mom. She wraps her arms around me and hugs me tightly, supporting my weight as I fall against her and make myself hoarse from crying.

"It'll be okay, sweetie. I promise it'll be okay." She kisses the top of my head and rubs my back. She's trying to help, but she's not. It won't be okay; it'll never be okay.

I'm experiencing my first heartbreak, and she is saying that it'll be okay?

Her words make me furious.

I don't stop crying.

Not even when I go home.

Not even when I shower.

Not even when I go to sleep.

Even when I wake up the next day, I am still crying.

My heart is missing, and I continue to feel the ache every single day. I am living without a heart.

My heart has been stolen from my body and is living in England.

Little do I know that I wouldn't get my heart back until many years later, and the person who returns my heart would be a baby boy named Luca.

And little do I know, all our promises would be broken.

TWENTY-FOUR

NOW

Camille

When I woke up the morning after Dean kissed me, I scrambled to get dressed and left his hotel room as quickly as I possibly could. I didn't know what the actual fuck I was thinking. My mind had been fucked up all day long, and when Dean came to my office, I snapped. My walls came crumbling down, and I let him see me. See the me that I've been hiding from my family and Dr. Reynolds. I had a breakdown, and it was utterly embarrassing.

I wasn't surprised that he stayed to help me calm down rather than leaving when he saw what a mess I was.

As if admitting my feelings toward him weren't bad enough, I fucking told him about my thoughts of jumping out of my office window. To be honest, it is something I think about. Sometimes, on the really bad days, I want to close my eyes and fall. Not even jump, just let myself gracefully fall. I want the rush. I crave the adrenaline. It's not even about dying; it's about feeling something.

God, I want to feel again. I miss the person I used to be. Before the manic episodes, before the highs and lows. I worry my medication isn't right for me, but I don't want to admit that or ask for help in fear that any new medication I may get might make me feel worse about losing Luca. I already feel bad enough, but my current medication numbs me enough that I'm not in constant agonizing pain and crippling with guilt over the fact I'm the reason for my son's death.

I want to feel without being scared. I panic when I start to feel anything, which leads me to take another pill that'll numb my heart.

I want to feel so I know I'm alive and living, yet I don't want to feel anything because then I'll feel my pain too deeply and may not be able to cope with it.

I'm a walking contradiction.

It's now been two full weeks since the kiss, and I haven't been able to stop thinking about it since. The feel of Dean's lips against mine ignited a spark within me that I've been missing for so long.

Now, I don't feel numb anymore. I feel alive, and he's the one who made me feel this way.

It's also been two weeks since we've spoken to each other.

We've been avoiding each other. Or rather, I've been avoiding him. He's texted me a few times, and unless it's been business-related, I've ignored it, leaving him on read. I don't see the point in speaking anymore when we both know there will never be anything between us again.

Whatever it is that we once had died the day he left Seattle.

He wasn't there when I needed him the most.

Dean is my past, and it's painful to be around him when I'm so obviously not over him and still seeking some type of closure.

I may not be in love with Declan the way I should be, but I am still married and have already crossed too many lines.

Our history will not repeat itself. What we had has to remain in the past.

"Camille? Are you okay, dear?" Lydia's voice snaps me away from my thoughts. She called me yesterday and asked me to lunch today, and I couldn't decline. It's been too long since I've seen her, and I'm happy to catch up. She's been lonely since her husband passed a year ago, and I've been too preoccupied with grief that I haven't reached out to her even once. It was so good seeing her again at the gala last month.

I reach across the table, take her hand in mine, and give it a gentle squeeze. "Yeah, I'm okay. I was just thinking of what a horrible person I am for not reaching out to you sooner. I'm so sorry, Lydia." She covers my hand with hers and gives me her sweet, motherly smile.

"Don't apologize to me, dear. You were going through a difficult time, and I don't blame you. Now, let's order before I die of starvation." She sits back in her chair and places the back of her hand on her forehead dramatically. "I can already feel myself beginning to wither away." I sit back in my chair with a giggle.

God, I love Lydia. She's been like a second mother to me since I was a child.

I pick up my menu but don't look at it right away. Instead, I watch her. Lydia has never looked her age, and the only telltale sign are the few gray hairs that are beginning to peek through her short brown hair and the wrinkles around her eyes. She'd kept her hair long when I was younger, but now it's cut to her shoulders but still just as shiny. She's always been a beautiful woman, and Dean takes after her a lot. He is the perfect mix of both his mother and father.

Her brown eyes snap up to mine, and she smiles. "What's on your mind? Something is going on up there." She taps a finger against her temple.

"I was just thinking how great it is to see you. I've really missed you." She grins.

"I've missed you, too, sweet girl. Please don't disappear on me again. I need my girl in my life." I laugh and give her a nod, mentally kicking myself for allowing so much time to pass between us without speaking

"I won't, I promise."

"Good. Now, tell me what's going on with you and my son. I want to know everything about how you two are getting along

245

working together." She reaches forward for her glass of water. "Spill the tea, girly. Is that what you youngsters say?"

I burst out laughing. "Oh, Lydia." I wipe at the invisible tears at the corners of my eyes for dramatic effect. "Hate to disappoint, but there's not much to tell. We were able to finalize the designs fairly quickly, and construction has already started." The waiter comes over and takes our orders and menus.

With a sigh, Lydia taps her middle finger against the table, choosing her words carefully before she opens her mouth and speaks. "You both followed each other around like lost puppies. I know your parents never let you two date, but you never needed that title. You were both so young but somehow already knew what love was. It's such a beautiful thing to find that type of love and to find it so young. You two are fortunate to have experienced that. My Paul and I had young love, too, and we had a beautiful, full life together." Sadness softens her features, and I know that she misses her husband beyond words. "I know you're grown and married now, Camille, sweetie, but I truly hope one day you find happiness." She sighs. "I know you're grieving, and will be for a long time, but one day I hope you can be happy again."

Is anyone ever truly happy, or do they just try and convince themselves that they are?

"Let me tell you a secret. Love isn't easy, and it's not pretty like you see in fairytales or movies. Love is complicated and can be ugly. It requires a hell of a lot of patience. Nothing worth having comes easy, love included. Paul and I didn't have an easy start to our relationship. We went to school together and broke up before we went away to college. Yes, we loved each other, but we wanted the chance to explore and make sure we'd never have any regrets later in life." She takes her napkin and dabs at the tears that are forming at the corners of her eyes. "We spent two years apart, and I missed him dearly every day. Finally, he said enough was enough and transferred schools to be with me. He had a new girlfriend at the time, but he was mine, and I knew in my heart we were meant to be together. So, I told him how I felt. The next day he left her and proposed to me. We were together from that moment on."

With a sigh, I open my mouth to speak, but a familiar voice catches me off guard and silences me. "Well, good afternoon, ladies." Dean's eyes roam over me, a smirk forming on his lips.

What the actual fuck. Why is he here?

"Son, hello, join us." Lydia smiles, gesturing toward one of the empty seats at our table. With his eyes on me, Dean leans down to kiss his mother's cheek before he claims the open seat. As usual, he looks handsome. He's dressed in a navy suit that looks phenomenal against his bronze skin.

"What are you doing here?" I ask.

"I was in the neighborhood, and Mom mentioned you two were having lunch today, so I decided to stop by and say hi. Such a coincidence that it just so happens to be my lunch time as well. I'm starving." He smirks, waving a waitress over to get a menu and place his order.

I roll my eyes. This sly motherfucker.

"I'm happy you're able to join us. Karina keeps you all to herself, and I never see you anymore." Lydia smiles, moving her napkin from the table to her lap when the waiter returns with our meal. Dean sits back in his seat, getting a little too fucking comfortable.

I'm uncomfortable around him. It's been two weeks since we've seen each other, and the last thing I want to do right now is see him and try and make meaningless small talk in front of his mother.

My phone beeps, and too eagerly, I grab it and check the new text message. It's a text from Declan asking if I want him to make dinner reservations or eat at home, but they don't need to know that. "Shit, I have to go," I lie, grabbing my purse hanging on the side of my chair.

"Is everything okay, sweetie?" Lydia asks with concern in her soft brown eyes.

From my peripheral, I see Dean, and I urge myself not to look directly at him.

"Yes, well, it will be. There's an emergency at work, and I must go." I stand, and lean down to give Lydia a quick hug, promising to plan lunch for another time.

On my way out, I fail and glance at Dean. The glare on his face tells me that he knows I'm lying.

Oh, well. I lied because I didn't want to sit here with him at lunch and pretend everything is okay.

I don't want to be his friend, and I don't want to pretend I do.

Fuck him.

Operation *Get Over Dean* starts now.

AFTER RUNNING OUT OF THE RESTAURANT DURING LUNCH, I stop by my office to grab a few things and take the rest of my work home for the day. I had a suspicion that he'd show up at my office, and that's why I chose to spend the rest of the day at home. That way, I wouldn't be around for any surprise pop-ins.

It's 6 p.m. now, and I hadn't realized I've been buried inside my home office for so long until Declan knocks on the door and lets himself in. "Hey babe, you plan on coming out anytime soon?" I look up at him and shrug, sitting back in my chair.

I've been here for nearly six hours, buried between my sketchpad and laptop. I've been emailing back and forth with Sadie for a few hours, going over different designs. She even emailed me a few attached images, and I responded with ideas and images of my own that better fit my vision for the décor of my headquarters once the build is complete. It'll take months to get in a few of the pieces, so we have to order things much earlier to ensure they'll be here in time.

"I guess I got lost in my work a little bit." Which isn't unusual for me. Especially with the transition of my operations from New York to here, I am swamped. I must work twice as hard to manage both locations. Thank fucking God for my incredible staff in New York for their assistance.

"When am I going to get my wife back? I miss you, you know." He stands behind the chair in front of my desk, his hands holding onto the back of the chair. It's been two weeks since I let Declan touch me. Every night he tries, and every night I have an excuse already prepared. Sex has always been the main thing we've had between us, and now that we barely have it, I'm not sure what's left. If anything. We don't talk much, I'm too busy working, and he does... whatever Declan does. At least he's not doing drugs.

"I'm sorry, I'm just busy trying to ensure my fall launch goes smoothly and managing two locations." I'm stressed the fuck out, and the last thing I need is a guilt trip for ignoring my husband.

"What if we go back to New York for a few weeks, or until your new building is complete and you can move operations here?" My eyes snap to his. No, that isn't an option. Sure, it would be easier to be in New York. I can easily communicate with my staff and construction from New York, but I can't go back there. *I can't.*

I shake my head. "No. I need to be here to oversee the build."

"Do you, though? *Dean* seems to be doing just fine." He says his name with such malice. "Listen, I've been talking with Adam and the rest of the band, and we want to start recording again now that I'm back. I've been writing again, and I think getting back in the studio and on the road is exactly what I need." Adam is Declan's best friend. The two met at sixteen, and two years later they started Riot, and their once small-time rock band blew up practically overnight. Adam was at the courthouse when we got married and drove us to the hospital when I was in labor with Luca. He was even the one who helped convince Declan to go to rehab. He flew all the way here when I'd called him. He's always been such a great friend to us both.

I'm surprised to hear that Declan has been writing songs again. It's been a while since he wrote anything new. A year to be exact. And even longer since they've been in the studio together and have toured. I know recording new songs will mean touring, and I have concerns about him traveling and being around drugs and alcohol. He isn't strong enough to resist his addictions yet.

"Dec, I'm happy that you're writing, but you should wait before thinking about a tour."

"Why? Because you think I'll do drugs again?" He scoffs, and I shrug. It's a very valid concern. "I'm not thinking about a huge tour, just something small, just a couple of shows in New York. I wrote songs about Luca, and I want to share them." His words cause my blood to practically boil with rage.

We've discussed this before and agreed we'd never bring up Luca to the public. Our family is private; his death was private. We don't need the death of our son to be exploited. Declan already has enough haters and crazed fans that we didn't want our son exposed to that, and I don't want his death exposed to the lunatics out there either.

"No fucking way." I shake my head, dropping my pen on my desk. "Besides, you need to focus on your sobriety. You haven't even gone to therapy, which you're supposed to do." Declan promised he'd start seeing a therapist, and I even found him several that specialize in addiction recovery counseling.

"He was my son too, and the songs are good. They're about loss, and I know someone out there will be able to relate." He rolls his eyes. "I don't need therapy. I'm fine!"

"You do! And you're not going to use the death of our son to get a fucking paycheck. This isn't even up for discussion. You know our fucking deal. Luca stays out of the media!" I snap, turning my attention back toward my laptop.

"He's gone, Camille! His memory will be out there, and this is a way to honor him." I see red. How fucking dare he!

"I know he's gone! I live with his loss every single fucking day! I dealt with his loss while I was saving you from yourself so you wouldn't fucking overdose. You were too high to function. Meanwhile, I was the one who was mourning our son alone!" I yell, standing to my feet quickly, my chair slamming into the wall behind me. The shock of seeing Dean again brought me away from my grief for just a moment, but being near Declan is bringing up too many emotions for me.

His eyes narrow at me, but I don't let him speak. "You left me alone! You chose to get high while I was alone, unable to properly mourn because I was too worried about you. I carried him inside my body for nine months. I felt his kicks. He heard my heartbeat from the inside of my body. I birthed him, he got nourishment from my breasts, and I got four perfect years with him. Every time you went on tour, we stayed behind, and I took care of him. I lost my baby! I lost my baby because you were too fucked up and didn't see that goddamn car! It's your fault he's gone!" I scream, my body shaking with anger. Ever since the night of our accident, I've bottled up my anger and resentment toward Declan, and it's finally coming out. I can't hold it in any longer. He's triggered me, and now I've reached my breaking point. I can no longer ignore the elephant in the room. "While I was here dying inside because my heart was ripped out of my chest, you checked out! You chose drugs, and I lost you too. You don't fucking know shit about mourning." I yell every word to him until my voice is hoarse, and I can barely see through my tears. "It's your fault he's gone. You should've been watching the road." It's a low blow, but I need to hit him where it hurts. "You killed my son, and I will never fucking forgive you. It should've been you." Misery loves company, and I need him to hurt just as much as I'm hurting.

His eyes harden, and his brows pull together in a scowl. I succeeded in hurting him. The evidence is clear on his face. "You are a cold-hearted bitch, and I don't know if you always have been or if this is a new thing. You think you're so fucking much better than me. Why? Because I went to rehab?! Perfect Camille doesn't know what it's fucking like to struggle because she's always had a silver spoon up shoved up her fucking tight ass. Fuck you, Camille." He spits at my feet. His words were pure venom. Before I know what I'm doing, my hand flies up and slaps him across the face. His head snaps to the side, and I see my handprint on his bright red cheek.

Declan slaps me right fucking back. My cheek stings, and I know I have a matching handprint on my cheek. Over the years, we've had our fights, our struggles, but they were never physical. Never once have we put our hands on each other until now.

"You want to hit? Then, babe, let's fucking hit. Nothing you do or say to me will ever hurt me worse than I already feel." He grabs the back of my head, tangles his fingers in my hair, and yanks my head back so that I'm staring up at him, our chests brushing against each other. "Do you think that you're the only one who is hurting? Do you think I don't miss our son every goddamn day? Do you think I don't blame myself for his death every fucking day? That day when you found me passed out with a needle? It wasn't a fucking accident, Camille; I was trying to overdose! Why do I get to live when our little boy doesn't? You can't possibly blame me more than I blame myself!" His face is red as he screams in my face, saliva landing on my cheeks from his screaming.

We stand toe to toe, staring at each other. "I want a fucking divorce!" I scream the words that we've both been too afraid to say.

Hot tears stream down both of our faces. I open my mouth to speak, but Declan shuts me up by yanking on my hair tighter. "I'm so fucking angry right now it's best you shut the fuck up."

Without another word, Declan leans down and kisses the cheek he had smacked, then turns and walks out of my office, leaving me standing there.

I stay staring at the door long after he leaves.

Even when I hear the front door slam, I stay standing.

I'm not sure how long I stand there staring at the doorway, but eventually, my feet move, and I rush out of our apartment.

Declan and I are broken. So fucking broken and beyond the point of redemption.

Right now, I want to be selfish and do something for myself.

I'm so tired of doing what everyone wants and being who everyone expects me to be.

A wise man once said to take life by the balls and make it my bitch, and that's exactly what I'm going to do.

I'm doing something I want, something that'll make me forget and make me feel good.

Before long, I'm handing my keys over to the valet, and standing in front of a door. The only person I want to see is just on the other side.

One knock is all it will take to feel better.

So, I take a deep breath in and knock.

TWENTY-FIVE

NOW

DEAN

It's been two weeks since I kissed Camille and her taste still lingers on my lips. I've texted her multiple times but only received a handful of replies. I've noticed that unless it's business related, she doesn't respond. I can see that she reads my texts, but she doesn't reply.

Things with Karina are the same. She acts as if we're perfect and there's nothing wrong, but we're far from okay. She's a robot, and I fucking hate it. The only time she seems to show emotion is when we fight, and we seem to be doing a lot of that lately. We fight, she storms out of the room, and minutes later, her mask is back in place, and she acts as if nothing ever happened.

I checked out of the hotel and returned home the day after kissing Cam. When I woke up, she was gone and ignored my calls, so I went home. I'd been home for two weeks when Karina and I had another fight that led me to sleep on the couch. Our guest room isn't put together yet, so I have nowhere else to sleep but our ridiculously uncomfortable couch.

Who the fuck buys an uncomfortable couch? They're made for sitting and should be comfortable, but ours is anything but.

Last night after dinner, Karina started with her shit again

about having a baby. She was drinking heavily and being denied a baby led to her crying and bitching about how I once promised to give her everything, but I'm breaking that promise by not wanting a baby.

We fought, I yelled, she cried, and I said I was done and wanted out of our marriage, then I left. We were going in circles, and I couldn't stand to continue having the same fight, so I was an asshole and left instead.

I don't know what led me to text Camille while driving to the hotel, but I did. I texted her twice.

Once to tell her that I was going back to the Rutherford Hotel, and again after I checked in to tell her my room number. As usual, she read the message but never replied.

And that's where I am now. Sitting in the living room of my hotel suite, a glass of liquor in my hand, staring at my text thread with Camille to ensure it says *read* and my eyes aren't playing tricks on me.

I'm so focused on my phone that I barely register the sound of knocks coming from the door. Odd, considering I didn't order anything, and the staff wouldn't come by unannounced.

It must be Karina. Great.

Downing the amber liquid, I set the empty glass down along with my phone and make my way to my hotel room door, all while dreading it and hoping it really is the hotel staff. I don't bother checking the peep hole. Instead, I swing the door open, ready for another round of fighting with my wife. Except to my surprise, it's not Karina. The last person I expected to see is standing at my door.

Camille.

"What are you doing here?" The question comes out harsher than I meant.

She doesn't say a single word. Her glossy green eyes find mine as she walks into my room, closing and locking the door behind herself.

"Camille?" I question, arching an eyebrow at her. She looks

disheveled, and by the sight of her, I can tell she's been crying. Her eyes are red and glazed, and tear marks have streaked down her face and dried. What angers me the most is her bright red left cheek with a very identifying mark. Someone hit her.

My body heats in anger, my hands balling into fists at my sides. I will fucking kill the person who put their hands on her.

She steps toward me, grips my now wrinkled white undershirt, and presses her plump lips to mine, stealing the air from my lungs. Her kiss sets fire to my skin and awakens a feeling that I haven't felt in a very long time.

Her kiss feels like pain, love, and loss all in one. It makes me dizzy.

"Cam," I whisper breathlessly against her lips, my hands finding her hips and squeezing them tightly, so I know she's real.

"I need you." Her voice is soft, her words spoken in a plea. If I were a better man, I wouldn't take advantage of her vulnerability. I'd push her to talk, find out what happened and what's bothering her. I'd do anything other than what I'm doing right now, which is pressing my growing erection into her soft stomach so she can feel what she does to me.

Her lips collide with mine once again. This time it's frantic and filled with lust. It's as if we can't get enough of each other. I lean down without breaking our kiss and lift her, wrapping her legs around my waist. She's wearing jeans, but I wish like hell she were wearing a dress so I could feel the wetness that I know is flooding her core. She always got so wet when she was turned on.

So wet, so needy.

With my hands tangled in her silky dark hair, I carry her to the bedroom and lay her small body in the middle of the bed. Her eyes never leave mine from where I stand at the foot of the bed, watching her like she's my prey.

"Come here." She reaches for me, but I shake my head, staring her down.

"You want me, Camille?" She nods.

"Prove it. Undress and let me see how wet you are." My words shock us both. Her green eyes widen, and she takes her plump bottom lip between her teeth to hide the smile threatening to curve on her lips.

She obeys, stripping herself until she's lying in front of me as naked as the day she was born. Her body is beautiful. The sight makes me so painfully hard that I have to remove my pants to loosen the pressure on my dick. My eyes never leave her beautiful, golden body as I unbutton my shirt and let it fall to the floor silently, leaving me standing before her in only a pair of boxer briefs. I palm my dick through the fabric, groaning at the touch.

It takes every ounce of self-control I have not to pounce on her and plunge myself so deep inside her that she feels me every time she walks. I'm forcing myself to go slow, and it makes my fucking dick ache.

"Spread your thighs. Let me see all of you."

She does as she's told.

Camille spreads her legs, giving me the perfect view of her pretty pussy that's glistening with her arousal. A mixture between a moan and grunt forces its way from my throat at the sight of her spread out before me.

I've never seen a cunt look so fucking perfect before. She had shaved herself bare the first time I'd ever seen her, and now she has a small patch of dark hair. For that, I'm thankful. I hate when women are bald, it's too pubescent looking for me. Karina gets waxed, and I hate it every time she does.

Fuck. I shouldn't even be thinking about her right now or even comparing.

With a sigh, I step closer to the bed, grip Camille's ankles, and force her legs further apart.

Her right hand trails down her perfectly soft body and brushes through the landing strip, then her index and middle finger land on her clit. The other hand goes to one of her breasts, pinching and pulling at her hardened nipples.

The sight of her on my bed playing with herself is enough to cause pre-cum to leak from my engorged boxers, my heavy manhood springing free and standing proudly between my legs. Her lust-glazed eyes widen, and a look of hunger washes over her.

She's so fucking exotic and beautiful when she's like this.

Camille circles her clit once more with a single digit before moving on to her hands and knees, crawling toward me. With darkened lust in her eyes, she sticks out her tongue and flicks it over my cock, causing it to jerk. She licks the pre-cum away from my slit, looking at me with a smirk.

I open my mouth to speak, my words forgotten at the sight of her swallowing my cock down her throat. Her eyes stay on mine, and if she's not careful, I'll blow my load in her hot mouth right now like a damn teenage boy.

"Mmm," she hums against my shaft. "You taste so good."

Her head bobs up and down, her tongue circling and sucking my head. As good as her mouth feels, I need to get inside of her as soon as possible.

I need to be buried in her perfect pussy as much as I need my next breath.

I push her shoulders, and Camille backs away willingly, settling herself on her back, spreading her legs for me, as if she knows exactly what's next.

Smirking at me, she takes a breast in each hand and begins massaging them and playing with her taut nipples. My self-control goes out the window, not that I had much anyway.

Jumping between her legs, I place them over my shoulders and devour her wet little pussy. I lick all the way from her little puckered asshole up to her clit, the flat of my tongue lapping at her wetness. She's still so sweet, tasting just like she did all those years ago.

Salted caramel.

My lips close around her sensitive bud of nerves, and my tongue flicks it while I roughly shove two thick fingers inside her tight entrance. Her moans are music to my ears. They're as sweet as her.

I want to be inside of her. I *need* to be inside of her. But right now, I also need her to orgasm in my mouth. I need more of her taste. I want her cum in my mouth.

"Dean," she gasps, her fingers tangling in my hair. "I need you."

I pull back. "Don't worry, baby, you'll get to feel my cock stretching you very soon, but first, I need to taste your cream."

"Please," she whines when my tongue flicks over her clit.

"Please what, baby?"

"I need you inside of me."

"Tell me exactly what you need, Cam. Maybe I'll give it to you." I smirk, diving back between her legs. With my fingers still inside her, I begin moving them, thrusting them in and out of her wet core slowly while my tongue licks, flicks, and sucks at her pussy lips and clit.

"I need your hard cock to slide inside of my wet pussy." To my surprise, she doesn't hesitate to tell me what I want to hear. "I want you so deep inside of me that it hurts." She pulls at the roots of my hair, replacing the pain with pleasure when she begins massaging it and scratching my scalp.

Pushing my fingers deeper inside of her, I curl them upward to find her G-spot and massage the area that has her body shaking and her core flooding. She squeezes around me with a vise-like grip, holding my fingers so tightly her pussy makes a gushing sound when I thrust them inside her.

"Oh God, I'm going to come!" she yells, her back arching off the bed. "I need to come in your mouth and have you lick me clean," she cries out, her body shaking with the threat of an oncoming orgasm.

Continuing my work, I keep my fingers curled deep inside her and give the sensitive bud the attention it deserves, my mouth sucking while my tongue circles the bud. By the way she's writhing and the way her pussy is pulsating, I know she's ready to come. I give her G-spot one more massage, then stop and pull my hand away when I feel the flood of fluid squirt from her.

She's always been an easy squirter. All it takes is the right touch.

Camille screams her release, her fluid dripping down her ass crack and pooling around her bottom. It'll be an uncomfortable wet spot to sleep in, clear evidence of her body shaking orgasm.

With a smug smirk, I kiss up her soft body, stopping at her hips to kiss over the faint silver marks etched in her skin. Beautiful stretch marks, a sign that she created and carried life inside her body, proving how fucking incredible women are.

I reach her face and crush my lips against her, forcing my tongue into her warm mouth. Her legs widen to accommodate my body.

Reaching between us, I take my cock in my hand and guide the tip to her entrance. "Are you sure about this? Take a minute to think about what you're doing because as soon as I sink my dick into you, that's it, you're mine," I warn, teasingly rubbing my head against her sensitive clit.

"I've always been yours. Now shut up and fuck me."

I thrust my hips against hers roughly, plunging all my inches inside her at once, not allowing her to adjust to my size.

She cries out, her arms wrap around my back, and her nails sink into my skin. Careful not to pull her hair that's spread wildly on the pillow, I cage her in, my forearms on either side of her head, my hands cupping her beautiful face. We're nose to nose, as close as we can possibly fucking get, yet I still need to be closer.

Moving my hips, I pull out of her warmth, the cold hair hitting my wet cock. With my next breath, I plunge myself back inside of her, my length disappearing into her slick heat.

"For eleven years, I've needed to be balls deep inside you and have your tight, greedy cunt around my dick. I've thought of it every single day," I grunt, showing her just how badly I've missed and needed her by pulling out and slamming back inside of her.

She's so fucking perfect that she just yelps and takes it. She takes everything I have to give her, everything I've needed to give her. "For so long, I've needed to have you wrapped around me, coming on my cock."

Cam fuses our lips together, our moans vibrating against each other. My hand slips between our connected bodies until I find her clit and apply just the right amount of pressure, strumming her in a perfect rhythm that makes her body convulse.

"Ah, fuck, you're so deep." She whimpers, clawing at my back, causing me to jerk and thrust harder into her core. The sting of pain mixed with the pleasure is exactly what I need.

The sounds of pleasure Cam makes while being fucked are loud and sultry. Having her be so vocal about what she feels and what she likes only makes me want to lose complete control and fuck her clear into next week. It's nice to finally have someone in the bedroom that matches my energy, and Camille does. She matches my energy on every level and always has.

Her green eyes darken with lust, her pupils dilate, and I feel the pulse of her insides, a telling sign she is nearing her climax. Her pussy squeezes around my length, the feel of her warmth sending a spark down my spine. This is it, the moment I've been craving. She's going to come on my cock.

I apply more pressure with a quicker rhythm to her core, and Camille tilts her head back, her body shaking as she comes with a scream, her walls so tight around me that she's practically fucking choking my cock.

"Oh God, oh God, oh God!" she chants. Her face and chest are flushed, her cheeks rosy, and the lightest beads of sweat have formed around her hairline.

"You're beautiful when you come," I whisper, pressing a kiss to her swollen, parted lips. "I'm not done with you yet." A smirk forms on my lips.

Pulling out of her tight body with an audible pop, I raise myself to my knees and bring her spent body up to her knees, her back against my chest. Using my thigh to spread her legs, I carefully push her forward until she's on all fours, then line myself up with her cunt and ram back inside of her where I belong.

The thrust knocks the air from her lungs, and I take pride in knowing that I can bring her pleasure. She needed pleasure and comfort, and she came to me.

I pull her body up to her knees so that once again, her back is against my chest. With one arm wrapped around her hips firmly to hold her against me, I snake the other hand around her body and grip her throat. "I need you wrapped around my cock every day. Can I have that?" I rasp in her ear, her head falling back onto my shoulder, her lips parting.

I'm a bastard, but I want her.

I need her.

Having her once isn't enough. Now that I've felt her warm pussy wrapped around me, there's no way I can go without. I've been willing to destroy everything in my life for her.

For the feeling of her being in my arms a moment longer.

"Shut up and make me come again." I don't need to be told twice.

She doesn't answer my question, but that's okay for now because I plan on having her again regardless.

With one hand between her legs, I strum her clit roughly while the hand that's wrapped around her neck applies enough pressure for her to keep still. Our flushed skin is dripping with sweat, the air in the room becoming as hot and heavy as our breathing. The sound of skin slapping against skin can be heard.

In the distance, there's a faint ring, but my only focus is on the ethereal woman wrapped around me. I don't pay any attention to the phone that's ringing. I focus on the sounds of sex that fill the air.

Pants, moans, grunts, groans, slaps.

And then a scream.

Camille screams her release, her fingernails digging into the sides of my thighs as her soft body violently shakes from her release, her cunt pulsing around me and choking my cock as she soaks me a second time.

"Dean! Ahh, fuck!" she cries, her spent body nearly giving out on her. Her orgasm sends me over the edge. I feel the familiar ache in my balls and the bottom of my spine. I can't hold back; I'm so fucking close that my thighs ache. Moving my hands to her hips, I grip them firmly and selfishly, not caring that my grip may be too tight and cause bruises.

One thrust.

Two thrusts.

That's all I can manage before throwing my head back and roaring my own release. My cock twitches as I shoot hot ropes of thick semen inside her. "Get on your back and open your mouth," I demand. Panting, she does as she's told. With a sparkle in her eye, she spreads her legs for me as if she already knows what I'm about to do.

With a smirk curling on my lips, I climb between her parted legs and use my thumbs to spread her glistening pussy. "Squeeze your walls together," I instruct before I vacuum seal my mouth over her entrance, sucking our mixture of cum from her still pulsing pussy. Camille clenches and pushes, forcing my semen out.

With a mouthful of cum, I climb up the bed beside her and lean down to her face. She's waiting just as I told her to, with her mouth wide open. She arches an eyebrow and sticks out her tongue, a look that's both curious and waiting. Slowly I move a hand down her flushed, sweaty body and shove three fingers inside her without warning, massaging her G-spot while my thumb circles her overly sensitive clit.

Smirking, I spit my cum and saliva onto her waiting tongue. "Swallow it all," I demand once my mouth is empty.

Like the good girl she is, she obeys and swallows what I give her.

To my surprise, the dirty girl sticks her tongue back out for more. I spit on her tongue again, but before she can gulp it down, I crash my mouth against hers, swallowing her moans as my hand coaxes a final orgasm from her body.

Camille breaths heavily against my mouth, her chest rising

and falling rapidly, her heavy eyelids struggling to open each time she blinks. I've taken all her energy, she's exhausted, and I can't wait to sleep with her in my arms.

I press a final kiss on her parted lips before climbing off the bed. I stand at the foot of the bed to admire my now sleeping girl. Her dark hair is messy and spread out beneath her over the white pillowcase, her legs still parted with her beautiful pussy on display for me and only me. She's in my bed with my cum still dripping from her pussy, and my cum all over her mouth. I take one final moment to look at her before going to the bathroom to get a warm, wet washcloth to clean her.

When I return, I carefully wipe her face, chest and between her legs. She doesn't stir. She stays peacefully asleep. Once I have her cleaned up, I return the washcloth to the bathroom and then pull down the covers on the bed, shifting Camille slightly so her naked body is under the sheets with me. She doesn't move until I turn the light out. Then to my surprise, she scoots closer to me and pulls my arm around her waist with a contented sigh.

We're both lying on our sides, spooning. She fits so perfectly against me that each time she moves, her ass wiggles against my cock, but I ignore the fact she's getting me hard again. I have all the time in the world to fuck my girl; I'm not letting her get away this time.

I fucked up eleven years ago. I should've never suggested we spend time apart. I know that she doesn't regret it because of the things she got to experience, and sometimes I don't either. But fuck, I missed her. Being with her now feels right. It feels like coming home after being gone for so fucking long.

She is my home, and I've been homesick for far too long. I'm ready to be home.

No matter what I must do, no matter what consequence I face, I will get the girl.

Camille will be mine.

TWENTY-SIX

NOW

Camille

I wake up with a familiar ache between my legs and guilt on my conscience. The second my eyes open, it takes me two seconds to realize I'm still in Dean's hotel room, and the body heat beside me and morning erection pressing into my bottom tell me that we're both still in bed naked. His warm flesh feels like heaven against me. But as good as it feels, it feels wrong.

I'm in bed with a man that isn't my husband. I had sex with a man that isn't my husband. That fact weighs heavily on my chest.

Despite telling Declan I want a divorce, I'm still legally married, which means I cheated on my husband... for the second time.

"Good morning," he mumbles behind me, his voice raspy from sleep.

"Morning, I need to get going. I have work." I attempt to sit up only for his hand to grip my hip and pull me closer to his body, thrusting his erection against my ass crack.

"Not yet." He trails gentle kisses up my arm and shoulder until he reaches my jawline, then he kisses it slowly, nuzzling his face into the crook of my neck. With a sigh, I relish in the feeling

267

of his hands on my body and allow his hand to snake around my body and between my legs to my cunt.

"Dean, I need to go. Last night... it was wrong."

"If it's wrong, why did it feel so right?"

"Stop, we can't do this. You know that we can't."

"But you want to." I don't deny it. I can't deny it. Not when his fingers can feel the proof of the effect he has on my body.

Dean grips my leg and raises it, moving it back to rest across his hip. This position exposes me to him, and he wastes no time slipping two thick fingers inside me to explore my arousal. "Your wet pussy tells me that you do want this. Want *me*." What does he expect me to say? Of course, he's turning me on. Anyone would be turned on in this situation.

Dean curls his fingers inside me, and once he finds my G-spot, he massages it. My body betrays me by coming on his hand too quickly.

Before I can protest, he guides his cock inside of my still pulsing channel from behind, using the same two fingers that were just inside of me to strum my sensitive clit.

"I dream of waking up next to you and taking you just like this every single morning," he rasps in my ear, biting and sucking my earlobe.

"We... we can't..." My words trail off with my moans of pleasure. "This will never happen again. It can't. We're married. Never again." I can't tell if I'm trying to convince him or myself.

"We're not married for much longer," he rasps, his thrusts become deeper and quicker, both of us in a race to the finish line. I'm determined to get there first and get the fuck out of his room.

I open my mouth to speak, but my words fall short when the familiar warming sensation starts at the bottom of my stomach and tightens. My climax is so close, and as wrong as it is, I desperately want to come on his cock again.

"You feel so fucking good. We can't stop, not when we've only just begun."

"Dean, oh God, Dean." I'm not sure if I'm crying his name

because I want him to stop or go deeper. After all, he feels so fucking good inside of me. Stretching me. Owning me. Claiming me.

"This isn't a mistake. You came here for a reason. You needed me, just like I need you." He pinches my nipple and clit simultaneously, sending jolts of electricity through my body.

"M-mistake!" I cry out, my climax ready to consume me.

With a grunt, he stills before I have the chance to let go and give in to the pleasure. With a slap to my ass, he pulls his still hard cock out of my pulsing pussy, leaving me wet and aching with need.

"Why did you come here?" he growls, demanding an answer.

"Fuck! Why did you stop?" I whine, grinding myself against his rock-hard cock that's pressing against my ass, slick from my juices.

"I asked you a question. If you want to cum, you must answer me." He pinches my nipple again, tugging at it in a way that is both painful and pleasurable. "Why did you come here last night?"

"Because... I wanted to see you."

"Why?" His fingers find my clit, brushing over it teasingly. I groan in frustration, desperately needing him to rub my clit and let me have what I both need and want. An orgasm. "Why, Camille?" he demands.

The bastard always knows exactly why I showed up at his door last night, but he wants me to say it.

He's making a point.

Asshole.

"I came because I wanted to see you! I had a fight with Declan, and the only arms I wanted to be in were yours! You were the one I wanted to comfort me, and I wanted to feel you inside of me!" I yell my admission.

He's silent for a moment, but my answer must please him because the very next second, his fingers are back on my clit, while he glides his cock back inside of me easily and begins piston fucking me like a crazed man.

My body twitches, and it doesn't take long until I'm shaking and crying out my orgasm, flooding him with everything I have. I come with a loud cry, my head falling back on his shoulder. I'm a boneless mess, still floating on cloud nine when he reaches his climax and roars his release, shooting his hot semen deep inside of my throbbing pussy.

"Oh, God," I groan breathlessly, a grin curling my lips.

For a while, we lie beside each other, his cock still inside of me, but he's no longer moving. His arms wrap around me tightly, and the only sound in the room is our heavy breathing. It's peaceful, and I temporarily allow myself to forget our mistake that doesn't feel like a mistake.

Dean could never be a mistake.

How can he be?

He's my first love. My first kiss. My first sexual experience.

He owns all my firsts.

I remember when I thought he'd own all of my lasts, too.

It's been eleven years since I've seen him, and sometimes it feels like no time has passed. Sometimes I think he knows me better than I know myself, and that thought is scary. Sometimes I wish he didn't know me so well so he wouldn't know everything I'm thinking and feeling.

Like now.

I'm overthinking our situation, and I need to leave. Dean must know what I'm thinking and planning because his arm tightens around me, and his body tenses.

"Stay." One word that feels more like a plea rather than a demand. I don't move. Instead, I remain where I am, wrapped in his warm embrace.

We remain silent, but I know he is also thinking about the mess we made and what we did. We should've been stronger and fought against our lust. Instead, we fucked.

Multiple times.

Our moment of silent overthinking is interrupted by a cell phone ringing in the distance. Dean tenses behind me, letting out a sigh. His grip on me loosens, so I take the opportunity to sit up and wrap myself in the sheet that we'd been tangled in.

I can't bring myself to look at him because I can't face him.

Not right now.

Not when I have a good idea of who's calling him.

He shifts to the other side of the bed, a sigh leaving his lips and confirming my suspicion of who's on the other end of the phone.

Clearing his throat, Dean answers the phone, and I hear him stand and leave the room. While he's in the living room having a conversation with his wife, I take the free moment to gather my clothes from the floor and step inside the bathroom to clean myself up as much as possible.

I'm taking a whore bath in the sink, cleaning his cum that's dripping down my thighs while he's in the other room talking to his wife.

A shower would be nice, but I can't bring myself to step inside the massive glass shower that's calling my name and offering to set me free and allow me to repent. Showering would mean being here even longer, and I can't.

Instead, I dress, wash my face, pull my hair into a neat bun, then use his toothbrush to brush my teeth.

I've just set the used toothbrush on the counter when Dean steps inside the bathroom and stands behind me. He doesn't touch me, but he's close enough for me to feel the warmth of his body that's only covered by the black boxer briefs he wore last night.

Our eyes instantly find each other in the mirror.

My shoulders sag. "We fucked up, Dean." I close my eyes, unable to look at him or myself any longer, a tear rolling down my cheek. "We made a mistake, and it can never happen again." This isn't who I am.

I'm not a cheater. My marriage may be in the shitter and at a dead end, but that doesn't change the fact that I *am* still married, and right now, my husband is probably at home wondering where I am.

When I open my eyes, they lock with Dean's in the mirror. Wiping my tears away, I turn and rush past him, bumping his shoulder on my way out.

Thankfully, he doesn't follow me out of the bathroom.

I'm able to grab my shoes and purse from the living room and get my car from the valet without him following.

Judging by the look in his eyes in the bathroom, he, too, knows that we made a mistake.

A huge fucking mistake.

But how can it be a mistake when it doesn't feel like one?

I feel guilty. Guilty because I cheated on my husband and betrayed our vows, but if I had the chance to do things over, I'm still not sure I'd change a damn thing.

ONCE I REACH MY OFFICE, I POWER MY PHONE ON AND check my missed notifications. As suspected, I have multiple missed calls and texts from Declan asking where I am, if I'm okay, saying he's sorry, and begging me to come home.

My heart pounds in my chest, guilt consuming me as I read all twenty-three worried text messages he sent.

As I scroll through, reading them all again, my phone vibrates in my hand, and his photo pops up, showing that he's calling.

I stare at the phone, stare at the contact photo that I have set for Declan. It's a photo from a few years ago, a candid photo I took during one of his concerts. I was backstage, and he'd just turned to face me, and his face lit up with pure happiness. His smile was wide, all his straight white teeth on display, beads of sweat lining his forehead, and his dark hair damp, stars bright in his brown eyes.

At that moment, he was so fucking happy, and I loved him more than ever. I snapped that photo and set it as his contact photo. It's always been one of my favorite pictures of him.

Wiping away the tears that I didn't realize are streaming down my cheeks until I taste the salt, I answer his call and press my phone against my ear, unable to bring myself to say anything. The only thing I can semi-manage in my current state is breathing.

"Baby girl, I'm so fucking sorry." Declan sighs into the phone, his voice causing more tears to stream silently down my face. "Where are you? Come home, please, or I will come to you." The remorse in his tone is evident. I know he didn't mean to hit me, and I don't even blame him for it. I hit him first, and he only returned my action. Two wrongs don't make a right, but I don't blame him. I can't, not when my pussy is still wet with another man's cum.

"Please, please, come home. We need to talk and figure things out."

"Okay," I whisper, not trusting my voice enough to betray the fact I'm crying. "I'll come home."

He lets out a sigh of relief. "I'll see you when you get here."

I don't say anything. I hang up as quickly as possible just as my phone vibrates with another phone call.

This time, it's the last person I want to speak to.

Dean.

Wiping my tears away with a Kleenex, I power down my phone, gather my items, and get the fuck out of my office, ignoring my assistant when she tries to speak to me.

Twenty minutes later, I'm home. My tears are long gone, but I wonder if Declan will be able to see the guilt written all over my face. I've never been good at keeping secrets from him.

I've never been a liar, but with each passing day, I'm becoming more of one.

I cautiously step inside our condo, unaware of what I will find inside. I've witnessed the aftermath of Declan's temper before. The broken TVs, the holes in the wall, broken picture frames and vases, and empty bottles of liquor. I've seen it all before with him. Although he's never hurt me, I can't say the same for our furniture.

Stepping inside, I'm relieved to find nothing is broken, nor are there liquor bottles anywhere.

What I do find is Declan sitting in the middle of our gray sectional in the living room with his head in his hands. I close the front door with a soft click, causing my faithful husband to look up at me with sad, remorseful brown eyes.

Quickly, he stands and rushes toward me. Dropping my purse to the floor, I fling myself at him. We collide, our arms wrapping around each other in a tight embrace.

Losing Declan would be like losing my best friend.

But losing Dean would be like losing a piece of myself.

I'm in the middle of two men I care deeply about.

One man I'm in love with, have always been in love with, and the other, a man I love deeply... but a man I'm not in love *with*.

And I don't think I ever have been.

"Camille, we need to talk." Declan cups my face, pressing his forehead against mine, his breath fanning against my lips. My hands find his waist, fisting his T-shirt tightly.

I know what he's going to say. It's a conversation we've been avoiding for far too long, and it's inevitable. When two people are not meant to be, there's no way to prevent the ending that's bound to happen.

A wave of guilt washes over me. "Declan, I love you." I choke on a sob. He doesn't deserve an unfaithful wife. We have our issues, but we never stray outside of our marriage.

"I know you do, baby girl. I love you, too." He presses his lips against mine, stealing my breath with his kiss. "Let's shower, and then we'll talk." I nod, letting him guide me into our master bathroom.

With gentle fingers, he undresses me slowly, then undresses himself. He even takes the time to untie my hair and let it fall down my shoulders.

It doesn't occur to me that I might have evidence of Dean still on my body until we step under the shower spray and Declan's eyes roam my body inch by inch.

He doesn't look in my eyes. His dark eyes stay focused on my bare body, and his eyebrows are pulled together tightly in a deep V. Silently, he grabs a washcloth, squeezes soap onto it, rubs it between his hands to create a lather, then massages it gently over my body, focusing primarily between my legs.

His eyes never leave my body.

The body that only hours earlier was being kissed and worshipped by another man.

Declan still cannot look at me as he washes between my legs, taking extra time to clean my cunt. With the way he's cleaning me, I realize that he knows.

He knows where I've been and what I've been doing.

He straightens to his full height, his eyes finally connecting with mine for the first time. In his dark brown eyes, I see my betrayal. His face is stoic, but his eyes give him away.

With a gulp, I open my mouth to speak, but he shuts me up by shaking his head. I remain silent, not wanting to push him, watching his movements closely.

Declan removes the shower head and sprays it over my body, rinsing away the soap subs. Once I'm clean, he hangs the shower head back up and steps toward me, backing me against the corner.

Goosebumps spread across my body, and a chill shoots down my spine when my back touches the cold shower wall.

He surprises me by picking me up. With a gasp, I wrap my legs around his waist and my arms around his neck, my fingers tangling in the hair at the back of his head.

Reaching between us, he grips his already hard cock, and guides it inside me, curses falling from his lips when he enters me. His forehead falls against mine, our focus on the sight of him sliding in and out of me repeatedly.

We moan in sync, our eyes remaining focused on the sight of our joined bodies.

One of his hands holds onto the back of my thigh while the other grips my hip. His fingers dig into the soft flesh of my hip that

I hadn't realized is adorned with fingerprint bruises from Dean until now.

Declan fucks me nice and slow against the shower wall. I should've been ashamed of myself and rejected him. I should've denied my husband entrance to my body because I couldn't keep my legs closed and let another man enter the sacred space that's supposed to be reserved for my husband only. But instead of rejecting him, I give him what he needs.

It's not about me; it's about him right now.

We come together, and he slowly sets me back on my feet as soon as our breathing evens.

We complete the rest of our shower in silence, then step out and dry ourselves. While I'm drying my hair and covering myself with my candy apple red silk robe, Declan slips into the closet to get dressed. We don't say a single word to each other, but I can hear him fumbling around in the closet and bedroom.

After pulling my hair back into a bun and putting on clean panties, I make my way into the living room, stopping in my tracks when I see the duffle bag and suitcase waiting by the couch.

"Dec, what's this?" I point toward the luggage as he steps out of the kitchen with two water bottles in hand.

"I'm going back to New York for a while." My heart stops. This is the conversation we've been putting off for far too long. I know what we need to do, but seeing his bags packed and hearing him say the words crush me. He steps toward me, sets the water on the table, and takes my face in his cold hands.

"Baby girl, we both know that this hasn't been working. It hasn't been for a while. Our problems started long before we lost Luca, and we both know that something must change." He wraps me in his arms, his chin resting on the top of my head. I wrap my arms around his waist, hugging him against me tightly, inhaling his musky spice scent.

"You had the right idea asking for a divorce, but first, I think we need to take some time apart and decide if this is really what we want to do."

I love Declan, and as rough as our marriage has been, and as much as I've thought about ending things myself, now that I'm faced with our marriage ending, I'm heartbroken.

I'm losing my best friend.

My lover, my husband, the father of my child.

"I'm so fucking happy that I'm able to call you my wife, and I'm so sorry that I wasn't there for you when you needed me to be. After we lost Luca, I was selfish. You are so strong and incredible, and you held us together. You took care of me and everyone else, and you were all alone. I'm sorry I did that to you, baby girl." He sighs, taking a step back so he's able to look at me. He grips my chin and tilts my head. "I'm going back to New York to meet up with the band and record some new music I've been working on. We need some time apart. It'll be good for us."

I can barely see him through my tears. "We had time apart while you were in rehab."

"Babe, I wasn't good back then. Now that I'm sober, I must focus on staying sober and mourning Luca properly. I can't be around you every day because all you do is worry about me. You resent me, and you have plenty that you need to work out on your own right now. Go see Dr. Reynolds. Take time to heal yourself." He wipes my tears away, kissing my forehead slowly. "Our relationship is very unhealthy, and until we work on ourselves, we'll never be good for each other."

I nod because that's all that I can do. I know what time apart means. We're going to end in divorce, and we both know it. Once again, we're delaying the inevitable. We know what's going to happen, what our ending will be, but neither of us wants to say the big ugly D-word, so we'll call it time apart.

Time apart that'll eventually end with us permanently living in two different states.

"When are you leaving?" I ask with a frown.

"I'm going to the airport now. I'll call you after I land and get to our place." I nod, pressing my lips against his for what may be the last time. We stay lip-locked for several minutes, our lips moving in sync and our tongues tangling.

"Goodbye, baby girl. I love you forever."

"I love you forever, Dec. Please call me." He nods, kisses my forehead, then he's gone, the door slamming shut behind him.

I collapse to my knees, tears streaming heavily down my face as my heart cracks open and spills all over the floor.

Maybe I was holding on to him because he's my connection to Luca. He's my connection to a time in my life when I was the happiest I've ever been—when I was Luca's mother.

Lying on the floor in the fetal position, I take my phone out of my robe pocket and call Spencer, hiccupping into the phone as soon as I hear her voice.

She hears my cries and says, "I'm on my way."

Forty minutes later, she's here. She doesn't bother knocking, instead, she uses the key I gave her and lets herself in. She lies beside me and wraps her arms around me, letting me cry until I'm all cried out.

Only then does she ask what happened, and I tell her everything. I tell her about how I'm still taking medication to suppress my emotions, how my head has been in a fog since seeing Dean again, how I'm so fucking depressed and broken that some days I can't stand to exist. I tell her about what happened with Dean last night, and lastly, I tell her about Declan leaving. I don't spare a single detail; I tell my sister everything I've been suppressing for far too long.

She doesn't judge me, which isn't a surprise. She never has. She lets me tell her everything, and once I finish, she wipes my tears away, helps me to my room, and then helps me into my bed, where she climbs in next to me.

"I've got you, little sister. I'm here now." She sniffles, brushing my hair out of my face, the same way she did when we were children and I would get upset.

"My heart hurts so fucking much. I thought the medication was helping, but it's not. I hate the way I feel every single day. I hate being this depressed shell of the person I used to be." I sigh, wiping my face with the back of my hand. "I don't know what I need. Talking to a therapist doesn't help." I don't tell her that I've canceled my appointments and haven't been in a while.

"I had no idea you were hurting so badly. I'm sorry for being so blind." I don't blame her. I'm great at hiding my emotions. No one knows that I haven't coped with the loss of my son or all the shit that happened with Declan and his drugs. He checked out, and I was left to pick up the broken pieces of our lives, and I was the one who had to be strong for the both of us while he was getting high. I was the glue that held us together; therefore, I never had time to mourn properly. Instead, I hid my emotions, burying them down so deep that now they're starting to explode.

"I think we should have your doctor check your medication. Sometimes, the side effects can do more damage than good. Perhaps she can change the dosage or put you on something else," she suggests.

Nodding, I say, "You're right. I'll talk to her at my next appointment." I lie easily to her, knowing I have no intention of saying anything. I don't need any more doctors giving me anything else. I can manage on my own. I'll stop taking medication altogether.

I'll be fine.

Stroking my hair, Spencer whispers soothing words, telling me repeatedly that she'll be here for me, begging me to open up to her more and tell her how I'm truly feeling. I agree, happy that I have my sister by my side. I would've called our mom, but I'm not ready for that yet.

For now, I just need my sister.

And to stay away from Dean while I focus on myself and think about what I will do about my marriage.

I cry myself to sleep, saying a silent prayer that when I awake, I'll be someone new and feel different.

TWENTY-SEVEN

NOW

DEAN

Camille left.

She walked out on me when I needed her to stay the most. I want to say I don't understand why she left me, but come on, of course, I fucking know why she left. And I can't blame her.

She thinks we made a mistake.

Maybe the way it happened was a mistake, but I don't regret what we did. I don't regret feeling her silky skin under my tongue again or seeing how her face contorts in pleasure right before she comes. Her sweet cunt is already tight, but when her climax is building and she's seconds away from coming, that's when she's the tightest. Her pussy squeezed my cock in a vice grip, and that's something I want to experience every day for the rest of my miserable goddamn life.

I've never once considered cheating on Karina; that's the honest-to-God truth. I've never looked at another woman the entire time we've been together. No one ever captivated me and held my interest. My eyes were always only ever on my wife. My gaze never strayed away from her until now.

Had Camille not come back into my life, I can't say where my future would've led. I'd probably still be a coward and stuck in my marriage. Camille has given me the strength to man the fuck up, and this time actually proceed with a divorce.

I know I'm still married and a piece of shit for cheating, but God help me.

Camille is my undoing. She's my beginning and my end. The in-between doesn't matter. As long as my life ends with her, that's the only thing I care about.

Because of my feelings for her, it makes my decision all the easier. I'm going to end my marriage to Karina. I'm going to set us both free. I'll leave her so she can find someone who sets her soul on fire and makes her feel the way Cam has always made me feel.

I've already found my person, and it's time Karina finds hers.

Before Camille left, Karina had called me, begging for me to come home, wanting to talk things out, not believing that I was serious when I said I was done.

I told her I'd come back to talk face-to-face about it and hung up.

Home. Such a funny thing, really. I think home is more of a person and not a place. I don't feel at home in the house I share with Karina. I feel at home whenever I'm sharing the same space as Cam.

God, I'm a lovesick fool. I always have been.

It's been a week now since Camille walked out of my hotel room. Sure, I've spoken to Karina a few times, but I can't bring myself to return to the house we share. Perhaps part of me secretly hopes that a certain raven-haired beauty will appear at my door again. Wishful thinking, I know.

One week without speaking to Camille feels like a lifetime, and I wonder how the fuck I was ever able to go eleven years without talking to her. I'm wondering why I even decided that it would be best to leave Camille in the past after graduating high school and moving to England for university.

I'm torn between thinking we wasted many years by being

apart and wondering what our lives could've been had we been together all that time. I never think about the what-ifs, but now as I'm sitting in my office staring out the floor-to-ceiling window at the buildings surrounding me, I can't help myself from thinking about them.

What if I had gone to school locally instead of going to London? Or, what if we had stayed in contact the entire time I was away at school?

What if she had joined me in London after she graduated high school?

Every possible scenario I think about leaves an uneasy feeling over me. We weren't meant to be together during that time. I know it. We experienced things that made us who we are today, and had we not had that time apart, we would be completely different people.

I shake the thoughts of what-ifs from my head when I hear my assistant's voice over the intercom. "Mr. Jameson, I have the information you requested. Would you like for me to bring it to you?"

"Email it to me. Thanks, Marjorie." Marjorie is my sixty-five-year-old assistant who moves slower than a snail but is as sharp as a nail. When I took over the previous company, the owner's only request was that I keep Marjorie as an employee. It was a no-brainer decision. She's been working for the architect firm for over thirty years. It saved me the time of having to hire and train someone.

My computer pings with an email notification from Marjorie. I open it and scroll through, locating the website and phone number she attached. Within seconds, I've got my phone in my hand and I'm calling the number on the screen. When the young lady on the other end of the phone answers, I schedule a rush same-day appointment and pay the hefty fee over the phone.

It's worth every single penny for what I'm about to do.

Twenty minutes later, I'm pulling into an empty parking spot in the front of Camille's office building, smirking when I see her standing outside with a scowl, looking very confused. Before I left my office to come here, I had sent her a rather vague, panicked text message telling her that there was an immediate issue with her build that we needed to address and to meet me out front. We haven't spoken in a week, but as usual, she read my text message without replying. I was taking a risk, but I knew if I said there was a problem with her building, she'd do as I said.

And look, she did.

I roll the passenger window down and unlock the doors. "Hurry and get in. We don't have time to waste." She opens her mouth to argue but instead closes it and does as I say. With a huff, she climbs into the passenger seat of my car and buckles up. The second her seat belt is clicked into place, I speed off in the opposite direction of her building.

"Where the hell are we going? If there's an issue at the site, you're going the wrong way," she says with clear annoyance in her voice.

"You wouldn't respond to me, and I needed to see you."

"So you lied about there being an issue with my building because you wanted to see me?" I glance at her in time to see her roll her pretty green eyes.

"Yes." There's no point in beating around the bush. That's exactly what happened. "Do you remember our adventures as kids?" We were always wandering off and getting ourselves into mishaps. As children, Camille dragged me off with her somewhere to explore something, and vice versa. Anything I thought was cool and wanted her to see, I'd drag her off to see. Every single time, she followed without hesitation and without questions asked.

Years later, I'm once again getting to take her somewhere I know will mean something to her.

"Of course, I remember our adventures. What does that have to do with anything?"

"Well, we're going on an adventure. So sit back and be quiet." She huffs but doesn't say another word the entire drive.

It takes nearly forty minutes to reach our destination, but once we do, I see Camille shift in her seat after I park, her eyes going wide when she sees the big sign above the small white building.

Titanium Skydiving.

"Dean." She looks over at me with wide eyes. I can't help the grin that curls on my lips. "What are we doing here?" I don't answer her. Instead, I unbuckle my seatbelt and climb out of my car, walking right up toward the entrance of the building, knowing that she's following behind me.

My hand is on the handle of the glass door when she abruptly stops me from pulling the door open. "Why did you bring me here?"

"You told me that sometimes you feel like jumping." I bring up our conversation in her office not too long ago when she broke down in tears and told me that sometimes she looks out her window and feels like jumping out.

Her green eyes glisten with unshed tears. "You can jump, but I'll be beside you." She blinks. I blink. Then the next second, she throws herself at me, her arms around my neck, and our lips are smashed together. She nearly knocks me over from the sudden impact, but I keep steady to support us.

Camille is the first to break our kiss. She backs away with a shy smile, gripping the door handle and walking inside with a level of confidence that makes me admire her even more than I already do. If she's nervous, she doesn't show it.

I follow behind her like the lost puppy I am.

"Hi, I have an appointment for two. One is a first-time jumper," I say to the girl behind the front desk after she greets us. Camille looks at me with skeptical eyes once I say that only one of us is a first-time jumper. Little does she know, I'm rather familiar with skydiving. Another piece of information that she'll be surprised to learn is that it's just the two of us jumping. Usually, when you're a first-time jumper, you must have an instructor with you, but money talks. She'll be attached to me, her precious life literally in my hands.

"Awesome, fill out this paperwork, and I'll let Tyson know you're here!" she says in an entirely too cheery voice, handing us both a clipboard containing a packet of paperwork and a pen.

Once our forms are complete and returned to the blonde girl behind the desk, a second worker leads us back into a small room where he plays us an informational video on skydiving to educate us and then delivers a PowerPoint presentation and speech of his own. I zone out during his speech, my sole focus on the breath of fresh air beside me and how she watches him so intensely, soaking up every word he says.

Thirty minutes later, Tyson has completed his presentation of who does what, the tandem equipment, and safety features.

"All right, Dean, I'll get your rig, and then we can head out and get the show on the road." I nod in response before he leaves us alone in the room.

Camille looks at me, raising one of her perfectly arched eyebrows. "What did you mean by only one first-time jumper? Are you saying that you've been skydiving before?" I nod.

"A few times, actually."

Her mouth gapes open like a fish out of water. "When? Why? With who?"

"My mom." Her eyes nearly pop out of her head with that news, so I explain, "A few years ago, when I came home to visit, Mom told me about this place she heard someone talking about at the club. My dad, of course, said no, so she asked me. She loves it. We've been here quite a few times."

"How did I not know this?"

"Why would you? We haven't been a part of each other's lives for a while." A frown curls on her perfectly plump lips. I reach out toward her and swipe my finger across her bottom lip. "You jump, I jump." Without thinking, I lean down and press my lips against hers. We're in public for crying out loud, but at this moment, I don't care about possibly being caught with someone who isn't my wife. I'm with *my* Camille, and that's all that matters to me.

Since Cam came straight from work and was still in her dress, she ran into the gift shop to purchase a pair of sweatpants, a T-shirt, and a pair of sneakers. Every piece of clothing is embroidered with the Titanium Skydiving logo, but at least she's wearing suitable jumping attire now. The clothing may be ridiculous, but she can make anything look good. Besides, it doesn't matter anyway because she's now covered it up with the tandem gear that Tyson gave us.

After changing into our gear, which consists of matching jumpsuits, Tyson leads us toward the airstrip and into the small awaiting plane. I don't think Camille has yet realized that she will be jumping with me rather than the instructor. It'll be a pleasant surprise.

The pilot introduces himself as Jeremy. While he goes through his safety checklist before we take off, Tyson again goes over safety protocol, handing us goggles that we slip over our heads and adjust around our eyes, along with earplugs.

Based on Camille's body language, I know she's anxious. She's trying to play it cool and not let her nerves show, but I know her too well. She's never been the type to second-guess herself or question her decisions. Cam has always jumped headfirst into anything and everything she does. She's completely fearless. She craves the adrenaline as much as I've been craving being in the same vicinity as her.

Moments later, the small plane takes off, and we're making the short journey into the sky, climbing higher and higher until we reach our maximum altitude.

Tyson grabs the rig that contains our parachute and helps me into it, placing the straps on my shoulders and the straps around my chest to secure it.

"Okay, Camille, you'll stand in front of Dean with your back to him, and I'll strap you to him," he announces, clapping his hands together.

Her jaw drops at the revelation. I smile smugly.

"What do you mean strap me to him? No way in hell!" She crosses her arms across her chest in protest.

"Come on, Cam, you'll be safe with me. We jump together, right?" She pulls her plump bottom lip between her teeth, and I refrain from leaning forward and pulling her lip away and biting it the way she currently is.

With a huff and an eye roll, she does exactly as Tyson said. She places her back against my chest, and then he secures the straps around her, securing her to my chest. Once she's secure, she ties her hair back into a bun at the base of her neck.

We're in this together now more than ever. There's no turning back. She jumps, I jump.

Soon the door opens, and it's go time. We shove the earplugs into our ears and step in sync until we get closer to the edge of the plane. I wrap one arm around Camille's waist while the other holds on tightly to the handlebar above us.

Tyson gives us the thumbs up to let us know it's time to jump. My hand around her waist tightens, and I lean down to place a kiss on her cheek. She won't be able to hear me, so I don't say anything. The kiss says all I need to say. I want her to know I'm here for her; no matter what, I'm here.

Camille surprises me by turning her head and capturing my lips, kissing me so deep that it makes me temporarily dizzy, and I get drunk on her. Everything about her is so fucking intoxicating. Her beauty, her scent, her laugh, her taste.

I realize in this moment that I never want to sober again. I want to be drunk on Camille until my dying breath.

When our kiss breaks, she gives me a smile that would've brought me to my knees had we been on solid ground.

With a deep breath, I grip onto the backpack strap, and without a second thought, we jump, our eyes on each other the entire time.

We free-fall through the sky, my heart galloping in my chest. We're falling fast, but it feels like we're in slow motion. The further down we go, the clearer my mind becomes.

The clearer it becomes that there's so much more to life that I want to experience.

It's been so long since I've been genuinely happy, but right now, I can say that without a doubt, I'm happy.

I tilt my head up toward the sky, close my eyes, and let the feeling of being weightless and free take over.

TWENTY-EIGHT

NOW

Camille

I can't explain my feelings while skydiving for the first time. Falling through the open sky makes me feel like I'm being reborn. It's the most exhilarating moment of my entire life. It's the most alive I've ever felt.

It's as if this entire time, I've been going through life barely existing, and now I'm here and have an entirely new level of appreciation for the life I've been given.

I don't want to disappear anymore. I want to live.

Life is full of experiences. Some cause us to change, while others don't, but without a doubt, I can say that this experience has changed me.

For the first time in a long time, I'm wide awake.

I choose life.

I choose happiness.

I choose myself.

I'm high on adrenaline. High on the feeling of my decision to live life unapologetically and high on the feeling of being reborn. It's because I feel so fucking good right now that leads me to jumping Dean as soon as we get back to his car.

After our jump, we didn't say anything. We went back into

the office to return our gear, and I took that time to slip into the restroom to change out of the ridiculous outfit I purchased at the gift shop and put my dress back on since I need to return to work.

But the second we both get back into his car, I pull my dress up to my waist and climb across the middle console to straddle him in his seat.

Thank God his windows are tinted because people would surely be getting a free show right now.

We don't speak. I know that we're both feeling the same thing right now. The lust darkening his eyes tells me everything I need to know. We both need this.

Dean makes quick work of undoing his pants, unzipping himself and exposing his rock-solid cock while I lift my dress higher and pull my little red thong to the side to expose my pussy that's glistening with my arousal.

I've been wet since we kissed before our jump—all it takes is one touch from him to get my panties flooded.

He strokes his fingers down the length of my cunt, hissing when he feels my arousal that's all for him.

"Is this all for me?" he taunts with a knowing look. I nod, grinding myself against his fingers.

"I can't wait. I need you right now," I rasp, so desperate for him. My entire body aches with an insatiable need for him. Need for him to stretch me and fill me so deep to the point I'm able to feel him in the back of my throat.

Leaning back against the steering wheel, I raise my hips, wrap my hand around his warm solid shaft, and guide him to my wet opening, slowly sinking down on his length, taking him inch by inch.

His cock fills me to the hilt, and only then do I lean forward and wrap my arms around his neck and crush my lips against his in a searing kiss. It's sloppy. Our teeth clatter against each other, but we don't have time to be graceful right now. We both need this dirty fuck.

His grip on my hips is so tight it's painful, and then he's lifting me so he can fuck me from the bottom.

And holy fuck does he.

Dean thrusts his hips up each time I move down. We work together, moving in perfect sync. The windows become foggy with our heavy, heated breathing, and the air in the car feels hot and sticky.

This position in his car isn't the most comfortable thing ever, but I don't need to be comfortable to take dick. I just need to be steady while I'm getting pounded.

Our skin slaps together, and my pussy sucks him in like the greedy thing she is. There's no good way to explain sex with Dean. It makes me stupid and speechless. It's fucking amazing! Hands down the best sex I've ever had.

Sure, my sex life with Declan is great. He's excellent, we have passion and great sex, but with Dean, it's simply out of this world. I shouldn't even be comparing the two, but I can't help it.

I don't want to go without this feeling again.

Dean was amazing our first time, but now that we're both experienced and know what we're doing, it's beyond my wildest dreams.

Unable to control myself, I let out a shamefully loud sound that's a mix between a cry and a moan.

"That's it, baby. Let me hear you, let me hear how badly you want this dick," Dean groans, kissing a wet trail down from my lips to the sensitive spot below my ear, where he nips and licks at it.

His thumb slips between our warm bodies to where we're conjoined, and he presses it against my clit, rubbing over the sensitive little bud.

I cry out, my head falls back, and my pace quickens, as does his. I'll have bruises from his grip on my hips again, but I don't care. I want his marks on me so I can reminisce later.

Dean's cock drags along my G-spot while his thumb rubs my clit viciously, my climax building quickly. I'm positive that he will have a sticky mess on his lap that'll need to be washed, and I like knowing that he'll be wearing my arousal for however long.

I'm slick with my wetness and can feel it dripping out of me and drenching his cock. I would've found it embarrassing if I weren't the type of person who enjoyed getting dirty during sex.

With one last flick of his thumb, I fall off the cliff edge I've been climbing and let my climax take over, soaking him even further. I scream my release just as he pounds into me one final time and stills, spilling his hot thick release into my pulsing pussy. His cum leaves me so full that I can feel it dripping out of me.

With a smirk, I adjust my dress and climb off his lap and back into the passenger seat.

"Take your panties off," he orders, his voice husky and eyes still full of lust despite just coming inside me.

I don't question him. I do exactly as he says and remove my panties, placing the damp fabric in his waiting palm.

With a smirk, Dean reaches over, spreads my thighs, and wipes me between my legs, showing me the panties that are now even further covered in my wetness and our joint climax. Heat creeps up my cheeks at the sight of the white cream on my red panties.

My eyes follow his movements closely as he places the damp fabric in his pocket before shoving his semi-hard cock into his briefs and zipping up. With one hand on my thigh, he brings his car to life and drives us away from the place that has forever changed me.

Later that night at home, I find a neon pink Post-it note in my purse from Dean.

You jump, I jump.

TWENTY-NINE

NOW

Camille

It's been two weeks since Declan went back to New York. Two weeks since we've last spoken, and one week that I've been spending a ridiculous amount of time with Dean.

Any chance we get, we're together.

We have lunch together daily and text nonstop about both business and pleasure. He's still staying at the hotel, and I've visited him there more than a few times for either a quick fuck during the day when we've been so horny we can't wait, or at night when he has time to ravage my body and explore it piece by piece thoroughly.

Nights with Dean are my favorite.

We talk about anything and everything, well, almost. There's one topic we avoid like the plague.

Our marriages.

That's a topic that neither of us is willing to touch with a ten-foot pole. It's a messy conversation waiting to happen, and I'm not foolish enough to think it'll never happen. I want to continue living ignorantly in our perfect bubble where no one can touch us, nothing bad can ever happen, and no one will get hurt.

That's inevitable, too.

My marriage is over; Declan and I both know it. As for Dean and Karina, I think he's the only one who's aware their marriage is over and is willing to accept it.

I don't know what he's told her, if he's yet to tell her that he wants out, all I know is that he promises a future with me. Only time will tell. Everything looks better at night when we're between the sheets and our minds are taken over with lust.

For example, right now.

Right now, I'm with Dean in his hotel room after a long and tiring day at work. It would feel weird bringing him to the condo I've shared with Declan. I just want to be around him, and this is where he is, so this is where I want to be.

At least the hotel suite is nice. It's located downtown, so it's near both of our offices and on the top floor, meaning a great view from the balcony, which is precisely where I'm at right now.

We just finished eating our room service dinner, and now we're both sitting on the balcony enjoying the view of our city while drinking an ice-cold beer.

It doesn't get better than this.

"So, baby, I was thinking." His husky sex-laced voice snaps me from my thoughts. I look at him with a smile, taking another drink from my beer bottle.

"Careful, don't hurt yourself thinking too hard," I say with a wink. Dean throws his head back and laughs.

God, I love hearing him laugh.

"You're a fucking smartass. I'm being serious here."

"Okay, fine, I'm listening. Talk to me." I set the beer bottle on the balcony table between our chairs and give him my full attention.

"We can't stay in his hotel room forever. So, it would be nice to have you come to my place and spend the weekend with me." Now it's my turn to laugh.

I know he's joking; he must be joking. Surely, he's not crazy enough to suggest something that fucking stupid. My eyes search his face for answers, looking for the slightest movement to indicate that he's joking and only trying to get a reaction out of me. But I come up short. He's not kidding. He's serious.

What the actual fuck?!

"Are you fucking crazy?"

"I'm serious, Cam. I'm checking out in the morning and going back home. I can't stay here any longer. I'm one night away from filling out a change of address form and becoming a permanent resident."

I stand and walk over to him, placing the back of my hand on his forehead.

"What are you doing?" he snaps.

"Checking to see if you have a fever. That would explain your ridiculous idea!" He swats my hand away and stands, his hands reaching out to grip my waist.

"I spoke with Karina a couple of days ago. She's going home to London in the morning and will be gone for about a week. It's my house, and I'm returning home." He says it so casually as if it's the most normal thing in the entire world that he just asked his mistress to come home with him while his wife is away. "I've asked her for a divorce, and when she returns home from her trip, I plan to begin the official process," he explains, as if that makes it any better.

I hate the M-word. It's so ugly and makes what we have seem so small and insignificant, and our relationship is anything but insignificant. But the bottom line is we're having an affair. We're cheating on our spouses, and I'm his mistress.

A woman is at home alone, wondering where her husband is, when he'll be coming back, and what they can do to save their marriage, and he's in a hotel room fucking someone else.

Me.

Regardless of us telling our spouses that it's over, it's still cheating. We're still having an affair.

I should feel guiltier than I do.

I did at first, but now, not so much.

I'm a bitch, and a horrible person, I know. Though I'm doing something I know is wrong, I can't stop because it feels too damn good.

"This is news to me." I wrap my arms around myself, tilting my head back to look up at him.

"She won't be there, so please, come home with me."

"No."

His face falls. "What? Why?"

"I'm not going to the house you share with your wife. No fucking way. Believe it or not, but I do have some morals." Maybe not enough morals to keep from cheating on my husband with a married man, but having an affair under his wife's roof is where I draw the line.

"She won't be there."

"I don't fucking care. The answer is still no." Placing my hands on his rock-solid chest, I push him away from me. "Dean, have you ever had an affair before? Even when you two were dating, did you ever cheat on Karina?" His eyes lower. He looks at me as if I offended him deeply by even asking the question. I'm sure the answer is no, but I still feel the need to ask. I have every right to, considering we're currently having an affair.

"No. I've never once cheated on my fucking wife," he dead-pans, his eyes narrowing into glaring slits. "I've never wanted anyone else until I saw you again."

I roll my eyes, unfolding my arms and moving them up to wrap around his neck. "You're ridiculous. We're ridiculous."

He shrugs, his lips curling into a grin that nearly makes me swoon. "You like it, though. You like the thrill of being together, and you like being with me."

Rolling my eyes, I lift my shoulders in a nonchalant shrug. "Eh, it's whatever. The sex is okay enough, so I stick around."

"Okay? Just okay?" he growls lowly, his lips crushing against mine in a painfully searing kiss. His hands grip my ass firmly. He picks me up and my legs automatically wrap around his waist.

Dean carries us inside the room, kicking the balcony door shut behind us, all the while his tongue dances with mine, never breaking our kiss. My grip around his neck tightens, and I cling to his tall, muscular body like a damn koala. I have this insatiable need to be closer to him, as close as I can possibly get.

We tongue fuck each other's mouths, and I press my core against his shirtless stomach, knowing he can likely feel the heat gathering between my legs.

We'd taken a shower together before dinner; he never put a shirt on, and I didn't put on pants. I'm wearing his gray T-shirt and a white lace thong, while Dean only wears gray sweatpants, sans boxer briefs. Bet if I were to look down, I'd be able to see his cock clear as day.

Once in the bedroom, he gently lays me in the middle of the plush bed and stares down at me with a mixture of darkness and lust in his eyes. His grip moves from my ass to my thigh, and he grips firmly, spreading them apart. I watch as his face contorts into pure lust.

Holy fuck. I'll never be able to get used to the way that Dean looks at me. He looks at me with such an intensity that it could literally set me on fire. He looks at me like I'm responsible for all the stars in the sky. Like I'm the reason that the most beautiful things in life exist.

He looks at me with love.

Arching my back, I waste no time gripping my shirt and removing it from my body. I love when he looks at me, but I need him to touch me right now. I need him to fuck me.

I take my heavy tits in my hands, squeezing, kneading, and rolling my nipples between my fingers. His gaze is focused on my hands, watching me play with my breasts and pebbled nipples.

"Dean," I groan, my back arching slightly off the bed from the feeling I'm bringing upon myself.

That small groan is enough to snap him into action. He makes quick work of removing his sweatpants and letting his big cock spring free and stand between his legs proudly.

Fuck.

His cock is a beautiful sight. I never thought a dick can be beautiful or perfect, but his sure as hell is. Dean standing in the nude before me makes me want to snap a picture of him and set it as my wallpaper so I can see him every time I use my phone.

"'What do you want, Camille?" The way he says my name sends a shiver down my spine and causes a flutter between my legs.

"I want you to touch me."

"Where?" I let go of my tits and remove my panties, spreading my legs and exposing my bare wet pussy to him.

He groans at the sight, his fist wrapping around his hard velvet shaft. "Touch yourself." I don't need to be told twice. I'm already aching for release.

Slowly, I trail my fingers down between my tits until I reach my pussy. My fingers circle my clit, my movements slow and teasing.

"I want your cock in my pussy, Dean. Fuck me until I can't walk and forget my name." He growls, fisting his hard cock from root to tip in what looks to be a painful grip.

"Don't worry, baby, I got you." With quick movements, Dean climbs on top of me and positions himself between my legs. He shifts his hips and drags his cock through my wetness, eliciting a groan of pleasure from us both. "Hold on, baby," he warns with a devious smirk.

His cock stretches through my entrance and fills me to the hilt with one hard thrust. He knocks the air from my lungs. It's both a perfect blend of pain and pleasure. He doesn't allow me any time to adjust to his size before he starts thrusting. He's a tight fit, and it's borderline painful, but it also feels so fucking good.

Luckily, it only takes a few thrusts for my body to adjust to Dean's massive cock being buried repeatedly inside my soft tissue. Not that it stops him from rocking his hips against me at a devilish speed. My nails sink into his back, leaving crescent moons in his flesh.

The soft light from the night moon shines through the

window and illuminates our bodies that are already adorned by sweat, causing us to glow together.

God help me; this is what I want for the rest of my life. To run my fingers over every inch of his skin and have my pussy filled with only Dean.

He grabs hold of my hips, pulls me close to him, then flips us over so he's lying flat on his back with me on top of his body, his throbbing cock still inside me.

His index finger curves under my chin, bringing me closer to him. A new fire ignites in his eyes, this time much darker and fiercer, almost demanding. "Start moving," he insists, voice deeper than before, filled with an ominous hint of that same darkness that also adorns his eyes. "I want to hear you say my name." I simper at his demand, a familiar ache returning to my stomach as I straddle him.

My hands grip his shoulders, and I slowly move my hips against his. With this position, he's right at my G-spot. Each time I grind my hips, he grazes my clit.

Circling my hips against his, I sit up straight and slowly raise myself, then slam back down, letting out a loud cry of pleasure.

Three drops later, I'm already on the verge of a climax, my sex squeezing his pulsing cock like a fist. It's so close that I can feel it.

I reach between our bodies and find my clit, rubbing it quickly to send myself over the edge. "Come for me," he demands, and right on cue, I do.

"Dean!" I scream, my climax sending me into another galaxy where I see stars. Dean tenses, his body becoming rigid. His hands grip my hips tightly as he thrusts up into me from the bottom, not allowing me to come down from my high and climax. He takes no mercy on me as he fucks me further into oblivion.

I gasp and scream, my release squirting out of my body and drenching him as he thrusts into my pulsing body, not caring that I just squirted all over him and soaked him and the bed.

Dean lets out a roar of his own as he stills, his eyes rolling into the back of his head, and I know he found a release of his own based on his expression.

Not even a second later, his hot, thick cum spurts into my tight core, and I take every drop he offers.

Every drop of his thick fluid.

I collapse onto his chest, my chest rising and falling rapidly as I struggle to calm my breathing. We stick together by the sweat on our bodies.

Dean wraps his arms around my body and kisses the top of my head, his cock still hard and inside my pussy.

"I'm not done with you yet." He groans in my ear, chills lining my body with the promise of more. He wastes no time flipping me onto my back and shoving himself back inside of me, leaving me breathless and overly sensitive. He throws my legs over his shoulders, grabs my hips in a bruising grip, and fucks into me until I scream, likely straining my vocal cords. I'll for sure be hoarse come morning.

I grip the sheets so hard my knuckles turn white and I arch my back, letting his name fall from my lips in a repeated scream. He pounds into me like a man possessed. Each deep thrust hits my G-spot, and it doesn't take long for the pressure to build in my belly again, especially when his thumb presses against my clit and he begins rubbing the sensitive bud, circling his thumb perfectly in sync with his thrusts.

Suddenly it's all too much. I'm falling off the edge I've been trying to hold on to, and yet another orgasm leaves me shaking and crying for God and mercy. Despite my pleas and throbbing sex, he doesn't stop. He continues rubbing my clit and pushing into me.

Each rough thrust pushes me farther onto the bed; my hands move to the headboard, and I weakly attempt to pull myself away from him but fail. He's much stronger than me and easily grips onto my hips and pulls me back toward him.

I'll likely be unable to walk in the morning, but that's a challenge I'm willing to accept.

My body shakes and thrashes around the bed, clawing at the

damp sheets beneath me, my voice raspy from my constant screams of pleasure, but he doesn't stop. Dean is determined to fuck himself into my brain so I'll never forget him, not that it would be possible anyway.

"Take it, Camille, take all of me." I don't realize that I'm crying until he leans closer to me and his warm tongue licks at the corner of my eyes, licking my tears away. The back of my thighs ache from the stretch. His weight is pressing them back against me with the way he's leaning toward me. My knees are nearly to my chin.

There's a burning sensation in my muscles, and if I weren't on the verge of passing out from too many orgasms, I'd laugh at how *not* flexible I am.

Luckily for me, he drops my legs from his shoulders and wraps them around his waist, his forearms on either side of my head caging me in. His thrusts remain consistent and punishing. Even as I claw his back to the point I know I'm drawing blood, he still doesn't stop or let up on me. I'm unable to hear the slap of his skin against mine because of my loud cries, but I can feel it.

"You're mine, Cam, all fucking mine," he grunts. "This pussy, your lips, your body. You're mine. Do you understand me? Or do I need to continue fucking you into submission?" My jaw drops, my mouth hanging open. I'm too stunned to speak, too out of my head to even think of anything to say.

With a smirk, Dean closes his lips and spits into my open mouth.

"Do you fucking understand?" he growls, beads of sweat dripping down onto my chest. Lifting my arms, I tangle my fingers in his damp hair and tug him closer to me, crushing my lips against his, swallowing the saliva.

My mouth is dry, our kiss is dry, and our lips stick together when he pulls away. We're a complete and total fucking mess.

My mouth may be dry, but at least my pussy is wet, and that's all that matters.

Instead of speaking, I nod frantically. He understands what I'm nodding about. He doesn't need me to say it.

I've never had sex so rough before, and now I don't know how I'd be able to survive without it. His head dips between us, as he sucks a nipple into his mouth, sucking and biting it so hard that it will leave a bruise.

"Oh fuck! I can't take anymore!" Finding my voice, I scream, my pussy fucking throbbing with another orgasm.

"Yes, baby, you can. Give it to me," he growls, the headboard hitting the wall with each thrust. Our skin sticks together where we're connected.

I love that I'm the one who's able to turn him into a wild animal.

His thumb finds my clit, and with one flick, I become dizzy while my orgasm takes over, causing temporary blindness.

"Fuck, fuck, fuck," he groans, the salty sweat from his forehead dripping onto my face and in my mouth. "I'm going to come in your pussy right fucking now," he says through gritted teeth, and true to his word, I feel his warm seed fill me yet again.

Dark spots cloud my vision, and his voice fades and becomes softer and softer, fading into the darkness.

I'm positive that I passed out from being fucked too hard because as soon as I come to, I realize I'm sitting between Dean's legs in a bathtub filled with warm water with no idea how I got here. His hand is under the surface between my legs, gently washing me with a washcloth. His touch isn't sexual. It's careful and caring, washing away the sweat that adorns my skin.

After our bath, Dean dries us off and carries me to bed, climbing into the sheets and holding me against his naked body, careful to avoid the massive wet spot we'd made on my side of the bed.

A content sigh leaves my lips. I'm so exhausted that I can barely think straight or keep my eyes open.

"It took us long enough to find our way back together," he whispers into the darkness of the room. I'm not fully able to comprehend what he's even saying. "I would do it all over again because the result is worth it. I've waited eleven years for you, Camille. I'm not letting you go this time, and I'm done waiting. From this point forward, you are mine."

"I've been yours since the day we met." My lips move on autopilot before my mind has a chance to catch up. With a sigh, I roll on my back. Our lips find each other in the dark and lock together like magnets. "Never let me go," I whisper against his warm lips, his arms wrapping around me protectively.

"Never," he promises, reclaiming my lips. "It's always been you. There's never been a moment in my life where it hasn't been you. You were born to be mine."

We fall asleep wrapped in each other, stealing kisses in the dark.

My heart is full for the first time in a long time, and I'm happy.

THIRTY

NOW

Camille

A few weeks ago, I had canceled my therapy sessions with Dr. Reynolds. I felt I no longer needed them, even though she insisted on it. She's been persistent, so when her assistant began calling me daily to insist I set up another appointment, I finally caved and scheduled an appointment. I figured I owed it to her to tell her face-to-face that I don't need her or the medication right now. I'm good, I'm happy, my mind is clear, and I don't want to go back to being foggy and numb.

I feel things, and I want to feel. Feeling is how I know I'm alive. Whatever the emotion is, I don't want to be numb to it. I fully stopped taking my medication the day I went skydiving with Dean, and I've never felt better. My mind is clear.

So, here I am, back in Dr. Reynolds's office for my regular Tuesday morning appointment.

In the entire year I've been seeing her, I don't think that I've ever made her speechless, but that's what she is right now after the bomb I just dropped.

Speechless.

Perhaps if I'd been a little more honest about my marriage in the past, she wouldn't be surprised with my news, but there's a lot about Declan that I've failed to mention in the past. For example, I've never told her that I've never been *in* love with him and always loved him like a best friend but never in the way a wife should love her husband.

I love him because he's the father of my child.

I love him because he makes me laugh and we're forever connected. What we share is truly an unbreakable bond.

Have I ever been in love with him and loved him with every ounce of my heart and fiber of my being? The answer is easy—no.

Love makes you feel insensible. It's messy and unapologetic and makes you feel weightless. Being in love is an extraordinary feeling. It's two souls coming together and becoming one.

Declan isn't the other half of my soul.

The truth is I found my missing puzzle piece when I was only eight years old.

I should've been honest with Dr. Reynolds all along, but there's nothing I can do about it now. No point in dwelling on the past.

"Are you certain this is what you want to do?" she asks, sitting a little straighter in her brown leather chair.

With a smile tugging at the corners of my lips, I nod. "It's been a long time coming, and I'm sure. I'm going to New York. It's the right thing to do."

"Be careful, Camille. You don't want to rush into anything you will regret later."

"Don't worry, doc. I'm doing what feels right, and this feels right. I know that I'm making the right decision." I'm aware the timeline looks a little suspicious with Dean coming back into my life, and now I'm ready to get a divorce, but honestly, the decision has nothing to do with Dean. This is the right thing to do. I know it is. Declan and I both need to let each other go. We're not right for each other.

I decide not to tell her I went off my meds, too worried she might blame my sudden mood change on the fact I'm no longer medicated. I also don't bother mentioning the fact my meds didn't work as they should. I know I promised Spencer I'd talk to Dr. Reynolds, but some promises are okay to break.

At the end of our session, I inform her that I won't be back. She wishes me luck and tells me that she'll be here should I ever need her again in the future.

I hope I won't, but just in case, I keep her number in my favorites in my contact list.

I've told one person about my life-changing decision, now it's time to tell my family my news and hope like fucking hell they'll be as accepting as Dr. Reynolds is.

"Hey, sis!" Spencer beams the moment I sit down at the table across from her at our favorite Mexican restaurant. As soon as my appointment ended, I'd texted her and asked her to meet me here for lunch. I've been locked up in Dean's hotel room for the past week. I've been neglecting my sister, so sister time is very needed right now. Especially with the bomb I'm about to drop.

"Thanks for coming, Spence. I missed you."

She rolls her eyes, takes a tortilla chip from the basket on the table, and dips it into the salsa. "Perhaps if you stopped having so much sex and came up for air once in a while, you could reply to a text so I know you're okay." She shoves the salsa-covered chip into her mouth.

Her comment catches me off-guard, but I shrug it off. "I'm sorry my communication skills suck. I'll work on it."

"Yeah, yeah. Anyway, what's up? I know you need to tell me something, so spill." She sits back in her seat, her brown eyes narrowing as she studies me slowly from head to toe, her eyes zoning in on my stomach. "Are you pregnant? Is that what you're about to tell me?"

Now it's my turn to roll my eyes. I roll them so dramatically it's a good chance they'll get stuck in the back of my head. "Fuck no." She laughs.

"Well, what is it then?"

"I'm going to New York for a couple of days," I say casually, reaching forward to get a chip.

"Why? Is there a work issue?" Shit. I realize now that I haven't told my sister that Declan went back to New York. Damn, my communication lately really does suck.

Wait... if she thinks Declan is still here, then maybe she thinks that's who I'm having sex with. She doesn't know that Dean and I are still involved.

"No, I'm going to see Declan. He went back to New York." I inhale slowly, preparing to share my news with the second person today. "We're getting a divorce." Her eyes widen, and her opens, revealing her chewed-up chip.

"What. The. Fuck," she whisper-yells, chewing her food and washing it down with a large gulp of water from her glass. "Tell me that I misheard you."

I shake my head. "We've separated, but I'm flying out tomorrow to see him and tell him I want a divorce, not a separation. Plus, I need to check in and see how my New York office is doing anyway, so I kill two birds with one stone." I shrug my shoulders.

"How are you so calm right now? You're leaving your husband, and you act as if it's just another day. What's your plan, little sis?" She sits back in her chair, her arms crossing over her chest and eyes narrowing on me. "Leave Dec and get with Dean? Is that your plan? Is he leaving his wife?"

"Oh my fuck, Spencer, Dean has nothing to do with my decision," I snap, rolling my eyes. "You know Declan and I have been rocky for a while. You knew this would happen one day. I've talked to you about this before."

"You mentioned divorce briefly years ago. How was I supposed to know that you've still been considering it? I knew you two were having problems, but I didn't know he left and that you separated." She sighs, looking at me with disapproval. "I don't think he's in a good enough place right now for you to spring a divorce on him. What if he relapses? He just got out of rehab, for crying out loud." My sister has always been understanding and seen my side on any decision I've ever made, so honestly, I'm a little surprised by her reaction. She knows how rocky my marriage has been, how shaky it's been since the day we said our vows.

This shouldn't be a surprise.

"You don't know him like I do. He knows it's coming; I've already told him I want one. That's why he went back to New York. I may be the one cutting the final string, but he's not going to be blindsided. Please support me, Spence. I need your support on this."

"Does he know that you slept with Dean? Is that why you're leaving him? Perhaps it's your guilt?" Her words confirm my suspicion. She has no idea I'm still fucking Dean. "It was only that one time, right?" I stay silent, not wanting to lie any more than I already have.

"Camille, it was only that one time, right?" she asks again, sitting up straighter. I chew on my bottom lip nervously, unable to meet her eyes. "Are you fucking kidding me?!" she hisses. "You're having an affair with a married man?" I know her feelings on the topic, and I haven't wanted her judgment—the judgment I see in her eyes right now.

Shaking her head, she scoots her chair back. "Your silence is my answer. I need to get back to work. Have a safe flight, Camille, and I hope you know what you're doing. But don't be surprised when Dean stays with his wife and doesn't choose you. It's not going to end well, and I'm sorry, but I can't be the shoulder for you to cry on when it all crashes and burns." She stands, grabbing her purse. "Don't call me for a while. I need some time." Without another word, she walks away, breaking my heart with every step.

My sister is my best friend. No matter what I've done over the years, she's never turned her back on me, walked away from me, or denied me when I needed her. Even if I was making a stupid decision, she still supported me and was there for me whether my plans failed or were a success. She's always been a phone call away.

Now she's turning her back on me and doesn't want any part of my plan. My chest aches. I've never experienced my sister turning her back on me before. But I should've known it would be too much for her.

I know Spencer's views on affairs. I was there for her every time she was cheated on in the past by several boyfriends. My sister hasn't had any luck in her adult life when it comes to dating. The longest relationship she's had was with Dallas in high school, and I still don't know why they broke up. Spencer doesn't have sex with strangers. She likes to take her time and get to know the man, and the men she's dated weren't interested in waiting for sex, so they cheated. After the third time being cheated on, she practically gave up on dating. Now, instead of going out and looking for love, she spends all her free time at her art gallery.

As for me, I have zero remorse for sleeping with another woman's husband.

What kind of person am I? What kind of person sleeps with another woman's husband and doesn't give two fucks?

Dean stood at the altar and made vows to this woman, vows to love and protect her, to cherish her and be faithful to her.

I made those same vows to my husband.

My marriage may be failing and nearly over, but that doesn't make what we've done okay. I'm a piece of shit, and so is Dean. And we're doing a very shitty thing and hurting two people who don't deserve to be hurt.

Can I stop? Do I want to stop?

Honestly, no. I don't, because I love him. I've always loved him. Even though he's not mine to love anymore, I still want him.

We've never discussed what would happen if he leaves Karina, same as we've never discussed what happens after me leaving Declan, but I think it's time we have that conversation. As soon as I get back from New York, we will need to sit down and have a serious conversation. There's no way we can continue with what we're doing. We owe it to ourselves to make a decision.

Either be together for good, or let each other go, but no more in between. I can't do it anymore. I'm trying to move on with my life, and being in bed with a married man isn't allowing me to move forward.

As much as I love him, I must choose myself.

After leaving the restaurant, I go straight back to my office just in time for my meeting with Sadie. I've previously told her about my ideas for modern theme décor, and she's been working hard to fulfill my exact vision.

Our meeting today is to review the final designs so she can begin ordering furniture, since some items will take a few months to arrive. Everything needs to be completed by the time I'm ready to open, so the final decision must be completed today.

Sadie has always been on time for every meeting, so when there's a knock on my office door, I don't bother getting up; instead, I yell for her to come in.

"I'm a genius, and you must see this. I've got everything completed." I appreciate the fact she doesn't waste time with small talk. She always gets straight to the point.

If you would've told me years ago that Sadie fucking Marshall, my freshman year bully, would be my interior designer, I likely would've laughed in your face and flipped you off.

Thank fuck people can change.

Sadie walks across my office toward my desk and holds her iPad out, showing me the 3D designs she'd been working on.

She'd worked with Dean's blueprints and his 3D design to show me what my building will look like once it's completed.

Inside the virtual 3D building, she'd decorated each room and is now giving me the virtual tour and showing me room by room what it will look like. She's taken all the furniture and items we'd discussed and decorated the rooms to show exactly how it'll look.

I can no longer say anything bad about her because holy damn. She captured my vision perfectly, and now I'm fucking speechless. She's captured everything I've ever envisioned, and seeing it all in 3D in front of me is a surreal experience.

My vision is coming to life, and I couldn't be more blessed and prouder of myself for making this happen. I've always loved drawing various clothing items and knew I'd be a fashion designer one day, but it still seems surreal that I'm living my childhood dream.

Childhood me would be fucking proud right now.

"Wow, this is incredible." If she weren't here right now, I'd surely be shedding a few tears. Yes, I have my New York office where my company was founded, but I didn't build that building from the ground up like I'm building my Seattle location.

"It is, isn't it?" Being humble has never been her strong suit. She's good at her job, and she knows it. "So, shall I go ahead and submit the order? The couch for your office will take about four months to arrive." I nod, watching as she clicks away on her iPad to bring up a new screen, showing what the total will be.

We're thirty thousand over budget, which she told me previously, but I'm willing to accept it because I want the best. If I must cut into personal funds and eat ramen for a while, that's fine. It's worth it to have my dream location finally come to life.

"Go ahead and submit the order. The price is fine." I sign for it, confirming my approval of the price and the items she will order.

"Perfect! I'll submit the order once I get back to my office and email you the final confirmation details. We'll be in touch." With a wave, she leaves my office as quickly as she arrived.

For the remainder of the day, I busy myself with my management team from my New York office and the HR team, discussing my need for employees to fill my Seattle location. I permit my office manager to upload the job posting, and she agrees to send me the applications she likes since I want a personal say in who will be hired, and who I'll be working with daily. I have a few employees in New York who want to transfer to Seattle, so that, along with hiring new staff to ensure both locations are fully staffed, will be a long, stressful process. But I work best when under pressure. And at this point, being stressed is just part of my daily routine.

Clearly, another part of my daily routine is ignoring Dean because I don't respond to one single text message or call for the entire day.

It's important for me to go to New York with a clear head, and in order to do that, I need to put some distance between myself and Dean. I can't be thinking about him while I'm having my conversation with Declan and having contact with him will indeed fuck with my head.

Perhaps I should reply to him and at least let him know I'll be out of town... okay, one text won't hurt. At least that'll stop him from texting me and worrying.

THIRTY-ONE

NOW

DEAN

Camille texted me last night saying she was going to New York for business. Since then, every call has gone straight to voicemail, and none of my texts are showing as delivered. It's Wednesday now, and I still haven't heard a word from her. I'm not worried, of course. She probably had her phone off while traveling, and she's likely in meetings. Of course she doesn't have time to talk to me, but that doesn't stop me from thinking about her and instantly checking my phone every time it beeps, hoping it's her.

Unfortunately, none of the messages I've been getting are from her. They're all from one person.

My wife.

Karina has been calling nonstop since she went home to London last week. As soon as she left, I went home. Spending the weekend home alone allowed me time to think about both the women and the relationships in my life. I realize how fucked up and wrong I was by asking Cam to spend the weekend with me in the house I share with Karina. She was right to reject me. Who the fuck wouldn't?

Why did I even fucking ask?

She went home the next morning, and besides endless texts

319

and a few calls, we haven't seen each other much. We went from spending every night for over a week together to not being together. I know a few days isn't that long, but when you have the love of your life back in your life after eleven years of separation, any time apart feels like an eternity.

I'm becoming pussy-whipped, thanks to her.

Karina got home last night, and like the coward I am, I stayed the night at my office, unwilling to go home and face her. Not willing to face my wife since I dropped her off at the airport last week.

We've spoken briefly while she's been away, but for the most part, I've avoided her phone calls. When we did speak, it was a short, probably less than a five-minute phone call; it was mainly Karina asking me not to leave, telling me that she loves me, and thinking if she gets pregnant, then we'll be happy and magically our marriage will be repaired.

I've been great with excuses and getting her off the phone. Now that she's home, I can't avoid her any longer.

In fact, that's where I'm going now.

Home.

I can't sleep another night in my office, and I can't stay at any more hotels. So, I'm going home. Home to face my wife like a grown-up. Home to make her come to terms with the fact I want a divorce and I'm not changing my mind.

Pulling into the garage beside Karina's car, I allow myself a moment of silence to be by myself and have peace.

I never get silence anymore. I'm reminded of what a piece of shit I am every single day I wake up—not to mention what a horrible husband I am. Since I've been waking up with a woman who isn't my wife, my guilt has been eating me alive, as it should be. I'm hit with a wave of guilt every time I open my eyes in the morning, but the moment Camille looks up at me with a sleepy smile and those intoxicating green eyes, I become numb to my guilt and lose myself all over again.

One look. All it takes is one single look for my entire existence to fall into place and make sense. She's my anchor, the one person who can make me smile despite all the shitty things I've done.

I never wanted to be this person. It's not like I set out to have an affair and totally ruin my wife. This wasn't planned, but fuck me, what do I do when the person I've always been in love with isn't the woman I married?

Lying makes me sick. No matter how ugly the truth has been, I've never been a liar. I've always prided myself on being honest, a good man like my father, and look at me now.

Now I'm someone my father would be ashamed of; someone I don't even recognize. I'm disgusting. I'm a bastard. I'm a fucking scum.

My internal badgering doesn't last very long before Karina interrupts me.

The passenger door opens, and my wife climbs into the seat beside me, a heavy breath escaping her parted lips. I turn my head to look at her. She mirrors me, and we just sit there staring at each other for a while.

"Why haven't you come inside yet?" I don't answer her immediately, instead, I allow myself a chance to look at her. To *really* look at her. Her blonde hair is down and hangs around her shoulders, and she looks smaller than usual. Her collarbones are more prominent, her jawline sharper, a sign that she's lost an unhealthy amount of weight. Dark circles reside under her eyes, her face free from any makeup.

She looks vulnerable, a look that I haven't seen in years. Her appearance is like a knife to the chest. I've done this to her. I've sucked the life and love from this beautiful woman. While I've been going behind her back, she's been making herself sick, likely trying to figure out where I am, what I've been doing, and how she can try and fix us.

I've been fucking someone else; that's what I've been doing.

"Karina," I whisper, unsure what to say or do, but I reach across for her hands and take them into mine. "Look at you." Raising her hands to my lips, I kiss each of her cold knuckles. As much as it guts me that our distance has taken a toll on her, I still can't be with her. Not anymore.

We're over.

"I've missed you, Dean, so much." A sob gets caught in her throat, her eyes turning glossy with unshed tears. If I'm being honest, I'm not entirely sure how to act. Karina doesn't show emotion. I'm seeing a side of her that she keeps hidden away. She doesn't allow herself to be vulnerable when it comes to me, and I've never been able to figure out why. She's always been the greatest mystery.

"Don't cry. I'm here now, and we need to have a serious conversation." Reaching up, I wipe away the tears streaming down her fragile face.

"I've been trying to talk for weeks, but you never want to be around me or be at home with me."

"Let's go inside, and we'll talk." Her appearance guts me. She's too beautiful to be dragged down and turned into a ghost of herself because of me, because I made a careless decision.

I follow her into our house, which has never felt like home. Perhaps subconsciously I knew that something life-changing would happen between us when we moved to Seattle, and that's why I never even tried to make our place a home. I didn't care about unpacking or filling the house with pictures and knick-knacks. I didn't care about any of it.

Maybe this is the reason why. My subconscious knew that our ending was inevitable.

Karina enters the kitchen and begins preparing herself a cup of tea. We're both silent, and for a moment, I wonder if she knows what I'm about to say. She agreed that we need to talk, so I wonder if she's thinking the same thing I am. That we've reached our expiration date.

We've reached our ending.

"Karina," I begin, prepared to tell her that I'm packing my bags and officially moving out because I do want a divorce, and I'm done avoiding it.

She places her hand up to silence me.

"Let me speak first, Dean. Please." I nod, waving my hand toward our dining room table. I lead the way, and she follows behind, carrying her cup of tea. We take a seat at the large white marble dining table that has never once been used but cost me a small fortune. I sit at one end, and she sits at the other. Somehow the space between us feels right.

"I know our marriage has been rocky lately, and we're going through a rough patch, but I know we'll be able to make it through. We've been here before, and we overcame our issues and ended up stronger than ever." A hopeful smile curls at the corner of her pink lips.

My chest feels heavy. We're not on the same page, and she's not saying what I thought she would say. Stupidly, I had thought she would agree that we needed to spend more time apart—this time for good.

Of course we're not on the same page. Have we ever actually been on the same page about anything before?

I tune her out, and even though I see her lips moving, I can't hear a single word she says. Not until she says those two words that I never want to hear again. Those two words that suck the air from my lungs and nearly cause me a heart attack.

"What did you just say?" I snap, more forceful than needed to be.

With a wide smile and glossy eyes, Karina says the one thing that cements me to our marriage, the same way it did years ago.

"I'm pregnant, Dean."

THIRTY-TWO

THEN

CAMILLE, 22 years old

"Riot! Riot! Riot!" the crowd chants, everyone around me just as eager as I am to see Riot perform live. For fucking months, I have wanted to see my favorite band live, but it never worked out with school. I was never able to take the time to travel out of state to see them.

They haven't played a show in their home state of New York in a while. When they announced they'd be having a show here, I was online the exact second the tickets went on sale.

Unfortunately, they were sold out within minutes of them going on sale.

When I saw the site reload and show *sold out* two minutes later, I felt utterly murderous. I don't want for much or ask for anything, but I badly wanted this.

I was lying on my bed wallowing in self-pity when Tyler called me and told me she had three tickets to Riot and was taking me and our other friend, Bree. The three of us met our first year of college and have been inseparable ever since.

I didn't know how the fuck Tyler managed to get tickets, but I wasn't questioning it. All I knew was she scored tickets and we were going.

That's how the three of us ended up here.

I turned twenty-two not long ago, and we just graduated less than a week ago. Soon we'll have to grow up and take on adult responsibilities, so being here with my two best friends and watching our favorite band perform seems like the best way to celebrate graduation and one last night of fun before I start my new job on Monday morning.

The venue is general admission only—and crazy packed. We're all standing shoulder to shoulder, bodies bumping into each other and stepping on each other's feet, but I wouldn't have it any other way. I've been to a few concerts before, but never anything like this.

The lights dim and the crowd goes wild, erupting in cheers and chants. I watch in total shock as the stage lights up and the music starts. I recognize the song just from the drum opening alone. It's the first song they ever performed live. "Rockstar."

The moment I hear his voice, my face lights up with excitement, and I lose myself to the music and the thrill of getting to experience something I've wanted to experience for the longest time.

Declan Valentine, the lead singer of Riot, is hands down one of the most attractive men I've ever laid my eyes on. He's tall and built and standing on the stage shirtless, which allows me to see just how muscular he is. I'm so close to the stage that I can see the veins in his forearms and how his muscles flex from his grip on the microphone.

He's pure sex on legs. He's not the man you bring home to meet your parents. He's the man you call to finish you off when the guy you brought home to meet your parents was unable to make you come.

When Declan smirks, he reminds me of the devil himself, promising to do something sinful. And I'm ready to sin.

That thought, along with all the tequila shots I consume, gives me the courage to go backstage with Tyler and Bree after the show ends. Tyler somehow got us backstage even though they weren't selling backstage passes.

Honestly, I think she blew the security guard to get us here, but I'm standing in the presence of the one and only Declan *fucking* Valentine, so I don't care what she did or who she had to blow.

Hell, I'd eat her out just to show my appreciation.

My hands tremble as I trail my fingers up my left arm and pinch it to ensure I'm not dreaming. Luckily for me, this is real life. This is really happening.

Brown eyes stare me down from behind a cloud of smoke as if I'm a piece of meat in front of a starved man. I gulp, my skin feeling like it's on fire.

Tyler and Bree are on the musty green couch across the room, spread across the lap of two men I recognize as members of the band, Adam and Miles.

My eyes trail from theirs back to the intoxicating brown eyes that belong to Declan, the man who's currently making my panties wet just by looking at me.

He's sitting on a torn brown leather couch, his long legs spread wide, eyes on mine, and a burning joint between his plump lips. He remains shirtless, his tattoo-covered chest on full display.

"Are you going to continue standing there giving me those fuck me eyes or are you going to come and get what you want?" he challenges, raising his eyebrow.

Cocky motherfucker.

My legs tremble as I walk toward him. A moment of hesitation washes over me. It's not like I'm a prude or unfamiliar with sex. I've had plenty in college. But never with a man like the one sitting in front of me. I've had sex with young, inexperienced boys, and Declan is anything but an amateur. He's all man, and if I'm not careful, I know that he'd be able to consume me entirely and drown me to the point the only person I see is him.

Finding my inner strength and giving myself a quick pep talk,

I walk toward him until I'm standing in front of him, suddenly feeling bare and exposed.

I'm wearing shorts that are swallowed by my thick golden thighs and accentuate my peachy ass. I've paired them with a ripped Riot T-shirt that's tied under my large breasts, exposing my midsection.

I feel I could be dressed as a nun and I'd still feel too exposed.

Declan looks at me with pure heated lust; his gaze sets my skin on fire, a feeling I've only ever felt once before.

I watch, frozen in front of him, as he takes a long hit from the joint and passes it to one of the four people sitting on the couch. I'm not sure which one takes it since I can't take my eyes away from him.

Holding the smoke in his lungs, he grips my waist firmly and pulls me down onto his lap. My legs stretch to accommodate his large build as I straddle him.

Declan thrusts his fingers into the back of my hair, gripping it firmly and pulling me toward him. My lips automatically part and eyes close, my stomach doing flips and full of butterflies.

His lips barely brush against mine as he blows the smoke into my mouth. He exhales, and I inhale.

Just as I exhale the smoke, his lips are on mine, and his tongue is thrusting into my mouth. He tastes like weed and mint, and I decide right here and now that it's my new favorite flavor.

He pulls away from my mouth long enough to look toward our friends on the couch. "Get the fuck out!" he roars, and thank fuck, they don't need to be told twice.

They leave us alone, slamming the door on the way out.

His mouth is back on mine, and we lose ourselves in a tangle of limbs, mouths, and heated breaths.

That night, in that dingy backstage room, Declan fucks me, forever claiming a part of me.

I'm so high on orgasms and the man giving me said orgasms that I don't deny him when he asks me to come with him to his next show in Los Angeles.

Like a fucking lunatic, I agree to travel cross country with a stranger.

The moment Tyler told me about the tickets to see Riot, I knew my life would change. It was just a feeling I had, but holy shit, I was right.

My life changed that night, just not how I could've ever expected.

Little did I know that nine months later, I'd be married and welcoming a son into the world.

THIRTY-THREE

NOW

Camille

I'm anxious the entire flight to New York. My nerves don't ease up any while on the taxi ride to the penthouse I share with Declan, either. I thought that I'd be angry or sad, but all I feel is contentment. I'm content with my decision to divorce Declan—and honestly, I'm eager. It has been a long time coming. We both deserve to be set free. I can't pinpoint an exact moment in our marriage when it all went wrong and I realized I wanted out. All I know is that's how I feel and I refuse to keep ignoring it. Perhaps I've always secretly known that our time together was limited, but I wanted to keep my family together.

Our son having a two-parent household was more important to me than my happiness.

I wasn't always miserable.

Were there plenty of times when I felt held back and unhappy? Yes.

But all it took was one look at my beautiful son's smiling face and that had me willing to push everything else out of my mind and ignore all the red flags in my marriage.

Instead of talking things out like any mature and healthy

couple should, Declan and I fucked until we couldn't remember why we were even fighting. It was the same routine, fucking and fighting.

Luca never witnessed us fighting; he didn't need to see his parents yelling at each and saying nasty things in the heat of the moment.

We tried to fuck our problems away without ever actually communicating. Obviously, it never worked. We were so young when we got married. It was a good decision then, but now, ending it is the right decision.

I know that Declan is aware this is coming, but I cannot drop that bombshell on him over the phone. He deserves me telling him face-to-face.

Maybe I'll be ambushing him by not telling him I was coming, but I hadn't wanted to call him and warn him that I'm coming, only for him to answer the phone under the influence. He's been doing good so far with his recovery, yet he's still so delicate.

If I were a decent person, I'd probably wait until he was in a better place before asking him for a divorce, but I think by now, we've already established I'm not a decent person. Besides, I've waited long enough. It's time.

My marriage was falling apart long before Dean returned, long before we lost Luca, and I've only been delaying the inevitable. I'm ending my marriage for myself. I want to feel happy again. Getting out of a marriage that mentally drains me every day will be best for me and make me happy.

I didn't tell Dean the real reason I had come to New York, only that I needed to check on my business. He doesn't need to know, not yet. I'll tell him once I return home.

The elevator dings, the doors slide open, and the smile I've been wearing fades the moment I step into the living room of the penthouse. I haven't been back here since I moved back home two weeks after the accident. The day we laid our baby boy to rest in the ground was the day that I packed everything I could and flew to Seattle. Declan stayed behind for two weeks to get his affairs in order with the band, and by the time he joined me in Seattle, I'd had our new condo already set up for us.

It's like stepping into a time machine and getting hit with a blast from the past.

My chest tightens as memories consume me. Everything is the same, and memories come flooding over me. The living room where Luca took his first steps, the kitchen where he said his first words while throwing his breakfast at me.

Tears sting my eyes.

God only knows how much I miss my baby boy. Living without him is like being unable to breathe, like my head is being held underwater, and I'm being forced to drown repeatedly. I can't get a deep enough breath.

Never would I wish this pain on even my worst enemy. The loss of a child is a pain no parent should ever bear. No parent should ever outlive their child. I spent months and months being angry at God for taking my son. Why him and not me? He was only four. He had his whole life ahead of him. I had lived my life, and I got to grow up and had plenty of experiences.

Experiences that he'll never have. For a year, I'd been so angry, looking for anyone to blame when there was no one to blame. It was a tragic accident.

I'm stuck in place, gripping the back of the couch, trying to remember what it feels like to breathe and have a heartbeat.

That's when I hear it.

The grunting, the moaning, the breathless words.

What the fuck?

Wiping the tears from my face with the back of my hand, I walk down the long hallway, my steps silent against the plush cream carpet. With a hand on the doorknob of my former bedroom, I open the door slowly.

The first thing I see is the bare back of a petite naked redhead on top of him. Her hair is fire hydrant red; clearly, it's not natural.

Declan lies on his back, his hands gripping the woman's hips as he digs his heels into our mattress, thrusting into her body. He grunts as his eyes meet mine, his eyes widening in complete shock at the sight.

Sure, I wish that I had a camera right now to capture his deer in the fucking headlights expression.

The fake redhead is too busy riding my husband's cock to realize they're not alone in the room anymore.

Without a word, I close the door and walk back down the hallway and into the new kitchen we'd remodeled just weeks before the accident.

How fucked up is it that I don't even care about what I just saw? I've just found my husband with his dick in someone else and I'm not even angry. I only hope that, for his sake, he's wearing a condom.

Even if I could muster a feeling, it wouldn't be hurt. I have no right to feel betrayed when I've been doing the same thing. We're separated, and I'm also sleeping with someone else.

Removing my coat, I hang it over a barstool in front of the island and remove my heels. I tie my black hair back into a pony-tail and scavenge the fridge for the items I need to make a sand-wich. I haven't eaten since last night and I'm starving; my growling stomach proves that.

I've just taken my first bite when the redhead comes running from the hallway toward the elevator, Declan hot on her heels, cursing under his breath. She looks at me, her eyes just as wide as his, and thankfully she doesn't say anything. She steps into the elevator and leaves silently.

It took them long enough to dress and get out here.

I wonder if they finished or not.

Declan's remorseful brown eyes meet mine, his dark brows pulling together, clearly surprised to see me sitting on the island eating a bologna sandwich.

"Oh my God, Camille, baby girl, I'm so sorry. I'm so fucking sorry."

"Sorry that you got caught, or sorry for moving on so quickly?" I ask, genuinely curious about what his answer will be. With a sigh, I swallow the remainder of my sandwich and chew it. "Is she the first you've been with since our separation?"

He nods. "Yes, I swear it." His head hangs in shame. I know he's telling me the truth. With a sigh, I hold out my second sandwich to him.

"Eat. I bet you're hungry." His head snaps up, and his eyes look ready to pop out of his head. "What?" I feign innocence, shrugging my shoulders.

"Why aren't you yelling?"

"Is that what you want? Me to get angry?"

"I want a fucking reaction from you!" he yells, throwing his arms in the air. He may want me to get angry, but I can't give him the reaction he's looking for. I'd be a hypocrite if I were to be mad over something I'm also guilty of.

Instead of saying anything else, I offer him the sandwich again. Of course, he doesn't attempt to take it, so I shrug my shoulders as if to say your loss and bite into it.

"Say something!" he snaps.

"Sit down, Declan. We can discuss this without getting into a screaming match."

He stares at me, his brown eyes becoming black as darkness takes over his features. The look that passes over his handsome face is a look that I know all too well. His anger is taking over, and he's getting upset that I'm not reacting as he wants me to.

"Fucking say something, Camille!" he screams like a child throwing a tantrum. In a flash, he grabs the island barstool and throws it against the wall, the wood shattering into pieces and falling to the floor with a thump.

Declan stands in front of me with a storm brewing in his eyes and his chest rising and falling rapidly with his heavy breathing. Neither of us moves right away; we remain staring at each other as if we're strangers and unsure how to respond after his outburst.

Except we're not strangers, and this isn't his first outburst. It's

Declan, and I know how to handle him. Regardless of why I came here and how I feel about being married to him, he's still my best friend, and I love him, and I hate seeing him battling himself the way he does.

"Dec," I whisper, hopping off the counter and taking a step toward him. He's stiff but doesn't stop me when I wrap my arms around his waist and hug him so tight that I wish it were enough to fix all his broken pieces and glue them back together.

Declan cups my face, his thumb brushing over my bottom lip, his eyebrows pulling together in a scowl as he studies me, and I wish desperately that I knew what was going through his mind right now to cause him to look at me the way he is.

"What are you doing here?" he asks.

"Now is probably not the time to discuss it."

"Why are you here, Camille? Answer me." I remain silent. Does he really not know why? How can he not?

Staring deep into his hazy eyes, a knot forms in the pit of my stomach telling me he's using again, but I don't want to ask him in fear that he'll be honest, and his answer will be one that I don't want to hear.

I roll my teeth over my lips, clamping them shut to keep me from saying something I'll regret.

"Fuck, Camille," he whispers so lowly that I almost miss it. "You shouldn't have come here." He presses his lips against my forehead, then attempts to pull away, fighting against me when I tighten my grip around his waist.

"Declan. Sit and calm down, and then we'll talk."

"Not right now." He pries my hands away from him, turning on his heel and walking toward the elevator, me following behind him.

"Declan! What the fuck? You're not going anywhere."

"Camille, stop talking. I can't hear your voice right now."

Yet again, history repeats itself, and he leaves when the going gets tough. We're like oil and water; we don't belong together.

Declan leaves me standing in the foyer of our penthouse with my mouth hanging open and a feeling in my stomach that's urging me to follow him, but my feet are heavy and rooted to the ground.

This time, I let him go.

I'VE PACED THE LIVING ROOM SO MANY TIMES THAT IF I PACE anymore, I'll wear a hole into the carpet. It's been nearly four hours since Declan left, not that I'm counting or anything. I've called him close to twenty times and left voicemails each time, begging him to come back home so we can talk like mature adults. I've texted him a ridiculous number of times asking for the same thing. He hasn't replied, but they've all been delivered, so I know his phone is still on.

Not that I'm proud of it, but I also tried to track his phone, but the fucker turned off his *Find my iPhone*, so that was a dead end.

After calling him again and leaving yet another voicemail, I throw my phone onto our plush gray couch with a soft thud, letting out a frustrated huff. I don't know what I expected to happen when I showed up here unannounced, ready to ask for a divorce, but this sure as hell wasn't it.

Without my phone glued to my hand, I allow myself to look around our penthouse, a place that holds so many memories between the three of us. We bought it when Luca turned one. He was about to start walking, and we needed more space. I'd spent my entire pregnancy touring with Declan, going to every show in every state and country the band traveled to. After the performances, he partied with the band, and I'd take my pregnant self back to our hotel and put my degree to use by working on my business plan and sketches.

I was seven months pregnant when Sinful Pleasures was launched. At the time, I only had a handful of clothing items, and they were only available online. I'm fortunate enough to have my family's support; my father is a significant reason I was able to quickly start my business and grow it to be as successful as it is. He backed me financially and connected me with other investors willing to take a chance on me because of their friendship with my father.

When we weren't touring, we lived in a small studio apartment in Queens. It wasn't until Luca was born that I told Declan we'd need more space. Even though I was usually home alone with Luca while Declan toured, it was still cramped for the two of us. When Dec was home, the space was even smaller.

We spent a year in that tiny studio apartment with a baby, eating ramen and saving every penny to purchase our dream home one day. Riot was becoming increasingly popular by the day, and luckily, we were in a better place financially and able to buy our Manhattan penthouse, giving Luca the space he needed to run around and have his very own bedroom and playroom.

We lived here for three years, and these walls have seen everything. The fights, the tears, the laughs, the good, the bad, and the ugly. I love it here.

I *loved* it here.

I stopped loving it when my baby boy died, and it no longer felt like a home. It became quiet and cold, missing the warmth of love.

It's been over a year since I've been here, it's hard to be here, and now that I'm here alone, I realize how difficult it is.

I'm not sure how or when, but my legs carry me down the hallway and to the one bedroom that has been closed for over a year.

I'm standing outside of his bedroom, with my hand on the doorknob, giving myself a mental pep talk to be able to open the door and go inside.

With a deep breath, my trembling fingers open the door with a creak, and my weak legs carry me inside his room.

Luca's bedroom.

The room is exactly as we left it that day, so I know that

Declan hasn't been in the room either. Unwelcome tears stream down my face, and there in the middle of the room, I drop to my knees, my hands covering my mouth as I choke on my sobs, my heart breaking all over again, my chest aching.

I'm in physical and emotional pain, and I have been for a while, regardless of how much I try and pretend that I'm not.

The room is untouched.

Luca's blue Paw Patrol sheets are in disarray. I didn't make his bed that morning like I usually did. The day of our accident happened to be his fourth birthday. He had been so excited that when morning came, he woke up and raced to my room asking to get ice cream from the shop near the park. I couldn't deny my birthday boy, so we got dressed and went out for ice cream, then played at the park. When we returned home, I was too occupied with planning his special day that I never made his bed or put away his basket of clean clothes that is still sitting in the gray laundry basket at the foot of his bed.

We walked out that day, closed the door, and never opened it until now.

Strong familiar muscular arms wrap around my shaking body. Declan holds me against his chest, pulling me between his legs and letting me cry the tears I've been holding back for far too long.

Wiping my runny nose with the sleeve of my sweater, I look back at him through my watery eyes. His remorseful bloodshot eyes stare back at me. Instead of scolding him for being intoxicated and ruining his sobriety, I keep my mouth shut and stare at him. There's no point in saying anything. I can smell the liquor on him.

A frown curls on his lips, his eyes softening as he looks at me, looking more vulnerable than ever before. "I'm sorry I'm such a fuck up. I'm sorry that I failed to protect our son. I never should've gotten behind the wheel that night, and I'm so fucking sorry that I failed you. You never deserved any of the shit that I put you through." Heavy tears roll down his cheeks.

He's hurting just as much as I am. We're both fucked up, and it's not entirely his fault. I'm to blame as well. We both fucked up many things over the years.

He's an addict, and I never knew how to help him. In the beginning, I made excuses for his heavy partying and late nights. I told myself he'd stop drinking and using once his tour was over. For a while, I was beside him drinking, and then I found out I was pregnant and stopped.

The signs were always there, but I ignored them, believing he had himself under control. He was sober around Luca and me, at least that's what I thought.

Once I realized how badly his addiction had gotten, I tried to help him by getting him into rehab, but clearly, that didn't work out, considering his current state.

What can I do when he's not willing to help himself?

The best thing I can do is walk away and hope that he gets the help he needs, more help than just rehab.

Declan has years of trauma that he's holding on to and unwilling to let go of. I've tried for many years to help and save him from himself, but he never wanted to be saved. He wants to continue the same self-destructive path he's always been on.

Instead of judging him like I'm guilty of doing so many times in the past, I don't say anything about him relapsing. I turn my body, so I'm facing him completely, then wrap my arms around his neck, hugging him so fucking tight that he may as well be my life-line at this point. His strong arms wrap around my waist, his face buried in the crook of my neck.

We cling desperately to each other, not saying a single word, only silently crying for many different reasons.

Together, we mourn the loss of our son and our marriage.

For the first time, we're mourning our loss together.

We don't need to speak; we know exactly what this moment means to us.

This is it.

This is the end.

THE SUN HAS SET, AND AFTER MANY TEARS, DECLAN AND I sit on the floor in front of the fireplace in the living room, both sipping cups of coffee. Our hair is still wet from the joint shower we took earlier. It wasn't sexual. We stood under the water holding each other while crying, and then we washed each other silently. He's still my husband, and we needed the bare physical touch.

"I know why you're here." He breaks the uncomfortable silence, finally addressing the elephant in the room. Suddenly, I feel too guilty and can't seem to look at him. "It's okay. We both know this has been coming for a while." He reaches across and takes my free hand, holding it tightly in his, giving me the strength to finally look over at him.

"I hope you know I love you, Dec, and I'm so sorry," I say, my voice hoarse from crying.

He nods with a sad smile. "I love you, too, and always will. But we both know that the love we have for each other isn't..." he trails off, looking for the right words.

"Isn't what we deserve or need?" I finish for him, and he nods. "We were young and high on life and excitement, but eventually that wore off and..."

"And we realized we're not each other's epic love story?" he finishes my sentence. "It's okay. I get it. Right off the bat, we made Luca before we even knew each other. I will always love you for giving me the greatest gift I've ever received. You are so beautiful, and you were such an incredible mother. I never deserved you. You were always unhappy. I knew this, but I was too selfish to change our situation. I kept hoping that one day you'd love me the way I love you."

"I do love you, Declan."

"I know you do, baby girl, but not how I love you. I won't pretend this doesn't fucking suck because it does. You're breaking my fucking heart right now." I open my mouth to interrupt, but he holds his hand up to keep me quiet. "Your heart was never mine to have, and that's okay. You're my best friend, Camille." He sets our coffee mugs on the table, turning his body to face me completely.

"We got married because of Luca, and I know that wasn't fair to either of us. We've never made a very great couple. But God, Dec, you're my best friend too, and I fucking love you." A tear that I didn't even know I had left to cry rolls down my cheek. He pulls me against his chest, kissing the side of my head.

"Stop. It's okay. This is the right thing to do. I won't continue being selfish, won't continue keeping you trapped in our marriage when your heart is already taken." I look up at him skeptically, raising my eyebrows in question.

He laughs. "We both know that you're in love with Dean. My guess would be you always have been, and that's okay because I know he's in love with you too."

I gasp. "What are—How do you know?"

"I saw how you two looked at each other the night we went on that whack-ass double date, and you turned into McGregor. You've never looked at me that way, and that's okay. There are no hard feelings, and I want you to be happy." I throw my arms around him again, letting my tears wet his neck.

He rubs my back soothingly, whispering promises in my ear that we'll always be friends and he'll always be here for me, both of us promising to stay in each other's lives forever.

As much as it hurts, I know we're doing the right thing. We're setting each other free, and I know he'll find his epic love story one day.

It's just not meant to be with me.

THE FOLLOWING DAY, WE DRIVE TO THE CEMETERY HAND IN hand to visit our little boy's grave for the first time. His large granite headstone is in the shape of a heart with a teddy bear engraved into the granite on the right side. It's beautiful and perfect for our baby.

"Hi, buddy." Declan squats down and sets flowers beneath the stone.

"Hi, baby boy." I kneel into the grass, setting a red firetruck beside the flowers. It was Luca's favorite toy, so I took it from his room this morning to bring to him. "Mommy and Daddy miss you so much, baby boy." I place my hand on the headstone, his photo sealed into the stone on the left side. Luca's smiling face stares at me, and my chest aches.

"We love you, buddy. We miss you so much." Declan sniffles, wrapping his arm around my shoulders.

We spend some much-needed time at our son's final resting place, talking to him and telling him how much we love and miss him. I don't know if I believe in heaven or if he can look down on us, but if he can, I want him to see that he is missed deeply—every single day.

After getting lunch, Declan takes me to his studio so I can see the rest of the band. It's been a while, and it's nice to see them again. Declan plays the songs he's written, and I agree to let him record the songs he wrote about Luca.

We spend most of the day together, except for a few hours when I leave to go to my New York office and check in with my staff. I'll be happy once my Washington location is complete so I can fully transfer my daily operations to Seattle.

New location to go with my fresh start. Exactly what I need.

Declan and I meet back at the penthouse and order in for dinner. We stay up all night talking about the past. Sharing stories from before we met. I even tell him about Dean and our childhood together.

This time with Declan is perfect and very needed.

On Sunday, he takes me to the airport and kisses me goodbye. It isn't a romantic kiss; it's a final goodbye.

Our decision to get a divorce is mutual, and we know it is long overdue.

With a final kiss, we say our goodbyes and close the door on our marriage.

Divorce isn't always a bad thing; sometimes, it's the best thing that can happen to someone.

THIRTY-FOUR

NOW

DEAN

My head has been spinning for days. I've also been drunk for days. Ever since Karina dropped her bombshell news on me, I've been drinking my feelings away, hoping that it's just a bad dream that I'll eventually wake up from.

So far, it's been four days and no such luck.

It's Sunday night, and I'm still drinking heavily. You'd think I'd stop and sober up, considering I have work tomorrow and spent the weekend intoxicated, but no such luck. I don't plan on sobering up any time soon. Right now, alcohol is the only thing numbing me enough to keep me from completely freaking the fuck out.

Camille has texted me a total of four times. Once to tell me that she was going to New York, once to tell me that she landed safely, once to let me know she was coming home, and again a couple of hours ago to let me know she landed. She hasn't asked to see me, and I haven't bothered replying to her texts. I know I can't keep this secret from her, but I also don't want to tell her. It would ruin us completely before we even have the chance to begin.

Fuck my life.

I was ready to tell Karina I wanted a divorce, only to find out she was carrying my child. History repeats itself, fucking with me and ruining any chance I have to ever get the girl I've been in love with since I was eleven years old. There's no way in hell Cam will have anything to do with me once she finds out Karina is pregnant, and I may be a piece of shit, but I'm not scum enough to leave the woman I impregnated.

Karina is pregnant. We're having a baby.

Fuck. I don't know how I feel about it. Children were never something I felt I desperately needed in my life. The timing is all wrong, and I'm struggling to be happy about it.

A knock sounds on the door of my home office, then the door opens slowly, and my wife appears wearing a pink silk robe and a seductive look on her lips that I've seen a handful of times before. "Are you going to be in here all night? I'm feeling lonely." She walks toward me, her hands untying the knot around her waist that holds her robe together. I remain silent, curious to see why her attitude has changed.

When she told me her news, I know I didn't react the way she would've liked me to. Like a child, I stormed off into my home office, where I've been ever since. At first, she tried to speak to me, but she stopped trying when I wasn't responding. This is the first I've seen her in two days, and she seems to be in a much better mood.

Karina stands in front of me, sliding the silk down her bare shoulders until it falls to the floor and pools around her feet, revealing her naked body to me.

"What are you doing, Karina?" I ask, my voice raspy from not speaking in days.

"I want you, Dean. I want you to touch me and make me feel how you used to." She forces herself between my legs. Her hands go to my shoulders, and slowly she climbs onto my lap until she's straddling me. "Touch me, Dean. I need you." Taking my hand, she places it between her legs.

She's dry and can't even fake it. She doesn't want me any more than I want her right now. "It doesn't seem like it." Placing my hands on her hips, I carefully shift her off me and stand, setting her on her feet. She grabs her robe and covers herself up.

"Then what will it take for you to talk to me?" She throws her hands in the air, clearly frustrated. "I tell you that I'm pregnant, and you haven't been able to say a single word to me! I'm carrying your baby. The least you can do is talk to me!"

"There's nothing to talk about!" I snap, my hands tangling in my hair and pulling at the roots. "You're... *we're* having a baby, and that's it. There's nothing else we need to discuss."

Her blue eyes find mine, and a frown stretches across her pale pink lips. "You should be happy. I'm finally pregnant again, and this is a happy moment." She reaches for me; I cringe, but don't pull away. She's my wife, pregnant with my child, and she needs support right now.

She's getting exactly what she wanted.

"I wasn't expecting a baby, Karina. Forgive me for being rattled by this news. Last we spoke about it, we'd agreed to put off trying."

"We did, but we also didn't use any protection either. I was at the doctor to get on birth control when they asked for a urine sample to ensure I wasn't pregnant. It's standard. To my surprise, the doctor returned to the room and shared the shocking news." Her face lights up with excitement. I don't know if it's too early for the glow everyone talks about, but she's practically fucking glowing with her excitement.

Is having an unplanned child the worst thing to ever happen? It's still my child, and I know I will love it and provide for it in every way possible. The timing and circumstances may be shitty, but it isn't the child's fault.

"Camille was right. She said if we stop trying, and for me to stop putting so much stress on myself and worrying about it, it will happen. And look"—she gestures to her flat stomach—"it happened." My eyebrows pull together in a scowl, annoyance setting in. I don't fucking like the fact that Karina spoke with Camille, of all people, about her trying to conceive.

"I'm going to call her to thank her for the advice and apologize again for what I said to her. It makes me sick that I upset her and ruined our friendship." The night of our failed double date seems like another lifetime ago.

"Don't. Stay away from her. There's no need to get involved with her again." Karina can't get involved with her because I'm already involved with her. It's best the two stay far away from each other.

Karina shrugs her shoulders, not responding to my request for her to stay away from Camille. Instead, she takes my hand and drags me into our bedroom, where she makes me shower because the smell of liquor on my breath bothers her.

That night, I lie beside my wife in bed for the first time in weeks. She falls asleep easily while I lie awake, my mind racing a million miles an hour.

When morning comes, I do something entirely out of character. I stay home from work. I call my assistant and ask her to reschedule my appointments and explain that I'm not feeling well, so I'll be working from home. I wasn't completely lying. I am hungover as fuck, and the thought of having to leave the house and go into the office causes me physical pain.

So, I stay home and work for half a day and spend the other half in our home gym working off my frustrations.

Apart from the call I made to my assistant in the morning, I stay off my phone the entire day. It isn't until night when I'm climbing into bed that I finally decide to check my phone, seeing several text messages and missed calls, all from the same person...

Camille.

Tuesday morning, the same routine. I work from home and ignore every call and text from Cam, too much of a coward to face her and share my bombshell news.

Wednesday morning, I go back to work, unable to hide away at home forever.

For the most part, the day is simple. I had two meetings when I got in this morning, but the remainder of my day is clear.

I'm sitting at my desk drafting an email to a client when the intercom buzzes, and Marjorie's voice comes through. "Excuse me, Mr. Jameson, there's someone here to see you."

With a sigh, I check the time on my Rolex. It's just after noon, and I don't have anything else scheduled for the day. I doublecheck my calendar and cell phone to ensure I haven't missed any meetings or texts from Karina. Pressing the green button on the speaker, I ask, "Who is it?"

There's a beep. "Camille, sir."

Camille. *Fuck.*

"Sorry, Marjorie, please let *Mrs.* Valentine know I'm unavailable today." It's petty to emphasize that she's married, but I don't care. I've been purposely ignoring her, so I'm not surprised she showed up here.

There's a moment of silence, then another beep. "Um, sir, she says she's not leaving until you see her." With a sigh, I hang my head in defeat.

Of course, she isn't going to leave. Why would she? She doesn't know why I'm avoiding her. Last we were together, I was balls deep inside of her, whispering sweet nothings in her ear. In her mind, nothing is wrong, and there's no reason I should be ignoring her. Can't blame her.

Standing from my desk, I walk toward the door and open it, looking over at Marjorie. "You can head to lunch now. I'll take it from here." She nods and walks away from her desk, a desk that'll remain vacant for the next hour while she's out on her lunch break.

My eyes painfully drag away from the empty desk and land on the raven-haired beauty standing before me with her hands on her hips and a scowl on her perfect face. She opens her mouth to speak, but I shake my head and lead her inside my office, locking the door behind us.

"What the fuck, Dean? Are you okay?" She throws her arms

out. Shoving my hands in my pockets, I straighten my posture and look down at her, looking her over from head to toe. She's wearing nude fuck-me heels and a black dress that hugs her curves in all the right places.

Camille Avery Lambert-Valentine is a true fucking beauty.

Even more so when she's angry.

"Why have you been avoiding me?" Our eyes meet, and just from the shift in her posture, I know she can see the lie coming before I even say anything.

"I've been stressed and busy with work. There's still a lot I need to do with the clients I've acquired, so I apologize for not answering your many messages."

"You can tell your bullshit lies to anyone else, but not to me, never to me." She walks toward me until we're standing toe to toe. Her hands reach up and cup my face gently. "What's going on, Dean? Talk to me." Her emerald eyes plead with me, begging me to let her in and tell her what's bothering me, but I can't because telling her means I will lose her for good, and I'm not ready to accept that just yet.

Instead of answering, I crash my lips against hers, shutting her up by stealing her breath and leaving her speechless. "I need you right now, Cam. I need you so fucking bad."

She gasps, allowing herself a moment to melt against my body before she pulls away. "Talk to me first. Tell me what's wrong and why you've been avoiding me."

"Stop talking. The only sound I want to hear from you is the sound of you gagging on my cock."

Her mouth connects with mine. "Take me. I'm yours." She pants against my mouth, her fingers working the buttons on my shirt. I need her like I need to fucking breathe. I pull away from her addictive mouth long enough to unzip her dress and shove it to the ground, and then I'm back on her like a starved man. Our hands move frantically between us, each of us desperately ripping away our clothing while our lips remain fused. She bends to take off her heels, but I stop her by gripping her hands. "Leave them," I say, wanting her to wear those fuck-me heels as I fuck her.

Only once we're both naked do we pull away to admire each other's bodies. Her green eyes are dark with lust, and I know mine are the same.

"Tell me what you need, Camille," I ask, my voice low and husky.

She doesn't hesitate with her answer or shy away from telling me what she needs. "I need you to make me come until I can't come anymore."

"Be a good girl, and I'll let you sit on my face later and fuck it until you cum on my tongue. Would you like that?" She squeezes her thighs together, looking up at me through hooded eyes.

"Fuck, yes." She practically moans her words.

Camille may be in control of everything else in her life, but when it comes to sex, she's been all too willing to let me take control. I've learned she likes to be fucked hard and loves dirty talk. She comes the hardest when the sex is rough and dirty.

"If I were to touch your pretty pussy, would you be wet and ready for me?" I look cockily at her. "Let's check," I say before she can respond. Slowly I slip my hand between her legs, finding her warm center. My rock-hard cock twitches between us at the feeling of her wetness on my fingers.

"You're wet and ready for me. Good girl," I praise, roughly shoving two fingers into her without warning. Her eyes practically roll in the back of her head at the sensation. Before she can enjoy it any further, I rip my hand away and spread her arousal over her lips, smearing her red lipstick across her face. Her lips part and I take the opening as my chance to shove my fingers in her mouth and down her throat. She sucks them, just like I knew she would.

With a devious chuckle, I pull my hand away and walk back to my desk, sitting my naked ass on the leather seat. "Crawl to me."

She drops to her hands and knees and makes her way toward me.

Cam crawls between my legs, her hips swaying with her movement. She settles herself between my legs, a smirk on her messy red lips, already knowing what she will be told to do next.

"Open your mouth and suck my cock like a good girl." I spread my legs wider so she can settle herself more comfortably. "I'm going to cum in your pretty little mouth, and you're going to swallow every drop. Do you understand?" Her pupils dilate, her big green eyes filled with pure lust.

She nods once, her tongue slipping out to lick her lips. By the way she squeezes her thighs together to create friction, I know she's worked up and will soon need release.

This fucking girl amazes me.

Camille lowers her head to my lap and swallows my dick whole without warning. My cock twitches with the sudden feel of pleasure.

Her mouth is warm and wet and sends chills up my spine. I don't know how the fuck I've lasted the last few years without having my cock in a woman's mouth. It's the most incredible fucking feeling, next to being inside of a pussy.

"I want you to wear my cum like lipstick."

My body jerks when she swallows, her throat tightening around me. I don't bother controlling the groan that leaves my lips; I want her to know how amazing she is and how good it feels. Gathering her silk black hair in my hands, I hold it back in a ponytail, keeping a firm grip. She knows what she's doing, so I don't control her movements.

Cam circles her velvet tongue around my engorged head, sucking me deeper into her mouth until her nose is flush with my skin. She gags, her eyes watering and throat constricting. Saliva drips from her mouth when she pulls back, removing me from her warm mouth with an audible pop.

Her tongue pokes out of her mouth, circling my slit and licking up a bead of pre-cum. Her swollen lips wrap around my crown, sucking it like a fucking lollipop. I'd do anything to spend the rest of my life rotating between being in her mouth and pussy.

My balls tighten, and a familiar ache begins to set in. She must realize it, too, because she swallows me down again, her head bobbing quicker, tears spilling from her big green eyes. Tightening my grip on her hair, I pull her head away quickly, replacing her mouth with my fist, squeezing my cock so tightly it's borderline painful.

"Come for me," she demands, batting her long eyelashes as she kneels in front of me with her hands on my thighs.

"Take it like a good girl," I grunt, lining myself up with her open mouth, just as thick ropes of cum shoot out of me and into her waiting mouth. Her mouth is so full that some drips down her chin and lands on her chest. She's a fucking mess with her red lipstick smeared across her mouth, mascara running down her face, and my cum dripping out of her mouth. What a fucking beauty she is. "Swallow it." She gulps down my load, then leans into me and licks my still hard cock clean, showing me just how fucking good she can be.

"As much as I want to taste you, that'll have to wait because I need to be inside you so fucking bad right now." She stands to her feet, wiping away her tears and black streaks of mascara under her eyes and bats her eyelashes at me.

"Whatever you say, Mr. Jameson." Her voice is laced with both amusement and lust.

I chuckle, taking a step toward her, only for her to take a step backward. "Good girl. Now stand in front of my desk and bend over so I can take what's mine."

"Yes, Sir." God, this woman is going to be the fucking death of me. I swear my cock gets even harder hearing her fucking words.

Like the obedient girl she is, she walks over to my desk and leans over it, spreads her legs, and flips her hair over her right shoulder, looking at me with a seductive gaze.

I waste no fucking time marching toward her, gripping her hips, lining myself up, and I'm in heaven inside of her warm wet cunt in one hard thrust.

The sight of her naked golden body leaned over my desk in

nothing but a pair of stilettos is a sight that can easily drive any man crazy.

"Use me, Dean. Let out all your frustrations on my body," she says through a moan.

So, I do. My hands grip her soft, curvy hips, my nails digging into her flesh, as I fuck her like a mad man. I let out the anger and frustration that I've been bottling up over the past week. I lose all control and fuck her to make myself feel better.

We both know I'm keeping something from her, but the secret I'm keeping is going to ruin us, and I'm so fucking selfish that I'd like to pretend for a little bit longer that nothing will change. I'm lying to myself, but right now, I want to forget everything else and lose myself in Camille.

For a moment longer, I want to pretend that we stand a chance and pretend that I'll finally have the opportunity to claim her as mine.

I'm only lying to myself.

THIRTY-FIVE

NOW

Camille

Getting fucked wasn't exactly what I had in mind when I came to see Dean at his office today, but I'm sure as hell not complaining. He's been avoiding me, and I know there's a reason why. It's been nearly a week since I've seen him, and my texts and calls have gone unanswered all weekend.

I came here to find out what his problem was, but I knew what he needed once I saw him and saw the vacant look in his eyes. So, I give him what he needs instead of making him talk it out with me and tell me why he's been ignoring me.

I give him my body to use as an escape.

It's not just for him. It's for both of us. We both need this. Especially after seeing Declan, I need a release just as much as Dean. I need to lose myself in him just as much as he needs to lose himself in me.

My stomach tightens with a familiar ache, my climax nearing by the second. Dean knows my body so well that he knows the signs and what I need. He slips his hand around to the front of my body, moves it between my legs, and finds my clit, rubbing it in sync with his forceful thrusts. That's all it takes for me to fall over the edge and cry out my release, coming all over his hard cock still pumping into me, not giving me a chance to recover.

With a growl, he pulls out of me and leads me toward the floor-to-ceiling window, positioning me to stand in front of it, the city falling at our feet below.

His office is easily visible to the neighboring buildings. I bet if someone were to look close enough, we could be seen standing naked together in front of the fully exposed window. That thought alone is enough to send a chill down my spine. What would happen if we were to get caught? If someone in the building across from us were to notice?

A smirk pulls on my lips. The thought doesn't stay with me long because with my next breath, Dean grips my hips and thrusts himself back inside me. Back where he belongs. Pressing a kiss to my shoulder, one hand wraps around my waist while the other laces with my fingers and rests against the cold glass of the window.

He thrusts into me from behind, fucking me so deeply and intensely that I can feel him in the depths of my cunt. My moans are uncontrolled and fall from my lips loudly. Our skin slaps together, our heavy breathing fogging up the window in front of us.

Dean fucks me as hard and deeply as he possibly can. I don't stand a chance with him and his perfect cock. The hand laced with mine moves down my body to settle between my legs as he begins rubbing my sensitive clit. Using the hand that's wrapped around me, he grabs a handful of my tit, flicking and pinching my hard nipple.

His skilled fingers rub over my clit, eliciting cries of pleasure from me while he plays me like an instrument. My mouth is dry from hanging open and my nonstop moans. My body feels as if I've been set on fire. Sex with Dean is the most incredible sex that I've ever had in my entire life. He's a fucking sex god.

A second orgasm racks through my body, leaving me shaking and ready to collapse. His strong arms wrap around me, holding me up; my legs are shaky and nearly useless to support my weight. My head falls back onto his shoulder. He turns his head and presses a kiss to my exposed throat, not losing a beat.

"God, you feel so fucking good wrapped around me," he rasps in my ear, his voice deep and husky, laced with lust. As if my body needed the reassurance, my cunt squeezes his pulsing cock, tightening around him in a vice grip. My eyes roll in the back of my head, and I go temporarily blind when another climax comes crashing over my body. By now, Dean is using me for his own personal pleasure, and I don't even care. I'll give him anything he needs for as long as I can.

By the time Dean stills and roars his release, filling my pussy with his warm cum, I've lost count of how many orgasms I had. He has fucked me all over his office. We've fucked on the sectional, his desk, against the window, the coffee table, and we've ended up on the floor near his desk where we now lie in a boneless pile of flesh. This man is a goddamn sex machine that never tires.

I struggled to continue allowing him to give me orgasm after orgasm. The orgasms were starting to become the perfect ratio of pain and pleasure. I'm exhausted, my body weak, and we are both covered in sweat from head to toe. Both of us sticky from sweat and bodily fluid.

We lie naked on the floor, Dean on his back and me beside him with my head on his washboard abs. The fingers of his left hand are tangled in my hair while his right arm rests behind his head. We stay here in comfortable silence, neither of us feeling the need to say anything. I'm too sedated from dick to speak or even think straight. The air is hot and heavy, and the entire office smells of sex and sweat.

There's no telling how long we've been at it, so I can only hope that his assistant is still away on her lunch hour, or else I'm sure the poor lady has been able to hear us. Surely his office isn't soundproof, and I haven't been quiet whatsoever.

"In a perfect world, you'd be mine. That would be my ring on your finger, and you'd be coming home to me at the end of the day.

Guess we don't always get what we want." Dean cuts through the silence, his words a whisper that I can barely hear over the sound of my racing heart. "Some people are put into our lives to simply tease us. To serve as a reminder of what we can never have." I'm too out of it to register what he's implying or question his train of thought. Instead of asking him what he means or what he's thinking, I remain silent.

A ringing sound pierces the air and steals our moment, forcing us back into reality. Despite the phone ringing, I would've been content to ignore it and continue lying here, but Dean shifts me off his body and stands. He grabs his briefs from the floor and pulls them on, grabbing his cellphone from his desk, a pained look crossing his face as he looks down at the device.

I take a moment to study him. His dark hair is messy and sticking up in places, his chest sparkles with a light coat of sweat, his posture is rigid, and his shoulders are tight with tension despite having just had sex multiple times. Something is on his mind, but he's not in the mood to discuss whatever it is. Still, that doesn't stop me from prying. So, I ask anyway.

"What's going on, Dean? There's something on your mind, and there's a reason you haven't returned any of my calls or texts." I stand, grab my clothing from the floor, and dress.

"Nothing, everything is fine. As I said, I've been busy." His guard is up. He's hiding something from me. I've never been the type to force someone into talking when they're not ready to, so I don't push him. When he's ready to speak to me about whatever is on his mind, I know he will. I'll take it at his pace and hope he opens up to me soon.

With a sigh, I say, "Let's go to the lighthouse tomorrow night. There's something I want to tell you." He doesn't know that Declan and I are getting a divorce, and I plan to share that news with him tomorrow. Hopefully it'll encourage him to open up about whatever is on his mind.

He opens his mouth to likely give me a lame-ass excuse, but I hold up my hand, shaking my head. "Don't say no, don't say you're busy. Just say okay and meet me there at six."

His shoulders slump in defeat. "Okay, Camille. I will meet you there tomorrow at six."

"Good. Bring dinner too." With a smug look, I walk off to his office bathroom to wash my face before leaving. His assistant likely heard us, but she doesn't need to see me completely disheveled.

After splashing some water on my face and attempting to fix my hair, I exit the bathroom and kiss Dean goodbye, making him promise to come to the lighthouse tomorrow. Luckily, when I leave his office, Marjorie's desk is empty, so I don't have to do the walk of shame after fucking her married boss.

From his office, I go straight to mine and finish my workday, all the while with a knot in my stomach telling me that something terrible is about to happen.

That everything is about to come crashing down.

THIRTY-SIX

NOW

Camille

After work, I drive straight over to my parents' house. My mom had called me earlier to invite me over to dinner. I was hesitant about it, not wanting to face Spencer after our failed lunch date last week when I told her I was going to New York to ask Dec for a divorce, but Mom insisted and wouldn't take no for an answer. Besides, if I declined, she'd be on my ass about it. Mom has always had a way of knowing when something is wrong with me, so instead of making an excuse and lying, I agreed.

Don't get me wrong, I love my family and spending time with them. They are the reason I moved back here in the first place, but sometimes I just want to avoid sharing things with them, especially regarding my marriage. They'll try to offer their advice, but I don't want it. Not about this, at least.

I pull up to the black iron gates of the community my parents live and offer a friendly smile to the security guard. "Good evening Mrs. Valentine. I'll buzz you in," Mario, the security guard, greets me, offering me a friendly wave once the gates slowly begin to roll open. I wave in return and drive through them.

Before, I never would've cringed at the use of my married name, but now it doesn't feel right. I feel like a fraud, like being called Mrs. along with Declan's last name is making me an imposter. Technically, I'm still married. I still wear a diamond rock on my finger despite ending things and being home for three days. I've worn it for so long, and it feels so normal wearing it that I'm not sure when I'll take it off.

Ideally, it'll be soon, especially since I plan to see Dean tomorrow night and share the news with him. It would be nice to share the news without wearing my wedding ring. I make a mental note to take it off when I get home.

My parents live in a small community that consists of wealthy, stuck-up neighbors and over-the-top luxury mini mansions. I grew up here and was once part of my parents' lavish lifestyle, so it doesn't shock me when I come to my childhood home for visits. My parents may be wealthy, but they're not your stereotypical rich bitches.

My mother enjoyed taking care of the house herself. Sure, twice a month, she'd hire a cleaning crew to do a deep clean and even a gardener for special events, but my mother took pride in doing things herself. She made our house a home, something I've always admired about her.

I pull into my parents' driveway and park behind Spencer's car, letting out a frustrated sigh. I knew she'd be here; hopefully, she hasn't said anything to our parents and she's over being angry at me.

It's been a week since we've spoken, but it feels like an eternity. We never go a day without speaking. She's angry, but I'm unsure how to make it right. She disagrees with my choices, not that I have any right to blame her. My recent decisions have been pretty damn questionable.

Realizing I can't spend my night sitting in my car, I suck it up like a big girl, hold my head up high, and walk into my childhood home, instantly being assaulted with the delicious aroma of Mom's homemade lasagna—my favorite.

Taking off my shoes by the door, I hang my coat in the coat closet along with my purse. I'm shoving my keys into my purse when a folded neon orange Post-it note catches my attention. My heart races in my chest, already knowing who the message is from. With shaky fingers, I pull out the note and open it slowly, my heart skipping a beat as I read the words written.

It'll always be you

Dean's message is cryptic and leaves an uneasy feeling in me. I make a mental note to ask him about it tomorrow. He must've slid it into my purse while I was cleaning up in his bathroom this afternoon.

Quickly shoving the note back into my purse, I shut the closet and follow the voices into the kitchen, my throat suddenly clogging with emotion when I see Spencer. She's standing at the island across from our mom, who has her back toward me.

I walk over as she eyes me skeptically, picking up her wine glass to take a long sip of the red contents. Mom turns around, giving me a wide smile before pulling me in for a tight hug. "Hi, sweetheart."

I return her hug with an effortless smile. "Hi, Mom." We pull apart. "Hey, Spence." I stand beside my sister, nudging her shoulder playfully.

"Camille," she greets me tight-lipped, her attention going back to her glass of wine. She uses my name rather than my nickname. A frown curls on my lips. She rarely ever calls me by my name. She always uses my nickname.

"I'm so happy to have both of my girls here. Where have you been, Camille? I've been calling you for a while trying to schedule time for our family dinner."

"Sorry, Mom. I've been swamped lately."

Spencer scoffs. "Yeah, busy in New York." She takes her glass and excuses herself into the dining room where I watch with wide eyes as she takes her seat, never once looking back at me.

"New York? Why were you there?" Mom asks, placing the homemade garlic bread onto a serving dish.

"It's a long story. Is dad home? I want to talk to you both." It's either now or never. I have to bite the bullet and tell them about my upcoming change in marital status before they hear it from someone else.

Mom doesn't have a chance to reply because dad comes walking into the kitchen just then, answering my question with his appearance.

"There she is. There's my little girl." Dad hugs me tightly, lifting me off my feet. He sets me down and kisses my head like I'm a child. No matter how old I get, I'll always be daddy's little girl.

We help Mom carry the food into the dining room and set it in the middle of the table, all while Spencer remains sitting in her seat, not once looking up at me.

We each fix ourselves a plate of food, sitting and eating in uncomfortable silence. Mom and Dad know something is up because I see how they exchange glances at each other as if they're each wanting and waiting for the other to break our silence.

Unable to take the awkwardness anymore, I surprise myself by speaking up and breaking our silence. "So, I've got some pretty big news to share."

"What is it, sweetie? You know you can always tell us anything," Mom says, giving me one of her warm motherly smiles.

"Well, uh..." I trail off, feeling shy for the first time in front of my family. I take a deep breath, reach forward to pick up my glass of water, bring it to my mouth, and take a large gulp. The cold water flows down my throat, hydrating my suddenly dry mouth.

After setting the cup back down, Spencer surprises me by resting her hand on mine, and I look over at her. She nods her head once, urging me to continue, already knowing what it is that I'm about to tell our parents.

Ripping the Band-Aid off, I share my news. "Declan and I are getting a divorce." Mom gasps. Dad stands from the table abruptly, only to return moments later with a bottle of tequila and four shot glasses.

"Here ya go, Cammy bear, I'm sure you need this." He pours me a shot, then slides it across the table to me.

"Oh, Harvey," Mom chastens, swatting his arm. She throws her napkin on the table, slides her chair back, and stands, disappearing into the kitchen.

Dad pours himself and Spencer a shot, but neither of us touches it, not until Mom returns with her small bamboo cutting board, a bottle of pink salt, a couple of limes, and a knife.

"We can at least drink the correct way," she says, reclaiming her spot and begins cutting a lime into four slices. Dad pours her a shot with a chuckle, then leans over and kisses the side of her head.

Mom passes us all a lime and the salt bottle, each of us licking the back of our hands and sprinkling it with salt. When we're all prepared, we count to three, lick the salt from our hands and toss the shot back. I quiver at the taste of the warm liquid, then suck the lime wedge into my mouth to soothe the warmth that's now floating in my belly.

"This was not the reaction that I was expecting," I say, shaking my head and suppressing a laugh.

"Oh, sweetie, you know how much your father and I love you. If you have decided to leave Declan, we know you put thought into it, and it's the best decision for you. We will always support anything you do." Unwelcome tears sting my eyes.

This is my crazy supportive family. The same people who let me have the freedom to make my own decisions and own mistakes. The same people who didn't question me when I ran off on tour with Declan and announced shortly after that I was pregnant and getting married.

My parents have always felt that Spencer and I need to make our own mistakes and learn from them. They've always said that you learn by doing, and they trust us enough to follow our hearts and do what we feel is right.

"Besides, we knew this was coming. Let's be honest, your marriage hasn't exactly been perfect. And this past year has exposed many flaws in the both of you," Spencer chimes in, holding her glass out toward dad for him to refill it.

"One more. I'm not going to get my girls drunk," dad says, looking from Spence, to me, and to Mom. We giggle in unison.

"Tell us more, Cammy bear. What do you need us to do?" dad asks.

I shake my head. "Nothing. Dec already moved back to New York. That's where I was last week. We had a long talk, and we both decided it's best that we part ways. No hard feelings. It's the right thing for both of us."

Mom sniffles. "You were so young when you got married. You both still had a lot of growing up to do. Sometimes, you grow together, and other times you grow apart. I'm proud of you for having the strength to make your marriage work and for letting go when you realize it would no longer work." She reaches across to me and takes my hands in hers. "But please know that Declan is still a part of this family. Just because he'll no longer be your husband doesn't change the fact he's family." My parents have loved Declan from the moment they met him. He doesn't have family, he comes from a toxic and abusive background, and the only people he had at the time were his bandmates.

My mom declared that he's her son, and he'll forever be part of our family. During his time in rehab, my parents spoke to him more than I did. Mom attended the weekly visits, taking him homemade meals and baked goods every week. She's always had the biggest soft spot for him, so it doesn't surprise me that she plans to keep in contact with him.

Of course, he's still my family. Us divorcing isn't going to change that. I know we'll be better off as friends, and we've already promised to keep in contact. He'll always have a piece of my heart and be a part of me.

After talking more with my parents about my decision and consuming more than the two-drink maximum that dad set, I agree to stay the night. Spence and I clean the kitchen after our parents go to sleep, making small talk as we clean.

As soon as we finish, we go upstairs to her room and bring the bottle of tequila with us.

Now, we lie in her queen bed in her childhood room, passing the bottle back and forth as we take sips.

"I'm sorry for how I acted that day at lunch. It wasn't cool. You can always come to me and cry on my shoulder," Spencer says with a dramatic sigh. "I love you, little sis, and I fucking hate when we fight and don't speak."

I giggle. "We never fight. I'm pretty sure that was our first actual fight ever."

She giggles, taking the nearly empty bottle from my hands. "Yeah, but still. We have to stick together. If you haven't noticed, you're my bestest friend ever!"

With an uncontrollable giggle, I shove her shoulder playfully. "Shhh! We can't wake them."

"God, I feel like a kid again. Having to keep quiet, so we don't wake the parentals."

"Except this time, it's me in your room and not a boy."

"See, I knew it! I knew you were the one creeping around every time I snuck Dallas in. He'd say I was crazy whenever I heard something, saying that he didn't hear anything."

"It was totally me. You would sneak him in, then right after, I'd sneak out and go to Dean's house." I sigh, reminiscing on our childhood days. The days when the only thing I cared about was getting to see Dean and earning one of his smiles that made me feel like the most special girl in the entire world. His special smile is what I called it. The smile only directed toward me that made my stomach fill with butterflies every time I saw it.

"You really have always been in love with him," Spencer says, now serious.

"Yeah, I have. I think that I always will be."

"Camille, he's married. I know you're getting divorced, but what about him? You know you can't carry on having an affair, right? Even if he says he's leaving her, he hasn't done it yet. If he loves you, then he'll choose you. You deserve more than being someone's dirty little secret. You're worth more than being the other woman. The woman he fucks on the side before going home and playing house with his wife."

I gulp, knowing she's right.

Never once have I thought about wanting to push Dean to make a choice.

Making him choose between me, the woman he hasn't seen for eleven years, or his wife, the woman he loves and cares for enough that he put a ring on her finger and gave her his last name.

I open my mouth to speak, but I'm cut off by Spencer's soft drunken snores. With a racing heart, I close my eyes and pray for sleep to take me, knowing that soon everything will be different.

The knot in my stomach telling me something is about to happen returns.

THIRTY-SEVEN

NOW

DEAN

I've been anxious and on edge all day, anxious for what's to come tonight when I see Camille. I could barely sleep last night. Every time I closed my eyes, I saw her emerald eyes staring back at me.

When she walked into my office yesterday, I hadn't planned on fucking her on every surface, but she looked at me with those eyes, telling me to use her body to pound out my frustrations, so I did. Without a second thought, I stripped her bare and fucked her all over my office, taking her raw and filling her with my cum repeatedly.

Now today, I can hardly sit still in my chair. She's everywhere in my office, and I can still smell her arousal and sweet salted caramel pussy in the air.

I'd agreed to meet her at the lighthouse tonight, and as much as I want to avoid it, I have to go and tell her about the baby. She deserves to know that Karina is pregnant, and we can figure things out from there. I'm not sure what'll happen and where we'll go from there, but I'm laying all my cards on the table and telling her.

No more lies. If she's going to be in my life long-term, a part of my future, then she needs to know. We've dug ourselves into a fucking mess, and it's time we face the truth, the harsh reality that we've spent so much time avoiding while we were busy tangled in the sheets and fucking all over my hotel room.

It's time we stop ignoring the elephant in the room and face the fact that we're both married. Except now, my wife is pregnant.

Fuck. How did things get so fucking messy and out of hand?

Somehow, I get through the day. I attend every meeting on time, send over notices and blueprints to clients, and get through the long to-do list of work-related things I've been putting off.

As WRECKED AS MY NERVES ARE, I SURPRISINGLY HAVE A VERY productive day. By 4:30 p.m., I leave my office and stop at a few stores on my way to the lighthouse in preparation to meet Camille.

I make it there an hour later, taking extra time to clean up the place. It's been years since we've spent more than five minutes here.

We were here a few weeks ago, but neither of us stayed for more than a few minutes. The place hasn't been cleaned in years. It's dusty and untouched; all the items we left here remain.

Blueprints and clothing sketches on the walls; the only thing that's been removed is the bedding and hygiene items we kept in the bathroom. Apart from that, everything remains—our books on the bookshelves. Magazines, papers, and pencils are spread out on the table. It's as if we walked away eleven years ago, closed the door, and never looked back or opened it until now.

Digging into the shopping bags, I set to clean up as much of the downstairs area as possible. Sweeping and dusting, setting up the battery-powered lamps I bought, and then spreading a blanket across the floor once it's clean enough.

I've just finished setting out our food containers on the middle of the blanket when lights flash through the windows, followed by the sound of rocks crunching under tires. A few minutes later, the door creaks open, and suddenly the space feels homier with Camille's presence.

She's wearing dark jeans, a pair of sandals, and a long-sleeved sweater, her black hair pin straight and flowing down her back. She clearly went home and changed after work, unlike me, who came straight from the office. I'm still in my suit, wearing dress shoes, navy slacks, and a white button dress shirt rolled up to my elbows.

"Hi," she says, breaking me from my stupor, giving me an awkward wave. I've been too busy admiring how fucking beautiful she looks.

"Hey." She closes the door and walks over to me, taking off her sandals before stepping on the blanket.

"I'm starving. Let's eat?" She gestures toward the food boxes spread across the black and white blanket. With a nod, I step out of my shoes, keeping my socks on, and sit beside her, opening the Chinese take-out boxes.

We eat in silence, and for the first time since knowing Camille, our silence is awkward and unwanted. You can cut the tension with a knife. It's clear we both have things we need to get off our chests, but neither of us attempts to speak.

Unable to take it anymore, I open my mouth. "I need to tell you something," I say, at the same time as she says, "I have something to tell you."

"Sorry... you can go first." I shove an eggroll into my mouth to keep myself from blurting out the burning words on the tip of my tongue.

Her shoulders rise with her inhale. She clears the food from her lap and sits a little taller, her hands resting on her lap as she prepares herself to speak. To share whatever it is that's been going on inside of her mind.

"Declan and I are getting a divorce."

I clamp my mouth shut, unsure what to say or if I should tell her what I have to share. She stares at me, fidgeting with her fingers and biting her plump bottom lip, looking more uneasy than ever.

Camille has always been sure of herself and her actions, so seeing her act shyly about this makes me feel awkward.

"That's why I went to New York. He moved back a couple of weeks ago. When I realized that's what I wanted, I went to tell him face-to-face. Telling someone you don't want to be married to them anymore isn't exactly something you should do over the phone."

A better man wouldn't keep such an explosive secret as I'm keeping. A better man would tell her he has a pregnant wife at home.

A better man wouldn't even find himself in this situation. He'd leave the past in the past, not have a wandering eye, and would be home with his wife, sharing her excitement about the pregnancy.

By now, we've established that I'm not the better man. I'm a selfish man.

The selfish bastard who takes whatever he wants without worrying about the consequence and without worrying about who can—and will—get hurt.

When I first found out Karina was pregnant, I told myself that I'd stay with her. But I don't want history to repeat itself, and why should I be unhappy just because we have a child? Our child should have happy parents, so I thought about it and realized that I still want a divorce. We can co-parent. I want Camille and hope she'll accept me with a baby on the way.

Instead of telling Camille any of the things I should, I pounce on her, laying her down until her back is flat on the blanket and I'm hovering over her. In an instant, her breathing intensifies, her lips part, and her green eyes become dark with lust.

We don't speak with words. Our mouths collide, and we let our tongues do the talking. Surely she knows me well enough to know when I'm hiding something or when I have something else on my mind, but she doesn't press me to share my news, so for that, I'm thankful.

Camille knows exactly what I need right now, in this moment, and she gives it to me without question.

What I need is her. All I need is her.

Her body.

Her mouth.

Her warmth wrapped around me.

It'll always be her.

"I need you, Cam. Need to feel your perfect pussy wrapped around me, need to feel your warm mouth wrapped around me, need your taste in my mouth. God, I need you so bad I can't even think straight," I admit, kissing from her lips down the length of her neck.

In the distance, I can hear the ping of a cell phone. It pings once, twice, then a third time. For a moment, the thought of checking my phone passes through my mind, but the second a soft moan escapes Cam's lips, I forget all about our phones. "I need you too, Dean. Right now, I need your mouth on me." I don't need to be told twice. We pull apart, both sitting up and frantically undressing, removing every ounce of clothing between us.

"Lie back," she commands, so I do. I lie on my back and watch her movements. She reaches toward her purse, takes something out of it, then crawls back toward me.

One thing I'll never get tired of is seeing this fucking girl down on all fours for me, crawling to me with a hunger in her eyes that only I can satisfy.

Once she reaches me, she opens her hand, showing me what she grabbed from her bag; a chuckle breaks free at the sight of the pop rocks.

This fucking girl amazes me.

Camille tears open the bag of watermelon pop rocks candy, tilts her head back, pours some into her mouth, and then sets the rest of the candy beside her.

Just as the candy starts popping loudly in her mouth, she

lowers her head to my swollen member and swallows my cock whole without warning. The candy pops and crackles against my shaft, my cock twitching with the sudden burst of pleasure.

Her mouth is warm and wet and sends chills up my spine. My body jerks when she swallows, her throat tightening around me, the candy popping against my hard skin. I don't bother controlling the moans and groans that leave my lips. I want her to know how amazing she is and how good it feels.

Gathering her silky hair in my hands, I hold it away from her face, keeping a firm grip.

Cam circles her tongue around my engorged head, the candy continuing to pop in her mouth and her throat as she sucks me deeper. She swallows, tightening her throat around me.

She gags, drooling from the sides of her mouth as she begins to bob her head, hollowing her cheeks, sucking me like I'm the greatest thing she's ever tasted. It's embarrassing, but with how great her tongue is, I don't think I'll be able to last, and I desperately want to feel her coming on my tongue at the same time as I come in her mouth and make her swallow it.

"Bring your pussy to my face," I instruct. "Right now. Let me taste you and make you come," I rasp, my voice deeper and unfamiliar. With my hand holding her hair, I pull her away from my cock that's now covered in saliva and candy.

Like the good girl she is, she straddles my face and lets me feast on her glistening pussy. My tongue swipes over her slit, earning a small moan from her swollen lips.

From between her thighs, I can't see what she's doing, but I can feel her body moving. "Stay still," I demand, slapping her left ass cheek, earning a yelp from her. She wiggles, clearly liking the sting. I slap her ass again, this time earning a moan. "Suck my cock, baby," I groan, somehow growing even harder from the taste of her sweet and salty pussy.

Camille lays down on my body and takes my cock back into her mouth. She must've put more candy in her mouth because I can again feel the candy popping against my painfully hard cock, the candy only adding to and intensifying the pleasure. She gags while she sucks me, her head bobbing quicker, working her fucking hardest to earn my cum in her hot little mouth.

I feast on her pussy like a starved man at a buffet while she sucks me off. My lips wrap around her hard clit as I begin sucking, using my tongue to flick the sensitive bud of nerves.

Moving my right hand to her core, I shove two thick fingers into her roughly, curling them down to reach her G-spot from the position we're in. Using her body's natural lubricant, I spread it up toward the puckered hole between her ass cheeks that's in my face and carefully work a finger in, pushing past the tight wall of muscle.

Her arousal drips from her pussy, dripping down my chin for me to lick up and savor later.

Camille's moans become louder, vibrating around my cock as she sucks me frantically. Her soft tissues tighten around my fingers, squeezing them in a vice grip. She bucks her hips against my mouth, pressing herself further down on my mouth, desperate for the pleasure I'm providing her greedy little cunt.

I flick my tongue over her clit rapidly, flicking it at the same pace as I fuck her with the fingers I have in both her pussy and ass. She's close; I can tell she is by how her body shakes, her moans become louder, and how tight she gets.

One flick of my tongue.

Two flicks.

Three flicks, she's crying her release, squirting all over my face and drowning me in her sweet juices.

I'm right there on the edge with her; my cock throbs against her tongue, ready for my release.

One flick of her tongue over my head.

Two flicks.

Three flicks, then I'm the one exploding in her warm mouth and being sucked dry.

I grunt my release, giving her every drop of cum I have to offer. My eyes close, my fingers pull away from her entrance while

I bury my face in her core. I grip her ass cheeks, my fingernails digging into the soft flesh, most definitely leaving crescent marks on her smooth skin.

With me in her throat, she swallows my release, then pulls back, my dick popping out of her mouth with an audible pop. In the distance, I think I can hear a phone ringing, but I'm not positive about it. I can't tell if a phone is ringing or if the ringing is coming from inside my head after having just came harder than I've ever come before.

Camille rolls off me and turns her body to lie beside me, her head resting against my shoulder. Our bodies are covered in sweat, our breathing heavy and erratic.

Neither of us speaks, but right now, we don't need to. All I need is her body next to mine. Staring at the ceiling, trying to get my breathing to calm, I reach down and take her hand to intertwine our fingers together.

The ringing starts again. This time I know it's not from inside my head. When I don't move to answer it, it continues for a moment longer, then silences.

As quickly as the ringing stops, it starts back again.

"You should get that, it must be important," Cam says with a sigh, pulling her hand away from mine.

I don't want to move, but I need to at least turn it off so it doesn't continue to interrupt our time together. Standing, I stretch out my limbs and walk toward the table where I'd left my phone. I plan to turn my phone off, and then I'll tell Camille about the baby and my decision to leave Karina.

Picking it up and unlocking it, I scroll through the notifications I missed, my eyebrows pulling together, seeing everything I missed.

Karina (12 missed calls)
Karina (27 unread messages)

I open the message thread and begin reading.

Karina: WHERE ARE YOU
Karina: 911!!!!
Karina: CALL ME

I only read three messages when my phone starts ringing in my hand, my wife's name and picture appearing on my screen. I answer the call, placing my phone between my ear and shoulder while I pick up my briefs from the floor and pull them on.

"Dean, thank God! Why haven't you been answering?" Her frantic voice comes over the line before I even have a chance to say anything.

"What's wrong?" I ask, suddenly on high alert. Goosebumps raise on my arms at the sound of my wife's voice.

"I'm at the hospital, Dean. I started bleeding. You didn't answer so I drove myself, but I can't be here alone." She hiccups on a sob. "Please, will you please come? I'm so scared. Please, I need you."

A chill runs down my spine. "I'm on my way."

"Thank you, thank you, thank you." She sobs into the phone.

"Send me your location." The line goes dead, my body turns cold, and my gut fills with dread.

With quick movements, I dress, running my fingers through my messy hair and wipe my mouth, trying to make myself appear somewhat put together before I have to face my wife.

"What's wrong?" Camille asks with a frown, sitting up and covering herself with her hands.

"I have to go," I grit out, unable to look at her, like the true fucking coward I am. Now's not the time to tell her that my wife is pregnant and might be having a miscarriage. While I was busy getting my dick sucked, my wife was sitting alone in the hospital, possibly losing our baby. A baby I wasn't sure I even wanted.

All I feel is guilt.

Guilt and shame.

Without looking back, I leave Camille alone in our special place.

I leave her to be with my wife.

I speed the entire drive to the hospital, swerving through traffic to get to Karina as quickly as possible. I pray to whoever will hear it, begging for Karina and our baby to be okay.

I'll end my affair.

I'll be a better husband.

I'll do anything for them to both be safe and healthy.

I've been here before; Karina has had multiple miscarriages. Since our daughter was born sleeping, she's been unable to carry a pregnancy past nine weeks.

I'm not sure how far along she is since we haven't had the first appointment yet, but I fucking pray this pregnancy will stick.

Once I arrive at the hospital, I jump out of my car the second it's parked and run inside, frantically telling the lady at the front desk why I'm here. It takes two seconds and a look at my driver's license for her to lead me back to the ER room occupied by my wife.

With my head hung in shame, I enter the room, our eyes meeting. Her hair is in a messy knot on top of her head, her face is bare of any makeup, and she looks so fucking tiny and fragile lying in the middle of the hospital bed.

This is where I should've been right from the start. I should've been at home with her, been there when she started bleeding, been the one to drive her to the hospital and check her in, just like I was there every time before. If I hadn't been so fucking distracted and busy with my own needs, I wouldn't have neglected my wife.

Maybe if I hadn't been causing her so much stress, she wouldn't be here now. Had I been a better husband, there's a chance she would be home right now, happy and not experiencing another miscarriage.

"You came," she says, her voice weak and raspy from crying.

"Always will, Karina. I'm so sorry that I wasn't there for you." I take off my suit jacket, tossing it on the waiting chair. Without a second thought, I carefully climb onto the bed beside my wife and take her small body into my arms, holding her against me while she cries.

"I'm so scared." She sniffles, looking up at me through her wet eyelashes.

"I'm here, baby, I'm here." She puckers her lips, so I kiss her. I kiss my wife with the taste of another woman's pussy on my tongue.

"Where were you?" she asks, pressing her nose against my chest and inhaling deeply.

The lie is already on the tip of my tongue and ready to go. "I was working."

"You smell like perfume." She raises an eyebrow in question, but I'm quick to lie about that too.

"Must be Marjorie's. She was in my office helping me prepare a few files to send to clients." She blinks, her expression unreadable. I'm not sure if she believes my lies; now unease sets in, and I worry that she can smell and taste Camille on me.

Clearing my throat, I pull away from her slowly and move to sit in the chair, just as the doctor enters the room.

"Good evening, Mr. and Mrs. Jameson. I'm Doctor Rion. I'd like to start with an ultrasound first."

I stay silent while Karina and the doctor speak, she tells him exactly what happened, when the bleeding started, and how much, and then answers other questions, but I don't pay attention. Instead, I sit there staring at my hands, saying silent prayers repeatedly that they'll both be okay.

The truth is, I don't want to be part of the ultrasound when the doctor performs it. I don't want him to confirm what I'm dreading. What I already know.

We lost our baby. Because of me, my wife lost the only thing she asked for.

Karina is a good wife and a great person. I love her, and I was in love with her once, and I wonder if I'll be able to get back there again if I really work at it and try. It may take some time, but I hope that I'll be able to fall in love with my wife again.

I fucking hope.

I'd been prepared to leave, but after this, I can't. There's no way I can leave my wife after she just had a miscarriage. I'm not that shitty of a person.

"Wow, we've got a very strong heartbeat." Dr. Rion's words pull me from my thoughts. On shaky legs, I stand and walk toward Karina, where she's getting an ultrasound. With a bright smile, the doctor moves the wand over Karina's still flat stomach and then turns the monitor so that we can see it.

A steady thump, thump, thump fills the room.

Our baby's heartbeat.

Our baby's very strong and steady heartbeat.

"Oh my God! Our baby is okay?" Karina cries, and once again, I zone everything out. The only thing I can focus on is the monitor that displays the scan of our unborn child and the sound of its heartbeat.

My prayers were answered.

Our baby will be okay, and I'll follow through with my end of the deal.

I'll end things with Camille, return to my wife, and try my hardest to fall in love with her again.

I can do it.

WE SPEND THE NIGHT AT THE HOSPITAL WHILE THEY RUN tests to ensure our baby is perfectly fine. Before we leave, Dr. Rion advised Karina that she was to be on bed rest until she could schedule an appointment with an obstetrician and be seen.

When she's discharged, a nurse wheels her out in a wheel-chair, and I help her into my car, stopping by a donut shop drive-through on the way home since she is craving a donut and smoothie.

Once at home, I carry Karina inside, help her shower, and dress her in pajamas. We don't speak as I place her in our bed, then return to our bathroom to take a shower of my own. She had asked me to shower with her, but I didn't trust being naked in front of her.

Good thing, too, because when I showered, I discovered that I did, in fact, have some remaining red lipstick smeared across my cock along with candy residue from Camille. Clearly, I did a poor job of cleaning properly at the hospital. The last thing I need is for Karina to have seen that, especially when she had already smelled her perfume on me.

I couldn't risk anything further. Not tonight, not when she is already fragile.

If she suspects already, she doesn't say anything.

She leaves me second-guessing myself, wondering if I've been discreet enough about my affair and covered my tracks.

There in the shower, I wash Camille off me for the last time. Our affair ended the moment I left the lighthouse, and any chance of us being together ever again goes down the drain the moment I wash her lipstick off my dick and brush my teeth, brushing away the taste of her sweet pussy.

I thought it meant something that we'd seen each other all these years later. That somehow, we were finding our way back to each other, but now I know that's not true.

We're over.

So fucking over.

ONCE WE'RE SETTLED BACK IN AT HOME, KARINA TRIES TO get an appointment with her obstetrician, but she is unable to see her for another two weeks.

I call Marjorie to tell her my plan to work from home for the foreseeable future, and Marjorie, being the best fucking assistant ever, is already putting a plan in place to keep the place running while I'm home. She even agrees to make a trip to my home to bring me some supplies from the office that she'll be unable to send over email.

I also choose to cut back on my workload, and after speaking with my partners at my architecture firm, they agree to take on a few of my clients so that I can have more time to spend with Karina.

Camille is the first client I pawn off on Anthony, one of my partners. Luckily, everything is already finalized, and her build already in progress, so there isn't much anyone else needs to do. All Anthony needs to do is follow my notes and detailed instructions to ensure everything finishes by the scheduled date. I trust him completely.

As expected, Camille blows up my phone and email with questions about why I'm transferring her to someone else. I have Marjorie respond to her inquires, being too much of a coward myself to speak with her. Too worried that if I do, I'd bow at her feet and go back to her; but I made a deal with God. He kept mine and Karina's baby safe, so now I must hold up my end of the deal and stay away from Camille.

Here's to hoping it'll be as easy as it sounds.

THIRTY-EIGHT

NOW

Camille

It's been two weeks since Dean walked out on me that night at the lighthouse.

Two weeks since we've spoken, and nearly two weeks since I received an email from his assistant informing me that Dean's partner, Anthony, will now be the new person in charge of my build. Apparently, due to personal reasons, Dean is taking a step back from work. Since we're already in the building phase and all the plans and blueprints have been approved, everything should flow smoothly with Anthony.

You bet your ass that that email pissed me off, and I tried to contact him multiple times—each call going ignored, every text going unanswered.

After about a week, I finally got the hint. Dean is done with me.

He took the coward's way out and couldn't even tell me on my face. After our history and all that we've shared, he couldn't man the fuck up enough to tell me to my face that he didn't want to see me anymore.

I told him about Declan and I divorcing when we were together at the lighthouse, and I was going to tell him that I wanted us to finally be together. I was going to lay all my cards on the table and hope that he wanted me as much as I wanted him.

Foolishly, I had wanted him to choose me. Instead, he chose her.

She called, he went running, and that's the last I've seen of him.

I don't have the right to feel hurt by his actions. Not when he was never mine to begin with. I knew our affair couldn't continue, and I was ready for it to end, but I didn't anticipate it ending like this, or hurting as much as it does.

Not sure what hurts the most. The fact he couldn't break up with me to my face, or the fact he pawned me off on his partner. My building means something to me, and he knows that but clearly doesn't care, considering he so easily sent me to work with someone else.

What the fuck ever.

I don't have time to wallow and be upset that the married man I was seeing is back home with his wife, acting as if I don't exist. I brought this on myself by having an affair in the first place, so I can't feel sorry for myself now.

Instead, I've busied myself with work during this time, which is where I am now.

I'm sitting behind my desk, reviewing employee files and resumes and looking through the internal applications I've received from my New York employees interested in transferring to Seattle. The head of HR posted the internal postings a few weeks ago, and the response has been mind-blowing. I hadn't been aware that I had so many loyal employees who would be willing to move across the country for the opportunity to work with me in Seattle.

I'm occupied reading over an application when my intercom beeps, and Emily's voice cuts through. "Excuse me, Camille, sorry to bother you, but you have someone to see you." I roll my eyes at that. When I got to work this morning, I'd asked not to be disrupted unless it was necessary.

With a sigh, I reach forward and press the green button on the black intercom that sits on my desk. "Thanks, please send them in." My fingers tap against the stack of papers in front of me. My nerves are shot; I'm anxious and on edge. Hopefully, whoever it is at my door will be able to provide the distraction I need to get me out of my thoughts.

Sadie had emailed me earlier saying she'd be sending over some documents, so I wonder if she decided to deliver them in person instead. When a light knock comes to my door, I don't bother standing; instead, I yell out, "Come in!" and sit back in my chair, crossing my legs underneath my desk.

The door opens, and my fucking jaw drops at the sight of the person who enters my office.

Karina.

What the actual fuck.

The beautiful blonde walks in wearing a snarky smirk on her bright pink lips. I stand, crossing my arms across my chest, instantly on edge and on high alert. What in the ever-loving fuck could she possibly want from me?

"What are you doing here, Karina?" She holds her hands up, keeping her distance.

Smart.

"I'm here to apologize for my behavior that night at dinner."

"You've already apologized. Coming here wasn't necessary."

"Yes, it is. I owe you an apology face-to-face. Please, just a moment of your time." I know I'll regret this and should say no, but instead of doing that, I let my arms fall to my sides and wave toward the empty seats in front of my desk, welcoming her to take a seat as I reclaim my own.

With a smile, she walks toward the chairs, pulls one out, and takes a seat, crossing her long slender legs. Her button nose scrunches up when she sits. "I like the perfume you're wearing. What is it?"

My eyebrows pull together in confusion, taken aback by her random interest in my perfume. "It's custom, a gift I got a while back from Declan." A ghost of a smile tugs at my lips at the memory. I'd been complaining because I had dropped my favorite perfume bottle and broke it, and since it had been discontinued, there was no way to buy another bottle. A week later, Declan surprised me with a new bottle of perfume that he'd customized himself. He chose the perfect scents that he said reminded him of me, and I've been wearing it every day ever since.

"Well, it must not be too custom because Dean's assistant has the same one. Maybe Declan just told you it was special," she says smugly, raising her eyebrow in challenge.

Her words are unexpected, but I keep a straight face, not wanting to show her that it affects me. Marjorie doesn't wear the same perfume as I do, and I know that for a fact for two reasons.

One, Declan created the perfume. You can't buy it anywhere. And two, Marjorie once complimented me on it and asked where she could buy it for her daughter. I'd told her the same thing I just told Karina; it's a unique creation. You can't purchase it.

Which means only one thing. If she smelled it on Dean, then it's from me. I don't know if he's told her about our affair, though I'm assuming he hasn't, or I'm sure she'd be here clawing my eyes out instead.

Clearing my throat, I sit up straighter in my chair. "Thanks for stopping by, but I have a lot of work to do."

"Understood, I won't take long. Again, I only wanted to apologize for my behavior and what I said. That was completely unacceptable. And as a mother myself, I should've known better." Her lips stretch into a wide smile, her hand spreading out over her flat stomach. "Your advice to pause and stop stressing really seemed to work. *My* husband and I are having a baby." The way she emphasizes *my* doesn't go unnoticed.

With a challenging look, Karina turns her phone toward me, showing me the gray and black ultrasound photo.

My heart stops beating and falls into my stomach. I feel the color drain from my face as a chill shoots down my spine and goosebumps spread across my flesh.

Karina's pregnant.

She's having Dean's baby.

He's been ignoring me because his wife is pregnant with their child.

I don't think I'm even breathing as I stare at the photo for so long, my vision becomes blurry, and my ears begin ringing.

"I hope you're enjoying working with Anthony. It's been so nice to have Dean home for a change and not have him distracted. He's been having so many late-night meetings. Good thing that'll no longer happen." The implication is evident in her tone.

Clearing my throat, I ask, "How long have you known? About the baby?" My stomach is rolling, and I'm more nauseous than ever. I say a silent prayer hoping that Dean recently found out about it and wasn't aware during our time together. My heart beats wildly in my chest, my hands shake in my lap, and I slowly wipe my sweaty palms on my legs.

"For about a month. I told him as soon as the test returned positive." She smiles, and I'm unable to tell if she's lying.

Karina stands, shoving her phone into the back pocket of her jeans. "Have a nice day, Camille. Tell Declan I said hello." Without another word, she exits my office. The slamming door behind her snaps me out of my stupor.

Karina knows, and I shouldn't be surprised. Dean and I haven't exactly been the most discreet.

I remain seated, unable to trust myself to stand when my entire body feels numb. I'm too in shock to move or form a single thought. I can only remain seated in my chair and stare blankly out at the city.

Even as it gets dark, I remain in the same position.

SOMEHOW, I MANAGE TO GET MYSELF HOME AFTER WORK. I don't remember how, but I was able to drive and stop at the liquor store on the way. I have no recollection, but the empty liquor bottles on my nightstand are all the proof I need, that and the fact I spent several hours hugging the toilet, puking my guts out. I dragged myself from the cold tile of my bathroom floor and put myself to bed, and I've been here since. Unable to move, unable to do much of anything besides stay buried in my blanket burrito and alternate between sleeping, feeling sorry for myself, and being angry at myself.

"It's two in the afternoon on a Sunday, and you're still in bed." Spencer's disapproving tone breaks me away from my internal thoughts. I didn't hear her enter my apartment.

With a groan, I roll my eyes, aware that she can't see me through the darkness of my bedroom. Except the darkness doesn't last much longer because she yanks open the black-out curtains, revealing the warm afternoon sun shining bright in the sky.

I hiss and close my eyes when the rays hit my skin. "I've never seen you like this before. This is unacceptable, and very un-Camille-like." The mattress shifts when she climbs beside me, scooting toward where I lie in the middle. "Talk to me, little sis. What happened?" I haven't told her about my breakup—if you could even call it that.

"Nothing, I'm fine. Just tired. Close the blinds and leave."

"Not happening. You're not fine, so start talking. Is it about Dean?" With an annoyed groan, I kick the blankets away from my body and sit up, leaning back against my headboard.

"Why are you here, Spencer?"

"Because, Camille, Declan called me and said he was worried about you, so I came to check on you."

"Declan? Why would he be worried about me?" My face scrunches in confusion.

"You don't remember calling him? He said you left him several voicemails crying and flooded his phone with incoherent texts. He said his phone was off at the time, so he missed them, but once he got them, he called me when you wouldn't answer."

My shoulders sag in defeat. I'd been too drunk that I don't

even remember drunk calling my soon-to-be ex-husband. Not sure what I even said on his voicemail. I probably don't want to know.

I pat across the bed in search of my phone, only to find it on my bedside table. With a groan, I pick up the device and tap the screen, instantly seeing the drained red battery icon. Reaching over, I grab the white charging cord and plug it into my phone, setting it back on my nightstand.

"Start talking. What's going on with you?"

Taking a deep breath, I close my eyes that are already filling with tears. "I've been thinking about a lot of things lately. My head is a little fucked up right now."

"Tell me, sis. Please. Fucked up about what?"

"Luca. Declan. Dean. Karina." I sigh, scrubbing my hands over my face and raking my fingers through the bird's nest of hair on my head. "I feel like a piece of shit for sleeping with another woman's husband. I met a lonely woman in a fucking support group for grieving parents who were suffering and just wanted a friend. What did I do instead of keeping my legs closed and being a friend? I fucked her husband the first chance I got. While she struggled to get pregnant and turned a blind eye to her husband's infidelity, I was giving him a blowjob at work." A humorless laugh falls from my dry lips.

"Let's not forget that I, too, have a husband. A husband who was fresh out of rehab and wanted to make our marriage work. A husband who loved me and wanted us to find a new normal and learn to exist together, as just the two of us. My husband was at home fighting his demons and trying to stay sober while I was sneaking around with some boy from my childhood, acting like we were both single and not hurting anyone." Spencer remains silent, letting me vent and get all my thoughts out. "What kind of woman does that? I should've been home with my husband grieving with him. Did you know that we never mourned the loss of Luca together? He turned to drugs, and I turned to controlling every aspect of our life and switched off my emotions. When it started to get too much, I took medication to fucking numb my emotions to get through the day. Dr. Reynolds thought it was helping me in the way it's supposed to, but she doesn't know I was taking it multiple times a day instead of just once like I was prescribed, and it was making me numb to everything." Her hands find mine, and she intertwines our fingers and holds my hands tightly, her thumbs rubbing along my flesh soothingly.

"I didn't tell any of you I was taking medication either." No one knew because I didn't want to be seen as weak. I didn't want to tell anyone that it felt like a fucking hole had been punched through my chest. A hole that only Luca could fill. No one knew that night after night I'd crawl into the fetal position and cry myself to sleep, praying that God would give my son back and take me instead. "Apparently, according to Dr. Reynolds, I have bipolar depression, but the meds don't fucking work, so I stopped taking them."

By this point, tears are streaming down my face. I only notice when I taste the saltiness on my lips. "When I went to New York, Declan and I got to mourn our loss together. For the first time, over a year later. It was what we needed, and finally, fucking finally, I was starting to feel better." That moment with Dec will forever mean everything to me. "Then, a couple of weeks ago with Dean, I had a cold wakeup call. Karina called him, he went running to her and left me naked and alone. That was the moment I realized what a true piece of shit I am." My shoulders shake with my ugly sobs. I half expect Spencer to tell me to fuck off for carrying on with Dean as long as I did, but she surprises me by pulling me close, wrapping her arms around me, and hugging me tightly against her.

"You made a mistake, and it's okay. We all make mistakes. It's over now, and it's what matters right now. You realized your mistake, and you're not going to make the same one again. It's time to let him go once and for all. Let go and leave Dean in the past where he belongs. Nothing good can come from it." I sob into her T-shirt, nodding my head, knowing damn good and well she's right.

"She's pregnant, Spence. She's having his baby. Dean knew she was pregnant while he was fucking me." She squeezes me tightly against her, knowing what I secretly went through years ago. She knows my biggest secret, a secret I made her promise that we'll take to our graves and never tell a single soul. A secret only she and I know about.

I know about Dean and Karina's history of going through miscarriages and a stillbirth, but that was all in the past. That didn't affect me. She's pregnant now, meaning they were sleeping together during the same time that Dean and I were sleeping together. He got her pregnant even after we reconnected and started our relationship. He told me so many times that they were no longer having sex. He lied.

Of course, he did. He was already lying to his wife. Why wouldn't he lie to me, too? I've been such a fool.

Shifting my body, I lay my head down on my sister's lap and let her stroke my hair while I bawl my eyes out, losing myself in memories of the past.

THIRTY-NINE

THEN

CAMILLE, *15 years old*

Dean left for his stupid fancy university in England two months ago.

Spencer left, too, leaving me all alone.

Both of my best friends are gone.

I have no one.

I hate being alone, and I hate that I'm experiencing my first heartbreak by someone who was never officially mine.

When I went to the lighthouse the day after Dean left, I found another Post-it note. The paper was blue and written in bold black letters.

Don't forget me.

As if I ever could. I'll never forget the person who made me feel more alive than I've ever been and made me feel limitless.

Everyone says the sky's the limit, but not Dean.

He's never once limited me.

I had hoped to find more Post-it notes, hoping that he had them hidden around, a reminder that he was still with me, but there was nothing else. I searched everywhere, and there were no notes.

I tried to talk to him a few times when I'd overheard him speaking with his parents, but I wasn't able to.

He was here one minute, then gone the next. It didn't help that both of our parents were always working or at the club more than usual.

Without Spencer and Dean here, I didn't realize how quiet and empty my house could be.

It's been two months, but it feels like yesterday.

Two weeks ago, I did a bad thing, and no one is here to even yell at me for it.

For the first time in my fifteen years of life, I stole.

Since I don't have my driver's license, I rode my bike to the corner store. The teenage clerk was too busy reading his comic book to even notice me when I entered or left. He also didn't notice when I grabbed the pink and white box from the shelf, shoved it down my sweater, and ran out.

I'd been sweating and shaking in fear the entire bike ride home, looking behind me every two seconds, convinced that I'd see flashing red and blue lights, but nothing happened. I made it home without being arrested and thrown into a cold jail cell for being a thief.

Just in case I was on the FBI's most wanted list for stealing, I laid low for a few days. I stayed home, telling Mom that I was sick when she tried to get me out of the house for school shopping. If the police came for me, I had hoped I'd be able to give the stolen item back in exchange for my freedom, so I didn't even use what I stole. I kept the sealed box wrapped in clothes and hidden in the back of my closet.

It's been two weeks since that day, and since I'm not in jail, I'll consider it now safe to use what I stole. That thought is on my mind as I grab the box from my closet and run into the bathroom with it hidden under my shirt.

Just in case Mom came into my room, I had to keep it hidden.

That's where I am now. Locked in my bathroom, anxiously waiting for the YouTube video to load. When I open the box, I read over the instructions twelve times but want to make sure I use it correctly, so I look up a video for reassurance.

Three videos and two hours later, I finally feel ready to do it myself.

With shaky fingers, I manage to slide my pajama shorts down my legs, sit on the toilet, and position the white stick between my legs.

After I pee directly on the fabric tip, I replace the cap and set the stick on the counter while I wash my hands and busy myself for the longest two minutes of my life.

When the timer beeps, my heart stops.

I hold the stick with shaky fingers and pray that the two bright pink lines are only my imagination. But I'm not that lucky. Since there are two tests in the box, I take the second one, convinced that the first one is a false positive.

Two tests. Both positive. They are correct.

I'm pregnant.

The first thing I do is call Spencer, and the second I hear her voice, the tears start. I'm barely able to get out what I need to say, but somehow, she can piece it together through my broken sobs.

She lets me cry to her as I lie on the bathroom floor in the fetal position, one hand on my flat stomach, the other hand holding my phone so tightly that my knuckles turn white.

This can't be happening.

I can't be pregnant.

I can't be.

"You have to tell Mom, little sis, please wake her up and tell her."

"No!" I whisper-yell, frantic at the thought of my parents finding out. They'll be so disappointed and angry with Dean and with me. Spencer is the only one who knows that I lost my virginity to Dean before he left, and even she is disappointed in me. She lost hers at sixteen but said even that was too young. I've asked her before if she regrets it, and she said no because she and Dallas were in love at the time. They're not together anymore, and she doesn't like it whenever he's brought up, but I know she still loves him.

"You have to, little sis. You can't keep this a secret. You'll need proper care that Mom and Dad can help you get."

"I can't have a baby, Spence, I can't." Soon, she's crying right along with me.

"Try and get some sleep. We'll talk about this later." Even though she can't see me, I nod anyway, hanging up with shaky fingers.

Soon, I cry myself to sleep there on my cold bathroom floor while my parents sleep soundly down the hall.

THE FOLLOWING TWO WEEKS GO BY IN A BLUR. SCHOOL IS starting soon, and my daily morning sickness is my constant reminder that I'm pregnant at fifteen and will be starting my sophomore year pregnant if I don't decide soon.

I've been thinking long and hard about my choices and what's best for not only my future but for Dean's future as well.

If I keep the baby, I'll eventually have to drop out of school and will be lucky if I graduate and get to go to college. Knowing Dean, he would rush straight home if he knew and give up his college education to take care of our baby and me. He'd be by my side. I know that for a fact. We'd become a family and eventually get married, but we'd never achieve all that we wanted to. I know the statistics for teen parents. I've done plenty of research over the last two weeks.

Keeping this baby means putting our hopes and dreams on pause and likely never achieving them. We'd have to get jobs to support ourselves, and we'd be too busy working that we wouldn't have the chance to focus on furthering our education and starting a business as we both want.

Dean wouldn't be upset with me at first, but I know that one day, maybe in five or ten years from now, he'll look at me with resentment because he'll be stuck at a job he hates, wishing he finished school and had the proper chance to become the architect he wants to become.

The point is, we're too young. Fifteen and eighteen is way too young to be having a baby. We have our whole lives ahead of us, and one day, I know that we'll become parents, but not now. Not when we have no higher education and would rely on our parents for financial support.

Now isn't the time.

It's not an easy decision to make, but I know what I must do.

It's just not the time for us.

SPENCER COMES HOME A FEW DAYS LATER.

We both start school in two weeks, but she wanted to see me before that, and I desperately need my sister.

Actually, I needed a driver and someone to hold my hand and support me with the decision I made that'll forever alter my life but allow Dean and me to finish school and follow our dreams.

It's Saturday morning, and my parents are at the country club. I'm sitting outside on the front step of our house when I see my sister's cab pull up to the front of our home. Her flight came in early this morning, and since our parents are not yet aware she will be home for the weekend, she had to take a taxi home.

She steps out with her duffle bag, and I run toward her, nearly knocking us both over. Hot and heavy tears stream down my face uncontrollably.

"Shh, it's okay, baby sis. I'm here now." She soothes me, rubbing the back of my head gently. "Let's go inside and talk."

"No. I need to go somewhere, please. Can you drive me?" She pulls back, giving me a questioning look, but doesn't press me further. She nods and carries her duffle bag toward the front door.

"I'll grab Mom's keys, be back." Our parents took my dad's car to the country club, leaving our mother's car behind.

Minutes later, the garage door creaks open, and Spencer is in the driver's seat, backing the car out of the garage.

Picking up my backpack, I throw the strap over my shoulder and rush toward her, climbing into the passenger seat.

She waits until we're exiting our gated community before she looks over and speaks. "Are we going to see a doctor?" I nod, digging in the front pocket of my backpack, and handing her the folded-up piece of paper containing an address. I throw my backpack into the backseat while she enters the address into the GPS.

"Something like that. Please, drive." With a nod, she does exactly that. She follows the GPS and drives me to the one place that has all the power to save my future.

Forty minutes later, we arrive at the small brown building with a white sign that reads On Your Timing Parenthood.

Reading the sign, Spencer's eyes widen as she places the car in park and shifts to face me, her brown eyes as wide as saucers. "An abortion clinic?!" she yells, shaking her head in disapproval. I cringe at the word; it sounds so aggressive and dirty when it shouldn't. There is nothing wrong with terminating a pregnancy. All women should be able to have the choice regarding their bodies.

"I can't have a baby, Spencer. One day I'll start a family when the time is right, but right now is not the time. I want to finish high school, go to college, and start my own business. How can I do any of that with a baby at fifteen?" Warm tears stream down my face. "I'm just a kid, Spencer, a kid who shouldn't have a kid." Her face matches mine, eyes red from crying, nose stuffy, and running. "I want to be a kid and grow up first. I don't want to be a mother right now." I don't regret my night of passion with Dean, but I regret not being more careful. I was on my pill and thought that would be all the protection we'd need. I now understand why parents say not to have sex until you're older.

"You are so strong for making this decision all by yourself. If you're sure this is what you want, I will support you and hold your hand. Are you positive this is what you want?" I nod, wiping away my tears and snot with the back of my hand.

"I'm positive. This is what I want." Without another word, she grabs my backpack from the backseat and leads me inside the clinic hand in hand.

We're greeted by the dark-skinned woman sitting behind the front desk with a friendly smile. Her brown scrubs blend perfectly with her beautiful skin tone. "Hello ladies, how can I help you today?"

"H-h-hi," I stammer, my hands shaking, more nervous than I've ever been. "I'm pregnant, and I can't have a baby." Her brown eyes are sympathetic and comforting.

"I understand, sweetheart. My name is Polly, and we'll take great care of you today." She helps me through the paperwork, and Spencer lists herself as my emergency contact and even pays for the service.

After everything is completed, Polly takes me back to a room that resembles any other exam room I've been in before. She explains everything to me in detail, no matter how graphic. I'm nervous, but at least I know what to expect now, thanks to her.

Spencer couldn't come into the room with me, but Polly, to my surprise, holds my hand the entire time.

Once it is over, Spencer brings me the backpack that contains extra clothes and helps me change into the loose-fitting sweatpants and sweatshirt I have brought. She helps me to the car and drive us home in silence.

Just like that, I am no longer pregnant and am determined to achieve every single goal I have set for myself, determined to do it in memory of my child. I feel guilty enough. The last thing I needed was to do what I did and not make my dreams come true. I did what I did for a reason.

I did what I felt was right, and once we arrive home, I never spoke about it again.

FORTY
NOW

DEAN

Two months.

It's been two months since I've seen her—two long, painful, horrific months.

Every day we are apart reminds me of how truly unhappy I am without her and how unhappy I am in my marriage. I thought I'd be able to stay with Karina for the sake of our child, but I realize that a child isn't a reason to stay in a marriage. A child doesn't save a broken marriage, no matter how much Karina wishes it does. She's four months along, meaning we still have a long and dreadful five months ahead of us.

Although it may not seem like it, I'm truly grateful that our baby is doing good and is healthy. Karina is still fearful that something terrible will happen, which is understandable given our history, so I stay with her. It's the least I can do after being a cheating piece of shit.

I've completely moved into the guest room, and we only speak when it involves the baby. We're roommates at this point, and it kills me that I'm here while my heart is living on the other side of the city, all alone.

While at lunch with my mother a couple of weeks ago, she

409

told me that Camille and Declan were getting a divorce, and he had moved back to New York, confirming what I already knew. My mom is a very intuitive person, she knew something was going on with me.

Unable to lie to her, I told her everything. I told her about Camille and me rekindling our flame and having an affair. She wasn't happy, but she didn't curse me out and judge me like I half expected her to do. Instead, she hugged me and told me that she loved me and would support me in any decision I made regarding my future and the future of my marriage.

That's my mother for you.

Supportive as fuck, even when I mess up.

I'm not proud to admit it, but I've driven by her apartment a few times, parking across the street or hiding away in the parking garage, hoping I'll see her. I need to see her like I need my next breath.

I need to touch her warm, soft body, need to hold her in my arms and feel her relax against me and rest her head on my chest, need her plump lips against mine, but most of all, I need to be in her presence. I thought I was doing the right thing by staying away and staying with Karina for the sake of our child, but I was wrong.

So fucking wrong.

To my luck, I did get to see Camille. Twice.

The first time, she was wearing sweats and looked utterly defeated. She kept her head down, and her dark hair covered her face like a curtain as if trying to hide from the world. She was a shell of the person she once was, and all I wanted to do was jump out of my car and go to her. To hold her in my arms and tell her how sorry I was for leaving her, for breaking her when I knew she was already fragile.

She was wearing jeans and a hoodie the second time and was walking with Declan, his arm around her shoulders, and she was tucked into his side, her arm around his waist, holding on to him like her life depended on it. It stung to see them together, but I had to keep reminding myself that they were divorcing and were probably preparing to go their separate ways.

After that, I never saw her again and stopped being a creep and hanging outside her building. Instead, I've sent her flowers. Every day for two weeks straight, I had flowers—a dozen red roses —delivered to her condo. Each time with the same handwritten note.

I'm sorry.

There is so much more I need to say to her, but I am not going to say all I need to say on a note. I had hoped she'd call me and give me the chance to tell her everything I need to say either over the phone or face-to-face.

Whenever my phone pinged, I hoped it was her... it never was.

One drunken night, I decided to man the fuck up and call her, only to immediately hear the robotic voice tell me the call was unable to be completed.

She blocked me. Camille blocked my number.

I even emailed her, only to discover she blocked my email address as well.

She had blocked me from her life completely.

Desperate to find out anything, I asked my mom if she'd heard from her, but she was tight-lipped and wouldn't tell me anything. Something was going on, it was clear that my mother knew, which wasn't surprising since she's been best friends with Cam's mother since college, plus they're neighbors.

I called her office. The receptionist told me she was on a leave of absence and would pass on a message when she returned.

She was going to great lengths to keep me away, but I only had myself to blame.

That was three weeks ago.

Since then, I've stopped everything. Stopped sending flowers,

411

quit trying to contact her, and stopped asking her family about her. I quit all stalking cold turkey.

I believe she will return to me when she's ready but needs her space until then. I let her go once eleven years ago, and I won't make the same mistake again. Space isn't the same as letting go.

I'm sitting in my home office staring at my computer screen, reading over an email from a potential client. My mind is elsewhere, and I can barely focus; I've had to reread the email six times already, still not comprehending what the hell it says.

This is how I've been lately. Unable to focus.

Deciding to give up and call it a night, I let out a sigh and lock my computer just as Karina walks into my office with a hand on her small, barely there baby bump.

"You left your phone in the kitchen. It won't stop beeping," she says with an eye roll. "You changed your password, so I can't even check it to make it stop." She tosses the phone on my desk with a thud. I changed my password weeks ago when I caught her snooping on it while I was in the shower.

Without saying anything, I reach a hand forward toward the phone and pick it up, entering my passcode to see that I have three unread messages. I ignore two of them, the ones from old high school buddies I'd recently reconnected with who were trying to meet up.

My heart skips a beat when I see the name and read the contents of the message the third person sent me. Taking a sharp breath, I lock it again and look up at Karina, already standing up from my chair. "Thanks. I'm going out. Be back later," I say, brushing past her as I exit my office and walk off toward the guest room that has become my bedroom.

Karina doesn't say anything, not that I care what she has to say anyway. Nothing will stop me from running out the door and getting to where I need to be.

After dressing in joggers and a T-shirt, I shove my wallet, phone, and keys into my pocket and leave our house, walking down the long driveway and toward the road.

It takes me about ten minutes running to get to the nearest park. It's dark out, the air chilly, and the full moon is bright and high in the sky, providing enough lighting to see where I'm going. The park isn't well lit; it only has one streetlight that glows a soft yellow. But, with that and the moon, it's enough to see her.

She's sitting on a picnic table, her back toward me, her head hung low. As if she can sense my presence, her head snaps up, and her posture straightens as if she's preparing for battle and putting her mask back in place to protect herself.

My heart is racing in my chest, my lips part as I breathe heavy, my palms are clammy. I've been waiting for two months to be this close to her and hear her voice again, and I'm going to finally, fucking finally, get my wish.

On shaky legs, I rush toward her until I'm standing right in front of her.

Her bright emerald eyes look directly at me, her stare is cold, and anger radiates from her. I can physically feel what she feels. My heart breaks at the sight of her. She's got bags under her hollow eyes, and her jawline is sharper, her cheekbones more prominent. It's clear that she's lost weight, though she is still the most beautiful woman I have ever fucking laid eyes on.

"Oh, Cam, I'm so fucking sorry." I sigh, taking a step closer and reaching my arms out for her. She hurries back from where she's sitting on the table, recoiling from my attempt to touch her. A frown finds my lips as I drop my hands, shoving them into the pockets of my joggers.

"I just want to know one thing. Why? Why didn't you tell me?" She crosses her arms over her chest, holding herself tightly as if she's trying to protect herself. "Why didn't you tell me yourself? You could've saved me the embarrassment of finding out from her." Her words are laced with pure malice.

What the fuck is she talking about?

My face scrunches in confusion. She must see that we're not on the same page because she's quick to explain herself. "You should've been the one to tell me your wife is pregnant!" she snarls in disgust.

Fuck. Fuck. Fuck.

Wait, Camille said that she told her... meaning Karina.

Karina told her that she's pregnant.

My mind races, trying to figure out when the fuck Karina would've even seen her and been able to tell her the news that I should've told her myself. The news I should've told her the night at the lighthouse before I let her spread her glorious thighs over my face.

"Do you know how fucking stupid I felt? She came to my office and showed me the fucking ultrasound, raving about how she's pregnant, and you two are stronger than ever. This was after you left me naked and alone and ignored me for two weeks." She scoffs, shaking her head, looking me up and down in pure disgust. "How long have you known?"

"Since you went to New York," I answer honestly, looking her right in the eye.

"Why didn't you tell me?" Her bright eyes darken with sadness and anger, her eyes becoming glossy, her bottom lip trembling.

"I didn't know what to do." Once again, I give her an honest answer despite how weak it sounds.

"You didn't know what to do?" She surprises me by laughing in my face. "You tell your mistress it's over, that you got your wife pregnant, then you go home and stick beside your pregnant wife. That's what the fuck you do." She laughs maniacally. "What happened when she called you that night? You ran out of there like you were on fire." She giggles, covering her mouth with her hands, her shoulders shaking with her laughter.

I don't understand what she finds so funny, but I keep my mouth shut, feeling as if she's on the verge of snapping at any moment. Plus, I don't want to say anything that'll upset her and cause her to leave. This is my first time speaking to her in two months, and I will enjoy it for as long as I can, regardless of whether I like our conversation topic.

"She called me from the hospital. Said she was bleeding and thought she had another miscarriage, so I left to go to her." My jaw clenches as I relive that fearful moment.

My answer causes her to stop laughing. She squares her shoulders, her eyebrows raising in question as if she's waiting for me to say something else. "She didn't lose the baby. She's still pregnant."

"She's having your baby." It's not a question but a statement. She nods in understanding, shoving her hands into the pockets of the hoodie she's wearing.

"I was so fucking scared, Camille. You know her pregnancy history, so I ran to be with her at the hospital. I'm so fucking sorry that I left you the way that I did, but I had to make sure my baby was okay. You don't know what went through my head when I heard her scared voice on the phone and even during the drive to the hospital." I shake my head, climb onto the table, and sit beside her, turning my body, so I'm facing her. To my surprise, she does the same so we can be face-to-face.

She doesn't speak, so I continue, "I felt like it was my fault. Like if I had been a better husband, then she wouldn't be at risk of losing our child. I wasn't sure about children, you know that, but seeing her in the hospital bleeding and then seeing the screen and hearing the heartbeat, it was so fucking incredible. I vowed every fucking day that I would be there for her if she could keep our baby. I had to go to her, Cam, I had to. She was alone and afraid she was going through yet another miscarriage. You don't know what it's like to be alone and experience that."

Her shoulders tense, her breathing becoming uneven as she stares at me like I've grown three heads.

"Fuck. You." She spits between clenched teeth. Her moods are giving me whiplash. I'm not sure what I said to anger her, but it's clear that I have. "You left me alone!" she yells, jumping down from the table.

"I told you why, because no matter what, she didn't deserve to experience that alone."

"You left me alone to experience something horrific when I needed you!" she screams, pacing back and forth like a madwoman.

Shaking my head in confusion, I climb down from the table and step toward her. "Cam, what are you talking about?" My brows scrunch together.

"I was fifteen, Dean! You got me pregnant, then left me alone! So don't you fucking dare tell me I don't know what it's like to be alone in that situation." Tears stream down her defeated face. My body stills, my blood running cold at her revelation.

Camille was pregnant. She was pregnant with my baby. Considering we don't have a living child together, I'm assuming she miscarried.

No wonder Karina being pregnant hurts her so much.

"Cam," I whisper her name in a plea, opening my arms to her. She runs into my arms, wrapping her arms so tightly around me as she sobs into my chest, her body violently shaking from her sobbing. "I didn't know, Cam, I didn't fucking know."

"I've gotta go." She sniffles, pulling away from me. She wipes her snot and tears away with the back of her sleeve.

"Please, don't go. Stay. We can keep talking."

She shakes her head. "There's nothing else we can say. We're over, Dean. I shouldn't have even come tonight, but I just needed to know why you left. Now I do, so I can move on."

"Cam—" She cuts me off by holding up her hand.

"Don't, Dean, just go home to your wife. This is goodbye." She looks me right in the eye, and I believe everything she says. She's telling me goodbye for good; she's done with me. That's it. We're over regardless of what I say. "Declan is waiting for me, so I should hurry." She looks behind me toward the parking lot, the black SUV parked there, a dark figure hidden behind the wheel that I hadn't noticed before.

"We can make this work. This doesn't have to be the end. I don't want her. I want you."

"I want you too, but we don't always get what we want, Dean. She's having your baby. Go home and be with her," she says, forcing herself to smile at me. "Sometimes, no matter how much you love someone, it's not enough, and you're not meant to be. No matter how badly you want to be together, it's not possible."

"It's always been you, Camille. There's never been a moment when it hasn't been you. You are it for me."

"No matter how badly I wish I could, I can't be, Dean." She stands on her tiptoes and wraps her arms around my neck. "We're toxic together. We're stuck in an unhealthy cycle, and we can't continue it anymore. You have unresolved feelings that you need to work out, and I need to focus on myself and my own healing." She presses her lips against mine, kissing me with every ounce of passion she has. I wrap my arms around her waist, press my body against hers, and kiss her, savoring how she feels against me and how her tongue tastes in my mouth.

Our kissing is frantic; neither of us can get close enough or enough of each other. My cock twitches and hardens between us, poking against her soft stomach. She must feel it because she presses herself closer against me, groaning into my mouth.

Fuck this.

If she's going to leave me, I need more than a kiss to say good-bye. I don't give a fuck if her soon-to-be-ex-husband is waiting for her only feet away. He can keep waiting.

Leaning down, I grip the backs of her thighs and pick her up. She wraps her legs around my waist, and I quickly carry her toward the bathrooms. It shields us from Declan's view to give us some privacy. The park bathrooms here are always disgusting, so I don't go inside.

Instead, I press her back against the brick wall near the bathroom door. My lips trail down from her lips to her neck, kissing any piece of skin I can reach. She moves a hand between us and grips my cock through the thin fabric of my pants.

"Tell me you love me," I rasp against her neck, inhaling her sweet scent into my nostrils, getting high on her smell.

"I do, Dean. I've always loved you." Her voice is shaky, and I can tell that she's crying. Raising my head, I press my lips against hers.

Breaking away from my kiss, she pushes against my chest and wiggles until I set her down. "Dean, I hope you know that I will always love you. You will always be a part of me," she says, her lips curling into a frown as tears begin streaming down her face. Reaching up, I use my thumbs to wipe away the tears from her devastatingly beautiful face. "I can't do this anymore. *We* can't do this anymore. It's so easy to give in to you, but I can't because giving in to you means losing a piece of myself." She kisses me one final time, our lips locked and lingering together.

Finally, she pulls away from me and turns, giving me her back as she walks away from me, taking my heart with her.

I REMAIN IN THE PARK UNTIL CAMILLE CLIMBS INTO Declan's SUV, and they drive away. Instead of rushing back home, I choose to take my time, walking home as slowly as possible, dreading having to walk through the front door. My lips are still swollen from kissing her, and I can still feel her lips against mine. A few of my knuckles are scraped from protecting her against the brick when I lifted her, but I can't feel anything. I'm entirely numb after seeing her. Unable to process anything that happened.

Unfortunately, it doesn't take long to get home. Once I do, I let myself in and head straight toward my bedroom, not even wanting to shower because I don't want to wash Camille off me. I want her scent to remain on my body. It's all that I have left of her now.

Sitting on the edge of my bed, I place my elbows on my knees, lean forward, and drop my head into my hands, my fingers tangling in my hair and pulling at the roots. The pain I felt when I left Cam standing in my driveway eleven years ago when I went away to school is nothing compared to the pain I feel now. It feels like a hole has been punched through my chest.

If this is how heartbreak feels, then I understand why some people choose to be alone and shield themselves from having to experience this. Watching the love of your life walk away from you, knowing there's not a damn thing you can do to stop her, is a pain I wouldn't wish on anyone.

My bedroom door flings open, hitting the wall behind it. The startling sound causes me to look up, my eyes landing on Karina, who stands in the doorway with her arms crossed over her chest and a scowl on her face. "Did you finally end it? Once and for all, is the affair over?" she asks, taking me by surprise.

She knows. How, I'm not sure, but she does. I thought I'd been discreet enough to hide it, but apparently not. I'm not going to insult either of us by denying it either. I can at least be man enough to own up to it.

"Yes, it's over," I admit painfully. Saying the words aloud is another painful stab to the chest, making the situation much more real.

Camille and I are over.

"Good. I forgive you for falling into temptation. You scratched your itch, and now it's time that you put that foolishness behind us so we can move forward and finally be a family." Karina has always been the type to hold a grudge over the smallest thing, so it surprises me that she so easily forgives me for carrying on an affair for several months.

For now, I don't read too much into her quick forgiveness. I focus on what upsets me the most. "She wasn't an itch, Karina," I state, narrowing my eyes at her.

"Yes, Dean. She was an itch you needed to scratch. You did that, and now you're home with me, where you belong." I press my lips together, allowing myself the chance to think about my words before I speak.

After a long moment of silence, I open my mouth and say the words that I should've said years ago. "I want a divorce, Karina."

Her face pales, her arms falling to her sides; she's taken aback by my words, surprised, though I'm not sure why. She knew this is where we've been heading for a long time.

"No!" she screams, taking me by surprise. She never loses control. "I'm your wife! You're not going to leave me just because you saw that woman again! I've known for years that you've always been in love with someone else. I understood that I was your consolation prize, the one you settled for, but I didn't mind because I have enough love for the both of us. I've been beside you, supporting you through everything, even moving to this horrible place to make you happy." She shakes her head, narrowing her eyes and practically shooting daggers at me. "You're not leaving me! I don't give a flying fuck if you're in love with her or not. You love me more, and I know you do!"

Quickly, I stand to my feet, rushing toward her. "Yes, I love her! I've been in love with her since the day I fucking met her! I will always be in love with her, regardless of if I can have her or not!" I roar, every single emotion I have rushing to the surface. I'm in love with her, and I always will be. There's no more denying or ignoring it. "I'm sorry, Karina, I never wanted to hurt you, and I do love you, but not the way you need me to. Not the way I love her. Not the way you deserve to be loved." She raises her hand, her palm connecting with my cheek. My head snaps to the side with the impact of her slap.

"Fuck you! All those times you looked me in my eyes and said you loved me, you lied." She scoffs. "Get the fuck out!" She's angry and has every right to be. She wants me to leave, so I will. It doesn't matter that the house is in my name and I'm the one paying for it. She can have it. I'm willing to call a lawyer and give her the house and whatever else she wants.

Regardless of what she believes, I do love her. I may not be in love with her, but I do love her. She's stood by my side as I built my business, helped me through sleepless nights as I focused on my career, and now she's carrying my child. Of course, I fucking love her.

Just not in that way.

Karina watches me like a hawk while I pack my bags, emptying out my closet and bathroom, fitting as much as possible into my suitcase and duffle bags. I can come back for the rest another day, but I need to go right now.

She doesn't say anything else as she follows me out to my car, watching me while I load my bags into the trunk and backseat.

"I'm not going to make this easy for you. You can't throw me away. I won't allow it," she says from where she stands in the driveway as I'm closing the trunk.

"Try to get some sleep, Karina. We'll talk later." I look into her blue eyes with a frown, looking between her face and her small baby bump.

Without another word, I climb behind the driver's seat and leave just like she wants me to.

I drive away with a broken heart, a massive headache, and a feeling in the pit of my stomach telling me something isn't right.

FORTY-ONE

NOW

Camille

Five months ago, Declan showed up in my room in the middle of the night. He had a late flight and never told me he was coming. I was sleeping and nearly had a heart attack when he slid in bed behind me and wrapped his arms around me. I screamed in fear; the fucker laughed at me. When I asked him what he was doing here, he told me that Spencer called him because she worried about me, and he was too after my drunken messages. I tried telling him I was fine and didn't need anyone, but he knew me too well and knew I was lying.

I wasn't fine, and I did need someone.

After confessing to myself and my family that my mental health wasn't good and hadn't been for a while, I allowed them to help me. My mom called Dr. Reynolds immediately and got me an emergency appointment for the next day.

Everyone cried when I opened myself up, became vulnerable, and told them how dark my mind could get. I told them I had been doing okay by taking medication, that it made me numb and made my days bearable, but I hated feeling like a robot and having to rely on it, so I'd stopped taking it. They were surprised. Mom knew after Luca's death, I had taken medication but had no idea I was still taking it nearly a year and a half later.

When I was too ashamed to face Dr. Reynolds again, Declan surprised me by taking my hand and going to my session with me. He sat on the couch beside me, rubbed my back, and urged me to talk about everything that I'd been holding in.

I couldn't explain why my mind sometimes went to dark places, but I did my best to tell her everything I felt, and this time, I was honest. A few things were hard for Declan to hear, but he never left my side.

Foolishly I'd thought my depressive episodes were because of Dean, but after talking with Dr. Reynolds, I realized it had nothing to do with him. I'm not depressed because of him. I am the way I am because of my brain chemicals and the fact that I've been keeping so much to myself.

For years I've held in my emotions, never telling a single soul how I truly felt. Not since my abortion years ago. That was the first heartbreak I kept to myself; since then, I've been piling on. Then when Luca died, I gave up trying to make myself feel better. I didn't want to feel at all.

I'm so thankful for the help of my family. With how dark my mind has been, I wonder how much longer I'd still be breathing without their support.

I'm incredibly thankful for Declan. He took me out every single day. He helped me get out of bed, helped me brush my teeth and hair, and would take me out of the apartment to get fresh air. Walking to the coffee shop on the corner felt like the biggest chore, but I did it because I owed it to myself to fight my depression.

Without fail, every day that we returned from our walk, there would be a dozen roses waiting for me at the door, all from Dean.

I ignored them, not ready to speak to him. He wasn't my priority; my mental health was.

Declan stayed with me for two months straight, escorting me

to therapy three times a week, taking me to refill my new prescriptions, and making sure I was well taken care of. We still planned on getting divorced, but it was put on pause until I was doing better. We'd discussed it, agreeing to make it as quick and easy as possible.

Three weeks later, we discovered an upcoming opening at an inpatient mental health facility in California that Dr. Reynolds had told my parents and me about. I'd been on the waiting list for a month when we got the call. It was bougie and expensive as fuck, but my parents wrote the check before I could even protest.

Everyone wanted me to go and get the professional help I deserved.

I wanted to go and get the help I desperately needed.

Before I left, I wanted to see Dean. Without question, Declan drove me to him.

We said goodbye once and for all, then the very next day, Declan and my family flew with me to California to check me into Ridge Creek Behavioral Health Facility, where I was treated for three months.

It took many sessions, lots of talking, and tears to work through everything I'd been holding in for years.

My depression started nearly eleven years ago when I made a life-changing decision at only fifteen. Since then, it's slowly been getting worse to the point where I could no longer pull myself out of my dark moods.

Declan had wanted to go to California and stay while I completed inpatient treatment, but I wouldn't let him. Instead, he returned to New York, and we FaceTimed every night, sometimes twice a day. Whenever I called, he always answered, no matter the time.

Last night was the first night sleeping in my own bed in my condo in Seattle. Since my treatment is now complete, I was able to leave California yesterday and get back to Washington.

My family had greeted me at the airport, and we went straight out to celebrate my homecoming with Mexican food. After, I went home to a cold and empty apartment, dreading what I had to do.

Part of my treatment is to talk about my short pregnancy, tell *him* what I had done, and confess the truth.

Last we spoke, I led Dean to believe I had a miscarriage. He assumed, and I didn't correct him, but my doctor says I have to now. Coming clean and sharing that with him is essential to my recovery.

So, that's what I'm going to do. I'm going to tell Dean I had an abortion so I can be free of the guilt, put it past me, and move on.

It's been three months since I've seen him or heard his voice. We ended things that night in the park, and I had planned on things remaining over between us and never having to see him again, but deep down, I knew that was impossible. Especially since his design firm is responsible for designing my building, I'm bound to see him again.

Plus, I'm still in love with him.

Too afraid to hear his voice sooner than needed, I text him instead, asking if he'd be able to meet me at a local coffee shop. He replies instantly and agrees to it.

My parents recommended I take some time before telling him since I only got home yesterday, but I need to do it now. I've waited long enough; I can't wait any longer.

After a long, hot shower and dressing in black skinny jeans with a pair of white Vans and a beige off-the-shoulder sweater, I pull my hair back into a ponytail and then leave to meet Dean at the coffee shop.

Luckily, I'm the first to arrive, allowing me time to order a coffee to calm my nerves. I've gone eleven years without seeing him, three months shouldn't have me as nervous as it does, but I can't get my hands to quit shaking or my stomach to stop doing flips.

I'm generally not a nervous person, but today I sure seem to be.

The bell above the door rings, indicating another person has entered the space. Raising my head, our eyes connect from across the room like magnets. A slow, seductive smile spreads across his devilish mouth, his eyes staying on me the entire time he walks toward me.

"Not going to lie, I was surprised to hear from you, but it was a very welcome surprise." He pulls out the chair across from me and sits down.

'Thanks for coming. I wanted to talk." He nods, remaining silent and allowing me the chance to say what I need to say. To finally tell him the secret I've kept all these years and refused to ever talk or think about. "So, I need to start by explaining where I've been. I know you've been trying to contact me for the last few months, and I haven't answered. I've been in California at a mental health treatment center. In fact, I just got back yesterday." His eyebrows shoot to his hairline in surprise.

Concern softens his handsome features. "A treatment center... are you okay?" I nod.

"I am now. For years I've been fighting depression, and most of the time, I've been able to pull myself out of that dark place in my mind, but after losing Luca, it only became worse, and instead of getting proper help, I took medication that numbed the pain. It wasn't the right medication for me, and I was only getting worse." I sigh. "I'm taking the right medication now, and I'm good. I feel much better, like myself again. I went through something traumatic when I was fifteen and never properly processed it, so for years, I've been bottling up my emotions and only damaging myself."

He reaches across the table and takes my hands in his. "The miscarriage?" he questions. Of course, he'd assume that since I hadn't corrected him then. Now it's time to fess up and tell the truth.

"Please understand that I was young and alone, and you had left for school, and we had our whole lives ahead of us. I made the right decision for both of us, but I was alone and had no way to work through the emotions. I became really depressed afterward, which was the start of my mental health issues. Since then, it's only been getting worse little by little." I sigh, squeezing his hands tighter and taking slow and controlled breaths. "Dean, I didn't have a miscarriage."

He blinks, his face contorting in confusion. "I don't understand. What happened, Camille? What did you do?"

"We were both so young, and a baby wasn't in our plans at that point in time. I did the right thing. I know it." He pulls his hands away, anger darkening his eyes.

"What did you do?" he rasps through clenched teeth.

"Dean, I had an abortion." Dropping this bombshell on him doesn't make me feel as good as I thought I'd feel after finally telling him the truth and getting it off my chest.

I can see the pain and confusion in his eyes. "You killed my baby?" His cold words stab me in the heart. "You knew that I wanted to have a family with you one day, and you killed the chance we had."

"One day, Dean, one day. Not at fifteen and eighteen. It's my body, and I chose what was best for me, for us."

"You were fucking selfish. Don't you think you should've called me and at least told me you were pregnant and asked for my input?" He shakes his head, looking me up and down in disgust, a look I've never seen from him before.

"My body, Dean. My choice. I didn't need permission from you or anyone else to do what was right for me and my future. I wasn't selfish. By not having a baby, we both got to go to school and become something. Do you really think you'd be where you are right now if I had had our baby?"

"Don't you dare, don't you dare fucking try and take credit for my accomplishments because you chose to be selfish." He stands, so quick that his chair falls back with a thud. "You're a liar, and you're selfish. The woman I loved never would've done what you did." He turns his back and leaves me sitting there with tears in my eyes and my jaw on the floor.

This is not how I expected him to react. Actually, I don't know what I expected, but it sure as fuck wasn't this. I had hoped he'd be understanding and realize what a tough decision I had to make at such a young age.

Instead, he got upset and left.

He can be upset, that's his right, but he doesn't have the right to accuse me of being selfish and killing our baby. I did what I could to save our future and give us both a chance in life. I didn't want to become a mother at that age, and I don't regret it.

Fuck him for trying to make me feel bad about it.

LATER THAT NIGHT, I'M LYING IN BED BESIDE SPENCER AT her apartment, telling her everything about my meeting with Dean at the coffee shop and how he reacted. She's been quiet the entire time, letting me vent to her and get all my anger out, ranting about his selfish behavior.

"Do you think it was selfish? Should I have asked him?" I ask, unsure of myself after ranting to her for nearly thirty minutes.

She takes my hand and intertwines our fingers, something she's done since I was a small child, the action soothing me. "I think you made the right decision. At the time, I remember thinking it was wrong, and you'd regret it. But I realized you made the right choice. You were smart and strong enough to make such a hard fucking decision." She lets go of my hand and sits up. "I'm in awe of you, little sis. You are the strongest person I know. You have been through so much, and it amazes me that you're still standing." Unshed tears shine in her eyes. "You've been through teen pregnancy, losing a child, having a drug-addicted husband, and now you're going through a divorce. You're unbreakable, and I admire your strength."

I sit up and mirror her position. "You don't think losing Luca is somehow payback for doing what I did?" My chin trembles as I ask the question that's been weighing heavy on me for a while now.

"What? No, of course not. Losing Luca was a horrible and tragic accident. It's not payback for anything." She wraps her arms around me as we cry against each other.

Spence pulls back, looks me in the eyes, and smiles. "I think it's time you find out who you truly are. You went from having Dean at a young age to having constant guys in college, then marrying Declan soon after. You've never been single for more than two seconds. Now that you're getting divorced it's time to ask yourself, who is Camille?" She's right, like always.

I had boyfriends in college, but those relationships were just to pass the time. They were never anything serious.

Dean had been by my side from the time I was eight until I turned fifteen, and he went off to college.

Declan has been by my side from the time I graduated college at twenty-two until now at nearly twenty-seven. I'll forever be tied to him, he'll always be a part of me, but our romantic relationship has ended.

As an adult, I've been married longer than I've been single, so Spencer is right.

Who am I without a partner?

Who am I on my own?

I'm not sure yet, but I do know that I'm determined to find out.

I've always thought Dean was my soulmate and hoped that one day we'd find our way back to each other, and we did. But I know now that sometimes your soulmate is put in your life only for a temporary time.

Dean entered my life like a thunderstorm in the middle of the night. Eleven years later, he walked back into my life with a smile and those dreamy eyes, and our hearts reconnected like no time had ever passed. I'll always love him; I know that, but I'm no longer holding on to the hope that we'll end up together. If we do find our way back to each other, I'll accept it, but I can't sit around hoping and waiting anymore.

I only have one life, and I'm going to live it. I'll live it without wondering what he's doing, without obsessing, and without seeing his hazel eyes every time I close mine.

For now, I'll be living for me.

It's time to figure out who I am.

FORTY-TWO

NOW

DEAN

It's been six months since that day in the coffee shop with Camille. Six fucking months since I've seen her beautiful face, and even longer since I've had the privilege of tasting her mouth against mine.

That day plays on repeat in my mind. The way I acted haunts me. It took me a few days to cool off and understand why she did what she did, and I accepted that decision, which is why I had sent her a dozen red roses along with an apology note. I didn't expect to hear from her after that, and I'd been right.

Camille never called, texted, or even emailed me. It was as if we no longer existed to each other, except we did.

She had told me that I had unresolved feelings that I needed to work on, and she was right. I'd been selfish with her, and our relationship was toxic. The way I was behaving and continuing on wasn't healthy for either of us, and I understand that now.

When my daughter was stillborn a few years ago, it fucked with my head, and I haven't been the same since. I suppressed my emotions and kept them buried until I became a man I didn't even recognize.

Camille called me on my shit, and because of her, I've been

meeting with a therapist once a week, working on myself and striving to be better.

Even though Camille ignored me, she continued working with Anthony to complete her building. Last week was the grand opening.

It turned out fucking beautiful, and I went to the grand opening party, hoping to see her, but there were too many people, and I couldn't get through to her. She was lost in the sea of people. I could feel her but couldn't see her, so eventually, I gave up and left.

Today is the day Cam's clothing company, Sinful Pleasures, opens for business. I only know this because Anthony told me that she and all her employees would be having their first day of work in the new building.

Even if he did finish it for her, it's still the blueprint I created for her when we were younger, at the exact location I chose for her. We created it together, even if I'd been too stupid and had my head stuck up my own ass and missed the opportunity to complete it with her and be by her side when she opened.

I have so many regrets.

"Congrats, man. To freedom!" My buddy, Nick, breaks me from my thoughts. He raises his glass in his air, toasting me on my now finalized divorce. It had been a long and messy road to make it happen, but it finally fucking happened. I am now officially a single man.

I never went back to Karina after I asked for a divorce that day. Instead, I hired the best damn divorce lawyer in the state, Ash Grant, the father of my high school best friend, Dallas.

I had hoped that Karina and I would be able to come to an agreement civilly but should've known that would be impossible with her. She wanted me to pay and suck me dry because I was unfaithful in our marriage.

Ash had discovered something interesting in my bank statements when I brought them in for him to review my financials.

We had hoped the discovery would speed up the process, but I wasn't that lucky. But it did save me money.

We found out Karina had used a sperm donor and had artificially inseminated at a clinic. She had her baby and thank fuck it wasn't mine. She refused to sign the papers, wanting every single cent I had.

She got the house, her car, and a hefty check. It wasn't nearly as much as she wanted, but considering she used my money to inseminate herself and claim the child was mine, I didn't feel she should be entitled to everything I had. We agreed, and she finally fucking signed.

Now, I'm out at Trinity nightclub celebrating the great news. My divorce was finalized today, and I'm free.

Clanking our shot glasses together, we all throw them back, and my friends erupt in a roar, cheering for me.

"Congratu-fucking-lations!" Ash Grant, my fucking wonderful divorce attorney, enters the bar, clapping his hands together. He's a shark of a lawyer, the best in the state. Back in high school, I remember when Dallas would talk about his father and how great he was. So, when it came to needing someone to represent me, it was a no-brainer that I'd ask him.

Nick, Logan, and James are friends from high school with whom I've stayed in touch with over the years. When news of my divorce spread, they became some of my biggest supporters.

Ash is old enough to be our father, but you'd never be able to tell by looking at him. It's funny how different he and Dallas are. He takes after his mother rather than his father.

Man, I sure do miss my high school best friend, and being around his father reminds me of the good ol' days.

"How does it feel to be a free man?" he asks with a chuckle, patting me on the back.

"Feels amazing, thanks to you." God, it does feel amazing.

"It was my pleasure, man. Glad it's finally over. It sure as fuck got a little ugly." He chuckles, sipping the amber liquid from his glass. Ash knows firsthand the details of my divorce, well, he and

Nick since I had called him one drunken night after I found out Karina had used a sperm donor. Even though I knew about the donor, I still requested a paternity test after Karina's son was born to be certain.

It hurt to find out he wasn't mine, but then that resentment faded, and I felt happy. I was happy that I wouldn't be tied to her and didn't have a child with someone I didn't, and couldn't, love anymore.

She got the one thing she always wanted, a child, so I'm happy for her. She's out of my life, and I'm happier now without her. I should've divorced her a long fucking time ago, but better late than never.

I'm occupied chatting with my group of friends when the hair on the back of my neck stands in awareness the same way it always does when I'm near *her*. I've always been able to feel her presence.

I feel her before I see her.

Our eyes find each other through the crowd like magnets. Camille walks through the door wearing a little black dress, red fuck-me heels, and matte red lipstick that instantly gets my cock hard, remembering how I smeared it the last time I saw her wearing red lipstick. I had spread it all over her face when she swallowed my dick and sucked me dry.

She walks toward me with Spencer on one side and Olivia, Spence's friend, on the other.

"Hello, boys." Spencer looks devilishly at my friends, takes one of the drinks from the tray the waitress just brought, and swallows it back. I see the moment her eyes land on Ash, and I try to keep myself from laughing. She coughs. "H-h-hi, Mr. Grant." How awkward that must be for her, seeing her ex-boyfriend's father after all these years. From what I've heard, she and Dallas never got back together, despite how we all swore they would.

Everyone around the table starts making small talk, but my eyes easily find Camille again, only to discover that she hasn't taken her eyes off me. A smile spreads across her red lips, and I know I'm wearing a matching smile of my own.

She's more radiant than I've ever seen her before. Her emerald eyes are bright and sparkling, her face lively, and her golden skin is glowing.

"Fancy seeing you here," she says, her tits brushing against my chest as she leans in to me to speak. Fuck, if the little vixen isn't careful, my cock is going to spill right here.

"What are you celebrating?" Her eyes sparkle with mischief as if she knows precisely the gutter my mind went to.

I choose to give her an honest answer, even if it's risking reminding her of the past. "My divorce. I'm finally free." I search her eyes for her reaction, only to find her pupils dilate and her green eyes darken with a look I've seen time and time again.

"Congratulations, that makes two of us." Her lips curl in a smile, and her small hands brush over the growing bulge in my pants, tempting me like the tease she is.

I'd heard from my mother that Camille's divorce was finalized a few months ago, and I believe that was my mother's way of hinting at me to see Cam or do something about it.

My saint of a mother has heard me complain enough about Camille over the last few months. I've told her everything, all about the affair and even about her abortion and how I reacted poorly when she'd had the courage to tell me about it.

"Dean," Camille purrs, her arms slipping around my waist. I can smell the alcohol on her breath. She's been drinking before coming here, though her eyes look clear. It's a contradiction, really. "Fuck me." She keeps her voice low enough that no one else from the table can hear her.

Her words take me by surprise, but who am I to deny the gorgeous woman standing in front of me in a dress that's too short? I look down at her and smile. She clenches her thighs together.

"Are you wet, Camille?" I wonder out loud, matching her smirk.

"Take me to the bathroom and find out." She brushes past me, walking straight toward the sign that leads to the bathrooms. Without a second thought, I follow her like a lost puppy, following her straight into the women's restroom.

Luckily, the bathroom is empty, so I flip the deadbolt, locking the door. "What do you want, Camille?" I rush toward her, my cock painfully pressing against my zipper, begging to be freed.

"I want you to fuck me like you hate me. Fuck me like I'm nothing." She turns, facing the sinks, and stares at me through the mirror, her hands fisting the sides of her dress as she shimmies it up around her waist to reveal her naked bottom. "Dean, be a good boy and fuck me until I forget my name." Her hand disappears between her thighs. A groan comes from my throat at the sight of her playing with herself while staring at me in the mirror.

Jumping into action, I undo my pants and shove them down my legs along with my briefs, my heavy dick springs free, pointing straight toward the woman in front of me, as if it knows its way home.

Gripping her hips, I pull her back to me, pressing my length against the crack of her ass. "I don't have time to taste you, baby. I need to be buried inside your sweet cunt so fucking bad." She nods, her head falling back on my shoulder, her lips parting as she continues playing with her clit, bringing herself pleasure.

"Fuck yourself with two fingers." She obeys, sliding two fingers into her wet entrance, spreading her thighs, so I have a better view of her in the mirror. Her thumb strums her clit while she fucks her hand. "Fuck, you look so sexy when you do that."

"I need you, Dean. I need you now." She moans the sweetest moan. With one hand, I yank her fingers away from her body, earning a frustrated groan. With the other hand, I fist my swollen cock, line it up with her entrance, and I slip inside her soft tissues in one powerful thrust, finding my way home. We groan in unison, her eyes closing from the pleasure.

"Keep your eyes open, baby, watch me fuck you." I pull the thick straps of her dress off her shoulders and help her remove her arms out of them, then unsnap her strapless bra and let it fall, her heavy breasts spilling free.

Camille grips the counter with one hand and brings the other to my mouth, sticking the fingers that were inside her pussy inside my mouth, allowing me to taste her sweetness.

I suck her fingers, swirling my tongue around them, lapping up every trace of her flavor. She lets go of the counter, uses that hand to slip between her thighs, and starts rubbing her clit, all while watching ourselves in the mirror.

One arm wraps around her waist, holding her back against me; the other hand finds her breast, kneads it, and tugs on her nipples exactly as she likes.

The sound of our moans and skin slapping against each other fills the air. She's panting, her body shaking in my hold. She rubs her clit faster and faster until her walls tighten around me and squeeze me, letting me know that she's reaching her climax.

With a final flick of her finger, she falls apart, going limp in my arms from the burst of pleasure provided by her orgasm. I hold her body up, not letting her get away until I'm satisfied.

Her cries of pleasure fill the air, and her pussy pulses around my cock, forcing me to reach my own climax. She's so fucking tight, so fucking warm, and so fucking perfect. It's hard to last when I'm inside her, no matter how badly I wish I could be buried inside her for hours and hours.

"Dean!" she cries, her body shaking as I force another orgasm from her before she's even had time to come down from her first one. I know Camille's body like the back of my hand, and this is what she needs. She needs at least three orgasms to be fully satisfied.

My hand replaces hers between her legs, and I rub her swollen bud, fucking one more orgasm out of her. She wanted hard, and that's what she gets.

I keep her body tight against mine, not allowing her to move while I pound into her repeatedly, whispering praises in her ear, telling her how good she is and how amazing she feels.

After a third and final orgasm, I pull out of her tight body, forcing her to turn around and shove her down to her knees. "You wanted me to fuck you like I hate you, well, I want you to suck me like a whore." Her eyes sparkle with lust. She opens her mouth and takes me down her throat, moaning at the taste of herself.

"Yeah, baby, you like that? Do you like how fucking good you taste? I've missed that taste." I thread my fingers through her hair, holding her tightly in place, bucking my hips to fuck her mouth.

She gags and drools, her hand squeezes my flexing ass, and I'm willing to bet when she moves, I'll find a puddle from where she dripped all over the floor. I can see in her eyes how turned on she is. "Are you going to swallow me like a dirty fucking whore?"

She nods as much as she can with her throat full of me. My balls tighten, and soon I'm exploding my load into her warm mouth, groaning at the sensation of her sucking me dry, forcing every drop from me that I have to offer.

Camille pulls back, and my length slides from her mouth with a pop. She stands in front of me, her little dress bunched around her waist, her perfect tits on display, and my cum dripping down her chin.

"You made a mess and need to clean it up," she says with a smirk, walking backward until her ass touches the counter.

My dirty girl wants to play.

Stalking toward her, I lick my cum from her chest where it dripped and then lick it up from her chin. I press my mouth to hers. She parts her lips willingly, and our tongues connect.

"Where else did I make a mess?"

Smirking, she climbs onto the counter and spreads her legs, showing me her glistening pussy dripping from how aroused she is. Without being told, I drop to my knees in front of her and cover her cunt with my mouth, my tongue lapping up at her wetness, cleaning up the mess I made.

In two minutes flat, I'm able to claim a fourth orgasm I wasn't aware she had in her. When I stand in front of her after pulling my pants back up, I give her a smirk, leaning into her spent body that's still on the counter.

"Your turn to clean up your mess." She sticks her tongue out and licks up my chin and lips that glisten with her wetness. "God, the things you do to me." I press a quick kiss against her lips, help her off the counter, and clean her up.

Once we're clean and her clothing is fixed, she stands in front of me with a hopeful look.

We haven't seen each other in six months. The last time we did, I was a complete asshole and freaked out about something I had no right to freak out about. She never said anything after the flowers and my apology, but I need her to know how genuinely sorry I am and how I want her in my life and for us to be together. We've been apart long enough, she's mine, and I'll forever be hers.

"Camille, I'm so fucking sorry about that day in the coffee shop. I understand why you chose not to have our baby, and that's okay. I'm sorry I wasn't supportive and wasn't there when you had to go through it." I lean down and rest my forehead against hers, my hands firmly gripping her waist. "I'm so fucking sorry."

"I forgive you, Dean." Her arms wrap around my neck.

"I want you, Cam, for the rest of my life, I want you. We can't be apart any longer. I've been waiting long enough for you." She pulls away from me, sadness and sorrow filling her beautiful eyes.

"I'm sorry, Dean, I can't be with you. Not right now. I'm still working on myself, which requires me to be alone. Please, give me the time I need to focus on myself. If we're meant to be, then one day, we will be." Her words break my heart.

"We are meant to be, can't you see that?"

"Then we'll find our way back together, but I can't be in a relationship right now," she says. I know we're meant to be, and I have faith that she will be mine one day. I have enough faith for both of us.

"You're right, I'm sorry. I know we can't be together right now because I'm not the man you deserve yet. I've been going to therapy and have been working through a lot. I promise, one day, I will be the man you deserve, and I will be there for you in every single way, and every single day." She nods, not saying a single word.

"I'm hopelessly in love with you, baby. You're mine forever, so go ahead and take all the time you need. Just know that you have my heart in the palm of your hand, and I'll be waiting for you when the time is right for us to make our way back to each other." I kiss her forehead, wiping the tears streaming down her cheeks. "Now I'm going to close my eyes because I can't stand to watch you leave. You have ten seconds." With one final look at her, I close my eyes and count.

When I open them, she's gone.

EPILOGUE

ONE YEAR LATER

Camille

"I'm not interested in dating," I groan, struggling with the zipper at the back of my dress.

"You're going for moral support. I'm ready to date and need a wing woman." Spencer flips her dark hair off her shoulders and turns me around so my back faces her. She effortlessly slides the zipper up my back.

Rolling my eyes, I say, "It's speed dating. How exactly can I be a wing woman?" One of our mother's friends at the country club told Spencer about an elite speed dating event she was hosting, and she signed up both of us without my consent.

I'd never do something as ridiculous as speed dating, not that I'm interested in dating anyway, even if I am single.

Declan and I divorced on my timing. He waited until I was ready and had the time to really sit down and focus, and for that I'm grateful.

We're divorced and doing very well in our new role as friends. We still speak often and have our mental health check-ins with each other. He hasn't been doing great lately. He has his own demons he needs to work on, and thankfully he's agreed to start therapy.

"Stop complaining, just put your shoes on and let's go or we're going to be late." I've been relying on Spencer heavily over the last few years, so if she wants to go speed dating, I'll shut up and go with her.

We finish getting ready in silence and drive toward the rented-out restaurant where the event is being held.

We arrive and get signed in quickly.

The room is crowded, everyone is wearing a number instead of a name tag, and we've all been given a small notebook to take notes on our dates. We're supposed to rate our dates, and if we like them and match up, we'll receive their contact information to schedule something on our own.

As much as I dread it, I'm willing to do it to make Spencer happy. My poor sister has terrible luck with men, and it's time she finds someone to love.

Spencer is quick to find her groove and mingles around the room full of singles, leaving me to fend off the horny middle-aged men who seem to swarm toward me like a bee to honey.

Fifteen minutes later, a bell rings, and Claudia, the event organizer, announces that all the women are to find a seat, and the event will begin. Women will remain seated, while men will practically play musical chairs, only having five minutes with each woman.

Setting my glass of wine and notepad on an empty table, I claim it as my own. The fact it's near an exit sign is pure coincidence.

I'll be able to bolt without being noticed.

Two minutes later, another bell rings, and the men all take their seats in front of the women, instantly jumping into a conversation.

I'm looking around the room to find Spencer, not paying attention to the chair on the other side of my table. It doesn't matter who sits. I won't be interested anyway. I'm not interested in dating.

Lately, I've spent the majority of my time going to therapy, taking yoga classes, and focusing on myself and my mental health. I've been doing good, really good.

I'm happier than I've been in a long time, and for the first time in nearly two years, I can think about my son without breaking down, and I can get through my days without medicating myself.

I haven't seen Dean since that night in the bathroom at the nightclub. I know from his mother that he's still attending therapy and is doing very well. I'm truly happy for him, though I've yet to see him. I know that he wants a relationship, but I'm not mentally able to have anything romantic with anyone right now. My mind is still fragile, and being with Dean was too toxic. All I can handle right now is friendship.

"Well, hello there, pretty lady," a short bald man says, stealing my attention from the room and my thoughts. He pulls the chair out, ready to sit, when he's stopped.

"Sorry, this seat is taken." *His* voice sends chills down my spine. Instantly my posture straightens, and I reach for my wine glass, my eyes fixating on the red liquid as if it's the most exciting thing to ever exist. I refuse to look him in the eyes.

Baldie says something under his breath just as Dean sits in front of me.

"Looks like we only have four minutes left, so I'll try and be quick." He clears his throat. "Hi, my name is Dean Jameson, and I would like the chance to prove to you that I'm worthy of you."

What the actual fuck? What is he doing?

I choke on my wine and set the glass down, finally letting my eyes land on him.

Finding my voice, I finally ask, "What are you doing here, Dean?" curious to know what game he's playing.

He chuckles. "My mother forced me to come. A friend of hers is the one hosting this event, and she signed me up." Ah, of course she did. Lydia knew I'd be here.

Feeling bratty, I sigh, taking another sip of my wine. "I was very excited to get to know the man you just ran off."

He looks around to find the short fat bald man standing on the side. "Yeah, I bet you're dying to get him home and have him sweat over you while he pumps you with his pinky dick." His lips curl in disgust.

Unable to keep up the act, I burst out laughing.

"It's good to see you, Cam. I've missed you."

"It's good to see you too, you look very nice," I say grinning. "Did you sit down to say hello, or did you have something to get off your chest?"

He nods. "I want you to know that I've changed. I'm good now, and I would like the honor of being in your life again. I still have a long way to go, but I'm confident I'm getting there."

His words take me by surprise, but still cause my heart to skip a beat. "Let's start with being friends. That's all that I have to offer you right now. No dating, no sex, nothing physical whatsoever. Platonic friends, that's it." I love him, and I know that I always will, but I can't allow myself to fall back into the toxic cycle we were stuck in. Dean had a lot to work on, and he needed to grow for himself, not for me.

For now, we can be friends and get to know each other again, like we should've in the beginning instead of jumping into an affair. If he's truly changed as much as he claims, then we'll see where the future will lead us.

"I accept your terms. I'm happy with being friends for now. I've treated you badly, and I have a lot of shit to make up for. Sorry isn't good enough, and I'm prepared to grovel and spend every day making up for my actions and earning your trust and forgiveness."

Nodding, I agree. I'll give him a chance. "Okay. We'll start over and see what happens."

When it comes to love, you don't always get a happy ending. Sometimes, you're simply happy for now, and that's okay, because I know that our story isn't over yet. I don't know where the future will take us, if we'll grow together or grow apart, but I know that I'm willing to explore our options and see where we end up.

For now, I'm happy. I'm looking forward to growing a friendship with Dean. I know our story may be unconventional, but I wouldn't change it because this is us.

This is our story.

This is our way back.

The End

Declan's story will be coming soon!

SIGNED COPIES

Do you want to own a signed copy of this book?

Order yours today:

www.kylafayebooks.com

ALSO BY KYLA FAYE

Dollhouse (Down We Go Book #1)

ACKNOWLEDGMENTS

Dean and Camille's story has been on my mind for three years now, and I'm thrilled it's finally written. Telling their story took a lot out of me and came with many self-doubts. Doubt that readers would be turned off by their affair. Doubt that readers would hate it because the story didn't end with your typical happily ever after. I rewrote the ending many times, hoping to find an ending that would please others yet still feel realistic for Dean and Cam. Their relationship was unhealthy, and them ending up married didn't fit their story. Once I finally stopped worrying about what others might think, I went with my gut instinct and chose to end their story the way I did. It feels perfect for them.

Their story is finally written, and I'm thrilled with how it turned out.

Thank you for taking the time to read about these characters that mean so much to me.

Now, I'd like to thank those who played a role in bringing this story to life because it truly takes a village to publish a book.

To my readers, thank you for taking a chance on me. You all make living my dream possible, and if it weren't for all the support I've received, I never would've had enough courage to be able to tell Cam and D's story.

To my husband, thank you for pushing me to finish this book and keeping me as distraction-free as possible. We went through a massive change this year and had a lot of stressful moments, but you pushed me daily to focus on my writing. You came home and encouraged me no matter how long and tiring your day was. I love you forever. Please always come home safe to me.

To my editors, Tori and Zee, thank you both x1000 for taking my rough, rambled words and turning them into something great. You both have been amazing through this process, and I've truly found my dream team.

To everyone else who played a role in bringing Our Way Back to life, THANK YOU!!! Writing a book is never a solo project, and I'm incredibly blessed to have such a wonderful community behind me with endless support.

I look forward to sharing Declan's deeply personal story with you all soon.

XO,
KF

ABOUT THE AUTHOR

Kyla Faye is a twenty-something author of dark, adult erotic, and contemporary romance. When she's not reading about romance, she's writing about it, trying to give a voice to the characters that live inside her head. She has a caffeine addiction and always has a candle burning.

You can find her on social media.

- facebook.com/authorkylafaye
- instagram.com/authorkylafaye
- tiktok.com/@authorkylafaye
- goodreads.com/authorkylafaye

Printed in Great Britain
by Amazon

16903502R00264